The Rain's Falling Up

THE ITALIAN LIST

LUCA RASTELLO

The Rain's Falling Up

TRANSLATED BY CRISTINA VITI

LONDON NEW YORK CALCUTTA

The Italian List
SERIES EDITOR: Alberto Toscano

●

Seagull Books, 2022

Originally published in Italian as *Piove all'insù* by Luca Rastello
© Bollati Boringhieri editore, Turin, 2006

First published in English translation by Seagull Books, 2022
English translation and Notes © Cristina Viti, 2022

ISBN   978 0 8574 2 990 2

British Library Cataloguing-in-Publication Data
A catalogue record for this book is available from the British Library

Typeset by Seagull Books, Calcutta, India
Printed and bound in the USA by Integrated Books International

Contents

> But I'm scared that if I stop to breathe the story will rear
> up and stop coming out, be sucked back like toothpaste
> up the tube: so I'm telling it to you as it comes, scattered
> and uneven as it is.

With these words from the protagonist, a man who has lived
through the struggles of the 1970s youth movements and years
later is sharing his partner's shock and anger following the sudden
news of her unfair dismissal from work, Luca Rastello declares
his intention to de-structure the narrative by opening it to the
surges, flashbacks and jump cuts of memory, its unpredictable
incursions into daily life. Chunks of plot racing with razor-sharp
precision along a fine line of attention to language—not like the
prototypes driven in circles by Fiat on the parabolic curves of the
rooftop test-track at Lingotto, but like orbiting worlds creating
warped harmonics on elliptical trajectories. The warp of everyday
speech, the way it bends the language in sickness or in stealth,
its lulzy disregard for the conventions it has mastered, the weird

property by which it accumulates and composes details until personal recollection widens by excess into a clear vision of history— all this and more, transposed on the page without filters, rough like a first drink and elegant with neglect. For the translator to do anything more than jam with this mother of invention while providing a few contextualizing bridges would be to disrespect the author's decision to never underestimate his readers. Let her, then, simply thank the readers for their attention and her editors for their support, and dedicate this work to the memory of the author and of the friendships he so vividly brought to life in his pages.

September 2022

The Rain's Falling Up

1

Venus on the Half-Shell

(1974–1976)

SUBJECT: BASTARDS   That's right. Some boss will have told you he's sorry. That he has to make painful choices—or rather, that one has to make painful choices. A virtuoso of the impersonal form, so concerned about your future, affectionate even. And anyway you are precious, you're a high-profile professional. You've nothing to worry about. Meanwhile he's saved the part-time secretary he's hoping to prong sooner than later, the wife who works for a hobby and the wife's girlfriend. As for you, you can look forward to new prospects: flexibility allowance, Desk 1 on the 2nd floor at the Employment Centre, eighty or so people in the queue at any time, and you can see that many are fighting back the tears. So you go home and wait for a slightly better day to try again, catch your breath. At night you look at your son before you roll over, and all this is so far from the lives you were sharing only a few days ago, far from the desk of someone who's sacrificed you to the company's future while telling you you'll have more time for your children. Of course you have not wasted your fifteen years' national insurance contributions: you've paid for *his* pension, and now you're running to piece together the situation you no longer have—no matter that it was doomed anyway.

Look, I'll be back in ten days or so, we can talk then, I know age scares you, it scares me too, but for the moment at least I have a job, and for a while at least we'll make it work for us both. Here's the deal: we're going to stay angry, at least until we see each other again, we're going to try and get together when we're totally pissed off and we're going to wait until we get lucid. How can I tell you anything sensible from this far away? I'll be back soon, we'll figure something out together. Right now I can't think of anything less stupid to say. Will you be able to forgive me?

Here's a confession for you, to cheer you up a bit. An old story, dead & buried until it resurfaced from a shelf of Urania on the second-hand book stalls. I've thought about it a few times, over the last few years: sooner or later I'd have to tell you, but I've always held back, partly out of shame, partly out of a sense of ridicule. It's a case of plagiarism, words stolen to make myself look good, from a book I no longer remember but know for sure must have been a Urania—cheap science fiction, white cover with a red stripe and those drawings that scare you when you're little. Sometimes I wonder if I could ever read them again, and last Saturday I felt like giving it a go. You know how it is—that indulgent curiosity you have for yourself as a young man: that guy you no longer understand, who's an embarrassment but also someone you'd like to meet again for a chat from time to time. I bought four, one of them should be the incriminating one. Well, four books are a pretty good key: real books, with the values and dreams of those times in them, something much less fuzzy than what you'd get from a song or an old film you watch in summer at one of the open-air screenings. I read them at the time I was breaking my brain searching for a way out, but I wouldn't settle for a tame way out: I wanted it to be cosmic and outrageous. I was sixteen, more or less—and I wanted to scream. I wanted to take a clean girl into that world of screams and spikes and sharp edges in which I felt stuck fast upside down, and Urania books seemed to hold some secrets that concerned me. Our lives—except for those of us who died early—all began later, even though back then we felt like we were living inside history, not only inside our own stories. Listen up, I'm going to tell you those four science fiction stories, and may these days pass quickly. Then we'll think of something.

FIVE HUNDRED CHARGESHEETS   I had two friends for life, their names were Dino (Goffredo, in fact) and Ruben. That's where it should begin. I met Ruben first: I was eight years old and he was six, I was Seconder of a Six in the Red Wolf Cubs, and everything was whirling around me with me stock-still in the middle, and they send us those three new kids, two of them terrible: Buttigliero, who was the son of criminals and was always saying 'fookin 'ell', and Chiarenza, who I'm told is a policeman these days, and will be an old policeman by now. And then there was the well-brought-up one with the slightly bulging eyes: at some point we're reminded of the pig in Morty & Ferdie Fieldmouse, so he gets to be known as Pig from then on. Ruben aka Pig was the son of a journalist who worked for the national news network, a Catholic communist of the sort that existed back then, booming voice and a righteous paunch: I used to call him Donedilio and keep my distance, so shy of him I was. Pig's mum was the Professoressa, a Sephardic high-school teacher from Leghorn, her colours clear as water and the stench of the shag baccy she smoked strong enough to smell as I tell the story. Later the Wolf Cubs also acquired Pig's older brother, Dino: we made friends and went out with the scouts, and Buttigliero kept saying 'fookin 'ell', not least because we would play grim practical jokes on him in abandoned convents and mountain ditches and in taverns too, and Benedetta the Beautiful would get mad because whenever Pig and Buttigliero and the others were around we'd drink nothing but stinking plonk. We'd get back on Sunday night, and one Sunday night my parents came to pick us up at the station: that time I was too tired to be ashamed. Except that at the station we also found Dino and Pig's mum, Professoressa Fanny, who invited us all back to her place for a glass of wine and a chat. I remember my folks looking somewhat wary as she took them up to the last-but-one floor (the Schindler lift, glass and wooden bench, creaking loudly and stopping short of the fifth floor where they lived, in a luxury loft with skylights and a long balcony over the plane trees). And suddenly, on the stairs, a terrifying squeal: 'Yooooohoooohoooohooooo, Niki (their dog), Nikinikiniki!! Here is Fannee! Fanneefanneefannee!! My Fannee, my Fanneehe-heheheheheeee!', and Donedilio, three hundredweight in under-wear, rocks out of the door, hurtles down the stairs and turns to stone in front of my folks. But he manages somehow to stay inside his boxer shorts and blurt out an almost impeccable 'Good evening', shake hands, even bow, turn on his bare heels and get back into the house and into his clothes.

They were different, my folks—daunted by the culture gap: my mother was mostly self-taught, my father had left home as a boy for the military career. On a small trunk in a long corridor that led to the living room, a copy of the Quotidiano dei Lavoratori, the daily paper of Avanguardia Operaia: me and Pig exchanged

looks, and I thought how cool it would be to have   parents smart
as his. Donedilio's bellow was ringing out all over the house, and
it sounded somewhat too hearty to me. But he was a sort of curious giant, and couldn't believe his luck in having a carabinieri
officer at his disposal (my father was in the army, but was stationed
with the carabinieri legion in Turin at the time): something huge
had just happened in town, and Donedilio was working on it
through professional interest, and shaken by it through personal
passion.

'So, do you believe in these Red Brigades?'

My father had twigged: he was in a communist's house, and
was trying hard to keep his tone down. He was holding the conversation, but I could see that was taking a toll on him. Here were
two men just over forty, each well settled and centred in himself,
with opposite views of the world: each in his own way, two tribe
chiefs in their prime. That polite mutual interest was a duel.

He said they'd been keeping track of them for at least two
years, they knew everything about that lot, and now there was a
new commander who would bring the town back under control.
My mother was a smart woman, she had sensed in Donedilio's
question a concern that had escaped my father. Donedilio was surprised to hear they had been followed for years: after all, nobody
had heard much about them until a few months ago. My father
recalled the 'sifting' that had begun in 1971: how they'd covered
the 'high-risk cities' at the time of the election of President Leone,
how they'd trailed hundreds of people for months, until his direct
superior, Colonel Marchisio (Grasso, Marchisio, Ferrari—weird
how the names of perfect strangers who are Dad's colleagues
can stick in a kid's mind, for ever outlining the landscape of his

childhood), personally went through five hundred charge sheets relative to as many left-wing militants. Now it was simply a question of looking carefully through that archive, and the kidnappers of Cavalier Amerio would be caught in no time.

The head of personnel at FIAT had been taken as he left his house to go to work, held captive for eight days and interrogated: they had photographed him with a placard of angry slogans around his neck, and let him go when FIAT announced they would not put anyone on the lay-off scheme. The papers said the kidnappers had made sure the Cavaliere's wristwatch and wallet were returned intact, and Amerio himself said he had been treated very well. I'd found myself thinking of Robin Hood.

Donedilio was trying to be polite but there was that doubt, the one my mother had detected. My mother, in the way she had, contrived to agree as soon as possible: after all, those guys were only damaging 'the cause of the left'—that's what she said, more or less, and I thought I'd sooner sink into the ground than hear her sound so awkward. My father said nothing. Donedilio pulled out L'Unità and read aloud an article that said the Red Brigades were a murky circle of sick, addicted people; my father asked him if that was also his opinion, and Donedilio said no. He went to fetch the Quotidiano dei Lavoratori, according to which the 'self-styled Red Brigades' were 'an instrument of the strategy of tension'—as in, fascists in disguise. My father parried the blow, saying that FIAT had been negotiating an integration of the work contract and that something of this sort had already happened in Milan, at Siemens, during a negotiation: those guys knew the workers and their struggles.

Donedilio however thought that if anything, those guys were sabotaging the workers' struggles. He said the unions were mad as hell. My father said nothing. Now I know he thought so too— but they didn't make friends. They changed the subject, and the Professoressa was quick to pick up on the hint to the president: Naples was in the grip of an outbreak of cholera—archaic as that sounds—and jokes on mussels and seafood were everywhere. President Leone had been photographed during a visit to Neapolitan hospitals with his left hand pointing downward and arranged in the apotropaic gesture of the horns. But 'Fanneefan-nee' had become a war cry for us. I heard it again a few months ago, when Dino sent me a mail from America to say that Fanny, the last surviving protagonist of that scene, had joined the other three actors after years spent in a hospice for Alzheimer sufferers.

That evening, Donedilio proposed that in the coming summer my folks send me to the seaside for a few weeks, staying in his family house at the Argentario.

THE GODDESS OF CROSSROADS   Dino was butt-ugly at that time: cross-eyed, with thick glasses and too much hair into the bargain, a sort of precocious and asymmetric development mashing the rough traits of a man into the fragile features of a puppy. You could see at a glance that he was intelligent—very intelligent—a genius: which meant that occasionally, for a moment, by a one-liner or a joke, he managed to have me doubt my own central place in the universe.

Ruben, on the other hand—you wouldn't know how much his brain weighed. But he was cool, and could flare up like a real lout. Dino once goes off to see his Aunt Magda in Jersey City,

USA—a lady in her sixties who treats him like a grown man. Intelligence can also play nasty tricks, it can be harmful, confuse those who meet you, ultimately hurt you or authorize others to hurt you in good faith, as if you were an adult. So Dino goes off to the States aged eleven and he comes back grim, but with a knapsack full of magical gear: T-shirts, records and gadgets, including a baseball bat & ball. We go to the Giardino Pietro Micca to play baseball with the other kids and strut our stuff like we're Americans; then towards evening, on the doorstep, Pig has the bat in his hand, and before turning in we are chatting under the high, windy arcade of Via Cernaia. That evening Juventus were playing Bulgaria, and this lardy guy sidles up to us, points at the bat: 'Good for braining those commies playing Juve this evening.' Ruben looks at him and says: 'I support Toro.' Then he looks at the bat, looks back at the lardy-ass: 'And I'm also a commie.' Ruben was nine years old, and a Juventus supporter. We began to hang out together: we were discovering so many things, at home, out with the scouts, in the parks, wasting time in the street, widening our world, feeling slightly thuggish and very brave. Mostly we were discovering the green shade that lights up the underside of horse chestnut leaves as it gets dark. Life at that time flowed entirely inside a big nineteenth-century square of dust, barracks, sunlight and large courtyards, arcades or plane trees to mark the boundaries, the pillars of Hercules I never passed, ever since primary school when after class I would follow Benedetta, the fear in case she turned around, heart leaping at every crossroads, standing flat against the wall whenever she carefully turned her head this way and that to check on coming cars and then walked straight on with her nose in the air (what a nose, a comma ending in a right angle) up to the pillars of Hercules proper—but I never followed her all the way to her house. Still I would dream of that, and I liked to think what I might find down there, among plane trees and conker trees, where you could see gates and window grates. Corso Vittorio—that's where the world began.

And so those autumn evenings roll on and you can smell a strange smell, and only much later will you find out it's from the conkers crushed under the trams and summer's really gone, and coming out of the scouts HQ you take the longer route because the guy at the dairy under the arcade makes godly ice-cream, because you've a hundred more things to say to each other, because Ruben, like me, like all of us, is in love with Benedetta who in the meantime is growing more and more beautiful and lives right over there. But not Dino—Dino and I never loved the same woman or the same books, never. Strange, because Dino is a guy I shared a girlfriend with—but that comes later. Two girl-friends, in fact, and he married them both: one was the mathe-matician, the other, Giuliana. On evenings like those, you just have to keep talking, walking home via the wider loop, stretching time like a rubber band and avoiding crossroads, then you're over the boulevard and here are gardens, small petrified villas, sphinxes, street gates with ancient lamps and heaps of dry leaves. The magic islands of the Crocetta.

We try to make it ours, that zone, we cross it in the fog like sailors fishing for mermaids, we want to capture it. And we find a way: the paint shop. A spray can of red acrylic, nice and cheap—all you have to do is skip the ice-cream a couple of times. Our first one was 'Bourgeois Watch Out': I'd even learnt to draw a fist clutching a monkey wrench, and so most nights in winter and autumn, seven o'clock or thereabouts, we were writing on the walls and running away, winded, veins going spare and then this calm, this icy calm, so much so that we got as far as scrawling threats in gloss paint at ten o'clock on a Sunday morning on the wall of the carabinieri HQ. We were good at shoplifting too, often at La Rinascente, in the afternoon—my masterpiece: a football (I bounced it all the way to the door and out).

DABBAAR   Right, so this was the year of Donedilio's invitation. First stop, Grosseto: wide fascist boulevards flattened by the heat right in front of the station, the scorching air stopping your lungs for a moment, smell of crushed tobacco and also of trees different from those at home. And me thinking, well only yesterday morning I was in school. Ruben and Dino's cousins were there: Carla, the elder sister, and the other one, Giulietta. Carla was our age, her hair was scraped back so tight it hurt but then it fluffed back out onto her shoulders like a mess of whipped chocolate cream. She was one of those girls on the threshold, legs still a bit stocky and stuffed like sausages inside her jeans and a breast that seems to be falling down any minute because her body cannot support it despite the low centre of gravity. In short, gorgeous.

In fact the house at the Argentario belonged to the girls' father, Donedilio's brother, a Christ-Dem shark, bare chest & silk shirt, who took a shine to me, probably by contrast with the children of his communist brother. Donaurelio, I think we called him. Grosseto was like a homage to Donaurelio and to Carla's breast. Then Orbetello, barely time to clock the cinema, rushing straight on to Santa Liberata where the villa was. Dark water, trees, a wide path of dirt and gravel, dry stone walls and a swimming pool where Signora Recalcati, the wife of the great basketball player, would go to sunbathe every day. With her tits out, and there's us clambering up the roof to see from far off. Dino would also climb up, but wasn't that interested. The smell of sage, the cicadas and those trees you always find at the seaside, what's their face—oleanders. At night we would go down to the pier, perhaps for a late dip, but it was more about the need to be there, listening to the water's noises and talking no end.

Some days, instead of the seaside, we'd hitch to Orbetello to watch Fantozzi at the local cinema in the afternoon. One evening we hatched our plan—something to impress Carla, I guess. She of the tiniest, daintiest feet. So we hitch to Orbetello, late in the day, as if for the cinema. We know where the poster case is, but finding the stone is not as easy: we need a big, sharp one. The one we find is round. But big enough. Let's go. If we hurry we can smash the Christ-Dems' case too, but the first target is the MSI. Except the stone bounces back, once, twice, three times, and the glass—not a scratch. And we're making noise. Run off, start again. After ten or so hits, the poster case is cracked, but we can do no better—not stupid, these Maremma fascists. Better go home. A lift with a guy in a Ferrari who gets us to sit on the edge of the open windows with our legs on the seat, or we wouldn't fit, and then takes off at 100 mph and we're shit scared. 'So where you been lads? Dabbaar?' Dino explains to me that Dabbaar means 'to the bar'.

Night at Santa Liberata.

I wasn't that bothered about the poster case, and Carla wasn't so much as looking at me anyway. I cared more about Fantozzi, and cared to keep clear of Donedilio, who was living his own discreet holiday and keeping us on a long leash, our breakfast already set out by Fanny when we woke up, Mass in Orbetello on Sunday mornings (Dino wouldn't come), spending his evenings talking to us and making us talk: I admired him too much, our Donedilio, to be able to look him in the eye, and at first I didn't even realize what he was talking about in such precise, hard tones that evening in June, while Dino kept his eyes stubbornly fixed elsewhere. On such occasions Donedilio liked to handle a bundle of newspapers, and that evening, with a determination that seemed in no way casual (but who had grassed on us? Carla?), he was speaking of antifascism, the real stuff. He was trying to meet our eyes, his eyes were hard, his big voice calm, until the punch-line. With the papers. In Padua, at an MSI section, two men, one aged thirty and the other sixty (old, I thought) had been killed in cold blood. The paper said they'd been tied up and killed, the murders had been claimed by the Red Brigades with a leaflet that spoke of a gun fight in which two fascists had died. So did they die shooting or while tied up? To me, watching at least one western a week as I was, that made a difference. The police were saying nothing. I was looking for a way to escape Donedilio and his papers, thinking of my films, there was one Pig had recommended, they'd screened it at the Reposi last winter, you could see this huge billboard through the traffic, a billboard three-storeys high closing in on the Via Gramsci, with three sun-baked faces and a few pistols in the foreground: 'It's beastly good, there's at least ten thousand dead in it.'

INNOCENT   Of the years before the stone episode at Orbetello, I've forgotten mostly everything. There's only one ghost resurfacing from a Ligurian sea: the ghost of Milena Sutter, a girl found dead on the beach years ago. Her story recalls another one over which I'd lost sleep as a child: Ermanno Lavorini, he might have been my age, tortured and killed in a pine grove in Tuscany. The story was on TV for weeks: the doors of evil had opened before me. He was playing outside, when they got him. Later the senseless evil had become more specific, in the form of what had happened to Milena Sutter on a Ligurian beach. By then I'd started to understand why such things were happening, I'd followed the news and the story of the blond lad in a red sports car who had given the girl a lift after school. I had an older cousin, her face like a sun with blue eyes, secretly engaged to a blond lad riding a Suzuki, and I was very worried about her. Then I forgot about Milena and my cousin Marianella, and returned to my universe made of spaghetti westerns and TV films at 7 p.m. But that spring, the blond lad in the red sports car had appealed his conviction, and a late-evening news show had broadcast a long interview with him. I had sat looking at him: he was cool, much more normal than Marianella's Suzuki guy. He was funny, and I very well recall the last question the journalist asked him, after a long, friendly chat: 'Do you think I consider you guilty or innocent?' Strange question. The blond lad, who had an oval face and looked bald to me on the black-&-white TV screen, had glanced at him and then said with a smile: 'I think you consider me innocent.' The frame froze on that smile, then the end credits started rolling.

CROSSROADS   Tricky things, these females. An afternoon three years before, slow glare of boredom, at my house with the Gastaldi cousins. It all hangs on Vittorio, the eldest: a standoffish, maudlin idol, freckly blond, big-cat feline and complete with a slot-in record player. For a while I'd been trying to imitate the way he said 'Tess' when speaking of Tex—but suddenly he was done with comic books, and the slot-in player appeared. That sort of guy could even get engaged to Marianella, if only he cared. Then there's his brother Maurizio, my near-brother at primary school: shared desk shared class shared school shared Sunday school shared afternoons because we lived on the same block and one mum over two managed to snatch a few spare hours and we'd run away from catechism to smoke under staircases or just for the thrill of getting lost in town. Anyway, Easter Day, afternoon—pale April sunlight, the grown-ups in the living room talking about austerity and the one & only Vittorio hypnotizing four girls who terrified me and Maurizio. Three of them living on the floor below, and me praying every day I would not meet them on my way upstairs. And then the daughter of Mariano the gunner, a great friend of my father's and of the Marello sisters', the same dynasty of officers' wives as my mother belonged to. Mariano: a ski champion, a Fifties beau with Jimmy Fontana specs, a man of the world, sort of—the guy who can mix a negroni, to give you an idea. He had married a maths teacher, a sharp, alert woman. And two kids had popped out: Marco, the younger, an indolent, off-kilter pup, one look and you could see he'd come to no good, and the elder, Alessandra: a prodigy of cant-be-assed-with-you-ness. Perfect, dress-perfect, nose-perfect, small and enclosed in a prodigy of grace. And the right age for Vittorio: the downstairs trio must have got pretty pissed off that day. Maurizio and I had run off to the Capitol to watch *Anche gli angeli mangiano fagioli*: one of those Sunday afternoons without cars in that year of the crisis, picturing the city's hero, Avvocato Agnelli, as he's pulled along in a hansom cab, picturing a future made of fist fights cigars fast cars—picturing, most of all, a bunch of teenagers going to town on my room while we're excluded and even a bit ridiculous.

So that's my take on girls, but in a few seconds it's spring '76 and my father has a word with old Mariano who starts asking around in fields and small towns and finds this place laid out on the plain of Saluzzo: Lagnasco, farm yards and corn cobs, silence, cockerels and plumb-line heat, glass-front bars and huge salami sandwiches. And then that big industrial shed: Lagnascofrutta. One evening we set off, me and my folks, and drive to Mariano's house in Saluzzo to have dinner and see if we can get it sorted. It's all very easy: Mariano will put me up at his house, Lagnasco is only four miles away, he can lend me a scooter. Embarrassing evening: she's there, the daughter from three years earlier, that Alessandra who's going to sit her high-school finals that summer and is showing a certain feminine disdain for the whole business. But I'm fresh out of Quarta Ginnasio, and can't very well just sit there like a dummy. So I start a generation-gap argument with the two old troopers, and Mariano really gets into it, winding me up, challenging me, and I hold my own, I can rant and rave and then I get mad, and when I get mad there's no stopping me. I've a model: for years I've been waiting to repeat words I can hardly remember, words from Marianella, the older cousin who in one of those distant-past summers at the seaside in Sicily scandalized our uncles and their friends, all of them drivelling at her bikinis but uneasy when she bit their heads off with the style of the Milanese university student she had become. They were trying to come on slimy but she fended them off blow on blow and called them swine, and once my aunt had slapped her right in front of everyone and dragged her away.

So now here is that Alessandra who's stayed sat at the table, she's perfect, pluperfect, all dressed up and womanly in her pencil skirt and sheer tights, high heels even, and her hair cut smooth in a bob, not a strand out of place. Drop dead there & then—or later, from wanking. My father is arguing hotly now, he's on about a judge who was shot in Genoa, he says my guys like guns these days, and I say no, we leave that to you guys who put yourselves in a uniform so you can become something. Yes, I'd thought of hanging the Red Brigades star in the house just to make my father mad—but that murder in Genoa stank of gun oil, fascist ways, corpses like that of Ermanno Lavorini, the child who'd stayed out to play in the pine groves. And here we were that evening, late June, driving home a bit drunk, my folks joking on how pretty Mariano's daughter was, but thinking back on themselves, on a young woman among grown-ups, rather than teasing me. Me, I was thinking of the revolution and of her mascara.

MAURO   His name is Signor Lovera, and he's scary even though he tries to be kind. It's clear this is a hierarchical relationship, formally and factually and harshly hierarchical: the hierarchies of work, not those of age, of school, of the scouts camp. Deep-end harsh. I thought I would learn something—and money is money after all. First of July, Lagnascofrutta shed, getting up at five lest I got there late, sleeping at Mariano's in Saluzzo the night before. Alessandra was not there. They've put a camp bed for me in a long, narrow room, it's all right once I close the door, but Lagnascofrutta is heavy, like a juggernaut slamming into your face at 100mph. Dour sky, swollen clouds, the huge entrance door slamming wide open, the shed inside with conveyor belts, countryside Fordism and a thought trepanning my head: the thought of those who get into the factory for the first time at fourteen, except they know they'll never get out again—or if they do, it'll be forty years later, with a gold wristwatch and a pension, their bones broken and arthritis in their hands. I think of the devil and his fat hard belly, I think 'I'm bricking it' and 'I'm fucking lucky' at the same time: I know autumn means I'll be back at the Liceo Classico, back to my mates, to the conkers of the Crocetta, to Dino & Pig, to Benedetta.

Lovera is sitting on a sort of rebar tower inside the shed, he looks like a guard on a panopticon as he checks the work on the conveyors: he gives people hell, takes the piss, but is not violent. I climb up the metal ladder and introduce myself, and he doesn't pretend not to know me, he might even be smiling a bit. He's wearing a white shirt: a man's shirt. He gets down with me, shows me the work. If you don't waste time you'll learn real quick. Real quick: I'm to stand at one end of the double belt. On the upper belt the peaches are unloaded from the lorries; on the lower one, wooden crates with moulded blue plastic trays. The girls standing along the conveyor take the good peaches from the upper belt, place them in the blue trays filing by on the lower one, and throw the bad peaches over their shoulder onto the floor. At the end of the line the full crates are loaded back onto the lorries and taken to the markets, and a power shovel sweeps up the bruised and rotten peaches from the floor and dumps them into the autoclave to be shipped off and made into jam. 'So look, your job is easy—on the left you've got the pile of blue trays, on the right the crates.

You put the middle and ring finger of your left hand into the moulded tray and pull it up, as if you're making a horns sign with your hand, and at the same time, with your right hand, you pull up a crate, then lower the tray into the crate and lay the crate on the belt. Have a go. No, not like that—I'll show you.' Smart, our Signor Lovera, well-practised, well-placed moves. I learn right away. He pats my shoulder, half man-to-man, half father-to-son, and goes: 'Seventeen a minute.' The minimum.

Eight hours. Lunch break at twelve. My hands are going by themselves, locked in the moulded-tray move, I've to remember to keep them still while on break or the older workers will get ideas. The women workers, especially. There's a freckly guy who's in charge of the cleaning, he's been looking at me with a funny smile on his face since this morning. On the first break he walks up to me and points at the women working on the belts and they all crack up. 'You know,' he goes, 'they've noticed you've been touching yourself between crates . . .' 'What? What the . . . !' Now he's splitting his sides—a sort of initiation rite. 'Come, I'll take you to a bar I know under the arcade, they do the best sarnies ever.' It's drizzling, the bar has a tinted glass front and it's good to sit behind it. Time, when you have no time, has a way of flowing by lovely and slow, rocking you, giving you respite. Huge sand-wiches with thick-sliced countryside salami, yellow peppers and anchovies in sauce. Can't for the life of me remember his name— Mauro, it must have been, they're always called Mauro in those places. And the girls, Steffi. One of the workers in the factory was his mother, they were my first workmates, and Mauro's old lady had a soft spot for this townie cub. At the end of my first eight hours I was in pieces, a nervous wreck: here I was, still at Lagnasco and already dreading the alarm going off the next morning.

Almost dark, pouring with rain, and no sooner have I left the place than the scooter stops. Dead. I want to cry: apple trees in rows all around, the sky booming. So I tie the lovely scooter to an apple tree and walk all the way back to Saluzzo. They'd had their dinner already, and were worried about me. But my father calls to ask how it was, and when I tell him about the scooter: 'Are you mad? It's Mariano's! You'd better go back and fetch it.' 'But it's dead!' 'So walk it.' And off I go, the rain has let up, almost stopped—a long, long night walk, magical even, and the pride of not letting anyone have one up on me. Mariano got me a bike for the next morning.

I was getting used to cycling along the road to Lagnasco. By now, I was ace with the trays and could act big with Mariano's young son. Alessandra looked on with curiosity, so I would pull out some abstruse theory on availability exclusively for her benefit and she would ask me if I wanted anything to read, and I'd get on my high horse and try to think up a way to impress her. Once I asked for 'some sociology texts'—no shit, 'sociology'. I think that gave her the giggles, but she was a sport, so she did find some sociology books and gave them to me, for my bedside table. I was nicking her wee brother's Mickey Mouse comics on the sly. At night, I dream of piles of crates as Alessandra observes me like an entomologist, and she offers me some wine to drink, red wine from the cellar. We go and fetch it—down, in the dark. As soon as I was left alone, I'd start massacring myself with my hands. I had this record I'd bought back in Turin—I knew the first thing I'd do that September with the money from Lagnascofrutta: buy a record player. There was one in Alessandra's living room, and in the evening, if she went out, I would play my record on it. Bob Dylan's Desire, with that song I was learning by heart: your breath is sweet, your eyes are like two jewels in the sky . . . your loyalty is not to me but to the stars above.

And that other verse, the one still visits me at night: your daddy he's an outlaw and a wanderer by trade, he'll teach you how to pick an' choose and how to throw the blade . . . he oversees his kingdom so no stranger does intrude, his voice it trembles as he calls out for another plate of food . . . He'll teach you how to choose the blade.

Back at the factory we laugh and joke, but it's a dry year, bad harvest, fear that the season might end too soon. I stand to lose my stereo—Mauro and his mum, much more. There are people who live like that, who depend on the harvest, the season, and if that goes badly they have to get set for a hard winter. Or at least, there were people like that back in 1976.

Alessandra's had it with staying home listening to the same record over and over again: she takes me out, and out means Saluzzo, a magical, vertical town, arches, vaults, squares, fountains, gargoyles, sharp corners and taverns like La Drancia, leaping out at you in the middle of the night as it stands bright yellow on the last slope in front of the prison, over a square with a convex, windswept surface. She has a secret table by the door, hidden by a wooden shutter painted green, where she shelters when she wants to play the troubled beauty and escape the stares of the students from the lower town, all crazy about her, her perfume, the way she walks. Some evenings she takes me along, and I'm starting to lose even the fear of not sleeping enough. I act the townie communist, speak of revolution and say it can be done, it will be done—before long, I reckon. You can no longer hear Alessandra's steps ringing out on the paving stones of Saluzzo because for a while now she's been burrowing into oversize sweaters and trousers and has stopped dressing the way she had when my dreams were clogged with the beauty and the hurt of her. One more cup of coffee for the road, one more cup of coffee 'fore I go, to the valley below, Bob Dylan says. Climbing and dipping, in the shadow. Yes—yes please, one more coffee 'fore I go.

DIOXIN   There are words that pop out from nowhere one morning and then are left nailed to the calendar, marking out past years: in the Dioxin Year, mid-July, Alessandra's friend Mariella has her birthday. She has made dinner—just the three of us. We drink and drink, then go out drunk, walking around. Alessandra is watching her step: we might be singing and shouting, we might be laughing all right, but we're not going past La Drancia tonight—she might no longer be dressing like a female, but she knows how to take care of her image. That night we ended up on a bench in front of the new school building, a threadbare little green outside a metal fence, and over the fence the playground, beer bottles and more beer bottles and me chucking them at the school pretending they were molotovs, then we would collapse back onto the chewed-up old bench, each of the three holding the other two up, Mariella in the middle. If either buttress collapsed, it would have been straight onto Mariella's thighs. And me so drunk I got hit by the blues—no it wasn't about the crates waiting for me the next morning, it was for mankind, for the tragedy of living, and under an empty sky, and all that stuff that only really means you're fifteen and you've never been with a female. I took up my position on the bench—belly down, which can mean universal torment or exploding guts, you choose. Lying there, face down, counting the rounds of the pavement as it spins beneath me.

Like that—and with the strangest feeling in the tip of my right middle finger, something like velvet but vague and faraway, nothing material, a sort of illusion just this side of touch. Just the booze, I say to myself—but that something takes my ring finger as well, it's moving, it's a wave of warm air, like having the tips, just the tips of your fingers in water. Coming and going, going away again but at times brushing past another finger and I'm damned if I open my eyes to find out, because it's climbing over my fingers and turning into a caress and taking my hand, so I roll over and I've Alessandra's hand in mine, no I can't believe it, I can't believe it. I don't know how Mariella went away, but she did go after a while, and after another while I was fully clothed but lying in Alessandra's bed, staring wide-eyed at the ceiling and she sleeping light, the way she does, and me with a headache and this crazy happiness looking at her, fully clothed too, sleeping easy, loose and beautiful, and all around the bed there are heaps, mounds, towers of wooden crates and blue plastic trays, haphazardly stacked and teetering, about to topple.

The morning after that mid-July, I look at Mauro, and maybe Signor Lovera too, with different eyes. And your pleasure knows no limit, your voice is like a meadow lark, but your heart is like an ocean . . . look, I'd like to learn the guitar just so I can stop right there, hit the wood softly, pause and then say: Mysterious and dark. The noontime sun is dry-varnishing the marble of the arcade outside a co-op building on the square that has been maimed by post-war rebuilding but never freed from the dust swirling around in the heat. We are playing with the shadows, me and Mauro, and I'm thinking and thinking, and for sure looking weird, and I hope he'll notice my looking weird. Still I don't believe it. I don't believe it, I just can't: I know she was just drunk, and now my real problem is, how am I going to look her in the face the next night: carry on regardless? Yes, that's best—she'll see no point in wasting time on someone like me. No point me wondering, even. Best to let it go. That's best. Sometimes, in the evening, she comes home after me, and in the meantime I've already slipped unseen into her room to look at her things, and then come back out so she can find me busy playing with her young brother, reading books on Leninism, grooming myself. I don't want anyone to remind me that she's a woman and about to go off to uni, I don't want her to swat me off like a fly, I've stashed my bone away and am trying to divert attention. I'll hold on to the memory of that drunken evening, and the best way is to never speak of it again. Each time Bob Dylan plays, I'll hold my nerves tense so as to slip past that cup of coffee, that damn cup coming round three times: three for the Road and three 'fore I go, to the Valley Below. There's still La Drancia, slashes of light on the ground, stairways spiralling round and round, the smell of night and the shrubs in front of San Giovanni with the Gothic frescoes and the dog pee. Until the day when Signor Lovera says there's no more fruit so no more work and packs us off home, he says we're going to be away for just two weeks and come back when the new harvest's in—I wonder about Mauro's mum, and I wonder about Alessandra: probably better this way, just about. Too scared she will wake up, or that I'll wake up, like Wile E. Coyote who's already walking well past the edge of the cliff and only falls when he realizes: thank you, Signor Lovera—or just about. Home, then: packing, Dino and Ruben somewhere at the seaside, maybe I'll catch them up at the Argentario, dunno, or maybe go up to Colleretto to see my folks, all right that's a balls-ache but it'll make them happy. Out of here before any illusions set in, the most important thing is no illusions: staying awake, awake, and in this stairway town you risk falling asleep at every step and falling for real and dreaming your life away until you wake up with nothing left but shame, or in fact, first the shame, then the nothing. So out of here, throw everything into the rucksack, relief, and the factory's just a nightmare after all, maybe I'll manage to avoid even coming back in August, hopefully, maybe.

THE GHOST OF SIGNOR LOVERA   But I did go back—except there was no Alessandra. Work and piss-takes from the women workers, and sleeping, sleeping, she's gone to the seaside after her finals, that's right, all right, and . . . better not think about it, but all right, that's all right. Better that way. Morning and night, like a nail through the chest, awake staring at the ceiling, was I not in love with the other one, what's her face—oh yes, Benedetta: my sense, my centre. TV in the evening, Christian soldiers have stormed the camp in Tel al-Zaatar, in the autumn there will be a poster for sale with sixty rows of fifty Palestinian silhouettes, each with the words: 'These Are the Dead of Tel al-Zaatar'. And the second harvest's quick, we can run away into the autumn: get changed, turn yourself over like an octopus when they kill it to eat it. Over this long summer, I have learnt to tell a prayer from a curse. 'Wanting to work' is a curse. I don't want to work—I want money. At the co-op, with my mate Mauro, I eat the cheapest sandwiches, and I can see the gate yawning open for him before long, this autumn in fact, and swallowing him once and for all, my quality-control mate, my lunch-break, peppers-in-dust-sauce mate. Once past that gate, all his life he'll be grabbed by the skin of his balls over and over again by someone who'll put him on the scales. Want to work? Pass. Not quite? Fuck off & die. Nice lad, he was—really wanted to work. Oh—how'd he die? Honest lad, a right grafter—ah well, the best get taken. 'If I get up one morning wanting to work, call a doctor.' That's right. Even though I'll continue to say and believe that revolution means working your ass off, sweating, making sacrifices, my feet are wiser, they've already shot forward and my head can't quite catch up. But we're on a roll, the autumn is marching straight into our faces with the fullness of its rich smells and I've a wodge of money in my pocket, all mine, lovely and heavy with the envy from my townie schoolmates, the bourgeois ones I mean: now I can even venture out on the side of certain comrades none can touch—Enzo the railway man, Ciro D'Amore, Cocò—the guys who get listened to and respected, because they work their asses off.

Meanwhile here I am, Quinta Ginnasio, it's a barracks, a lesser seminary, a torture of Greek verbs, received opinions, afternoons broken over a book useless as the grammar of a dead language. After the summer's colours and hard work it's tough to go back into high-school captivity, the stench of a lifetime, a slog. By now, Mauro must be walking, with some new mates, through that great gate in the city. All right, I'm having it easy, I'm lucky. Lucky.

BASICALLY   And luckily there's much to do, there's still the scouts, there's Benedetta at every crossroads—but also, there's the dealer & pusher, there's new and awesome friends, seductive, criminal, chemical, electrical, coercive and explosive, there's collectives and self-management of school structures, you're in school all day, setting up study groups: on work in the factories, on archaic metrics, on Marx's thought, and then you've just got to be in a committee, no two ways about it. Teaching committee: a young girl called Federica, always in that good-family-girl uniform, blue skirt & jacket with white stockings, always belly down on the desk swinging her feet in the air, which means that after each teaching committee session you've got a job pulling your dick down. She's in the same year as me, but will only mix with the older guys. The big guys, all of them busy with a spiel to sell you their newsletters, taking the mickey and trying to pull you into their party. What was that you said? Bureaucracy in China? Ah ah ah! Everyone, you've gotta hear this one!!! Shit—too late, it's come out now and you've put your foot in it, that guy's never going to speak to you again, in fact he'll be laughing with his mates as you pass them along the corridor of the new wing (Royal Lyceum Gymnasium). So you buy his newsletter, you read and can't understand a fucking word, and on your way upstairs you have to climb over the lovebirds, motionless like chequers players, for ever glued to the same step. Giulia and Paolo, they're called. She's the prettiest in the school, a carpenter's daughter, and was in Avanguardia Operaia last year; he was in the Pdup and has a famous father. Not sure if they love each other, but this year they've made a shocking choice: they've the same slightly lost look on their faces, but they've shed their old skin and joined

Autonomia Operaia—nasty adventurists, violent, ready to take up arms. And they're both still sitting there, alone together on their step, so when Giulia gets a rash on her face a permanent-marker message appears on the step: 'Live to rage and fight, die by the itch mite.' Because no one from Autonomia had ever shown their face at the Royal Lyceum Gymnasium. Paolo became a scholar lecturing on some of those rarefied, boulder-heavy German poets, and Giulia spent many years in jail, because there was a time when any scumbag could grass on you and get you sent down and who knows if you'd get out and what you'd be like if you did. And inside, Giulia lost it. She tried to grab on to something and ended up grabbing another girl by the throat, or at least trying to. Probably got ousted after that, struggling badly, and meanwhile the killing of the other girl, fiancée of the super-grass, will be someone else's job. But Giulia still ends up in solitary, where no one knows anything about you except that eye stuck to the spyhole every minute. There are pickets and collectives every hour: one for each class, each floor, each section, one for the Gymnasium, and then the assemblies that go on all morning, their heroes speaking and looking out into the distance with the superb verbal tics that you'll try to import into your own speech patterns. There's one for instance who always repeats the word 'basically' twice over. That's right, he goes 'Basically basically,' and then starts. And there's always that moment's silence when everyone's casting about for just anything to say, and sure enough there's always the shitface who goes: 'We've still to hear from Comrade Miasco on this,' and oh fuck, Pietro Miasco, that's me, and here I am about to look like a dick. I really can't recall how I used to wriggle out of all that—the only thing frozen in my memory is the moment when I'm about to look like a dick. Yet the group, the red horizon and the coded languages of politics have the power to shelter me.

WHITE FLOWERS   And the other day Mao Zedong died, so Ruben and I went to buy great big bunches of small white flowers, some of the money from Signor Lovera and some from Donedilio, and then towards evening got on the trams to give them away to people, explaining that white is the colour for mourning in China and listening to what everyone had to say, and everyone was nice to us, the old ladies looking at us with tenderness, perhaps thinking that a bit of the century they'd got used to inhabiting was gone with that old Chinaman. That's it—the kindness of old ladies on the trams. Maybe I can talk to Alessandra about that. Come on, there's no way she's going to turn up, fool that I am, standing in the rain and half an hour early. Her folks have a house in Turin and she stays there now that she's at uni— a gloomy old house in a fin-de-siècle block with stained-glass cathedral-style windows, rugs, heavy black furniture, and even a grandfather clock, I think. A medium's house in a neighbourhood of ghosts. Nearby was a bakery that sold these huge chocolate-covered biscuits I used to call niggers' dicks—one of those bakeries with paper bags stained with grease and lollipops in a big jar on the counter. No, she won't come, she won't come at all but she does, she comes in the rain, Come I'll show you the house, look it's pouring, put my jacket on—perfect, makes you look like a mushroom. Really. Yes. A poisonous mushroom? No, no! No, really! Well, yes, maybe—oh, I don't know—a pretty mushroom, anyway.

And then I never saw her again, and who knows why, at some point she starts writing me letters and I almost don't open them, or won't answer anyway, not because I don't want to, but because Alessandra is too important, surely there must be some mistake if she's still writing to me.

PHASE   My mother doesn't want me to go to demos. My mother, a sticky substance on my skin, and when I get to school I'm scared someone might see her. So I've stopped talking about my secondary-school exams, and I get the feeling that the scouts, well—maybe not. Everyone's talking about a coup, and it seems to me they're all thinking my father would be happy to be part of it if he could. My father has a wide face, a loud laugh: I can't quite imagine him on the TV news, watching the military parade from the dictator's box. But he doesn't know a thing, and neither does my mother, and everything's rushing headlong towards a time of hard work, a better world where neither of them has any place. Dino, Pig & I are widening our field of action, perfecting our spray-painting art, discovering small cafes and hot chocolate that's only good if you can stand the spoon in it. Meetings every night, at the neighbourhood committee where there's a wood stove and a big glass pane so you can watch the snow, or in some mouldering loft or other, and more often in the houses of the rich comrade girls at the Crocetta, with tropical plants behind large windows, blond wood and pianos, and long corridors leading to secret rooms and lives you can only imagine. And icy mornings at Mirafiori, afternoons on the parade ground, Greek and Latin and the monarchist bearded lady teacher summoning the mothers of my classmates Franz and Franco and Ciccio and telling them to keep their children away from me because I'm a drug dealer. At the scout groups the talk is of politics, 'territory', there's no more going to Mass even: we're all reds—except for Benedetta, of course. And we fight about everything, all the time, I love shocking her with my bottles and violence and god who's not there and if he is he's a bastard, and whenever she was away I'd feel like the world should be blown apart and rebuilt afresh for the simple reason she would be in it—my highly private reason for revolution. Except she can't stand me not believing in god and can't stand herself laughing at my jokes. One night, in some wood in the Val Susa, we're all in the same tent, she's next to me and I put my head on her shoulder, we spend the whole night talking, just me and her, softly, and I hold my neck stiff not to weigh on her. Only Dino can hear us, and yowls: 'The lovebirds are cooing!' And the next day, sleep in my bones, the sleep of when you've not slept from emotion and the heart racing, a hundred thousand revs. Chiomonte, that place was called—and I thought I would probably be saved.

BATMAN   My father is saying stuff like 'your murderer friends'. He's obsessed with the judge they've killed in Genoa, talking about him all the time, clearly it's something to do with the strange summer of 1970 that's always coming out in his conversations. 'The judge,' he says, 'had been investigating the death of one of my friends'—a journalist who disappeared one day in August—or maybe not the journalist but a judge who also got killed, who was looking for the journalist. Oh I don't know and I don't care, and I tell him so. But I remember when I was a kid and someone said the journalist must have been walled up alive inside a motorway pylon, because that's how the mafia do it—or they might have made him some concrete shoes and thrown him into the water at Palermo harbour.

I was at primary school back then, and spent my summers in the moraine arc of Colleretto. There was a great meadow and a dog called Poldo, a farmer kid who'd teach me his tricks, and the rooms opened onto a long corridor made by a wooden partition painted white. I shared with two cousins more or less my age, and we were all crazy about Batman comics. My father had made me a box of red wood with a glass sheet on top and a lightbulb inside: a tracing machine. I'd made posters for our room by tracing Batman covers with a marker: all I had to do was put the covers on the glass, place a sheet of paper over them and light the bulb. There was one with Batman & Robin tied inside a wooden frame, and a gangster in a double-breasted pinstripe suit and Borsalino hat pouring a load of cement sludge over them and jeering. We took it off the wall almost immediately, me and the cousins—too scary.

These days, all my father will do is mutter something like 'You imbecile', and that'll be it. The carabinieri have dumped him and he's full of rage. They've disbanded his boss' special squads and packed him off to run a fuel depot in some shithole north of Novara. In the morning he fucks off before sun-up, and he's back at night just moments before hitting the sack. He's the perfect enemy: old, uniformed, stiff and prejudiced—a right shithead. I stop even saying hello to him, try to hurt him as much as I can by using the power of my growing body against his. I've the whole world right ahead of me. If I'm at home, I'll be shut up in my room listening to Radio Città Futura in the dark, the window open and a mass of blankets heaped on me. There's a fuck-around phone-in called Non è la gelosia, and one evening I call on behalf of an orthodox micro-party and launch into a Stalinist-Maoist tirade that I think is very funny. They are not amused. I never called again. On air, they only said that one listener had phoned in to complain about the freshman humour.

SEAGULLS   Sure, I too would like to track back to one precise point along the line of those days and see where the war of the living and the dead was decided. The fact is, I've a private question tangled up with all that, messy like all the stories spinning around me, and I get confused. At one point I even commissioned a murder. But I'm scared that if I stop to breathe the story will rear up and stop coming out, be sucked back like toothpaste up the tube: so I'm telling it to you as it comes, scattered and uneven as it is.

The seagulls—yes, there they were in the city, and left wakes of strange cries on the tarmac as they scavenged for garbage along the drains of the Dora, which was culverted back then—a river walled alive into a coffin. Below the seagulls, water rushing towards the steel-cement belly of FIAT Ferriere, a bridge of pride and enterprise the city had built in its drive to swallow and climb over, because the future won't stop for a natural border, and the future, back then, was throng and toil rushing over the tamed water and every day, every night, punctual and relentless, three shifts in, three shifts out, loading and unloading millions of blue toy soldiers. And so the river bends, she flows into the factory's belly and does her duty, sheltered from the prying gaze of those who live in the city. Each time I watch Juve play on TV, sooner or later the camera will pan over to the elegant figure of Avvocato

Agnelli smiling in his box—the clock that regulates each movement in the city. As for Benedetta, I couldn't stop thinking of her. Then, a short while later, I saw her again: I was walking along Corso Matteotti, making straight for Corso Vinzaglio and the western arches of my first homeland, when a yellow bus rolls by, groaning with scratches & varicose veins as it heads for the weekday markets or the workplaces of office clerks and cleaning ladies. And behind one of the windows, a luminous spot looking at me, standing up and smiling: and she was beautiful, so beautiful that I . . . No, I'd never forget her, I'd silently dedicate my all to her, and she'd be back in the end, back to an innocent place somewhere west of a few massively urgent things I had to sort out, a place where we'd understand every single thing, the two of us—above all, the two of us. So I smile and raise my hand and she beams again and laughs and flashes her eyes, and the air all around is shimmering and buzzing, and then she lifts up the baby for me to see.

Right. But I still think you can get out any way you want, whenever you want, and you can go back, even, if you want to. Right. So let's try to live up to these high skies I'm aspiring to: first of all, I decide I'm going to learn to swear. It's not hard to do: the first one was Dino, thick specs, checked winter jacket, toothpick in his mouth, always in heavy boots these days, and at assemblies he likes to jump on a desk and land on his heels with a thump accompanied by a resounding 'mother-fucking-god'. Not hard to do—try it: motherfuckinggod. See? It's coming on, it sticks. There's Pasino, the blond guy—tall, calm, ethereal and relaxed, a former patrol leader in the Foxes, who's finding it harder, he can't get the hang of it—I don't think he managed to get it out nice and rounded once in his life, not even later—and so he pulls a funny face, eye-brows lifted and a safety-distance smile, and chuckles it all out in one go: motehrfuckinggodfuckinggodfuckinggod. Me, I get it in no time—I've the gift.

The streets keep throwing up fog and snow, thousands of doors open, and I can walk along the threads stretched between the rich colours of those interiors, I'm light as a tightrope spider, Alice in progressive wonderland.

VOUCHERS   My parents travel a fair bit, it's a voucher thing, sometimes they're away for a whole fortnight, and then I fill the house with important people, clear eyes and guitars, and spin out the night. My mother is a residue from a useless world, she's bour-geois and cut off from everything, but she likes to find ill-concealed traces of those human flood tides when she's back—she likes it, that is, from the second day onward, because right out she gets completely pissed off and we scream at each other until my father goes to bed to get away from it all. Still, she always finds a way to get stories about a life that's escaping her while giving her a whiff of dangerous ideas. She had me at twenty-one, before she could start anything—and sure enough she never did start anything after that. She'd do anything to hear a few words from me—so I keep well buttoned up. But sometimes, at night, she gets me. She has the knack: she grew up the fifth of ten children, beloved of her father but born too late to be able to study. She got her 'vocational' qualification, the one that stops you getting any kind of further education: high school was for her older sisters—the family was still needing to make that sort of choice, when she was six. She's shifty, like those kids who'll hide in the cupboard when it comes to clearing the table or take for ever pooing when it's homework time. Probably a liar, too—but she's hungry for the world, no matter how she tries to shoehorn herself into the wife that she is. At a certain point she dug out an old teacher's training diploma she'd got godknowshow, and reinvented herself as a secondary-school arts & crafts teacher. She got despatched promptly to Mirafiori Sud, a disaster area of a school called something like Gramsci or Rosa Luxemburg, which says it all, really. In the morning, the southern edges of Turin are blurred in the fog coming up from the flatlands around Pinerolo, and on those mornings too she makes the effort to remain the colonel's wife, oozing away at the crack of dawn along Corso Unione Sovietica in her maroon Cinquecento, wide passageway in front of Mirafiori, Gate 5, staff lane, and off she goes for another ten minutes of traffic lights and fog and counter-lane, she's never so much as seen the edges of town, it looks like, but now she's taking the terroni kids out to play in the scraggy grass around the mausoleum of the Bela Rusìn—as in Pretty Lil' Rose: the neoclassical tomb of one of the king's lovers, lost in the middle of a park ruined by effluents beyond the banks of the Sangone. I know why she's taking them to the mausoleum, but I also know that's not going to wash with those little guys. Sometimes she'll stay with them through the afternoon, dodging the hypodermics that litter the ground, because these kids can't go home, their parents might be working on the same shifts. These are scary little adults, they know the blackmailing, whining and violence that are the law on the streets of Mirafiori. But she's found charming colleagues, guys with names like Linus, Capranico and the like: they've beards and scarves and strange ideas she despises but listens to, turbulent thoughts that shake her bother her nudge her to read. She knows everything about a few things and a few things about everything, a self-taught woman's knowledge flaring up here and there, and maybe that makes her interesting. My father adores her, and she takes advantage, throws tantrums. When I was small, all through the endless house moves and relocations young officers and their families are forced to live with, she would take me for walks around the ruins and tell me long, long stories—stories of geese waking up the warriors as the barbarians arrive, or Mucius of the burnt hand, Coriolanus the renegade, or Collatinus the banished, wandering hero. She would use anything that came to mind, talk of the empires of the sun gods across the ocean and the Spaniards who destroyed them, or a sick boy who had a magic lantern and magic lime-flower tea that stirred memories. She would use all she had, and I would chew and digest unawares. Who knows if any of the terroni kids were listening as she spoke of the Bela Rusìn.

She's brought me up without any means, and now she can only get entangled. Nothing worse than getting entangled with a teenager, especially when you're still so young: all you'll get is frustration and grief. And sure enough I am making her eat shit, making my father eat shit, simply out of biological right. And she gets anxious, and breathless, and starts drinking. And when she does, she goes blind with rage and lashes out at the weakest link: the colonel my father. But she loves the thought that I'm growing up in a garden wider than our housing block for state employees and servicemen, with its gravelly yard and its puddles: we've landed in the town centre by chance, and she thinks this will save me just like it saved her when she was small, and she gloats even as she hurts herself with the image of what she could or should have been. Sometimes, at night, she starts breaking things and shouting that I'm suffocating her, my father rushes over to take her side and I retreat more and more into my room with the window open onto the hill. All the more so when she tries to re-establish contact, because then I feel the pleasure of revenge— I feel it in my body, a rush. And I take advantage, play on my trickster skills, plant clues and counter-clues, sometimes drop a casual truth or two. One evening I pretend I've left my precious Red Diary, the journal of all my adventures, in the living room, so she can read all about my flight to the occupied Statale.

That Saturday, I'd plucked up a rucksack with the red & cream kerchief of my scouts troop and told her I was going into the mountains near Cuneo. A fib: I'm meeting Ruben and Dino at Porta Nuova. Our destination: the national conference of proletarian youth circles in Milan, at the occupied Statale: State University, workshop of the new world. Words and more words, sandwiches gobbled down to keep out the fright of facing that particular unknown, the fear of landing at the centre of the world.

WHO GETS HER FIRST   Fancy finding Bruno Pizzul at the centre of the world, beyond the station with its nuts and bolts and stanchions, toing & froing of wee men along tracks filled with crazy AC/DC running across living bodies, dragging them out of the sheds, slamming them along lines of buildings at the wrong speed, street signs are a violet blur and as soon as you're out everything's moving. We've grown up in a world of vectors and energy flows, a world scrunched up by speed, a sphere harnessed in the network mesh of cables and waves, where everything's near and what's near is known. But out there we are looking at the night as it slowly draws in, at a world that's long and wide and mineral, boundless and calm, and a sign from the sky comes to bless the portent of celebration. We've dived into the streets without directions, any time now we'll ask a passer-by or a tram conductor, but for now we're happy surrounded by crossroads, any street will do, so we take Via Vitruvio heading for Corso Buenos Aires, our eyes filled with taxis and on the pavement we run across a tall guy in a tweed coat walking stooped beside another guy and talking to him, and Ruben touches my elbow: 'Look, that's Bruno Pizzul,' and I get a shred of the joke or the cheat-on-the-wife story he's telling the shorter guy. They're almost running, the voice he uses for commenting slo-mo takes or second-division games as if leased to him by elder colleagues. He does not notice us, he's chatting away as he turns the corner of one of those big buildings.

And we get there by concentric circles, following the outline of the Duomo, because we know everything's kind of clustered in the town centre, and sure enough by walking close to the side of the cathedral building we arrive at Piazza Fontana—and have to wonder just where the actual piazza is: what we see is a stunted little roadside green, a sort of casual aneurism in the middle of the traffic. And straight after, Piazza Santo Stefano—heart of the nation. The sign advertising Apulian wine and the shop window glowing yellow point us back to a past tense of scouts groups and taverns, because you're always home at the centre of the world. On the step there's a few people singing a song called Stalingrado, and we're invincible. The wee men spat out of the station are here now, they're moving, but there's nothing mechanical left, the sky is full of signal lights and we know everyone. The house has numberless rooms and corridors with huge windows. There are bivvies on desks and writing tables, banners along the walls, cracks of open doors through which you can see lines of sleeping bags— won't those get nicked? One door opens and a stout guy jumps out, his face is like the oval of a rugby ball set sideways, he goes: 'Yo!' I know his face, we've walked side by side in some demo, his name is Igor. He walks over: 'We ought to find out how these guys make their tin cans.' 'Tin cans?' 'Molotovs—over here in Milan they don't use bottles but cans—the bang is something else.' That was the moment Igor earned his lifelong nickname (relative to the lifetime of this story, that is): Tin Can.

He pulls us into one of the classrooms: 'The comrades from Turin are nearly all in here,' and the three become four, we dump our sleeping bags in a corner and Igor shows us around: permanent assembly, smell of sweat and ganja, the red of checked shirts, army green, faded blue. And a sense of glory, of siege and tower and knightly duties: around the walls are 1,200 armed police, which goes to our head a bit. Igor introduces us to his comrades: two who are called Carletto or something, plus Zio Lupara—as in Uncle Shotgun. There's Cocò, he has a flick knife without the flick, he slides his thumbnail along the blade to open it then flicks his wrist to spring it out, when he wants to move about he starts pulsing and going: 'Well, fo'fucksake, well, well, fo'fucksake . . .' No one knows what he might be doing for a living. Though we all know what Billy does: he makes ice-cream at the Nuova Cremeria, the one that's just opened under the arcade. It's full of chi-chis, and Billy warns us against eating his ices, because he likes to—uh—cream into the vanilla. There's a big guy called Giambranco—as in Johnnypack, because when he lays into someone it's like a whole pack of bruisers coming down. And there's Albertino, who looks at you from behind a half-fringe and has you hypnotized. And then Johnny, thick arms, eyeglasses that look like they're resting on a stone—a guy you can listen to, and if he smiles when you say something, you feel you're in.

There was also a kid with long fair curls and eyes clear as water, his name was Tano. I never saw him again—except in a dream one night in 1983, after Cinema Statuto burned down and a lot of people, almost seventy, died suffocated from the poisonous fumes of the plastic walls as they sat watching Knock on Wood, which is a French film but funny. Turin was left in shock and mourning for weeks, the film posters stayed on the front of the blackened building bereft of its cinema for years: everyone had a friend, a relative, some even a wife or child who had died in there. I knew Tano, who'd decided to spend his evening watching Knock on Wood. A few months later, I dreamt of Via Po on a night of comets and shooting stars like the one at the occupied Statale, and just where the arcade starts there's Tano, sitting cross-legged on the ground and playing a flute. I recognize him, say hi, tell him he can't sit there playing when he's dead, and he says he knows but has something to tell me, so he gets up and we go off to the dead men's bar which was a real bar called that, overlooking the river on the far corner of Piazza Vittorio. A place where you could find yourself say on May Day and they'd give you a shot in the hours it took for that monster of a demo to come uncoiled at the belly and stretch out towards the final rally, a huge demo every time, short and fat like a chestnut maggot. And in carnival time the piazza was invaded by carousels, there were shooting galleries with balloons and the haunted grotto, and the old guys remembered that time when they'd set up the rollercoaster right above the water, level with it, so you'd feel like you were going to be pitched into the river and drown, and there were gangs of local yokels spoiling for a fight, and if you knew anything at all you knew you could nip out between the sideshows and go for a drink at the dead men's bar. But that night, the night of the dream I mean, there were not many people in there, just two guys playing draughts and one talking to the barman, no one's looking at us so Tano says, 'Let's go into the little back room,' and on the right there's a door with the place for the empty crates, mops and spare bottles. Tano locks up and he has something important to tell me, he says I'll not be able to remember it when I wake up, since it's clear I'm dreaming. Except that from behind the door come the voices of those guys who'd been drinking and minding their own business and not looking at us, and now we can hear people yelling, 'You bastard! You're dead, you don't belong here, you want to ruin us?' and pounding on the door, and I'm scared. Tano is calm and says, 'Listen to me,' but they kick the door down. I never saw him again.

But here at the Statale he's alive, scouting around for girls. There's one from my school, a bit older than me: Marina. Hers is the smell of skin, a soft smell, one of those smells you'll remember for ever, the sort of smell you'll wish you could forget for ever if she has hurt you. Her hair is black, near-blue, her eyes an even deeper black, she's a tiny little thing with springy legs and a big bosom pushing out straight at you. Her face is sweet, perhaps a bit dumb, like she's just woken up, and her nose has a tiny dent, as if broken, and is lost in a sprinkle of brown freckles. And then

43

she speaks with a lisp, which is enough to give you thoughts as soon as she opens her mouth.

Marina at the occupied Statale, dazzled by Milan that much later will become her dream of a safe harbour—much later, as she drowns in a toxic sea, she will dream of Milan as the stage set for a normal life where she will step back in time and become a physio, she'll be married, perhaps unfaithful but in a normal way, with a white coat and a study, in Milan. That was her dream as she was drowning. But now—now she's a child with the smell of biscuits and warm bread still lingering in the parting of her hair, her womanly shape screaming to escape an outline that's still blurred, a kid with a fringe in mid-forehead and the tarmac of her hair stubbornly trying to curl. Wondering at everything: her eyes are not just black, they're wide, wide, open wide. Igor passes me a bottle of beer, he's laughing quietly, and I want to measure up to him: 'Let's see who gets her first.' At which he puts on his serious face, like an entrepreneur or a gambler. He nods, stretches out his hand, shakes on it: we're in business.

LEGALITY WITH NO THEFT   He could be a leader, Igor could—except he doesn't take himself seriously: he goes to some sort of high school because of that Seventies miracle of social mobility, but later on life will throw him back into the circus, drowning him in heavy labour. After which, being a bright lad, he'll wind up in some office or other, then perhaps some bad investments, a flunked degree, disenchantment with politics and a woman—one woman after chasing many, never needing to work too hard at it because he's a laugher. He's the sort of guy who writes piss-take songs on the feminists, which shows an outsider's courage, because that lot will put you straight on trial and expel you from each and every thing: from collectives, from demos, you name it. They'd throw you out of the world if they could, they're the types who on weekend outings will come up with stuff like: 'You guys do the dishes, we've been doing that for two thousand years.' So the dentist's daughter from the pedestrianized area— but Igor will just laugh and sing, and you can see he'll come to no good, because he's had no schooling in the 'good-manners-at-all-times' form that cradles us, the scions ready to take over from our daddies at the wheel. Before long, he and I will joust for Marina.

But right now, our problem is food. Ten days ago they stormed into two supermarkets in Milan with loudspeakers and started telling shoppers to wake up, to get mad, to see to the inflation for themselves and slash the price of their own shopping. They helped themselves to all sorts, and left without paying. Proletarian expropriation. Like what I do at La Rinascente, except this was done by a bunch of people shouting out loud. Adventurist stuff—more like thieves than avant-gardes: Johnny says these actions carry the risk of mistaking individual interest for collective need. What we're going to do tonight is different: proletarian price reduction—as in, the same thing, but at the restaurant, and leaving a symbolic sum. The plan was hatched by Ice-Cream Billy, and he knows the place too: you just walk around the campus, past an Argentinian or Indian or Sicilian restaurant, then down Porta Romana where there's an alley with a perfect pizza place, wood-fired oven, dark matchboard cladding, quiet chatter and bright checked tablecloths. We're at a long table by the door, on the corridor that bends into the next room. And here we go, cold cuts, salad and cheese for the thirteen of us, sixty-one thousand lira, we'll pay ten thou: we make the sign, a fist slammed on the table, one of us stands up, boshes the money down and shouts out: 'This is . . .' It comes out wheezy, but he rallies and resumes as everyone looks on. 'This is a proletarian price reduction—we accept a politically fair price and we're paying it, anything on top of that is legalized theft. We are for a different legality, legality without theft.' Great. Except look at the waiter, he's coming at us with the mother of all pizza shovels in his hands and the sort of mother-fuck-ing-god in his mouth that'd put our leaders' leader to shame, he's got the longest legs and he's running, fucksake how he's running, omigodomigod this is it, this time I'm for it, but he throws himself after another small group, there's three or four of us, I've a sword spiking my spleen, I rush down a small street—dead end. No, worse: ends against a barracks wall. A tower, an armed gate. And a man in uniform standing in front.

And again, I don't know how we got out of it, my memory is freeze-framed on that split second of no breath in front of the barracks down a dead-end street. I don't even know if that street was actually there, if it was really a dead end, and if that was really November '76.

BARABBA   What do you mean 'what are they'? Where have you been? They're liberated territories, and that night the campus in Via Festa del Perdono was the federation of liberated territories. Yes, of course we've had the Dutch guys and the house occupations and the communes: but that was old stuff, the stuff of high ideals and dreams of a remote future. The circles are different, they've come out of the edge of town, out of park benches and bar doorways, among those uncool packs of kids who jump on the uptown buses on Sundays to come strutting down into central and line up outside the windows of locked-up shops and ice-cream parlours.

Spare time. It had always sounded like some sort of blasphemy—the workers worrying about spare time? Like fuck they do. Our elder brothers in '68, engaged in a training course for the ruling classes, had no time for spare time. Their plan was simple: to take power. In their world, spare time is something like a stupid brother-in-law, a tic, a non-standard sexual habit, a wodge of ill-gotten money. But these days there are people who are no longer ashamed, people who while away empty afternoons as we do on the steps of certain monuments, no money for the cinema, and work is no longer a value. Yes, there's the future of the body politic, no question about that—but meanwhile we've got to sit through an endless Saturday afternoon, and that's enough to do your head in. To get through spare time and come out alive: there is lucidity in a kid of eighteen who sets himself this goal. Revolt is still dressed in red flags, but it comes out of a human bunch that has the stench of sweat and cologne, legs brushing past one another with each movement and if you've got a boner there's always someone who'll notice. It comes out of murderous boredom, bivvying by low walls or flowerbeds or the steps on the square, whole nights spent deciding where to go and then not going. Or it comes out in the most elementary form: finding a place to get it on. And on Sundays there are neighbourhoods where you're either shooting up or you're an idiot, cause if you live in places like that and you've got half a brain, the least you can do is waste it. One evening, a guy who usually infests the station at Limbiate gets his ass off a bench and sees that his jeans have left a blue stain on the wood. He and his mates are the sort that gets thrown out of bars before long, yes it's the long hair, but also they tend to take the piss, plonk themselves down at a table with half a white wine and expect to veg out for the whole afternoon and there's the boss behind the counter dreaming of the customers who'd come in droves if only that hairy little git would fuck off. Well, these guys in Limbiate started keeping tabs on the empty windows of some of those big town houses, the dusty old sort you can find anywhere in the near-suburb belt and no one's been in there for ten years at least—or the big abandoned sheds that had belonged to some dashed entrepreneurial dream, or even decommissioned garages with broken or boarded-up shop windows. You've got the map in your head, you know where they are, know the moment when not many people pass by, know how to get in as well. The avant-garde goes straight for the archetypes, no mental superstructures: these guys are looking for a place to get laid. Guys who know how to twist a bit of wire around a forgotten lock and slide into those unrented rooms to get covered in dust as they cover their date. That's the avant-garde for you, in 1976.

In just a few months, there's hundreds of squatted dens, each with a name. In Turin: Cangaceiros at the villa in Santa Rita, Montoneros in a dump at San Salvario, Fantasma—guess where? In the far-off mausoleum of the Bela Rusìn. Pavone at Borgo Vittoria, Malembe, Zapata whoknowswhere. And Barabba. Barabba has been looking for a place and decided to occupy the sports hall belonging to the convent school at the bottom of the hill: we thought it was a council sports centre. Pretty well kept for an empty hall, mind you—no dust anywhere, the climbing frames nice and shiny, the poles, the mats . . . bah, we dump our sleeping bags and begin the assembly. And in comes the tiniest of all nuns, she's probably dying of fright as she stands at the top of the staircase at the entrance and says: 'Sorry boys, this is the girls' sports hall—you know, the girls with no family.' Oh fuck. So we fold the sleeping bags up, not much arguing even, except that one of us has disappeared: Gino Bonetti—now a Catholic MP—has run off to Palazzo Nuovo, which is occupied. Bonetti—we'd met him on one of our spray-painting afternoons, Dino, Ruben and I: we were going to swamp the election posters in paint, and Bonetti comes up, carrying a haversack, and says, 'Watch out—police at the other end.' We'd never seen him before. That's how you made friends, back then. After that meeting we took to going out in his neighbourhood, the Crocetta, to slash the tyres of luxury cars. So anyway, here we are sheepishly making our way out of the hole in the fence of the nuns' sports hall when four cars turn up loaded with steel pins and iron bars, with ugly mugs and hooligans: 'So what's up? Were you not being evicted? Forced out?' Turns out Bonetti had whizzed out to see someone he knew and come back with reinforcements—which should have made it clear there and then what a dickhead he was.

So Barabba moves into the nursery-school building on Via Plana: we did manage to occupy that, with its flooring made of wide wooden boards, the warped eighteenth-century windows, the dust and the porch, the small hall on the first floor full of bottles—the ones that Igor of the Tin Cans says are not good enough—neatly lined up in a row. We younger ones know what they are and how they're made but don't know if those ones are full or empty. Inside, in the rooms we've cleaned and washed with bright paint, there is music, there are people and endless discussions full of fuck this and fuck that and knowing looks exchanged on the sly and all the press you're beginning to read the better to give the universe a shape. Writings on politics, on drugs and music, snatches of California: Tim Buckley, Grateful Dead, Zappa, weed smoke and recesses partitions screens for love stories, small intrigues, tangled bodies. Blood, sweat, tears—not our business. The revolution can wait: yes, of course that's where we're going, don't get me wrong—but we've got to get there in one piece, and the body is crying out for some appetizers in the form of a party, hours snatched away from the weekday order, from timetables, roles, hierarchies. Bodies twisted together to dance or couple, or to hallucinate and stay stoned. The revolution comes down to earth, it loses its curse of waiting and projecting into infinity, it's in your hands, your nerves: you can take the pieces and eat them up, fill your belly and even get fat. We're still parsing the vocabulary of our elder brothers: 'Struggle', yes, 'Class'—but every other one of us is thinking of throwing a party or gatecrashing a party, or of some girl, you might get her at a party. Among our elder brothers, the grim ones are thinking of steel and palingenesis—the best ones, of partying and palingenesis. As for us, we're pretty much fucked off with palingenesis. The soldiers of the revolution raise their gaze to the sky—as for us, we're aiming low. The actualized mystery of the whole world is here: but its strength is only complete if fleshed out on earth.

Yes, there is violence in our bellies, and you can smell it in the streets. Out on patrol that same night, other avant-gardes can smell it. Not the avant-gardes on the benches, I mean, but those of the guns, ancient as a Russian novel, symmetrical—a cop's dream. At every drunken party where eyes are filled with chemical colours and utopia, there's always someone in a corner bartering that mighty here-and-now communism with a snippet of the eternal promise made by a structured mind to our minds looking for structure—the promise of a hard and magnificent 'then' to which we should aspire, all the way to self-sacrifice.

Soon they'll start calling it 'Geometric Power'—and how can you resist a formula telling you that the strength you feel as it courses through your arms and legs and into the paving stones rising under your rubber shoes is a lucid metal force, that it is cogent and metallic and can smash the world? How can you resist the lure of a powerful, geometric insight? The recruiters know that well.

PILLS   These you can hear walking are spirits from the lower heavens, because I'm making a roll call of the dead, and they're coming.

Anyway, that morning at the Statale, after our proletarian price reduction and escape and an endless night spent on the teacher's dais, we end up with rashes around our eyes despite splashing water on our faces in the toilets, and we're desperate for a sandwich or anything that might shut our stomachs' gaping mouths: we go downstairs and find a group ransacking the canteen, Igor says that's not the way and he just can't take it, we go upstairs to call Johnny and a few safe Milanese and throw together a sort of security crew on the spot. It's a sentimental thing, I reckon: the security guy at the Statale canteen is a face we all know, he's stayed all through the occupation, he's a good old devil and probably has a family to support. So we kick out the vandals, clean up as best we can and organize a collection for the guy. And later, in the afternoon, when the talking begins in earnest, when the circles that have come from everywhere in Italy start sharing their stories, the strategies, the attempt to keep drugs out, when there's someone setting up a library and someone trying to come on as a situationist circle, there: just when the talking starts, it's suddenly so late and so Sunday that Dino and I and Ruben have to go home, take the train, take our refocused ideas on the borders of legality with us.

And then in mid-December something happened in Sesto San Giovanni: a police squad broke into the house of a young engineer who'd just got his diploma from the State Technical Institute for Industry. The engineer reacted, fired some shots, jumped out of his window. He killed two policemen and died on the way to hospital. His name was Walter Alasia. Later, one of the military units of the Red Brigades in Lombardy will be named after him. We tell one another he was alive and well when he got into that ambulance. I think there's a big difference between him and that fascist accountant who last year killed two carabinieri and got away. The difference is in the funeral: a partisan's funeral. Walter's mother has tied a red kerchief around his neck, the people of Sesto are singing the Internationale, a comrade from Marelli goes up to speak and all raise their fists. That's when you can see the difference—after death. That young man in Sesto had to die before I could understand the difference.

And then there's Marina's smell, it clings to the sweaters she wears, they're big and shapeless, perhaps she's still too young and a bit ashamed of her tits. She takes my hand, we sit together at meetings. And when we get out there's always Igor, Gino Bonetti

THE RAIN'S FALLING UP

too, we go to bars and drink white wine and hot chocolate, but
Marina calls me little bro and I call her little sis and we muddle on
through a mix made of sugar and misconstrued friendship.
Cinema Roma has midnight screenings, that's a religion for us
four lads—but first Igor walks Marina home, every evening, tenth
floor, balcony, three rooms plus kitchen, her dad with his black
leather griefcase. Then Igor walks back and we carry on to the
Roma for the night's science fiction. Igor's not well, Marina says—
I think he lives alone with his mother who's not in good health
either. He loves Marina—for love's sake, probably: and despite his
work-strong arms and wide face, he's of the age at which you like
suffering and are not content with irony. He's on three or four
Valiums a day. He shows me the little pill as we stand in front of
the solitary stall that breaks the span of the arcade on Via Cernaia:
that's his secret—plop, down it goes, and you're not sick any more,
you just wait a bit and you get calm, you're even smiling. Not right
away, you just wait a bit, that's all. No, they don't sell it just like
that, but there's a way, there's always a way. And if you're in really
deep shit you can do a couple. So much cheaper than acid, too.
Me, I'm always in deep shit of course, but then, a Valium and a
midnight movie, it's like the morning will never come, it's like you
can lose yourself without getting hurt. I remember a film called
The Blob, swathes of deadly fluid swallowing up small-town
humans—all except Steve McQueen—and looking at all that red
jelly, Pig came out with Jamancipation. That's all he said, but with
so much giggling to do I got home so late that my folks had been
up waiting for me and worrying themselves sick. Them—ih ih
ih—selves sick.

CANON   'Bonetti says he's in Lotta Continua.'

'Bonetti's a jerk, Lotta Continua was disbanded, what the fuck can he have to do with Lotta Continua, jerk that he is?'

Bonetti is not worried about the details, he moves lightly from one world to the other. In the last stretch of 1976, the dream of taking power is rotten through: it remains the specular problem of the PCI and the Red Brigades, both of them military worlds very far from our dens. Bonetti has not noticed—never mind, he'll be in Lotta Continua even when there's no Lotta Continua, waiting to go up in the world. At Barabba there's Igor, Ruben, the guys with American names and cowboy dreams like Billy or Johnny and others, pretty much out of reach but just to see them in there makes you feel safe: Ciccio, big belly and Nero Wolfe brains, and the magnetic Albertino. And Giuliana, the hard-core Giuliana, whiskers under her nose, green eyes and hair twisted tight over her nape, Giuliana who pinches my cheek one day and says 'Pretty boy—like Giuseppe Arduino as a kid,' and who knows who this Giuseppe Arduino might have been. But she's the direst of all the feminists, the one who shouts at meetings and everyone all around keeps shtum. And then Rosy Caciottella—as in Creamcheese Rosy, big bit of all right, and Marcella, rake thin, the melancholic lines of her face stretched even longer by her big flowered skirts. On stage, permanently, are the ways of bodies and desire, as compressed by the city. 'I'm going to tell you why I'm here, what this meeting does for me,' followed by streams of words flowing along the basic need to have a destination. The language is the ancient one we have inherited—not so the opinions: there's always someone who will lean on a quote from Mao or Lenin for authority, but that's not the point. We've no time to put the past on trial and no means to plan the future: so we make do with the present, awkwardly, with a strange courage that scrambles words and alters meanings. The present is made of flesh, and Mao is not any more venerable than Donald Duck—in fact, quote Donald Duck and you're sure to be heckle-proof. Anyone trying to set up a hierarchy will find a mass of jelly and be absorbed and gobbled up and soiled. 'Comrades, there's been talk in here of braining anyone who smokes, but I know people who went about saying that six months ago and they're on heroin now. I mean . . .?' The problem is to give ourselves some code, the tables of a new law. Heroin is the crux: never seen so much of it around, a river in spate, and not only in the suburbs—you'll find it anywhere, whenever you like, and cheap: 'Comrades, I think the problem is not do we brain those who do heroin or not, or do we allow smoking joints inside Barabba or not—the problem is finding a way to make heroin useless, so that a proletarian won't see shooting up as the only way out of despair. I'm saying we've got to change relationships among us, among people.' A shout from the back of the room: 'Well done—just like the Pope says.' Laughs.

LEMON TREES   So: the summer I turned nine, that summer bathed in the dazzling light of my older cousin Marianella, who one evening had squared up to her father's creepy friends. 'Well done, all of you,' she says to the ladies and the gents in their neckties (I remember one, a garish red under a fat, up-thrust chin, and my father saying, 'That one's just out to shock people') sitting around on the terraces over the sea, 'You've grown into a woman' the catch-phrase on those scented evenings. 'That's right, the beach is lovely,' Marianella says at one point. Every head turns towards her and her white miniskirt. 'It's good fat soil—you've only to look at it and it'll bear fruit.' What does she mean? My aunt is alarmed, Marianella motor-mouthing now: 'You can lie around with your negronis while the goodies get offloaded like a dream, right here, down at the big beach, no?' Ah, it's the negroni, my uncle says, the girl's too young for it still. 'Comes in every night and you know it, don't you? It's your mates bring that shit in—new stuff all right, but you're not going to like it in the end, no you're not.' My aunt puts a stop to it with a slap, 'Negroni goes to the girl's head,' says the deep voice, patient tone of the double chin in the red tie. And my aunt with her Sicilian accent: 'Marianella is so shy,' as my uncle drags her away by the arm, the male guests craning their necks slightly for a private farewell to her little white skirt. It's 1970, Gigi Riva's World Cup dream run has come to an end, Marianella is angry all the time. What was that to her, up on the verandas, if stuff was coming by night on the boats putting in at the big beach? 'She's struggling with the weight of her new tits,' someone says after her. Muffled laughter, and maybe it was now that my father said 'That one's only out to shock people', maybe he hadn't been talking about the fatso with his red bunting but about his 'catwalk niece' as he sometimes called her. Marianella has blossomed, she feels her new body as it leaves onlookers breathless, that's why she threw that number, blonde as the sun and tall as a lamppost. What do you mean, 'that shit', Marianè? She looks at me with a savvy older-cousin sneer and says nothing. The abstract fear of a young boy on the beach at Terrasini, same as when you're watching a TV film and the Martian spaceship gets away from the SHADO fighter and touches down. Perhaps it was thanks to the scare I got that night among the lemon trees that I got away unscathed.

SMOKERS   As for joints, they disagreed with me on account of the smoking ritual, against which I had been unwittingly inoculated by my parents: sixty fags a day, minimum, between the two of them, neither had yet got even a cancer, a low curtain permanently hanging over the house. They'd been steamrollered under the pressure of work, inherited responsibilities, family structures, institutions, common sense and cigarettes. Whisky & negroni with their mates. They were holding out, creaking with the strain, sooner or later they'd fall to pieces, but in the end many did hold through, they had unpredictable changes of direction, escape routes and rebellious solutions for survival. Except we couldn't see those. Partly the fault of their system of values imposing a sense of guilt and decency, blunting the language: a system of values based on the threat of expulsion, with which we were unwittingly complicit, all the more subjected to it the more we judged them for it. So these were our parents: approximate humans, like us.

Anyways one morning I'm dozing over the heaps of books in the delegation room and skiving off classes as usual when there's furious knocking on the glass door. I open and there's Dino: 'You're fucked,' he goes. 'Your mother's just outside the classroom door—shoot.' So I dash up the stairs of the new wing and catch her in front of the fat receptionist lady's desk just a minute before she gets into the classroom to ask after me. She's trembling with shyness, confused, looking at me. 'Come outside,' I say, 'come on—I can explain.' So I take her to the ice-cream parlour in front of the lyceum and start spinning yarns, not very clever ones at that, and I can see she's at a loss, pissed off but desperate, she's not been told what's best to do in these situations and she's thinking of how expensive it's going to be to keep me at the Liceo Classico and me spitting on it like that. So that's your revolution? That's what she must have been thinking, and of her colleagues, of Linus and Capranico who worked hard and walked their revolutionary talk by teaching kids in Mirafiori Sud, building weapons for edge-of-town brains while I fail to understand or show respect, she must have been thinking that and more, but all she could do was cry her grey eyes out, cry and leave, pretend to believe me when I promised I'd go straight back to class and end the morning with my lessons. She kept up that pretence so as to be released, and all her life or what was left of it she'd never believe it but that's just what I did, walk back and head for my class, don't know what I said to the bearded lady teacher but I did go in and sat at my desk. It was as if I'd signed up to be formally failed that year. What could they do? It's not like you can throw out a fifteen-year-old son—they know they'd only come chasing after me, they know I'm all they've got. All they've got.

EYE SHADOW   There's water coming in from the mountains, avalanches of bad water ready to fall on our demos and on the smell of battle in our nostrils. The smell, yes—but no battles, only a few running escapes: the first one in Piazza Montanari, they say the villa in Santa Rita the Cangaceiros have occupied since autumn will be cleared by force, on eviction day the air is tense and everything's floating in a damp mist that muffles every sound. The cops are laying into people pre-emptively, indiscriminately, even people coming out of the Santa Rita supermarket or the Standa or Upim, whatever. Yes, them too if there's more than three and they've stopped to talk. So we go and nose around on the piazza, but we go prepared: file casually down Via Tripoli or Tunisi up to a small square piazza, one of those 1950s basins made of concrete and cheap glossy marble, a few drab flowerbeds and the anodyne baccy bar and the coach stands. It all happens in silence, even the truncheon blows, all you can hear is the caw-caw of crows reclaiming the winter sky. We think there's only a few of us, but people keep coming, people we've never seen and no one expected. And the storm hits: a storm of policemen and truncheons and rain to make you run along the tracks, and as you run, look down at the tracks so you don't slip and fall, and all the while they're speeding like crazy with their jeeps at full throttle, not the murdering jeeps, those will come a few months later, but powerful blue-black bodies against our bodies, masses running at you, not to scare, but to hit. And so windows in the neighbourhood open above our heads to look down, street doors open to hide us, even house doors open if they come chasing us up the stairs: shop-keepers come out on their thresholds to see what's going on and our flight turns into a party, we're scattered around the neighbour-hoods and markets south of the city, along the great boulevards touching the belly of FIAT and the families of workers, workers who've been swallowed by the devil and yet the families throw their houses open to shelter us, they hold us as their children in that last winter of peace.

That day it was us who scored, the police reaped a bad har-vest. I remember it was Igor who swept me away, like a godfather at my baptism. I ran off along a covered market held up by cement mushrooms and then down a wasteland slope on the edge of an old farmhouse that had survived the ring roads and the flyover, along big blocks straight out of boomtown planning, all the way down to the fruit & veg market on Via Baltimora, a strip of countryside torn from those Sixties vertical spikes with their bare bricks and balconies clad in blocks of reinforced concrete & glass shading the market stalls, and on the ground, crowd and bunches of carrots, peppers, bananas, oranges, voices of fat ladies and us with our improvised leaflets and our legs aching from the running, and it seems strange now but the ladies were putting their shopping bags down and hugging us, one gave me a tangerine of that perfect sort with the peel raised from the segments, and it's party time again, drying the rain off and feeling strong—it felt like a beginning, we were hidden in the crowd, we were pieces of that crowd, strong with that crowd.

Hell, Igor. I know what you're looking at: a stranded girl who turns her back on her tenth-floor flat with a useless mother and a father running around with a griefcase and a sullen brother to jump on the bendy buses out of the suburbs and come look for a home in the town centre, with you, with me, with her girlfriends, at the Barabba circle, sticking fast to people with the jelly of her complicit tenderness. Living on one another is part of the canon, her curvy body is also part of our alternative family, it's not something between you and me—wide-mesh Marina, her baggy jumpers and little or no learning, can't tell her Mao from her Marx, reads nothing, overhears something and shyly repeats it, almost apologizing for piping up. Her language is made of wheedling pleas for affection—but she's perfectly skilled in meeting our teenage passes by her ability to get along, to improvise, and above all to understand. She knows how to allay anxiety and guide you straight to the centre, and then she's on home ground, leaving the ideologies and the 'it's not done' to the other females, because you can ask anything of her without looking like you're asking. She has a way that brooks no argument of showing you she knows what you want, what you are, and fills your mental void about what you might like even as the Giulianas put you on the spot in meetings and explain to you what you ought to like. And so you no longer realize that Marina is like a vessel into which some of the heavy matter of the times is precipitated: even though her eyes are relentlessly begging for mercy, no one is really interested in her fate, and on the coach that takes her into town there's always someone chatting her up, and she responds, shortening distances, her wide eyes staring at some place outside the window. One thing you noticed was that she used too much eye make-up—a night-blue curtain all the way up to her eyebrows.

SUBJECT: COCKROACH SHIT   Listen up: everyone knows the ballad of Simon the Space Wanderer, songs tell his story on ten billion inhabitable planets, even the ones he has never visited. He never grows old. He wears Levi's and suffers from an old wound on his ass and thus can't sit down long, because at a certain point he had to grow a tail so he could make love to an alien dame and then had to cut it off, and the ballad begins in a Terrestrial desert where he's naked on top of the Sphinx with a lady, tourists swirling below and suddenly it starts raining.

It's the Flood: not the first, but the last one, covering the earth and sweeping away the whole of humankind, including Simon's lady. Having survived by grabbing on to his banjo case, just as he decides to let himself sink he bumps into a large, empty, coffin-shaped object: a case that does indeed contain a coffin, a Pharaoh, a pair of panties, a dried-up condom and a cheese sandwich—relics of a pleasant evening some museum worker had organized for himself. The other survivor is a dog who adopts Simon, clinging to the same coffin on the surface of the world. A dog can save your life, if you're the last man left on Earth: you can talk to him, smell him, stroke him and he'll wag his tail. All very well—but, one sandwich for two? As he opens the coffin before tearing off the Pharaoh's penis, he reads the tag: 'Merneptah, Pharaoh from 1236 to 1223 BC. Thirteenth son of Rameses II. He gave Moses a hard time.' Simon is happy to make a man so misjudged by history feel useful again, and the dog is not displeased either. A happy day breaks as Simon sees against the horizon the abandoned spaceship Hwang Ho—a strange spaceship whose shape reminds him of something the author avoids mentioning: a long torpedo slightly curving upward at one end, with a tip whose diameter is larger than that of the main body and two large spherical engine compartments at the opposite end. In the spaceship there's an owl, which Simon baptizes Athena. And so begins his quest for the reason to the end of the world. Simon thinks it might be a clean-up due to the Earthmen's proverbially bad smell, which had earned them the moniker of 'Stinkers' across several galaxies. When the water begins to wash away, Simon discovers he is standing on a saddle between Greater and Little Ararat—not bad, as coincidence goes. He finds a stone tablet that reads: 'The first German citizen who set off to climb to the top of Mount Ararat was here. This was 58 years before the pause that refreshes. Courtesy of Coca-Cola Co.' Simon looks at the writing that later travellers scratched on the tablet. One says: 'I WUZ HERE FURST. NOAH.' And another: 'NO. I WAS HERE FIRST, YOU ILLITERATE BASTARD. GOD.' And yet another: 'GRAFFITI WRITERS SUCK.' Here Simon meets another survivor, an ultracentenary spaceman who has returned to Earth to discover who had won the World Series back in the long-gone year when he had left the planet. The old spacer reveals that Earth was destroyed by the Hoonhors, the race that's been cleaning up the universe, the most altruistic of all species, who can't stand seeing people kill off their own planet and so they 'sanitize'. Simon is troubled, he thinks of the millions of years of conversations, poetry and quarrels about love, immortality and more. He decides to leave Earth and start asking the primal question: why are we created only to suffer and to die? The Hwang Ho is easy to steer, and Simon will get to meet scores of races—whether alien, hostile, friendly, rough-hewn or philosophical, and on many planets he will see the ruins of the cyclopic towers built by the legendary, extinct, enigmatic Clerun Gowph. In some cases he will be saved by the banjo case, in others by Anubis the dog, or Athena the owl. He will come across worlds where the dead survive by taking turns occupying the mind of the living, others whose inhabitants are highly flammable dirigibles. He will be loved by Chworktap, she who has come from the waves, perfect as Venus on her shell: she is an infallible robot with a woman's sensitivity, destined to save him at the cost of sacrificing herself. Simon will discover the pleasures of tail-driven sex before painfully shedding his tail, etc.

Until he gets to the End of the Line and meets the Clerun Gowph, who have the Answer. They kill living stars to power their spaceships. These giant cockroaches, and their leader, Bingo, have been waiting for him a long time. Bingo is dying, but grants Simon an interview in a cosy little room complete with the framed photograph of a blue cloud, with a dedication: 'To Bingo With Best Wishes From It'. 'It' is the creator of the Clerun Gowph, who were responsible for every other life form created accidentally through an evolution of the germs in the excrement they shed while on their scouting expeditions to planets whose climate conditions were unknown. It might have told Bingo where It came from and what It was doing before It created the universe, but Bingo is old and has forgotten.

It must be a scientist, and the Clerun Gowph a scientific experiment. It has discovered that knowing everything is no fun, and so has blanked out parts of Its own mind and invented oblivion —which is why It went out to lunch and forgot It was due back for an important meeting with Bingo. Bingo is sure that when the universe collapses into a big ball of fiery energy, It'll probably drop by and see how things worked out. At this, Simon begins to scream out his question, over and over again: 'But why? Why? Why?'

'Why not?'

That was Venus on the Half-Shell by Kilgore Trout. I had a mythologized memory of it, not least because when it came out people said no one knew who Trout was. Years later, having discovered that the author is named for one of Vonnegut's characters, I thought Vonnegut was in fact the author—which isn't the case, but never mind: I'd devoured it lying belly down on my bed while eating reinette apples. Later I'd stolen words from it, and now I can taste those reinettes again.

2

Forbidden Planet

(1961–1972)

RASPBERRIES   Actually no, you're right: it starts earlier. It
starts like this: you recognize your father by the raspberries. For a
while now he's been pulling his tongue out every time he looks
at you—calmly, so you can see him well—as he goes prrrrrr . . .
and slings you an instructive raspberry. You're doing everything
to partake in that secret language, making an effort to stick out
your tongue, but where's that tongue, how do you do it? It's
always getting stuck on your lower lip, which makes you come
out in a little yowl of joy mixed with annoyance. There are interludes, and you'll grow to understand they are long ones, when
he's away, but you don't know that yet: right now, everything's
right here, and he's blowing you a raspberry, which unites you,
the two of you in the whole wide world. You're so proud of that
secret bridge between you and the best man in the world that
you're growing up almost especially to improve your raspberry-
blowing technique and build up your repartee. And it's still a party,
even when you've learnt your way up to the table, along his legs,
around playschool routines, and you've learnt to tell the sequence
of weekdays until Saturday morning, and you begin to notice your
father's absences: you're still getting playtime with him, when you
get him at all, that is, but he's making you shy these days. You're

looking up at him, to him, and trying to find a way to rebuild the absolute ease of when he'd hold you in his arms and teach you to blow raspberries at the risk of getting a gob of milk spat up on his jacket. Everything is still revving fast enough for you to forget the interludes between one time together and the next, and at the same time so slowly as to hold everything poised.

But at a certain point along this protracted exit from certainty, my father changed: his face has grown dark and he's eating very little at supper time, he who used to cheerfully polish off any food left on my plate. Time was when in the evenings he'd make me laugh by playing gorillas: Batungo the nice gorilla and Baringo the bad gorilla, both disappearing behind the door frame and I never knew which one would pop out, and the whole block could hear me scream as I ducked under the blankets. I'd clap my hands for more and he'd sit on the bed and say beddie-byes now, or we know what we're going to look like in the morning. And he'd stroke my head and settle me in the right position for sleep.

In the morning he'd get me out of bed with riling energy, jerking the blind up all at once, the sun hitting my eyes and him shouting out his morning-time imperatives and epithets: 'A-wake! Up-getting! Lions at night, next morning a fright!' In the morning he's his own unalloyed self, and I'm grabbing on with all my might to the shreds of an endlessly festive time that's already cracked apart but still deceives me. I'm going to school now, milk and cocoa and mashed biscuits in big green-red plastic bowls with white polka dots, puffed-up eyes and the big paving stones, leather boots that your feet hate, ring the bell, wait for Maurizio, my cousin-brother since we were born in the same year, and then across the huge boulevard, three lanes and two long traffic islands, between buildings with their vertical panes in many colours and facades lively with small balconies and monsters of stone and metal on the arches and frames of street doors, look right, look left, carefully, hand in hand as Auntie looks down from her sixth-floor window. And we wave at her again from the other shore, two croissants in pink greaseproof paper from the corner bar, then two or three squares of straight street to the school pavement, all chewed up and broken, tarmac that's withstood decades of rain and running children's shoes, bumps and small marks that map out our continent: 'See you at the volcano,' a small dent in the tarmac that boils with bubbles when it rains hard, 'See you at the hillock,' a cement hump the size of a bread roll, small enough to be a shared secret, confidential information. And in school the verbs or times-tables competitions, I was struggling but like all children not realizing it, in those years you hold time together with your teeth, you stop it trickling away into the rosary of squares, weekday, holiday, black, white, black, white. You wait for Christmas, go to catechism, hide under stairways when you're chasing thrills. My father was working late, coming home in his uniform, I would wait for him but I knew the uniform is sacrosanct and he can't, he really can't pick me up until he's taken it off and put his briefcase down. So tall, he is—and my Mum so very pretty.

SCARED   I spied on them. And so I knew they had fights sometimes, or long serious talks, and it came out that my mother was not really at ease with the job he did. I think it was mostly about the moves. An officer has a hard life, at least until he's a major: you have to up sticks very often, at short notice, and if there's a family they'll usually tag along, and then the camps, the training, all those times when the husband and father is simply missing, for weeks on end, and all right, we did agree on that, we did choose each other, but this—this, Francesco—this is not quite what we had in mind, is it now?

I overheard all this because I couldn't sleep. Truth is, Channel 2 was showing The True Story of Pancho Villa and I didn't want to miss it. Sometimes I'd show up in the kitchen wearing my pyjamas and my best contrite face: 'I can't sleep . . .' I'd usually be packed off straight back to bed, but once in a while my father would smile and pick me up to watch the film snuggled up in his arms—that's when I understood he was all-powerful. But on that Pancho Villa evening they were talking thick and fast, and I'd have said my mother was crying except she never cries, so I went back to bed and started thinking. Then sleep got me, I reckon.

When I started primary school they decided it was time to settle down. The family in Turin would help us. This was my father's time to run—alone, and often away for long periods. My mother accepted his reticence when it came to 'matters of duty': these were part of their loyalty pact—and the less you know about some things the better, as I once heard her say to one of her friends. Womanly cunning. Still, when I was in year three or four, good fortune came to our house. It came in the form of a racing suit and a dark uniform. I was bursting with pride because my father was now in the carabinieri, and not to do any old job either: he was in the corps of the genies of engines, and he worked at the fast-driving school. Get it? He was going to train police drivers to do the chases: ever seen a TV film? He was in the alpini corps, not in the carabinieri, but the carambas didn't have anyone as good as he was and so they had to call him, and I was telling everyone, including that shitface De Luca, who always thought he was going to get me (in fact he did, once, in the classroom: taking advantage of my ignorance of market conditions, he got me to show him my doubles and then snatched up my Pelé and ran off. More out of surprise than revenge—I'd never been robbed before, it seemed unreal: what would my father do in such a situation?—I told the teacher, who forced him to give me back my Pelé. Except I was confusing the famous footballer with the rare card, and everyone, I mean everyone had Pelé that year: that year, it was Poland's Deyna you needed if you wanted to be god. In the end, I felt sorry for De Luca, maybe that was the last card he needed to complete his album, so from that day onward I agreed to all his exchanges, gave him any card he wanted and thought of him as a real friend).

But one night in the kitchen, not knowing I could hear him, my father had said: 'I'm scared.' I heard that very clearly: 'Scared.' That night he was calling my mother by her name—'You understand, Giulia?'—rather than any of the thousand nicknames they used for each other every day (their favourite was Cookie, in memory of the years spent in Verona with the Americans). This thing of my father being scared was simply not possible—so I started eavesdropping carefully and found out it was to do with his work: some colleagues had pulled him into a weird circle, they were looking for him because he was in charge of the vehicle fleet. One, he said, had even threatened him. How's that possible? In the carabinieri? Maybe it was because he was an alpino, I thought. But he was saying that things at the legion in Turin were turning ugly—very ugly. And my mother was holding him in her arms. That night, my father's week-day life fell open in front of my eyes.

AGGRESSORIA   Those were dark, heavy days. My mother
had a red face and always looked about to explode, I think that
'scared' thing had shaken her to the core, just now that things
seemed to be going all right, the workplace with the carabinieri
just round the corner, the family nearby (because on an officer's
wages, who's going to help you if not your relatives?) and the pro-
motion to major. She'd been holding on to life by the skin of her
teeth up to that point, and now she felt unable to accept yet
another form of precariousness. I fancied myself the brave kid in
the fairy tales, the one who solves all of the family's problems: the
youngest. And the eldest too, being an only child. And so, on and
off, in between thoughts of blotting paper, Sunday school and a
new watch, this 'scared' business became my game, a mystery to
be solved, a reason to listen out from behind doors and rummage
through drawers, all those thing I was doing anyway in those endless afternoons when I was man of the house, since my parents,
both of them, went out to work.

He never spoke of his work, even when I was small he'd divert
my attention by telling fables, soldiers' tales (my favourite was the
retreat from Russia), and if I asked him who the enemy was he'd
always say this was peacetime, and there are no enemies in peacetime. But I couldn't be satisfied with the sort of answer that simply
skipped over all the films and comics stories. So we made up some
games, and it's not like he spent too much time on them—he
never had time anyway—but he did look like he was enjoying
them: we'd pick up some toy soldiers, he'd take the unvarnished
ones (I'd buy them in cuboid cardboard boxes, whole plastic
platoons to pull apart and colour with the varnishes sold sepa-
rately) and play the baddie: his army came from a country called

Aggressoria, and the baddies were called the Oranges. My guys, no matter that they were varnished and mostly in green, were called the Skyblues, and they'd always win in the end, but it was hard, because the Oranges of Aggressoria knew a thousand tricks, they'd hide under the sofa cover or among the house plants, they had snipers lurking in the drinks cabinet and they were always scattered about, never all together, at most sending a few patrols along the armchairs or the coffee-table legs to try and get my divisions from behind. Luckily, the Oranges had really bad aim, and so when it finally came down to the two floor tiles, the shooting distance we'd agreed as the last stand-off, all their tactics came to nothing and I mowed them down: you'd flick one marble and the first soldier would die, and when all the Oranges were down, I'd start fighting back the hiccups and saying 'More.' I knew there'd be no more, but I was laughing like mad, and my father did look really happy.

If he could, in the warm season he'd take me into the mountains: he knew all the forts that had been abandoned after the war against the French, and we spent some nice Sundays exploring them, sometimes stopping on the way in some hotel or mountain hut or even camping out in the tent. Once I started crying from the tiredness and strangely he didn't get angry but lifted me onto his shoulders: we'd started out from Bardonecchia and it was still springtime, I'd never seen so many flowers or animals in the mountains, there were these bluebells, there were squirrels even, and he was walking in front of me, slowly, and after a while we even found an adder's skin. He was telling me to stop running around or I'd get tired, and sure enough about halfway up I threw this tantrum, bawling and shouting as if asking to be smacked,

71

but he stopped and looked at me and just picked me up and off we went. We were heading for Forte Foin, we took it slow and by the time we got to the top we saw everything was covered in mist: 'We've come into the clouds,' Daddy said—and that was just how I felt.

He was taking photographs, with me in them and without, and time was ticking on and I began to worry that he might want us to sleep there. We were walking around all those casements, sometimes we got in: he had keys, and he'd look at me with a twinkle in his eye, touch his index finger to his nose and say cheerfully: 'This is classified, Corporal.'

DOMES   It's a slow change, and by the time you realize, it's done already. The sequence of days stretches in front of you, sometimes shifting names: Holiday, Weekday, Turin, Milan, Milan: the supply chain of commuters, for instance. A warped chessboard, with not many black squares and the centre in disarray. It happened as early as primary school, but you didn't realize. Mine was a nineteenth-century school, the teacher in muted greys, specs perched on his nose, cycling to school every day and just about getting along—not that you'd notice though, because of that decorum he had. A widower, with a little girl barely older than us. He used a pointing rod, if he caught us talking he'd come up from behind and box our ears, led us to the toilet all together marching three by three and stamping on the 'left!', and even in the sports hall it's not like we did any sports—just marching, learning the form for the parade. If the headmaster arrived we had to snap at 'eyes right!', sometimes with our rods at carry arms like guns.

After the first two years in a smock, you could wear the blue pullover with pompoms at the neck—our uniform. Not sure what the rods were meant to be used for, or the skittle-shaped clubs in the sports hall. There were so many down there, under the wall bars: we knew what those were for, we knew that navy commandos also exercised on them, but we never once did.

He was a good teacher: I don't think I ever really needed to open a book in secondary school, I could get by easily on what I'd learnt from him. Except he was intimidated by important families, like a man from an earlier century: he very much favoured blond children, and in my school blond children often had two or three surnames. Yet his ethics could withstand the lure of social class, and we saw that when in our third year they decided to set up a 'differential' class. A beadle was running around collecting the names of those destined to the ghetto—graceless surnames, ugly mugs ill concealed under the smocks and pompoms, kids whose hands are big and hard already and you can see they're put to work after school. Still he had held on to all of us, and it was clear that had cost him a fight with Maestra Bessola from the girls' class. We had to call him Signor Maestro and shoot to our feet each time he got up from his desk. He kept discipline with an iron fist, and yet I remember the long, long breaks, and us boys venturing out to the farthest corridors in the school as if out on patrol while he acted absent-minded and the beadles disappeared behind their newspapers.

We'd crawl around in the shadows of airy vaults and the small busts of WW1 heroes in their niches: when you got to Sub-Lieutenant Gallino there was a bend leading to the guards' corridor—better run along that one as far as Artilleryman Maina where you could have a rest, then carry on as far as the antipodes (Corporal Major Bertot) where you'd find Maestro Baj, for instance, who would beat children in the toilets, or Maestro Borsellino, the older boys' teacher, who was so tall he bumped his nose against the ceiling lights. No one showed any sign of taking notice of us during those long, long twenty-minute breaks, and we grew brave and strong—and rebellious.

Signor Maestro also relied on the school trip that happened around Christmas time: a nice trip, always the same, to the sanctuaries of the Consolata and Maria Ausiliatrice, an orgy of devotion, mystery and labyrinths. The underground passages at the Consolata, ill-lit caves between twisted columns, small altars laden with dark gold and ex-votos clustered in tighter and tighter rows until they almost touch the ceiling or packed tight behind sacristy armoires, few words often scribbled in pencil, colourful stories with happy endings, mad horses, boilers that had exploded ripping whole squares apart (the tram toppled by the blast), miraculous healings. And workplace accidents: machines swallowing bodies, men turned into half-machines, scaffoldings crashing down and dragging bricklayers with them, sludge heaps collapsed, bodies writhing, arms in three segments, hands raised to the sky or shielding the eyes. And many wartime stories: people crawling under barbed wire, cannons, grenades, aeroplanes, daring and doomed actions, beds and nurses, heroes with bloodied bandages—in the half-light of those half-basements, under vaults that feel as if awash in some boiling fluid. And Maria Ausiliatrice, the opposite: corridors, huge bright window panes and a Sunday school with a basketball pitch, sports hall, exhibitions with photos of African children and nicely done drawings on glossy paper, smooth wooden banisters, spotless halls where each detail sings the omnipotence of the followers of Don Bosco, glory of the city of Turin and master entrepreneur, and of the Beato Cottolengo who heard confession from those sentenced to hang in a spot a hundred yards from here, which today is a bedlam of trams and angry carburettors. Maria Ausiliatrice makes you think the world knows where it's heading.

And so Signor Maestro had us grow amid the baroque secrets of the city, curves of air and shadows along surfaces designed to coax and snare, the hypnotic game of concave versus convex. All in step, catching glimpses of other temples. The crazy dome of San Lorenzo that denies the principles of keystone, arc and statics, holding itself up without knowing why, kept in place by spells and prayers, or the other temple, the frightening one looming like a black spider at the centre of the straight and narrow streets of the Roman square, where you feel like you're being sucked up and away and everything's dark up there, a dark cylinder planted on a starburst of underground tunnels fanning out in all directions, blind and mindless gods of nothingness screaming, the city's ancient defence system, tentacles of the mystic monster. The Chapel of the Holy Shroud, just a few yards away, seems to have been placed there to keep watch, to hold at bay that cavern whose name is unknown even to the people of Turin—who respectfully, without asking questions, just call it 'the Basilica'. As if they were saying 'the basilisk'.

LOUCHE   Like his domes, Signor Maestro entertained us—and he led us wherever he pleased: he made a point of finding out what was said in our families, and I remember one autumn in year five, when the TV was constantly on in every house for news on the election of the president of the republic: 'The chief of all chiefs', 'Higher than the minister of defence', 'Higher than the general'—'minister of defence *is* higher than general, you jack-ass'—so Maurizio and I, officers' children. We'd been told the honourable members of parliament were going to stay locked in there until this president came out. I thought they'd end up starving to death, because there seemed no way for them to agree, and spent my afternoons in a trance, as if watching children's TV, staring at that hall where a bald man with a loud voice was reading names off little slips of paper: Fanfani, Fanfani, Fanfani, De Martino, Fanfani, Fanfani, De Martino, De Marsanich. My father and I had a green folder in which we collected republic coins patinaed with the fingerprints of people who had disappeared in the post-war period. Sometimes he told me it would have been even better to collect stamps, but that was a sea we didn't know how to navigate: better stick to coins—and then he liked to say we had our very own 'pink Gronchi': that's what he called the rarest coin in our collection, an innocent-looking five-lira coin from 1956. 'This is worth two or three hundred thousand liras.' 'We're rich then, are we?' 'Filthy rich. And imagine if we find the five-hundred piece with the wrong flag!' 'What's wrong with it?' 'The flag is the wrong way round, it's pointing backwards but the sails swell forward.' All right, so the five-hundred coin had sailing ships on it—but what with this 'pink Gronchi'? So my father explained that was a super-rare stamp, it had gone wrong like the five-hundred coin: they'd given a pink background to President Gronchi's face, and I was laughing—fancy the president on a girly background! And of course they'd set it straight right away, in a rush, made a blue background and took the pink ones out of circulation. So I learnt that my father disliked that president, Gronchi ('Groan-key: just the name sounds like some sort of death rattle, doesn't it? Makes you think of something sick.'): sometimes he would tell me the story of the republic, right there over the coins, and whenever he got to the president on the pink stamp, he'd say 'the louche Gronchi.' He said that guy was hanging out with nasty people. I knew the word 'louche' because sometimes we played 'louche' on the street, walking around with dark frowns, hands behind our backs and necks craned out—just me and him, the big one and the wee one, with our tough-guy faces on.

One evening, during the endless election newscast, my father had pointed straight at the bald man who was reading out the scraps of paper and said, 'That's who I'd vote for—that's an honest person.' I'd asked him what the honest man's name was and he'd said: 'Pertini.' Our teacher had organized a game in class: we were the Right Honourables, and had to elect the president. He knew our handwritings, and so would easily find out what our parents' leanings were. Of course I wrote 'Pertini' on my sheet: he looked at my vote with slight surprise, but did not show that he had understood.

In class, Fanfani won by a landslide—not so on TV. On TV it all carried on for weeks on end, it had turned into a quiz show by now. There was this quiz show at the time called Rischiatutto, and on some of the breaks we'd play Rischiatutto in class. The smartest among us, the gang chiefs like Petrolito or Casalegno, had set up their own version, with the questions penned in a notebook and a board made from two reams of classwork sheets with tear-off subject tags pressed hard into the paper with a biro (strictly forbidden to us, who were only allowed fountain pens): early in the day we'd sign up to join Casalegno or Petrolito on either team, and in the break any three of us might be at it (the gang chiefs playing the quiz show host, Mike Bongiorno) while many more stood around watching. For a while we also kept the Right Honourables game going and elected all sorts, including Gigi Riva, but we got bored before long. The TV guys on the other hand did carry on for ever, in black & white, one evening after the other.

THE GREAT BALU-BALU   Of course I kept flashing back on that 'scared' business. I didn't dare ask, but thought about it before falling asleep, in the time it takes for the mind to set off on its weird pathways. I was spying, eavesdropping on the talks between my father and the In-Laws Gang (three out of five of my mother's sisters' husbands were in the military like Dad). They used to descend on our house at least once a week, together with a few friends of the family, perhaps those of my favourite kind, the guys who could show off their living-room devilries—a bright red necktie, a certain way of drinking whiskey, exotic cigarettes, left-wing opinions, fancy variations at the poker table, dirty jokes, passes at friends' wives.

I would listen in from behind the door. I was king of the hallway, where I almost had permission to write on the walls (small biro scrawls under the radiator), and where I would stage whole football World Cups playing both sides with a tennis ball: I'd spend whole afternoons preparing, listing all 128 teams by looking up names in my atlas and then setting the first knockouts (no ties in my world), so there'd be matches such as Germany vs Nauru and the scores would be far from predictable, since in the evening it was me who teamed up on the hallway floor as both Germany *and* Nauru, kicking hard, catching rebounds from the wall, running like a rabid dog to get at the ball, going from centre forward to full back in a fraction of a second, being Gigi Riva and Beckenbauer or if necessary even Balu-Balu, Nauru's awesome striker. Mostly I was my favourite, De Sisti, but if I wanted to I could turn into one of those big Dutch or Brazilian bullies, guys who could play so well that even the worst traitors among my schoolmates started rooting for them. Like those unfathomable kids—all invariably from poor families—who lived in the centre of Turin but supported Inter or Milan. After my matches, or in the breaks, as long as sleepiness allowed, I'd listen to the chitchat dragging on and dodge clouds of blue smoke as they filtered from under the doors—words punctuated by the tinkle of tumblers etched with square patterns where they'd poured their Whiskeys, Martinis, Negronis, Angostura (place names in a fantastic country I was going to explore before long). One of the guests even had an exotic name, like Christian: he was French and worked as a hairdresser, and was telling them about when he'd been a secret agent and an OAS terrorist and how he'd tortured people in Algeria. These days he wore loud baggy shirts, a thin moustache and a combover. My father took him on fearlessly, stopped him spouting stuff like 'you need courage to fight a dirty war'—ah, here was something I could at least ask my father: What is a dirty war? He knows more about war than all of them put together, he's here to wage war, in fact, and from the way he gets pissed off with the hairdresser you can tell his is a clean war.

PEARS AND TORPEDOS   There were judgements my
mother would rehearse at supper time in front of the TV, work
on for a while and then release in the living room—in a slightly
toned-down version, of course. I remember the one about this
guy who was a dancer, and hence certainly a homosexual—What
does homosexual mean?—and also epileptic—Mum, what's
epileptic mean? It had to be him, what else can a guy like that do
to take revenge on life if not plant a bomb in a bank, and I remember images of the blown-up bank glaring in the darkness of a cold
afternoon a little earlier than the Right Honourables game (how
long? how much earlier?), but not as a bad memory: I like darkness
and the cold and winter drawing in, Christmas lights and the fires
of roast-chestnut sellers under the arcades. Spring and summer
are old men's passions—not so the lit-up shop windows. And that
face in the papers, the epileptic dancer's (must be something to
do with drugs), the stubble and the eyes bulged up in the photo
as if to say 'I did it—so what?' And the taxi driver who said it was
him, no doubt about it, riding in his cab to the bank with the
bombs in a bag. Beagle Boys style.

My father had been a fascist child, and if there was anything
of the fascist left in him, that had stayed a child, going no further
than the wartime songs we'd sing in our Cinquecento on the way
to summer holidays at the seaside: 'Arm your prow, mariner /
wear your war colours for the battle's nigh / for Dalmatia and for
Italy / tomorrow we may die', or 'Swift and unseen / the sub-
marines gleam / torpedoes strike, sure-fire might / the sea is
howling and foaming white', or 'Down on your knees, cameleer
/ it's the saga of Giarabub'. Yes, because when he came out of
the war, aged eleven, he was little more than a child, but his elder

brother Mario had been old enough to enrol in the militia and start strutting around Alessandria in his black shirt—and there he was, the wee little guy, looking up to him and thinking, one day I'll be a big strong fascist too. But one fine morning that spring a routed Decima MAS column came stampeding into town, running any which way they could, on foot, on bicycles, on the few motor vehicles, and an officer came by to warn my grandfather who was chief of traffic at the Alessandria railway interchange: better jump up, take the children and head for Turin, there was a flood tide of partisans swelling behind them. Well, during that trip my father must have seen something he didn't like: his disgruntled brother was being shouted down by the fascists, they'd been fighting and losing, and were treating him like a dodger. They got to Turin during a clash: there was a German tank division nailed in Corso Peschiera, a riot of stuff being hurled down at them from the windows—and the boy my father must have started to think that those guys firing machine-gun bullets, potted plants and stones from behind the shutters were Italians like him, and the other guys, the arrogant blond guys, were taking a beating and holding on to their asses for dear life, and as he thought that he could see the tough guys of the Decima MAS taking off right behind the Germans. They'd gone when the city had decided to let them go—and this is the sort of thing a young lad can't help noticing. My father disliked communists: when Granddad had come home from the WW1, where he'd been one of the special force volunteers, the guys who went out under enemy fire to cut barbed wire, the reds had wanted to throw him into a blast furnace, and now in Turin he was up against the partisans: we'll give him a nice trial, send him back feet first if we see fit. So Grandma had taken the boys to Colleretto, back to the mountains where they'd come from so many years before. 'Daddy will be back if you wait for him—you'll see.' And everyone in Colleretto looked at Grandma in her fine lady's clothes like she was Queen Elena in person as she rolled up her sleeves and got down to work in the kitchen garden with her sister-in-law, a schoolteacher in the villages. The elder brother, my uncle Mario, had been breastfed, while my father had been sent to a wet nurse in the mountains around Cuneo. He was the wee one, so small and short, with those sad, wide eyes fit to break the hearts of the mountain girls who'd come down from the grazing grounds at daybreak on their way to market. So they'd stood him at the crossroads near the washing fountain, where the village path gives way to stone steps as it slopes down into the valley: there he was, with a sack of pears for sale, and the girls from the villages would stop and give him a wee pat on the cheek and a few bob in exchange for his pears. He'd make it like he was weighing them, give them some change, have a laugh with it. There he was in the fields, busy with two geese and Mirko the cat, busy realizing what horror the world really is when old Bianco, a guy who'd walk him into the mountains at daybreak by the light of a lantern, invited him to his house for stew and the stew was Mirko the cat—just like that, for a laugh.

In the end, Granddad did come back: two railway workers among the partisans had testified and said that yes, he was a fascist, but clean, and they'd let him go. And my father might have thought to himself that these partisan guys, after all. But Granddad had come back to a bad, long drawn-out death, and my father had shot up and become a teenage beanpole in one summer, and since he was not a lovely little nipper any more he'd had to stop selling pears and was spending his nights by the bedside praying it would end, for which he would feel guilty all his life. And partly out of that guilt, once back in the city, after the Liceo Classico and the girls smiling in their wide skirts and pearls, he'd dropped everything and gone off to the military academy in Modena: one less mouth to feed and one more wage packet, following my uncle Mario, who'd enrolled right after the war and was set for a brilliant career. Modena, bitchy cold and bollockings, but also horse riding and foil fencing and pride. Fifty minutes' leave in the evenings, but only if you'd earned it: the bed a perfect cuboid of blankets mattress & pillows, your shirt & tie neatly stacked on top, the knot well pressed, all properly folded and no pins allowed. One wee crease, you stay in the barracks. Modena— farewell, little pear boy: nothing makes a man like breaking him. In that post-war academy he had found enough fascists, sticking together by nostalgia in that bedlam, running in the courtyard, reveilles when it's still dark—in fact, he'd even got friendly with some, especially the great Majorelli, who got up in the morning with a hard-on so stiff he'd stick his combat helmet on it, stack towel, soap bar, toothbrush & paste on top and walk off to the lav.

Majorelli died, of cancer, and Zurlini died, and through the years I heard their names being rattled off and their widows speaking to my father with the affection of veterans. My father entertained no nostalgia—unless perhaps for the pears or for Mirko the cat, but he stifled that. He'd been cultivating the myth of the unbeatable flotilla, the successful combat, the military trickery, loved the feats of the 'swine torpedoes' in the Bay of Bakar and the courage of bersaglieri paratroopers rolling under English tanks with magnetic mines to stick in their bellies. But that was fun stuff, aesthetics—we'd sing the songs and watch these films together, Ice Cold in Alex or Only the Valiant—and I'd play alpini, or bersaglieri, or colonial war in the desert, with khakis and pith helmet. Those little myths—he had to reckon with them one night, in front of the box tuned to the Swiss TV channel.

THE BLACK PRINCE   In the living room, he would go along with the comments on the epileptic bomber: more than fearing anarchists, he could not fathom them—so it figured that they'd slaughter people just to do something, and also he was convinced that all extremists are the same, crazy bastards and all the same, as he'd say while watching the news. He was the sort of guy who gets mad watching the evening news, a show that cemented the complicity between me and my mother. It was a kind of religion, in our house, and the liturgy consisted in getting pissed off. Two channels are not enough, and at some point he got mad keen on Swiss TV.

It happened at times that my folks would lose their head for a certain gadget—it was rare, but it did happen: suddenly they simply had to have that thing. We had no space-age appliances, owned one small car, and my mother would keep me clothed by recycling my cousins' cast-offs—or, if it wasn't too embarrassing, her own. They stayed out of debt, but occasionally went off on a whim. Now all you had to do was buy a special aerial and fiddle around a bit with the knobs, and from Turin you could catch Swiss Italian TV programmes—a whole channel in fact, with films, new quiz shows and, most important, different evening news, broadcast a bit earlier than ours.

So here we are one evening, nailed to an image on the screen—an almost motionless face, lips that move slowly and muted words trickling down a clean-shaven chin. I can't make sense of those words, all I can see is a voiceless image, the face of a man injured by time. I can see words dripping off his cheeks and a smile of infinite contempt. My father had gestured sharply for silence, and I knew that in those moments the only sound allowed was the bzzzz of flies. I think I was making those mechanical little noises that came from being bored, like singing some ditty or gently hitting the rim of my glass—that's why I can still remember my father's stern look and the way he turned his chin towards the screen as if grabbing me by the ear. The man with the moustache is speaking of war, he's saying the enemy is using our children as a vehicle of infection, and even the children, who are sick by now, must be rooted out like noxious weeds: 'I have no compunction telling you that they are enemies, and that I would be delighted if I could exterminate them.' Words trickling down his mouth like the drivel of an alien slug. My father, stone-faced, is watching him: he knows him, has recognized him.

Archive footage from five or six years earlier, the slightly emphatic voiceover telling the story of that man, calling him 'the Black Prince'. They've pulled out that old interview because it's come out that one night the Black Prince tried to overturn the president of the republic and take his place in Rome. My father is bent forward as if someone's trying to steal his TV. On screen the man with smooth cheeks, white tie, waistcoat, combed-back hair thinning grey at the temples, continues to speak: he's calm, but it's his face that scares you. My father remembers that man: as a child, he tells me, he'd have followed him anywhere. And telling me so is his way to apologize for the threat of a smack that has hovered over me all through the interview. Dad, who is that guy? The Black Prince. The Black Prince—you mean he's bad? My father keeps quiet, he is stroking me. Dad, why does he want to kill the children? I think I must have dreamt of the Black Prince for weeks on end: clearly, princes looked nothing like that in my imagination, and certainly did not have drooping cheeks—there must be some bad spell at play here. Anyway this Black Prince guy was scary all right. Here's my plan: one night I'll slip into their bed (forbidden thing to do, my father would pick me up by the scruff and kick me out) and say I dreamt of the Black Prince . . . 'per vedere di nascosto l'effetto che fa'.

AUTOMATIC WORLD   I never plucked up the courage to get into their bed, of course. Instead I'm holding on to my tennis ball as I keep eavesdropping on the chitchat of the whiskey & martini living room until my mother arrives with her usual 'Isn't it time for beddie-byes now, young man?' and to hell with it. There's an army surgeon, a guy who has the nerve to turn up in the evening with highly tailored bell-bottoms, sideburns slightly longer than service guidelines allow and the beginnings of a paunch. He comes in plain clothes to drink whiskey under the ficus leaves in the living room and knows how to flatter my mother: he started getting busy at the time of the 1970 World Cup, staying back to talk to her while we all watched the game. When he gets mad, my father often speaks of 1970—maybe it's the army surgeon's fault? Italy vs Israel (admiring blah-blah from the officers: those guys know how to fight—all the Arabs in the worlds against them, and they flattened them in six days), Italy vs

THE RAIN'S FALLING UP

Sweden (close-ups of blonde women on the terraces), Italy vs Uruguay (these guys are bruisers—and spitters too), the endless one against Germany and then Brazil, 4-1, a slaughter. And the surgeon back in the living room talking to my mother, probably about epileptic dancers, or perhaps about fashion (or so I thought, because I knew my mother was interested in fashion). I think the surgeon guy loves to make my father mad, he's holding court and saying that difficult times call for difficult measures, one must protect the children (is he shooting a look at my mother? can't tell from behind the door). He loves to say the war is not over, he says that every time, my mother's listening, my father usually mumbles 'Oh, give over,' and pours a drink. We slacked off and now the reds have got it, they're using the kids, can't you see they're all communists? I'm a surgeon ('A dentist,' my father snarls), I know when it's time to cut.

My father was not built for hatred: as a boy he'd even admired those guys so full of wrong ideals that they'd taken off with spud guns to go into the mountains in the rain and fight the guys from his side who were after a beautiful death. In the martini & angostura living room they're talking and talking, drawing maps of Europe and the world with a scalpel: a line in the middle, on one side the sun, bright sea breeze, grilled fish and colonels, on the other grim Nordic people, rain, windscreen wipers, drab hills, institutions. And my father, ill at ease like one who understands all this as more than chatter, trying to change the subject with a joke, slipping a finger into the knot of his tie, mixing a negroni.

Can't you understand? Of course I can. Well then—do you prefer the communists?

All agree that we've got to move forward, look west, while in the meantime I'm doing all I can, whenever I can, to conquer a scrap of street and a scrap of the night: the world is changing, and on Via Cernaia they've opened this automatic bar, like on a starship. No barmen, no cashiers, just machines: you'd just slide a coin in and the contraption would start revolving, displaying layers of triangular sandwiches or bottles of fizzy drinks, then another click and out pops whatever you've chosen: a snack, or crisps, or a slice of cake. I had no coins, but could easily spend hours watching that. And I was a big boy now, I could easily go a couple of blocks down the road by myself—so one night I offered to go and buy ice-cream for the guests, and why not? But you must be careful— aw come on, he always goes to buy fags for me (which I found disgusting by the way, every time I touched fags I'd spend ages washing my hands), he's even walking to school on his own these days. All right, but you'll be careful, won't you, Pietro. And so I was out in the night, leaving them to their whiskeys and Black Princes and epileptic dancers and divorce referendums and the Christ-Dems who've been moving to the right and that's the proof, I'm out in the fabulous night, flares and Saturn in the sky just above the tram cables, all the way across the Cittadella garden and to the Nuova Cremeria on the corner of Via Cernaia. Only two blocks further, no, it's three, yeah all right three, and here I am standing in front of the automat with its fizzy drinks and sarnies, and so didn't get back until more than two hours later. The situation had been saved by Christian the hairdresser, who'd had the bright idea of asking the whores: round the corner from my house there were these fat ladies who always saw all sorts— no chance they'd miss a young boy out on his own at night in the early Seventies. So my mother got a good dressing-down from the whores, and I got found and taken back home.

The next summer, my father gave himself a wonderful present: an ice-cream maker looking like a flying saucer made of glossy plastic, and we'd put in eggs and milk and lemon, or cocoa or sometimes fruit, and make our own ice-creams—much better than those from the Nuova Cremeria, if I say so myself.

FILIPPO   Except that in the evenings I was getting less and less sleepy and in the daytime I was running in my leather boots along the pavement, chasing Poldo the dog or heading for the Wolf Cubs' HQ, the green world of adventure hidden in the hollow of a church crypt big enough for you to play football, poison ball, hawks & swallows. My father was still losing sleep, a Sardinian friend of his had been speaking to him of what he was having to do on the job, and Dad had a strange look about him at that time.

This was a colleague of his, a major in the alpini, a strong man with blue eyes and a grey beard who had returned to Sardinia on a special assignment. He stayed at our house for a few days. That happened often back then, and it was a splendid variation on my evening routine: I would give up my bed for a guest who'd stay a few nights and then disappear. Some were straight out of adventure books: there was one who had come from Somalia, one who was an Ecuadorian captain and in the evening would explain to me how to catch a watchman unawares in the middle of the jungle or how an infantry division can cross a river infested with piranhas; another, a mysterious gentleman with a frightened look, said he was an Israeli inventor who had designed a water or air engine, and my father said that would cause factories who made petrol engines to shut down and so the gentlemen who owned those factories wanted to kill him, so I mustn't tell anyone, anyone at all, about him. Not even Maurizio? Not even him. There was also one whose face or provenance I can't remember, but I still have a stuffed koala he'd brought me from the other side of the world, a soft, furry little thing that had once been alive. And then one evening they'd suddenly disappear, and I'd get back to my bed. But the Sardinian major was different: he was an old friend of Dad's, they had studied together at the academy, you don't lose touch with people like that along the way. He treated my father like a brother, and he was a brother: the man who always showed up of his own accord in the hour of need, all through life, wherever he may be. The only thing was, he had this fixed idea that bothered my father a lot: he wanted him to make up with Uncle Mario.

Even I had realized they'd fallen out, because at a certain point we'd stopped going to see him in Milan and he no longer came to our house on visits. After the holidays in Sicily, the year of the World Cup, they'd spoken on the phone a couple of times, but I remember my father one night yelling at him: 'Will you please stop talking crap now! Will you just stop it now, Mario!' and then slamming the phone down and saying something more, I think a swear word even, though that's impossible. My mother was watching him in silence, jutting her chin out towards me in reproach. Exasperated, he'd left the room, and she'd smiled at me: 'They've been fighting ever since they were children.' Later, Dad had picked me up in his arms and said: 'Say, you're not going to be a bersagliere when you grow up, are you? They're all crazy, the bersaglieri—all like Uncle Mario.' Since that evening, Uncle Mario had disappeared for us. Mum and Aunt Rosalba would speak sometimes, out of courtesy I think, and I was sorry, because I thought I'd never again see my supercousin Marianella, my passion, my pride and joy.

The Sardinian major was insisting, as if he wanted to convince my father to go back on certain decisions: 'Look, Francesco,' he'd say, 'you've screwed up, all right? You've blown your chances at the Scuola di Guerra for nothing—speak to Mario.' All I knew was that 'war school' was a thorn in Dad's side: it must be this thing that you either do or you can't ever be a general. My father hadn't got in, and this came up a lot in his arguments with Mum. The Sardinian major was commander of an American base on the coast, in his home town, Alghero. That's the training ground for the special corps (i.e., in my not-quite-eleven-year-old language, the commandos). 'That was your place, not mine—you were the gifted one.' I was happy the major said that sort of stuff, but my father would drop the subject—in fact he was beginning to look more and more annoyed. 'That's many people's opinion, Francesco. Even now.' Whenever he started on that, my father would stop him: he didn't want to talk shop in front of me. We'd eat in the kitchen, on a table with a lacquered red top, with the TV on, as you do with family, and I was dying to ask the Sardinian major about his special corps. And he listened to me, explained guerrilla tactics: there are enemies so strong that it's not enough to face them in battle, you have to outwit them, have the brains, the courage. This is guerrilla, and he was head of the guerrillas, smart guys—and I'll do that too when I grow up, for sure. Some evenings they'd lock themselves in my room to talk. A mistake:

as the good spy I was, I had one up on them. Now I was growing, my folks had made space in my bedroom by taking out a bookcase from against a wall adjoining the bathroom: through that bare wall I could now hear anything that was said in my room simply by crouching in the tub. Secrets of the house, things only I knew, things discovered through being my size, through the long after-noons making up games and stories on my own. 'What do you expect—you think we can talk about this stuff in the office?' 'I don't want us to talk about it here, with Giulia, the boy . . .' 'Think about it carefully, please, Francesco—Mario . . .' 'Don't talk to me about that shithead, please.' 'He's your brother, Fra,' 'I've no brothers, all right?' 'Right. But the problem's still the same—what are you going to do with Filippo?' 'You tell me. Did you swear loy-alty to the republic, or to Filippo?' 'Aw come on, Francesco—you're in now—that's not the sort of thing you can forget.' 'I did not swear. Talk about it with those who did.'

At which point the Sardinian major had really lost his temper: 'Let's get one thing straight: when the shithouse blows up, it's not like you're going to land any less deep in it just because you've backed away, all right?' Then they'd started whispering, and I couldn't hear anything more. I'd stayed there, my ear glued to the plug hole, and at a certain point it was my father who had raised his voice: 'D'you know where they're going to enrol them? Reggio Calabria, all right? Or further south, even!'

Ah, so that was it: Reggio Calabria was bad because they're terroni. Shows my father really can't stand terroni. Neither can Mum, for that matter. And anyway the city was still full of jokes such as: a man goes into the bar with a crocodile on a leash and asks 'Do you serve southerners?' 'Of course we do.' 'Then make it a martini for me and a southerner for the crocodile.' It's no longer written explicitly on the 'to let' signs on street gates, because shame is one of the souls of Turin—but just ask, and Mum can introduce you to any number of people who wouldn't let their place to a southerner. And Reggio Calabria was a peculiar thing with Dad, a bit like Bolzano. He spoke often of Bolzano, when the krauts had started setting bombs and shooting at the alpini because they wanted to be Germans and not Italians, and of that time in Reggio Calabria when the barricades had gone up and people had started shooting and throwing dynamite and yelling 'Boia chi molla'.

All in the same year, the Mexico World Cup year, all in that same summer—my father glued to the TV and everyone scared of travelling by train because they said there were bombs on the way. The terroni—my mother tutting, 'Look at these terroni,' my father shooting black looks at her, and I realized he was more interested in Reggio Calabria than in anything else, even the Cup.

Then after a while the Sardinian friend must also have seen something that wasn't to his liking: he had left the army and gone sailing around the world in a wooden boat he'd built himself, him and his wife, and he'd stayed friends with my father, so much so that when my father died he was there, at the foot of the bed, as if he'd arrived by chance.

PAPERS   I wanted to know more. There was one thing I could do, though that meant risking a punishment to be remembered. In my house, on the balcony, behind an iron rack with everyone's shoes and assorted junk, rags, broken toys and cuddly teddies I no longer cared for, there was a safe. I knew he kept his pistol in there, and the paperwork for it. He kept it there, disassembled, the magazine in his bedside drawer: he might have surmised I knew the combination, and didn't want me to get hurt playing with that black-iron toy. I did know the combination: my mother was always forgetting it, so they'd changed it to the birth date of her eldest sister, 8 September 1931: turn the wee crank anticlockwise to 8, then back twice to 9, then anticlockwise again three times to 31 and clack—the numbered dial pops out and the door opens almost by itself. The problem is putting everything back the way it was: if they find out I've been rummaging, I've had it. Nothing interesting: the pistol is disassembled and it's taboo anyway, there's an envelope with those booklets that my father called 'synopses' (with the strange language that went with them: 'Got the synopses?' in the morning, 'How was the questioning?' in the evening. Questions—verbs, times tables, argh). A set of folders and files with names like SME, RMNO, and my favourite, COMILITER. Plus one called US IV rep. (army people are crazy about acronyms), a handwritten note 'Give back to Stef.', a pamphlet in English with a famous name on it, Gen. Westmoreland, the hero of Korea; and one titled Mani rosse sulle forze armate—as in Red Hands on the Armed Forces. This might be it: sounds threatening enough. A disappointment: nothing inside except politics, and almost nothing I could understand. One interesting thing: the special force training courses. I'd heard my mother speak of those, some hazy time before school began, when we were living in Rome, I think. At that time I fancied myself going through the training, learning courage and dexterity, growing massively strong, unbeatable and loyal.

I came out of that search mission with the idea that the armed forces might have mysterious enemies, and that there were brave people fighting for their freedom. 'Red hands': the communists, clearly. In those days there were demos all over Italy, pretty much—the Friends of the Armed Forces, the Silent Majority: my mother had explained that the troublemakers who bring violence to our streets are not very many, and the fewer they are the more terrible stuff they have to do if they want to be noticed—but the others, the majority, in fact the vast majority, keep quiet and don't make a fuss, because they're going to win in the end. So the communists didn't have that much hope: firstly, there was no messing about with guys like my father; secondly, people in the streets were on our side and against them: not much chance of any communists frightening Dad. But one day he looked straight into my eyes and got me to promise that I'd never become a communist. No matter what might happen.

SUBJECT: ALIENS   A film I watched at my aunt's house, hiding behind an armchair so scared I was: the spaceship has landed on Altair 4 to find traces of the Bellerophon mission that had disappeared years before, but the planet has turned weird, as if visited by spirits, there's some good ones in the form of robots and bad ones in an unknown form. An invisible horror is slaughtering the crew, it kills a cook as he dips into his stash of beer hidden in a crater by the landing stage, and then at night climbs aboard the ship where the goodies are sleeping peacefully. All you can see is the rungs of the ladder bending under the weight of something invisible. The communists—something you can't see. And, of course, I did promise.

The time will come when I'll want to hurt him, and by then communism will no longer be enough for me.

3

Homunculus

(1977)

OBJECTS   She's a weird city, she protects her children—or at least preserves them. You always end up meeting again on her streets, even after many swings and roundabouts or whole lives lived along parallel lines. A tough city, as everyone knows: there's a shadow of distrust each time two people look at each other askance with something like 'I've seen you somewhere before' going through their heads. A city bewitched, the air in May condensing into transparent solids, masses of smooth glass planted on the rooftops like cubes, spheres, cones, pyramids, edges facing down as if to section the streets. A nursery that will kill off its seedlings, play with fear as only she knows, aggravate her men of power by indulging in the vice of nostalgia and upend each and every thought into a sequence of symbols governed by the thin light of crypts. And by a question, always the same question: Is it possible to turn back? Is it?

And in any case she's the city of the dead, where thirty-two thousand ghouls marching through the autumn have made history. The streets have the motionless quality of objects left in silence on a sideboard top or in the corner of a cellar. Houses, too, and certain taverns. Sometimes you look at an object and are amazed to find it's still there, present to your eyes and hands as it is present in your memory. Knick-knacks coming from a faraway time and surviving in your habits, so quiet, so discreet, until one day your awareness will unexpectedly clot around them and you'll pick them up and look at them and think something like: 'So it's you—still around?' And you're pleased with that meeting: it's like seeing someone who always minds their own business, but you know you can rely on them. And then the thought might jump out at you: it's objects will survive you. One day you'll be dead and the same old comb will have some of your hair snagged in it. And after a lifetime of just being there, one day when your nerves go slack and you'd be glad to fall back on habit, objects will sneak up on you from behind. Their rebellion has the cruelty young people show towards the old, something that's simply there, not needing to do anything at all. They will show you that your hands, your eyes, your step. They will show you up, with the cold logic of the irreparable. And there you are, butterfingered, knees almost gone. They're in no hurry for now, they can wait. You'll be the one stopping at their door, calmly, feebly. It's the time of coffee pots, of lightbulbs blowing up, knobs refusing to turn, keys lurking deep down in your pockets and laughing.

RUBELLA   Dino is wary of women, he understands them better than either Ruben or I do: he dislikes Marina, says she's stupid and sickly sweet—but respects Giuliana, the most fearsome. She can probably still surprise him, with her short-fuse intelligence made aggressive by the disadvantaged condition she turns into a loudly claimed privilege, and with the imperfection of her adolescent body. Giuliana is older than we are, she's authoritative, often angry. Igor fears her and keeps her at bay with the little smile of one who always knows how to skive off life's hard work, his eyes flashing in the sideways oval of his strong-boy face. One day Igor gives me a book bound in what looks like timeworn red leather, stolen from a street stall: 'Better than acid,' he says as he passes it to me like a secret only he and I can share. I start reading it lying belly down on the bed, on a sunny afternoon in March, and it takes me and sweeps me away to a place like a lost homeland of sorcerers and knights. Kids' stuff, and I'd be ashamed of it, except Igor and I are sure that anarchic secrets and the germs of a life that's possible in a radical elsewhere lie hidden under there, in the words of the story. And as I read the story, my face fills with blebs: rubella. So there I am, well pleased with being stuck in the house if it means I can be sheltered from my mates' looks and finish the big book of swords.

And Igor of the Tin Cans comes to visit every day, towards evening, to talk about it, to tell me things I don't know, things that have come before, after and behind the story I'm reading, and every evening it's a wonder, so much so that I send visitors away just to carry on reading, even if often it's Marina who comes (if Igor is around, they'll leave together). Marina—her smell, her baggy jumper, heavy eyeshadow and all.

Until the Sunday afternoon of that rubella spell: Marina has come with Giuliana, they've brought a present though I can't recall what it was, and something to say but they're not sure how, and I can't make head or tail of it either—until in the end they somehow manage to explain they've discussed this together (their word: 'discussed') and realized they both want a relationship with me (their word: 'relationship'). With me? Relationship—in what sense? That's what I must have thought ('in what sense?'). But it was a skin-deep thought: it's easy to get used to the absurd, especially if the absurd is stroking you. And so, yessir: with me, and they've discussed it, it was a good discussion between women comrades, and we've got to put ourselves on the line if what we want is really a different and clean life, if it's really true that we don't want to end up in those patterns with families, power, authority stifling every rebel's life, if we really, seriously believe this is the birth of a new humanity we've got to risk exposure, and where is the new man going to be found if you don't look for him inside yourself, or at least try to stitch him on over your self. New man? Would that be me? You, us, all of those who believe in something, and not only words but praxis, you understand? Oh, OK—praxis. I get it. Praxis is something that hits you right in the stomach and makes you feel inadequate: not a Sense of Guilt, that's Catholic stuff—but praxis, now, that's the thing that always finds you wanting. Praxis acts on me the way geometric power will act on my slightly older mates. I'm hungry for praxis—for Marina's hips, too, and Giuliana's prestige, yes, but above all I do believe in it, in praxis, I do want the world to see. And I'm feeling like Mandrake right now. And so it was that they informed me they had come to an agreement and had decided to get engaged with me. Both of them.

They announce that as if inviting me to a party, then go away reassured by my consent and experimental availability for the New Man workshop that starts there and then, as the year 1977 dawns on the living room of my house somewhere around Piazza Solferino, with the blessing of the Angelica Fountain, around six o'clock on a Sunday afternoon. No kissing, of course, and I went back to turning the pages of the Lord of the Rings without even wondering about l'effetto che fa.

ONE THAT LASTED LESS THAN A DAY   Over the following days, I was walking on eggshells, and as the rubella ended so did that doorstep of an adventure tale that had kept me company, and now I was stifled with emptiness and I thought that world must be there somewhere, there must be a crack through, I thought the story couldn't just end there, that one unexpected way or the other I'd get through the membrane, maybe exploding in the middle of an atom bomb, who knows, who can say. I had a secret diary, of course—the Red Diary, and the only record of the Saturday after, dated 2 February 1977, is the line 'blackest hassles': the unique, slangy identifier for the date of birth and death of the New Man. An afternoon in quasi-spring, spent stamping our feet against the cold on the garbagey green below Villa della Regina where we used to hide, the grass still too chilly, the air grimy, dust in particles, and Giuliana kissing me in the mouth, from above, like a game to be played in public, like political practice. Marina next to Igor, and standing around somewhere Pasino, Gino Bonetti, Pig, and two kids, Roby and Lauretta—he's dark she's blonde, both beautiful, he in the final year she in the first, he in check patterns and she almost bone china. Here we are, waiting for the sunset, discovering you can kiss Giuliana in public: it's like peeling off the 'underage' label that marks you, the way the older guys look at you at meetings where you try to lie low and watch the clock hoping to get out alive in the evening and go back to walking the streets in silence, with the certainty that all you are to them is one number in the ranks. But if you kiss one of them—

or, rather, if you're kissed by one—well then it might all be different, because that year goes under the 'personal is political' banner, and what that also means is kiss versus geometric power, kiss versus superior aim. The rest is clandestine looks shot at Marina, cold under your shirt and tangled thoughts. And the dark coming early, and good-byes, and how Giuliana dismissed me I don't remember. But I do remember Marina, getting me to walk her to the bus stop near my house, the last to go home, and standing with her back to the wall, a sad, intent look on her face, and I remember our hug, her smell: I couldn't find her, she was almost disappearing on me, receding and returning as if from far away and it was a caress, a game, something falling wide open and leading you inside, swathing without swallowing, and I remember a thought coming from far away, almost as Marina does when she reaches inside your palate, and the thought said 'I want all of me to stay right in here, I want to stay in here a long time.' The first emotion of that story.

That night, each and every thing had already fallen into the place allotted to it till the end of time: I had kissed Marina in hiding, Giuliana in public. This was a clandestine story already, and the New Man could relax—he wouldn't need to be born for many more centuries.

NUMBERS   'Look Dino, the Red Brigades are right—elections are useless.' Dino gets mad, he jumps and lands flat on both feet in his boots, he's smoking these stinking fags that come from France. He can be cruel when he hears that sort of stuff. 'Ommother-fuck-ing-god, I knew you were a cretin, but there's got to be a limit!' Last summer he thought we'd force the PCI into the alternative, into governing without the Christ-Dems. He'd said that and I'd believed it: if Dino says something I do believe it, even when he explained the electoral campaign had been quiet—all right, there'd been seven dead, but those were isolated episodes, Red Brigades or fascists, no violence from the masses or against the masses, so we'll win.

And look, the figures would work out: Dino gets pig-headed, he's adding up the secular parties, subtracting them, multiplying by the quorum, carrying the dorothees over, dividing the lot by the Union valdôtaine and hey presto, the Christ-Dems are in the minority: if the PCI had wanted to, they'd have got through. We'd all been watching and holding our breath, but more like you'd watch an adventure movie, really, cause no one really believed they would—not even they, the communists. And they opted for the strangest of solutions: the eternal Andreotti in power, while they stay out of the majority, and lest they be any trouble, out of the opposition block as well.

This is the government of the abstained. A strange whiff of sacristy in that word—the generous gift of the communists to the country's stability and to the effete, bovine Christ-Dems, soggy and stable as a mountain of mayo, that they're regaling with the manly culture of the workers' movement, injecting them with rigour, proposing austerity. Austerity—when the sheikhs closed the taps, people used to say 'austerity' like one of those filthy words whispered in French around drawing rooms. Now it's made it into the language: austerity, mother to firmness and sister to sacrifices. It's a lifestyle, a horizon, the ticket to power for the working class—you'll see, the workers will take the country into their own hands in no time, with the calmness of those embodying a destiny—that's right, yes, even those who right now are plunged deep into the pits at Rivalta, busy bolting engines into body shells. History marches with them, and they are pushing the undecided. On 8 October, the effete government rolled out the Austerity Plan: they can hit everywhere including below the belt, raise taxes and prices, snag the sliding-scale mechanism that pegs wages to the cost of living (it was called Scalamobile—as in Escalator. I guess it was something to do with a Sixties mindscape similar to mine, made of afternoon raids in the big stores like Standa or Upim). They've even knocked off the canonical holidays, snip an Epiphany here and a St Joseph there, let the accountants' scissors slash even primary-school holidays. 'Sacrifices': it's a mantra, a lexical slip—or a nod to the culture of the Catholic female, the mother of your children.

ROLLERBALL   These days, Marianella is a singer in Milan, at the occupied Santa Marta, and she's known to the comrades: she's doing backing vocals in a song that airs on Radio Città Futura. The code of conduct at Barabba is formalized: whoever wants to smoke a joint goes out on the green, respecting those who are against smoking. What about heroin. 'It's used to mow us down, comrades—whoever sells it is a fascist.'

But in Via Po there's a place with a metal shutter always halfway down, and right outside a load of rags and empty bottles. This is the Circolo Alice: they call themselves comontists. Anyway they're nasty guys, chemists, anarchic and violent, destructive and full of infiltrated cops, stuff that escapes any language, any term used to define them is scary, and the scariest thing is that one of them—the hardest to place, the softest-spoken—is Elio Mandrone, my mate from secondary school. I used to play handball with him, we went to see Rollerball and then he explained that in Via Pomba there were some distribution companies, you could ask and they'd give you film posters—thanks, Mandrone. And I did go, I was ashamed to ask but they did give me a poster: 'In the not-too-distant future, war will no longer exist. But there will be Rollerball.' That was my first poster after the Batman I'd done with my father's tracing machine, when the world was coming unlayered and splitting open and the films were all about catastrophes, and not by chance: Earthquake, with the bridge bending and wobbling and the coaches plummeting into the sea like peanuts; or The Towering Inferno, with the lifts melting and dripping from the sky like in my usual nightmare of the lift failing to stop on the top floor and going up for ever, or Rollerball, where the whole world is a shithole, an X-rated clockwork orange, and all that's left to do is get on your motorbike and mow down people or at least their Platonic idea, nice & white like my mother's beauty parlour. But eighteen centuries have gone by since those times—that is roughly eighteen months, I reckon, if you factor in the biological evolutionary rate of the cubs we were. Mandrone stops me one afternoon under the arcade, he looks into my eyes, too close, smiles and sings, 'Se c'è una cosa che mi fa tanto male / è l'acqua minerale'. So I struggle free with a fuck-off, I can hear him laughing from behind and threatening me—I'll get you anyway. With him is Cardillo, former scout, and I'm scared of that soft, sticky, sarky familiarity on them, and of the stuff they like that makes them so distant.

STONES   Igor says the city's made of stone. Not cement, brick and mortar, but real stone: quartz, or the pudding stone that stands alone even when hollow, a geode under the houses concealing indestructible natural vaults. Igor is my city master (there's only one subject we never brooch, only one name we avoid speaking). At night, he says, Turin is a book, it's written on the cornices, inside street gates, on the friezes in the courtyards: all you have to do is understand the language. He knows the passageways connecting houses through cellars, shows me a strange panopticon at the corner of a courtyard on Via Verdi, blind windows and wings of defunct barracks, he laughs at my obsession with Prague, derived from some book I must have read as a child and cultivated up to these early-revolution days: 'Look, that's like Prague,' I say each time I get swallowed up into a cavernous hallway, or stand on the crossroads at the end of an alley—not that I've ever seen Prague, of course.

But Igor knows I'll be going there, I've a second life there, an innocent life waiting for me. And so we get lost as we roam our way back from our nights at the Cinema Roma, as we build our book. There must be a secret between the paving stones, below street level, a good reason to prise open a manhole and climb down. We have sifted the old quarters, violating doors and stairways and finding a key that unlocks our excess fantasy: a thin book full of numbers, 1930s type, black & white photos, Miscellaneous section at the Civic Library. It says that the Angelica Fountain was not meant to be sited where it currently is, but in the middle of Piazzetta Reale: it shows calculations and original maps with the fountain in front of the kings' palace. We spend our evenings thinking about it. That's the way out: a plane crossing two-dimensional space and offering an endless escape route. The fountain's giants face each other: Gog and Magog, one looking east over his mate's shoulder, the other with his eyes fixed on the former's so he too can catch the eastern light, by reflection. There's a theory in the play of gazes bouncing off each other in the eyes of the fountain giants, as there is one in the flight of the basalt swallows, in the crowned putto and in that one lifting a fish towards the top spout: there's even a thought in the date, 1930, and in the dedication to the sculptor's mother. And if the fountain can speak, so can the streets, the whole grid of straight boulevards points to a different substance, signs are everywhere, on walls and cornices, in flowerbeds, on lampposts, look and you shall find, toil and you shall learn, gather and dissolve, in the good work. In the end, you shall find. Igor gathers useful and useless knowledge, gold and garbage, he shows me Giulia Colbert's serpent diving into a bowl of water in a hallway inside the Roman square and the portraits of witch medics faded along a huge square-section stairway guarded by dragon door frames, a street door you can open even in the dead of night, and hidden away inside is a church with an apse but no tapers. We are visiting the insides of the earth, and by trial and error we find many hidden things. One of the most overused expressions in those years was: 'a good comrade'. When is someone a good comrade? You'll speak of that without being quite sure what you're saying. But I've got my definition, here it is: a good comrade is someone in whose design of the world I could live well. The side door of a church on Via Bligny, set deep between two eighteenth-century jambs at the top of four steps, is lit by two street lamps whose shafts cross: the shadows of the jambs merge into each other creating the figure of a monk stood on the second step, his hooded cloak well defined, one arm stretched towards the bell by the gate. Igor says, it doesn't matter how it's formed, what matters is why. It's a good philosophy, allowing us to believe in ghosts without believing, and I think I'll be able to walk girls all over the city, prime them nicely with scary stories and go out with a bang by showing them the ghost. Except one day the monk's picture shows up in the local press and people start passing by on their evening walks and spotting him, and so some prudent civil servant decides to erase him: first they plant a floodlight in front of him, then move the lampposts. This is the logic of my city. Never mind, there's a secret street everyone's talking about but no one knows where it is.

Igor is nerve intuition hard head: the police are our enemy, and our nights must resemble our days. So he decides to take on the police. In his nocturnal way. The Turin Town Centre fleet park, blue-white 'panthers' and mechanical workshops. It lives behind an ancient street door with spheres on top of brick pillars and lions on top of the spheres: far inside, past the depot, you can see an arcade. Old cobblestone paving. Igor's rule is to look like you know where you're going: we walk calmly past the busy mechanics and the uniformed men, and suddenly on our right a great courtyard opens out, bordered by a huge, bare wall of dark bricks. A horse-carved portal leads to the two paved strips for carriages that skirt along the gate of a forbidden park—and hanging from the corner, high up, the small sign we were looking for: Vietta Roma. The second Via Roma—the smaller, secret one. There's a still, quiet atmosphere, like in a country village. The great mystery was guarded by the police.

The small hidden street will end up like the black monk: one picture in the press and the locals smashing up the sign to stop sightseers. But that doesn't matter—what matters is we've found it, on a winter made of girls, Valium and cinema, wine by the jug, conferences motivated by the animal hope for sex encounters, meetings and street marches, and the search for a cut-price philosopher's stone. Igor could have you believe that the city is a simmering pot—back then. These days, he doesn't care: he's an undertaker, blue tie & visor cap: sometimes I see him after a funeral and he still gives me a hug, we're always saying we must get together for a drink, and I swear we will, one of these nights. He asked to be taken off active service after the night he was called out urgently to bring a coffin to a house uptown and found a man cuddling the white corpse of his little boy who had drowned in the tub, he was stroking him, soothing him as if he'd been crying, telling him he'd be all right, he'd be nice and warm in a soft coffin, and then he'd introduced Igor to the boy, entrusted the little one to him, and on that night that's so close to where we are now, the stone city collapsed: Igor packed up his forty years, love perhaps, whatever he'd got left of the far-gone revolution, the useless sense of an honourable defeat, and stashed everything away somewhere inaccessible. He asked to be moved to an office job, names of the deceased and slim grey folders, and he got it, cause you'd never believe it, but even a town-hall boss can grasp certain things.

But then the city is something else again, it's enclosed in a different casing: a black sea that scares a literature professor watching from a hilltop as pools of darkness widen by the second, and the professor shows them to his elegant friend Avvocato Agnelli, and the avvocato gets the unspoken question in one and answers, calmly: 'Let them rest.' The palm of his elegant hand stroking the city's dark grid, long straight boulevards, clockwork lives.

ONE MORNING IN TIBET   The kids from the great party, oppressed by the mother house recommending sacrifices and moderation—you can tell they're sick at heart, they're peddling this little newsletter in schools, with a centrespread debate titled: 'Don Rodrigo or the Innominato?' Dino says there's no scandal, that it's just what it is, it's normal, even. They're scared of scaring people off, their newsletter is like those holy piccies of St Dominic Savio that are meant to stop you wanting to wank. Poor little Buffalo Bills who have made promises to the Injuns and to the colonel too—you can see they're looking for you at every step, wanting to reassure you that they too. Like fuck we care, if you too. So you don't want to be in? That's your fucking business. Your fucking business, dear PCI friend. Still, you have to understand them: they're part of a huge force made unstoppable by that industrial world of tamed rivers and seagulls scavenging over the drains, but now find themselves powerless as the world comes at them—calmly for now, resting as it does on an area that was once called, with good reason, Mirafiori, and watching them with the idle eye of a large animal stymied by the labours of digestion.

We bring germs of death, rotten bodies and rotten words on the edges of their demos, and we're rushing, rabid for partying and violence in the play of maggots urging our flesh along, we've no desire to join their world even though we were born and raised in it. Bare bodies shuddering with the anguish of labouring women fertilized by a monster. You're the lab mouse running inside your tiny maze and gathering experience, but you're aware that the sky has been replaced by a doctor jotting your movements down in a notebook. We'll look elsewhere for beauty—a chemical beauty, since the mechanical one has bitten the dust for ever in our cities. That's the point: that flexible paradise, this flexible paradise in which you now live was unmasked from the word go, in fact unmasked a priori by a mass of kids my age simply through going under, and that's why the dead of our generation are the most forgotten: they died giving birth. On campus, someone has written on the walls: 'Work will make you dandruff free', and the Don Rodrigo newsletter will discuss the offensive splicing of Nazism and shampoo.

The meetings are profligate with words, at Lang & Lit the women assemble to discuss a scrawl on the toilet walls: 'Considering the relational communication breakdown between male and female comrades, tonight we have called a wank-in.' One of the contributions: 'What I needed, as a male, as an oppressor, like, as the right-wing—as the right, I needed the left to bombard me, like, so I can understand when I'm being a male chauvinist, where I'm exploiting or marginalizing—it's not like I can get it by myself—' One of the replies: 'Comrades, we're talking about antifascism here—about taking antifascism into each situation, understand?' At Law, the Anti-marginalization Committee is speaking of loving affects, of those who are queer or have a scag habit. Meanwhile, the ministry of education sums up its view on the future in a terse circular: from now on it will no longer be possible to sit two exams in the same subject. A detail, and probably geared to making the workload of those skivers we know as the academic teaching body even lighter to bear. But what it does is abolish the freedom for students to plan their own studies, the margin of initiative inherited from that much-celebrated '68, that small chance students had to shape their own future and believe they had a say in their own education. This detail is what brings the university front together: occupations spring up everywhere, first in Naples and Palermo, then all over Italy. And one morning in Rome, a group of brave special-force fascists breaks into a meeting to smash up everything, and on the way out they turn around and plant a bullet in the head of a kid named Guido Bellachioma. So the students leave the campus and make straight for a section of the MSI, meaning to raze it. Halfway there they run into a group of men: plain clothes, big guns—no match. Shots on this side, shots on that side, on Piazza Indipendenza. Three people on the ground, serious conditions: two students and one of the plain clothes.

'See how they do it in Rome?' Igor says. 'They take their thunderbolts into the streets.'

'Yeah.' Images of funerals, murder.

'They don't mess about down there, you understand? The street does it for real—and on its own.'

'. . .'

'Bugger these shithead samurais.'

Right. I've not got a single word he's said. Better bone up on the slang—I can hardly say sorry mate, can you go over that again for me please.

'The university is in the hands of a handful of provocateurs,' L'Unità explains: they're 'faction squads' and 'diciannovisti': surrounding our Roman 'squads' is a cordon of five thousand policemen. But there's nothing like a siege to get a party going, and by 6 February, the huge, wild, endless party has started. There are people coming in to dance from the city's deepest reaches, L'Unità says it's time to 'close down the hideouts.' These are old partisans speaking, tough, gutsy men who had to start wearing ties. These are our fathers speaking, and it's them who shape the language: so we're 'diciannovisti' and belong in 'hideouts', and anyone not slating us is a 'Nikodemist', in memory of the man who was too scared to visit Jesus except by night. 'Hideout' is a word I first came across in Beagle Boys comics. That's OK, it's like going back to a colourful Disney world and living there. You can't get away from the fathers' language unless you gobble it and puke it back up inside out, bent and weirded up and stoned: 'Eating eating eating / is a vice / all we want to do / is work and sacrifice', 'We've had enough of working / nine to five / we want / to produce / and burn ourselves alive.' Those who have sweated through life battling starvation to build socialism are not equipped to tolerate the human merchandise teeming in our hideouts—and so the announcement comes: 'Luciano Lama will come in person to explain democratic life to you.'

And so he does, on the morning of 15 February. With a security cordon made of real factory workers—edgy, thick-set giants. There's a throng of people, electric with emotion, people weeping as he speaks of his toilsome democracy after landing in our midst with his big spaceship. Here comes the myth of the factory worker, the myth of labour, Everyman's myth, thudding down onto your neck and smashing your spine in. Loudspeakers blaring and booming so the students couldn't listen to that huge, bellowing father even if they wanted to: it's the noise that counts, the wall of sound indicating itself, and beyond that, the principle of order. Massive workers in their overalls come out of the security cordon, they have brushes & buckets and start whitewashing the slogans off the corridors, the toilets, the outer walls, the bright graffiti that had turned the walls of that sanctum into a conversation, and as they paint away, Lama is saying universities have to be saved just like the workers saved the factories in '43—what's that? You're calling us Nazis now? It's raining and many don't care, they're making noise to drown out the blaring loudspeakers, the Metropolitan Indians with white face paint and foam axes are singing as if in a mantra, their voices rise, 'Lama on the lam, love him love him not, Lama on the lam', 'Go back to Tibet', 'More work less wages', 'What do we think? / The bosses are too slack / What do we want? / A saddle on our back.'

At the edges of that carnival crowd, the workers' nerves were snapping—you could hear them pop. The first one is a guy with a fire extinguisher: he presses down on the lever, the white cloud goes up, aimed forward like a charge signal, the PCI security launches the attack, planks of wood flying, bludgeons circling overhead, bones are broken, heads even, as the charge runs all the way up to the edge of the fountain. Then they stop, scared of themselves, in front of the students scared of the rage they feel mounting inside their own chests, of the strength rising from that rage. A moment's lull. A wild silence in the middle of a morning of fury, of a venomous city. Like a heart missing a beat. Awe, as if each could count out the laps of the blood's race through the vessels, one by one, loosening the tangle of nerves, like bodies realizing their own being.

It lasts but one moment, and then the measureless, blasphemous wave breaks, the tide of kids laying into their fathers, the lightning-quick, merciless counter-charge sweeping away the toughs, the patient, the oppressed accustomed to winning out on the street, the tide strikes, smashes, devours, Lama's truck is seized on by hundreds of hands, it's rocked, overturned, submerged. The head of the unions, the guy with the pipe, the man who put the heat on FIAT, is running away protected by his staff's umbrellas, off through the uprooted wire fences, through the leaves rotten with rain. That's weird, some of the students say—none of us came with umbrellas.

JABBERWOCKY   On TV, Aldo Moro says there's no such thing as putting the Christ-Dems on trial: two of his ministers are in the dock—a matter of a few war planes, some wee little pay-outs. Meanwhile the language is spawning again, after the Hideouts here comes the Conspiracy, not much later it'll be a matter of finding the Grand Old Man—the heat is on, the police attack. On 12 March, there's meant to be a huge national demo in Rome. We slash it open: demo is 'manifestazione', so mani / festa / azione—as in hands, party-time, action. That's how we get to feel clever, slashing words open. We'll improvise our slogans, the main stage in Italian politics will host a rhyming contest: 'Petrovic, Vallanzasca, Turatello / Stealing is heaven / Working is hell-o'—or how about this one: 'Power is allergic / To tripping with lysergic'. Marina is coming, and Igor has a plan for our night on the train, hands / party-time / action on the tracks, he's flexing his muscle and his smile, stretching his wits to look his best. He'll be speaking to her all night, he'll be fun, he'll be sharp and subtle, caring even. The night on the train flashes away, we've no time to think about it because the rotten dawn over Rome is buzzing with wartime news that erase our slashes: in Bologna, the police have killed one of us 'squad' guys under siege on campus. A carabiniere steadied his elbow nicely on the bodywork of a parked car, took careful aim and bang—seven bullets, in the back. The guy carried on running like the cartoon coyote going over the edge, he didn't realize he was dead until ten or twelve steps later. At 13.30, lunch-break time, Radio Alice is telling Bologna what Bologna is going through: every street is invaded, people running, paving stones plucked up, policemen being hunted down, and Alice, in sorrow and pride, confesses that everyone, everyone together, got involved, readied the molotovs, chose violence.

Overnight, those who listened to Radio Alice and those who'd heard and those who'd heard from those who'd heard, everyone crammed into the trains, left by the carloads, found coaches, the assembly point in the same old sad Piazza Esedra now a bubble swelling and pulsing, like that instant of crossed stares on campus in front of Lama's spaceship, flesh moving and incubating the collective gesture of violence, an organic logic that frightens those caught inside. The long workaday street sloping towards Piazza Venezia is lined by a wall of police, we're negotiating in a grim silence broken by the thunder of slogans booming out in isolated explosions. No, after the death of Francesco Lorusso these are no longer the playful slogans we'd thought up on the train: the day has changed sign, the party will be a battle. And then a minister, a newspaper, a magistrate will think that all this has been ordained, and will call it a Conspiracy.

Slow, restrained, the demo moves along the parallel street, Via Cavour, rain falling from the sky, howls like a solacing ritual all along a route that takes you further than where you meant to be.

At the Coliseum bend there's still a dozen calm, collected kids with baggy shirts and haversacks: they're busy making tea in the middle of the street, a silver teapot sat on the pavement and a spirit stove. Behind them, a banner: 'Never again without lemon.' But everything's going to shatter before long, the cordons will shatter, the demo shatter, Rome's mind-map shatter: the city is big, and you can hear firearms going off everywhere, barricades are going up in the squares and there's shooting on all the bridges and nowhere's safe, not the police stations, not Piazza del Gesù, the heart of the empire, not Gulf Petroleum or the Chilean embassy, not the banks or FIAT, not the boutique of the radical-chic '68 lady selling evening dresses stitched by underpaid women prisoners. This time Rome is burning, not a single glass pane left in one piece, a group attacks an armoury, takes it and arms the ones following, police are retreating beyond the river for the last stand defending the prison, someone's thinking of the Bastille, here is the geometric power, straight from our guts. 'It seems very pretty, this Jabberwocky poem—but it's RATHER hard to understand. Somehow it seems to fill my head with ideas—only I don't exactly know what they are! However, SOMEBODY killed SOME-THING—that's clear, at any rate—'

And this is it: if the magistrate the minister the gazetteer had read these words spoken by Alice from behind the looking glass, they'd have got it in one about the Grand Old Man and the roots of the Conspiracy. Igor and I are stuck in the middle like tourists, at first we're sheltering behind big lines of security, joining in some of the attacks on police vans, then following small groups along narrow streets, across squares and boulevards, without under-standing, volumes in movement, faraway thuds, blood and pain that we guess at, we know about the fear but can't feel any, in the middle of the battle we can't see the battle, sometimes we find comfort in a bar, with the guy behind the counter asking, wanting to know. There are the wounded but there are no soldiers, what's exploding is a continent of flesh deranged with its own growing, kids who can't see clearly, who are low on subtlety and high on irony and have to work that irony off. Pity Marina said she wouldn't come at the last minute. 'She couldn't,' Igor says sharply. And with that he puts a full stop to our day of battle, right there on the river path, next to the classical columns of a ministry building that's been daubed with a message: 'Like '68? Nah, worse— we're in recession.' Winded, our red neck kerchiefs pulled over our noses.

AMENDMENTS TO THE LANGUAGE   Time to start lying. This is April, trees with swollen bellies, green bubbles in the air, the smell of meadows wafting into the city and new shoots pushing raw out of the branches like curled-up lettuces: tightly-packed green-ochre cones, solids that will come fraying into leaf as you waste your time watching them—and they make you hungry as well, even if the revolution has you rushing around like a lunatic. It's true that our relationships are abuse and cannibalism, because the law of desire is a merciless one, and seduction is a non-negotiable power; it's very true that our hidden code brings out the differences, the natural and hence the worst differences between those who are strong and those who aren't, and that we are all about exclusion—a different kind, but exclusion nonetheless. Yet we are experimenting: we're not any more or any less hypocritical than those who came before us. We're experimenting.

And when the experiment gets scary, here you are back on the beaten tracks of those who came before you: shame, lies, deception. Some are toying with dark powders and teaspoons: it's a way to go beyond, a sign of identity, the mark of curse or courage. And many are beginning to look at a pistol, take it apart, learn the correct names—drum, firing pin, rod, angle of grip, distance and calibre. And all of them still walking the streets, every day, every night.

Giuliana: snared in her self-representation, she is tracing my eyelashes with a long finger. The women comrades often mate with young lads. What they say to me is: 'You don't scare me.' She mirrors herself in my smooth cheeks and feels reassured. I don't scare her, she says, I wear jeans tight around curved hips, not one hair on my chin, long eyelashes and hair down to my shoulders. Marina has given me two bracelets that tinkle on my wrist, I like that and love the ambiguity that makes my father mad, the bracelets too are good for me to kill him with, that bastard with his back bent by the daybreak trains to Novara. Giuliana cherishes the same myths as other girls her age, the same pantomime of unspeakable sorrows inherited by exploited generations whose weight she thinks she's carrying on her eighteen-year-old shoulders. She deploys grim faces that want to signify her endless sensitivity and endless suffering for all the injustice in the world. And of course, she has a grandmother. The grandmother is a must for all the young women of my time: invariably wonderful, the grandmother is the only person even more splendid than they are, and worse oppressed still—a partisan grandmother, a betrayed, sculpted grandmother. If you want to get it on with Giuliana (or Mària, Giovanna, Valeria, Paoletta) you'll have to listen to all of her tales about the splendid grandmother; if you want to cheat on Giuliana (or Mària or Paoletta) you'll have to brace yourself for more splendid grandmothers of splendid granddaughters oppressed by all the injustice of the world. Giuliana is good at turning herself into an institution: without in the least reneging on our initial pact, she draws a curtain of friends all around me —caring, helpful friends, my fiancée's friends, welcoming and exacting in their respect of the brief.

Marina: smell and sweat, she tells fantastic lies heavy on the images, she takes me into her inventions, and never mind if it's rather crowded in there. Marina—can't take her anywhere, or at least not into certain circles: she'll write me little notes during meetings, full of drawings of kittens and hearts and fat dots over the i's, she wears a white cotton skirt hemmed with lacework through which her knees show, she cries in public, she's even got that cute chat-show lisp. Her father is a clerk and, yes, her grand-dad is a southerner from Calabria—but she couldn't care less. Sometimes she'll call and act the jilted fiancée, if I hang up in her face she'll call back again and again and come on friendly with my mother, who is scared of her: 'Your mother is a splendid woman.' You'd swear she wouldn't mind having a child of sin for all to see and a black veil to wrap around her hat.

In words at least, the New Man pact has never been abolished, and I follow the line of least resistance: whoever gets here first wins me, no questions asked. You got here first, girl: here I am. Easy. I never choose, the one who gets here second gets a fib—I'll say I'm playing football with my old schoolmates, we've kept a lit-tle team going and there's a proper pitch around the Barriera di Milano. Sling a wee fib to Igor as well, just to keep the peace. After all, I tell myself, I'm lying to build the truth, the truth on my love caged inside the New Man. Within the bounds of the pact, I can lie, expand, elide, elude. I'll fry Giuliana in words, then I'll fry Marina, for equality's sake, and inside I'm rock-crystal virgin. Hardly my fault if the true order of the world, peopled by New Men, cannot come alive inside humdrum realities snared in old men's miseries and petty jealousies: it's just that the world requires a little language amendment. I've a wife and a lover. And the vigour of my young age allows me to cultivate two parallel worlds without getting worn out—but the clot of the New Man is hardly keeping still in its egg of sealed glass: it's fermenting, stirring, and it's about to take on a new, grotesque form.

Meanwhile, it's blasting time: something blows up at night, a small fire outside the entrance of an office block or inside the SIP Telecom car park. But that's water, not fire: a carbide flame, like in the games my father played as a kid—like blowing a lunar, lunatic raspberry. Fake blasts. And the head of department, the prison doctor, the head of personnel, Doctor Dioxin from Seveso, the Christ-Dem notable, the journalist—if the proletariat deems them deserving of punishment, they'll get it, in the form of bullets through their legs, that'll teach them to meditate while they recover. What relief that their lives have been spared: my endlessly regenerating sixteen-year-old body knows nothing of pain or entropy, cracked bones or lameness, ripped femoral arteries or the decay of torn muscles. It sees a gesture that appears reversible and finds in that a relief that murder would preclude.

Igor is talking about some friends of his who one night got into the Singer offices—Singer, you understand? They're out on strike, at Singer. His eyes are shining. Were you there? No, not me—Kiko, Roby, someone else but I better not say. And then? Cocktail time: they burnt all the archive files. Johnny is grinning and winking in a corner. It's a festive evening in one of my favourite taverns, the sallow lights angled upward shadow-marking each angle of each face, and someone hiding away in corners and speaking low. About a section of the PCI: sixth section, sixth bar—named for the partisan boy, Luciano Domenico, a murdered child some of us will surely have mentioned with idiotic humour. The pergola, the long room below a shack made for dinner gatherings and the room of small tables with the drinks counter.

There's a guy from Milan, he seems to be the only thing Johnny's interested in this evening. They're talking of courage, of one gesture with the power to keep it going, partying, growing, the liberation of a corner of the city. I try to hook on to Igor, and he smiles and changes the subject, he's keeping me out of it—but he's a friend, and later, by the outhouse door, he opens up a bit: says there's a discussion going, 'We can't leave the use of force to the samurais alone,' he says: they're among us, they're old guys dressed and walking around like us but with military ideas, and they're standing up to power in the name of another power. We need to override them, take force back, think of something that will express the rebel logic of our bodies, or we'll be caught in the vice grip, between the nostalgic military dreamers and our own head-wanks as we try to pick up a woman. Good old Igor—maybe he's only trying to show me he's not bothered about Marina, that he's not hurt, that he's got more serious stuff on his mind. Then Johnny comes out and Igor follows him.

MAY DAY   'What does "Free Nonna Mao" mean?' Igor doesn't miss a beat: 'Nothing—a situationist provocation.' Meeting at the pillar nearest the river, where the slogan on the wall, 'Free Nonna Mao', is enigmatic as all the other graffiti along the arcade on Piazza Vittorio: 'Carlin the lamer is a rotter' scrawled in chalk (and here Ruben stops to read, well within sight of the punters at a bar, then limps off mumbling 'the bastards'—just for a laugh); 'Jonathan Scully', 'Zeus sees you', 'Who is Carlo Kredy?', 'God is with us'. God is with us is a sign for the users: fresh heroin available (and maybe 'Zeus sees you' stands for 'Watch out, Police'— but I'm not sure). As for the others, who knows. Anyways Igor is wrong about Nonna Mao: her name was Cesira Carletti, age 64, a partisan relay in the Resistance, now a stall keeper at Porta Palazzo, busted for aiding & abetting, two years before our meeting: Nonna Mao pillar, Piazza Vittorio, May Day 1977, a sparkling white at the dead men's bar.

The piazza flooded with wind, arches and the hill at our back, the great silent march waiting to unfold. The counter at the Dead's is jammed, a solid wall of shoulders and backs, you'll have to push and shove for your sparkling white, little groups of people talking, Walpurgisnacht behind us. Johnny, cast-iron muscles, sharp smile under the shades: he's hiding away in the back room, the one where I will see Tano after his death in my dream. Johnny's got a table with Ice-Cream Billy, Cocò, Albertino, Ninetto, Carletto, Maurizietto and a whole string of other pet names, and towering in the middle the Nero Wolfe curls of Ciccio the unattainable. I'd go say hi, but it's not done. Outside the arcade people are waiting for the cordons to form at the top, it's a holiday, morning time, no rush. Some are cracking jokes on the symbolic perversion of this city: 'One avvocato is dead, go shoot another,' one says sneering—as in, one avvocato is a warning to *the* avvocato, Agnelli. At the rally in Piazza Castello, Cardinal Pellegrino will be missing: he's at the Duomo, celebrating Avvocato Croce's funerals. Avvocato Croce—my mayor. The news is from the other day, I was with Igor as usual, letting lunch settle before going to Barabba—a breezy afternoon, and we're busy looking good with our windswept hair and big flannel shirts flapping. 'He was from my hometown.' I couldn't find anything better to say. Igor looked at me as if expecting me to launch into a speech, but I just shrugged. Turin is proud of its record as the European capital of crime, the set for TV films on the special squad: hardly the place to get upset for one cop killed, let alone a lawyer. Black & white images of Judge Violante in his raincoat, the dead man's colleagues, images in my mind of stairs and landings in Barriera, a woman struggling with the washing and the little ones. But Colleretto, now. People in Colleretto still call Avvocato Croce 'the mayor' on account of his mandate ages ago, they're proud of that old man who got ahead, they'll tell you about him as they wrap up your salami in the arcade shops, surely they'll give him a plaque or something, name a school after him, or a square. He was killed in his study on Via Perrone, above the corner bar where I'd learnt to play pool: two bullets through the head, three in the lungs. His secretaries are trying to describe the commando: one tall man, blurred shadows, a girl in buff high-heeled boots. That's right, only Red Brigades women wear heels these days. All I can think of is stupid stuff like that.

In the city there's a large hall furnished with steel cages, in the cages are the political prisoners, caught on camera in that strange hybrid gesture they have, the raised fist and the other hand hanging limp from the handcuffs. To stop the trial taking place, they've issued death threats against anyone who would defend them. Croce, the president of the Forensic Order, is tasked with appointing the court counsel. And he does so, with a devilish twist: perhaps a mountain man's sly turn, or perhaps he simply finds it natural to go to those who have been the loudest in the chorus of legality and firmness—but the upshot is, he appoints as court counsel for the Red Brigades ten of the best-known professionals in the institutional left. So all hell breaks loose, the firm and austere ones are loud for sure—loudly declining, that is, and accusing the old Canavese lawyer of wanting to burn them, now that the elections are near. A conspiracy, of course—him, too. The old lawyer has uncovered a bubble of truth that no one wanted to look at. Fulvio Croce of Colleretto appoints himself as a replacement for the fugitive heroes—and signs his own death warrant.

I no longer understand what the movement is thinking. Johnny is the movement—reasonable, solid.

'What's going on, Johnny?'

'Remember the GAP?'

'What the fuck's that got to do with anything? The GAP shot Nazis.'

'Calm down.'

'All right Johnny, I'll calm down—but the GAP were no snipers.'

'Look matey, cut the crap, will you.'

Matey. But then Johnny is calm, smiling even. 'Anyway I don't like it either. It's not this military logic that's going to get the movement to grow.' Johnny smiled—that's good enough for me. I'm beginning to feel better: that's right, executions are not what we're about.

The trial will be suspended, twelve of the 'people's judges' summoned to serve will bring medical certificates. The diagnosis: depression. Because no one in this city, no one who runs a shop, or might fancy going to the match on a Sunday, or normally walks the kids to school or likes a stroll around the arcade shops of a late afternoon—no one is up for being part of a people's jury that might acquit or sentence guys who shoot in the name of the people, turn farmhouses or cellars into people's prisons for the people, and set up (people's) tribunals.

The demo starts off sluggish, on the way there's time for a drink at Roberto's Bar: I'm next to Ruben, at the end of the stream, because that's where the angry ones start from, far from the PCI who are opening the march, hard-faced steelworkers who came down with whirlwinds of fist blows one morning, only a few weeks ago after the communists' chief, Giuliano Ferrara in person, rallied uptown sections by shouting that fascists had taken the university, and they came in like a red flying squad. The head was Mandola, big as a pillar, nose with fifteen bumps and wild eyes. They came down like furies, and Tancio of the student collective knows them one by one, partly because his dad runs the chemist's in front of the factory gates, partly because he's the leafletting king on the early shift and they protect him as one of their own when they see him in the daybreak frost of Mirafiori handing out thick sheets of paper with the letters spelling 'Lotta Continua' arranged to draw a fist. And that day on campus they go Tancio, what the fuck are you doing out here with the fascists?

And there he is, explaining those are not fascists but the collective—he doesn't get hit, but the others do. The first thing to go flying is an Indian tent made from flagpoles and toilet paper by the guys from Fine Arts. Ferrara was too fat already to lead that raid, but he was Ferrara enough already to gloat in the wings at his juicy prank. So you stay at the tail end of the march to avoid running into them, and there you get a break from Giuliana and Marina as well, they're righteously ranked in the feminist cordons, rigorously elsewhere. We've taken off with no regrets, and we're drinking white wine and the air is hanging over the city like a water bomb.

Pervers is a guy with an electric gaze and lightning-quick ideas, easily stirred to violence. He's bought a python, just like that, just because it normally costs seven hundred thou and he could get it for three—a bargain, and maybe he fancied he'd make some profit off of it as well. That was already some idea of traffic, and many of us young ones had no idea of how much market there was in the corners and passageways of that brave new world of ours. The revolution distracts us from the world, and love from the revolution: Ruben, for instance, is now in love with an older girl, Cinzia, Marina's friend (uh, I know her—her dad's a carabinieri colonel!), he wants me to speak to her, or to Marina, or to him at least. We want to move off, we decide to meet that evening at Pervers' house—just like that, to see the python maybe, and we walk away from the galaxy of humans scattered over the three main squares, climb up to the hill to smell the calm of those sloping meadows. Walking through streets called Porzio Catone or Marco Aurelio—strange names for us coming from the factory-city—we could feel the silence mounting, the air growing swollen and rarefied and a spellbinding voice rising from the kitchen gardens as we walked over iron fences and onto lanes that were countryside already as the city dissolved at our feet and perhaps we'd forgotten Marina and Cinzia and the others, and what we could hear was pipes playing, a buzzing like summertime bees. Gates and guard dogs, some close escapes, and then small scatters of houses hushed in the heat that invites you to find a pergola or a room in the shade where you are welcomed with stew and still wine.

We walked on without thinking, all the way out to a tavern called Anna la Pazza—as in Anna the Madwoman. You had to wash your own glasses, but you could sit there playing board games and always feel like family. And there was no more Giuliana, no more weapons or pills or anguish and hard-work meetings to build the future. Everything was buzzing in our ears.

PYTHON   So here we are wasting time till late under the pergola at Anna la Pazza, Ruben and I laughing and hitting the sparkling white and counting the bars to crawl home through that evening, forgetting that the day is slipping away, the air is tinged with colour and the sharp corners of the prisms on the houses are losing their edge, let's go down and see the snake, and I'm laughing out loud cause I've arranged to meet Giuliana and Marina at the snake house—together. 'You dickhead,' Ruben says.

On the way down, the gods are silent and other creatures sing, those who belong to the city as it gets to be at night, lines of energy and low-lying frustrations running along the tram rails, spiralling up the arcade pillars, slipping into those half-circle windows on mezzanines where as a small child I could sense great expectations and feelings and under-stairs adventures I would have loved to live through. The evening city is the city of taverns, of unsettled plans, of ideas for tomorrow, and Ruben and I are reaching it, going down calm, heading for Pervers'. But just outside his street door are Igor—pale, with rings around his eyes—and Marina, they're talking thick and fast and she moves off and walks determinedly towards me like one who has something to prove, we all go up together, after the kisses on the lips that we all exchange to say hello and show how different we are. A wealthy, modern house, marble & crystal. The snake is in a glass case, it's the beginning of a great collection. Pervers is elusive, allusive, never speaks directly, perhaps he likes to appear threatening and disquieting: an iguana, like the ones he'll buy over the years to keep the python company, smug at the idea of feeding it on live animals to scare the comrade girls.

Who in the meantime are busy discussing male and group behaviours, and have no time whatsoever to be scared of any snakes. Perhaps that's also one of the reasons why Pervers will turn into as cunning an entrepreneur as the business requires, opening cult venues for generations later than his own, hiring bouncers to bruise up the Moroccan pushers hanging out around the place. That's right, that's what they'll call them: 'Moroccan pushers'. That night we were counting out the pills and divvying them up, some disappeared for a half hour or two to dream their jagged dreams: but a few years later the bouncers will become a power in the nights of that same city, by a local council order that will file them under 'security' and get the citizens to put up with them and pay their wages. Until one night at the end of the millennium someone—a bouncer maybe, or who knows—gets a bit out of hand, and the new Moroccan pusher on the block falls into the brown water of the Orinoco-Po, just outside the venues run by the old comrades, and some bright spark will decide to kick him down, make it harder for him to get out, and then someone throws a toilet bowl at him—a toilet bowl, where on earth from?—and he plays along, goes under, glug-glugs and dies. And then, as always happens in this city, many things change—but discreetly: the councillor gets mad at the papers, turns catholic, goes up in the world, gets ready to move to Rome as a right honourable, the entrepreneur might pause a moment and think back on that evening, his first python, that time when we were all revolutionaries, the bouncer disappears and might go top himself by OD-ing in some downtown cellar, and some guy getting done for the crime will say the sentence is too harsh: What's all the fuss about? It was just some Moroccan after all.

But for the moment here we all are standing around the glass case, Councillor Bonetti, Entrepreneur Pervers, the comrade girls, Igor, Ruben, I and some others. There's Billy, hands on his hips and hips thrust forward, snicker-bickering with Albertino, Albertino losing it and shouting: 'The fuck we do! We're clocking in as militants for people who're sending us to the slaughter!' How does Billy have the guts to laugh in the face of the most charismatic one? Behind him, Carletto and Zio Lupara are playing gangster faces. Hold on, let's waste a moment looking into his face—Albertino's, I mean: he's different. The weirdest. With women he takes no prisoners, knows just what to do, he's the one who taught me the grandmother trick, says he himself was brought up by his grandma. He's grown into the art of surviving and understanding, learnt to look out of the window of a locked room to keep his optic nerve exercised, to keep his brain functioning so as to find an escape route, to never be outdone. They say he tells his stories sometimes, those who speak of him do so in hushed tones, women will put up with anything to be near him. Albertino once said to me: 'Can't you see we're all getting shafted—what do you think our circles are? Just Lotta Continua not wanting to give up the ghost.' He wears a long fringe that splits two thirds down his forehead, he has magnetic eyes, he has judgement. Once he told me not to trust Billy: 'He'd do anything to please people.' Albertino is different—disturbing. Billy is more normal.

Giuliana got here too. And I kissed her. The Unfinished Lab of the New Man is a golden opportunity for us to hurt one another—and we do: there's always someone who ends up weeping, with a boozy head and a mess of guilty feelings. Marina went away, crying like only she can. In the end, Igor and I are walking Giuliana home, along the boulevards of a wealthy pedestrianized neighbourhood. We say goodbye to her, in her doorway we kiss one another's lips, then it's Igor and I retracing our steps and we're pretty mixed up. We get to the petrol station and hear someone say ''xcuse, comrade.' I turn round just as Igor signals and grabs me by the shirt. At the first punch, I see red all round and taste blood, after that I can't remember much, except they're kicking me while I'm down, one of them sniggering 'Your friend's putting up a fight at least.' Then nothing more.

I was out already, no longer any fun for them. Igor found his courage and came back, but they'd scored one by now and walked off, and now he's at a loss, raises my head, wipes off a bit of blood, there's a pool of it and it keeps coming, he tries to wave a car down but they won't stop, then a cabbie does and won't charge us. Then Igor has a delicate idea: knowing that my mother would drop dead at the sight of the state I'm in, he takes me to the house of an older guy who lives nearby. And as I sort myself out and clean up, I can see clearly: one, that I'll be the talk of the town tomorrow; two, that my lovely little straight nose is fucked. Igor goes off on foot. And the next day it's the limelight, everyone hugging me, what my mother might have said I can't remember. The three-way-couple hell calms down for a few days and it's Marina who takes very good care of me, I go to her house every afternoon. On the seventh of May, I see Igor again: white-knuckled, eyes sunk even deeper: 'Just after the beat-up we did the rounds twice. Knocked out a few of them.' I've no time to rejoice: 'I've had it,' Igor says almost in a whisper. 'I'm going to lie low for a while.'

EIGHTH OF MAY, TESORIERA   Morning, in the park where the Zapata Circle is occupying the great ancient villa. They're raising the stage, this afternoon it's the Radical Party rally for the referendums: against public financing for political parties, for the abolition of insane asylums, against the Legge Reale that allows police to shoot at you and get away with it. Marina is stroking my bruised-up face and spreading her perfumed spoor around me. Igor has disappeared as promised, but so have Billy and Johnny—there's a lot of people missing, but then I can't feel anything when Marina plays around with my mouth and covers me with her black curls. She knows how to smile, and the wind is blowing. The eighth of May has begun, and we're on the lawn, counting flowers and thinking we can just carry on after all. Albertino has a magazine, Re Nudo, that has printed a long article

on a militant from the Nuclei Armati Proletari who was tortured
in jail. This is something that really gets him, he wants all of us to
see the picture of a man strapped to a restraining couch, the
clamps, the wounds, he shows us stories of violated bodies,
Argentinian, Chilean stories that are almost impossible to listen
to because they drag you down and leave you as if greased with a
sick stupor, the stunning fact of a body taking power over another
and violating it, and there's no redress, and the world afterwards
can never be stitched back up again, after torture there's nothing
but waiting for old age and death, and after death, hell. For those
who have fallen prey to that stunned disgust, bearing witness and
embodying memory are nothing but palliatives, a service provided
to others or a drill to sleep at night: temporary cleansing measures
in the hope of approaching oblivion. You can't think but you do
see, the bound and gagged body is disgust, unease and embarrassment before it is pity, the stunning fact of the first hard slap, of
limbs reduced to things, disgust at the ties that bind, at what can't
be redressed or rebalanced and will return every single night since,
whether for Aldo Moro in a few months or for the tied-up comrade from the Nuclei, for those stunned and lost for ever because
once or a thousand times they've been under the thumb of an
absolute power: a time has begun of nights invaded by that
stunned disgust, by the worst dreams.

Stealing, taking and buying, selling even, tearing down gates,
upending cars, taking the bandit and robber as brothers in the
paradox of innocence, the innocence of thieves and soldiers.
Without rules, and hence free: Jamancipation at Cinema Roma.
But give a man a gun, and he's joined an army, or if it's not an
army, it's a political party: the other violence is underway already,

the efficient, military violence. The sergeants have had their coup already, they're admiring the gleaming of their little cannons as they sit proud amid clusters of adoring women.

There's a lad hanging out in Turin, slinking about a bit: the right guys know him, I think I've seen him at the Dead's one day with Johnny. A while ago he got busted with three comrades while practising with a pistol on straw targets. Up to that moment, his life had been floating inside a strong but friendly current: Magneti Marelli in Sesto San Giovanni had laid him off together with the angriest guys, but every morning on the first shift he and the other banished ones would get wrapped into a march and taken into work by their mates. Now that was the sort of gesture we were looking for: a collective one, violent, effective, full of rebellious solidarity—armed struggle minus the firearms. For the logic of production, that's worse than anything, worse than people refusing to work. And this was happening at Marelli, in Sesto, every single day. Then they get caught with guns, there's a trial, and at every hearing the same march that had embraced them at the factory gates turns up like a court clerk's bad dream, and the carabinieri have to let fly with their bludgeons even inside the courtroom. And at the end of the trial, the bosses in Sesto get headaches thinking that rigmarole of the huggy mother march is going to start all over again for breakfast every morning. So they make an offer: 25 million per head and you can fuck off. Offer accepted: 100 million to get laid off, that's not bad. And they use the hundred million to build a crèche for the women workers who don't know where to put their babies—or who in fact don't usually know if it's even a good idea to have babies at all, the way the factory's run. And this time, the four laid-off guys with their mother-march have really passed the mark: that's counterpower. They've upended the social rules, altered the landscape, filled it with babies. They've proved there can be a rule other than the industry's rule, they've attacked the normal shape of the world and blasphemed productivity and its order. Right there, in Sesto, they've sent the laws of entropy into reverse for a few yards. So it is possible to turn things back.

And now I imagine that if you're young and have not fought a thousand wars, you might get dizzy when you've gone that far, you might need something familiar to hold on to, some form to ground you. Safety jackets in the shape of guns: someone got into the reception at Magneti Marelli and shot the head of security in the legs. The legs. Those levers by which you run, the ones you forget about while making love, one of the two is better at kicking ball, you can even dance on them if a woman asks you to, or bend them to follow your children's toddling steps.

Meanwhile people everywhere are quitting work: to face up to the tidal wave of suspensions and lay-off schemes, they leave the factory by choice. Bidding farewell to work—its great warm belly, the workers' movement, mother earth. That's all right, the wave of the new world is strong and carries right on, even if the world is a little harder to imagine. That's all right, except it's cold and you're feeling lonely, you need a newsletter, a word game almost, a shift in meaning, and the newsletter calls itself Senza Tregua, it's given away almost clandestine, in Turin—it's the workers of Borgo San Paolo, the guys from the Committee Against Repression, those nostalgic for the great security crews of Lotta Continua getting together in a room at Palazzo Paesana in the Roman square. Senza Tregua, as in No Truce—so it can be like

Giovanni Pesce, the commander who used to pop out from nowhere and leave a Nazi corpse on the concrete. A shadow in the city, the terror of those who would spread terror. And when the newsletter is no longer enough, a few kids arrive from outside: they have weapons and a system of thought, they know how to swim in the shallows of our dream of lawlessness, they are the carriers of a libertarian idea together with a fiery paradox. Some only have a taste for adventure and war, but none speak of people's tribunals, people's prisons or church truths, their ardent words lack the suffocating tone of Red Brigades communiqués: this looks nothing like an army—more like a pirate ship. They have meetings on the side of our permanent assembly, at different times, in the back room, in a corner, outside, they talk among themselves, they assess, meet up, have a word for everyone but certain special words only for some chosen ones. They've a merciless conscience, but seem to spread harmony.

Marina was on my belly, all of her fitting snug, and the world hollow like a huge gaseous bubble under the thin crust of the lawn. With the first howls and thuds we stand up and run off from the Tesoriera flowerbeds, ready to run, a girl shouts there's police charging, but strangely enough no one is looking for escape routes, everyone's heading for the entrance to the park. That's it: on the endless boulevard leading to the heart of the city in one direction and to the Val Susa in the other, black holes, tunnels, shadows and beyond that France—on the boulevard, there's shooting: pistols aimed forward, hands trained to shoot and black balaclavas, and we all stand looking from the park gateway, and the police have cut and run, far back, as far back as Piazza Bernini. And those guys are shooting and someone laughs—they've young, flexible bodies and sparks in those eyes I can remember though perhaps I did not even see. Sparks towards us who don't know if we can believe it. Eyes that I know I know. The toughs have come down from the Valle di Susa—and they shoot straight.

SWIVEL HIPS OF A GUY IN THE STREET   That's right, the body. It'll do you in, the body will. Might just work if you use it as a weapon—but use it as a judge, and sooner or later it will send you a pretty steep bill for all the stuff you got up to; use it as a measure of judgement, and it will escape you, turn volatile, shatter into smithereens, each reflecting the whole like fractal drawings or funfair mirrors: you'll lose it. The 9th of May, a Monday, and my parents would not be back till late: my father was running an army fuel depot way out past Novara and never got back till late every evening, my mother's Mondays were taken up with staff meetings or lesson planning or that sort of thing in her school in Mirafiori Sud named after some workplace hero where she learnt so much, where she wanted to stay as long as she could. Well, this Monday thing—I simply hadn't told Giuliana about it: only Marina knew, and we'd meet at my house around mid-afternoon, but that afternoon it was more like being in mid-question:

'Billy, you think?'

'I think so.'

'Are you sure, Marina?'

'Not quite sure—did you see his trousers, though?'

'Like I spend my time checking out people's trousers?'

'You dickhead.' Laughing, raking my hair with her fingers, covering my neck in kisses. That day we were laughing out loud, laughter like an engine pinking in your head, quick and urgent with each other, and she'd seen the hips of a guy who'd stopped in the middle of the boulevard at the Tesoriera—he'd stopped, steadied his wrist with one hand to take aim with the pistol, bending his knees and lowering his ass to shift his weight backwards and absorb the recoil, and all of us had seen his eyes and now we were trying to decide if they were laughing eyes, if we knew those eyes, and the women comrades also had something to say about those springy prosthetic metal limbs used by our guys' bodies to shoot at other bodies. They had more things to say than I wanted to hear. I felt anger—me, the fledgling in the back lines, unfit for combat, the one women don't find scary, the one on the side of the game, busy cultivating my ambiguous body.

No, not the body—the body is young and holds out, smooth like nothing else in the world can be, you can feel it pushing out of its bud, you can smell the scent of your own self, and this is something that'll never happen in your life again—to be stone and water, male and female, air and fire: not the body, they haven't got my body yet, and here it is, wanting to show the world all its might. Marina has eyes painted night-blue, her backside's small and pointed and cocksure, her smell is face powder, talcum powder, skin and tears. That day Marina guided me inside while lying on top of me and I didn't know anything like that was even possible, and her face was full of joy and I can't say anything at all, even if afterwards she said it was hurting but not too much and that was another thing she'd never done before and it felt right that it should be the two of us, Marina and I, right there, right then. And since I can't say anything at all about it, any more than I could have back then, the next night I'm in a tavern with Ruben, his eyes bulging out greedily as he says, 'Were you thinking about it as you did it—that you were fucking a woman's ass?'

So there you are: in a bar, talking bar crap with your bar mate, and Ruben's complicity was the same as a few months later, when I got back from driving a car for the first time and he asked hungrily: 'Could you feel her under your ass?'

GIULIANA IN HER YARD   Giuliana integrates the universal cult of the grandmother with the myth of some ancient tribe of hers lost somewhere in the delta of the Po, an imaginary continent peopled by images of old folk who firm up her image of her own self and the world—nothing to do with the embarrassing real-life version, the codgers who'll come across a girl with a grandmother myth and go straight for her ass, sometimes with their canes, you know how it is with the gimpy hand, love. Her hypothetical ancestors are there to remind her there is something to hold fast to and respect in a world that like all of us in her age group she wants to turn upside down: because of course the family is an institution, and as such must be torn down—but Giuliana's family has already seen to tearing itself down nicely, thanks very much, and so she can make an exception to the various palingenesis proclamations, a small exception each time she gets home and closes the door behind her to wash up, scrub the floor and make dinner for her mother's man. She lives in one of the last council blocks left standing at the margins of the city's richest neighbourhood, a few yards away from the pedestrianized areas. Behind the kitchen curtain is her mother, a girl-mother who had Giuliana back at the beginning of the economic boom and is now a Veneto-blonde matron, our lady of the pasta bake, a shy, principled woman who married a

FIAT worker when Giuliana was small. A middle-of-the-road guy, flat wide face, straight hair, not right-wing, not left-wing, and that'll do: he's never at home, out on shift, but has given her this massive son, her and Giuliana's pride and joy, a kid with a good left kick on him, he could even do well at football if life gives him a chance. They look good, this lot, in the slatted light that catches the stillness of dust grains in the air, the washing machine rumbling and a coffee pot steaming somewhere. And Giuliana might not be aware of it, cause she's eighteen and everything's rushing along fast as lightning, but her project is: a family. That's the image offered to her in the eternally present form of myth and in the eternally lost form of an actual past—and someone else's past at that. The past of a mum who fled as a girl from the banks of the Po, of a grandmother you see once a year at the end of a journey with luggage heaped on the car roof, and for all you know you're nothing to her but the child of sin, the daughter of her daughter who walked away.

She says her stepfather molests her, but she's not quite sure: she can't tell whether the attentions of that stolid, gentle guy are swerving towards treacherous ground, or if his is just the awkwardness of a guy who hardly knows how to approach the woman he's married, let alone this adolescent who watches over the house and its proceedings with the authority conferred upon her by a past made from the waters of the plains. And even the sick darkness she thinks is surfacing from a caress might be nothing more than an oversight of her mind, the reflection of one of those stories about scary ogres that come from the river banks her mother has left. She's not sure, she's scared, fragile as her solid mum is. I'm not scary—Giuliana tells me over and over again, as if that was a form of praise. She sees my face made up as a woman's in the fairy tales she tells herself. For her, it's a figure of calmness; me, as a child I watched the hermaphrodite, the two-faced monster rising from timeless darkness, planted on his two feet, the stony spreadhead of the books on alchemy my mother kept in the living room: it was the custodian of a landscape that was the scarier for being familiar and composed of alien elements, silent like the image in an enigma. If it speaks at all, I thought, its voice must be terrible—perhaps those who hear it will die.

But to these girls, it's a reassuring figure: they hurl themselves at girly lads with a self-protecting instinct that is more or less the same as pushes me towards stories of elves and gnomes. Androgynous forms that Giuliana smooths like a balm over the precariousness of her wide council-block yard. All around are coarse vegetable soups, fights, men in vests, sometimes murders, nearly always there is want and the struggle to just about keep on top of it, nearly never is there any future. Yet Giuliana is generous: when in doubt, she does heap insults on her mother's man—but they're the sort of insults you would save for your father, and she holds him dear, gets home before him to make his dinner, and later, when the time will come for him to die, she will be with him to the end, with a daughter's and a mother's gentleness and the forgiveness of his every trespass, and she'll be the one who soothes him and wipes away the sweat that comes from the ultimate fear when the last foothold's gone. And she uses her intelligence to pre-empt my needs, my whims even: in private she wears lipstick as none of them ever would in the daytime, and she's bought a pair of buff boots with Texan spurs that she keeps on as she kneels for me when I'm behind her.

TV FILM   The police have been raging mad since March, they're acquitting themselves, as per their work contract and as per the prime-time TV films with the misunderstood, betrayed, self-sacrificing cop, and standing around in disguise watching over the stall set up by the Radical Party to gather signatures for the referendums. They don't think there was much harm done (and a judge will agree) that time one of them whipped out his gun, took careful aim and found that girl on the bullet's trajectory. And anyway, we was under pressure, and the girl had already thrown away the flowers she was handing out to passers-by and was running away. There's a bullet shooting out of a TV film and landing smack bang between the vertebrae of Giorgiana Masi on 12 May 1977. And we stage our recurring ritual, our take on the circle of life. We take the dead on, still warm, and they become our dead: even if that girl was only giving out flowers to passers-by, we've enrolled her now. We are showing off our grief, our drums, the usual run in which you feel your body responding and hide your pleasure in it. Meanwhile, I'm watching the TV news with my father, like when I was small: Milan, Via Larga, a P38. A pistol, a gun—a Bertha, a Barker, a Thunderbolt, in the slang I can hear more and more often as it gets mixed up with our tightrope language of hype and irony. A gun pointed at the head of a very young policeman, Sgt Antonino Custrà. He was thrown backwards, his body corkscrewing onto the tarmac. Dead. I prepare my litanies on infiltrators, but no one in the house wants to listen to me—not even me. A shit month: trees swelling and bursting, the air full of light and strong smells on the boulevards in the city. And me, a virgin in virtue of the pact the girls are betraying every day, with every hour and every word and every lie—what can I do? I present arms to the altar of the New Man.

SOFA   Ruben and Dino's house is full of shadows and rugs, high over the plane tree boulevard that you can see from above as birds do, and behind you are long long bookshelves of blond wood, curving lines, coffee table and poufs, Marxist classics in their Mondrian-style covers, red circle & black line on a white background. Pasolini and Archie Shepp—but also those large colourful Adelphi volumes that signal open-mindedness, and higher up the Greek poets next to etchings and mezzotints. And then, the sofas. Modern, elongated—our legs all over the place and our variously hanging heads, clogs & flip-flops beached on the edge of the rugs. Shade, lots of rooms, no need to all huddle together all the time: there's space to hide, there's Billy and Marina, Albertino, Cocò—even Johnny, today, and we talk of nothing, make grey tea, listen out for the buzz of flies as trams go past ten thousands yards below. Heard about Igor? Someone laughs: 'He had a bit of trouble with a bus.'

'As in?'

'Got tangled in the tracks.'

'So was it a bus or tram?'

'Let's say both.'

The laughing spreads: a few nights ago something happened in a city transport depot, someone set some vehicles on fire and poured cement onto the tracks—like Giovanni Pesce had done. Right. So Igor was also there, it seems. Right. Then he's all right, it seems. Right, that'll teach them to put up the fares and send employed conductors home to replace them with little machines. Right.

No chemistry: no joints or pills, no time for pleasures. There's more urgent things in the air, I think, and yet we're spending whole afternoons lying around and talking—some of us because they live in these afternoons, some because they couldn't care less. Billy is good, he lashes out and hits, gets a laugh each time he speaks, says he can get them to bring us up some ice-cream from the arcade place where he works. No thanks, darling—no way of telling if your colleagues pull the same tricks as you do with the vanilla—uh—cream. And he deadpans, it's no laughing matter— you try wanking off while wearing a bow tie. Marina looks on, she listens and laughs.

Yet there's something wrong—with the pauses, or the looks, eye contacts long as sea-sickening waves, stymied smiles: or maybe it's just me seeing secrets everywhere. I never get asked to do any- thing like that on any of those nights, to be along for anything like the city transport thing, for instance. Maybe it's for the same rea- son as makes girls plan their love life around me: I'm not scary. Death has a hermaphrodite's face, and for me the hermaphrodite lies in a long gesture of Giuliana's fingers tracing the line of my eyebrows: 'What a sweet face you have—why do we always have to feel this rotten? Why can't we just have a quiet evening in a house somewhere, without panic, wasting our time, making up our faces . . .' Summer comes, burning and laying waste, every- thing dries up white, the earth is flat and nothing grows.

CHESSBOARD   En route to the Maremma again: on the train I can sleep well, especially when it rains, I'm free and easy, no responsibility and the track doing it for me, my head simmering like a cauldron of thoughts, I'm making friends, almost invariably I don't hear what people are saying but rather the music of their words mixed in with the rhythm of the tracks, and I stick a neutral gaze to the window as sleep comes down on me, merciless, like it does for children, with the flatline of the sea running parallel to the railway track and the line of my eyelashes. We've left earlier than the others, because the house at the Argentario has been closed for a year and we've to make it ready, get the keys from Uncle Donalfonso in Grosseto—and also because the train is the proper place to straighten out on a few points. And we do have some points, loose ends to tie up, we started out from the same place a while ago and left some baggage behind—ballast, people, memories. We've changed our names, dissolved clots of habit, committed some acts of violence without looking in one another's eyes, without stopping to check if we're using the same words for the same thoughts. On the train Dino is a stream of politics, and he's not talking like someone trying to chase away the heat or the flies, but like someone who's been thinking things over for a while and is beginning to find the words: he doesn't like what's going on, he believes in the masses, thinks we're getting shafted, says it's not about morals but strategy, all this Robin Hood stuff will do nothing but get us a long way away from the factories, from the place where changing the world really starts. He says guerrilla is a serious thing, not a question of concrete in the tram tracks, and those who are just dying for adventure do nothing but hand it to the bosses, and in the end the pawns are always moved by those in power. Dino is taking the long view, churning things over, using our weaker brains as sparring partners, travelling far.

First stop, China, where he thinks there is a real, solid project. Not the Soviet Union—lost, failed, oppressive, dangerous, inimical. Dino's China is asking to be taken seriously, not as a myth but as a programme. Dino is thinking back—years back, many years back, and I can feel my eyelids closing and the train lurching. Usually at this point I get a note from Marina and the comrades shoot nasty looks at us—but no, this is not a meeting, I can feel the track's rhythm and sense that Dino is packing up, his China is a step back leading to a side step, he's going to live someplace else out of his need for intelligence and results. He will get on the Marxist–Leninist train, he will study the canonical texts and hold on tight to the hard embrace of the working class. He's off searching for a land that will bear fruit: I'll get there too, but later, after a shipwreck, asking to be enrolled. I'll get there as one walks into a church after a murder. He will plant his feet on the Marxist–Leninist thought of Mao Zedong; I will look at it as you would look at the sky, in the hope of not finding it deserted.

Dino will make new departures after that one. But later, much much later: right now the train is running and putting us to sleep and we've no time for his communist logic, we wake up and here is Grosseto again, a warm drizzle drawing an ancient smell from the wet paving stones, the smell of when we'd stopped over on the way to smashing the noticeboard window at the MSI section, the smell of some earlier time, earlier than the earliest memory. The raccoons' cage at the zoo in Novara. I can't remember anything before that: I was three years old, my father was a penniless captain, in the afternoons my mother would take me walks around that flat, charmless small town, and I liked the dousers, I remember the edge of the pool where they would rub their food clean in the water, it's the first image I have retained. And then, throughout life, at times, you're caught unawares by a caress you can feel, it's coming from far, far away, from before the raccoons: that is the moment when the thought of the dead is honoured. Well, the dead are scary when they walk on earth: we chase the smell of the rain of Grosseto with an ice-cream and we progress via the ring-road underpass to the great villa of Uncle Donaurelio (still a Christ-Dem, still in a flappy shirt). Almost evening, and Ruben and Dino's cousins are there: Carla, the very pretty one with the weight of the tits toppling her over, and Giulietta, a new sister who's grown up at a stroke and has trouble manoeuvring her new body. The house is big enough for us to get lost in, Aurelio and his missus have disappeared hours ago in one of their tastefully lit rooms. I don't know how long I've been here on the poolside, stars and cicadas free-freeing, an empty glass under the deck-chair level with my ass, the rain has disappeared without a trace, Giulietta and Carla are swimming in the dark, and us three males whacked with the badly-mixed alcohol, busy looking at the garden lights hidden by the shrubs, laughing out loud to see how it sounds in the silence, and after each laugh all you can hear is the plash of slow girlish arm strokes in the water.

And then I don't know how it happens, crickets still going, spinning head, and Giulietta lying on my belly, in her birthday suit—or, more accurately, in the skin suit she has grown at fourteen, and she's moving like a lizard and I hear the noise of cold pool drops falling from her body onto the concrete, I turn my head and Dino is gone, Ruben is talking thick and fast with Carla and his eyes are pleading for help but none can see them in the dark, and the only thing I can feel aside from Giulietta's heat are those liquid sparks sliding along the deck chair and making noise under my back, time is standing still, I can see everything from a height, motionless, Giulietta's back curved into an S shape, something of me underneath, the wet concrete floor, the pool, the shrubs, the houses of Grosseto, the shore of the Tyrrhenian Sea and the other one, the curve of the planet and all is spinning and spinning. I go hedgehog, stop turning my head, keep my eyes closed and don't move a muscle, at least none of the voluntary ones, my mouth and nose shut tight against the smell of her breath. I remain motionless behind my eyelids, suspend even my heartbeat, and with the passing of strange aeons the young girl loses patience and slips away looking for a new game, the soft plop of drops following her, I'm shivering, it's cold in the deep night in June.

And the next day all is dry again, inert, sun-sanitized, and for once I've been faithful to the pact of the New Man, to the voice that says 'no more than two', for once faithful without ruses, out of fear: the drops I can hear as they fall on the fake-leather seat of the Grosseto–Orbetello Scalo train are friendly drops of sweat, the only evolving life form in the white heat. Then the coach, Santa Liberata, another villa bare and cold with tiles, and a noisy gang of mates to keep me safe from everything—one by one or in groups, here they come: Pasino, patrol leader in the Foxes, Giuliana and Marina in two different convoys, Gino Bonetti, Roby and Lauretta who look like they're made of bone china, a girl called Sara Levi whose veins you can see the colour of, and Cinzia, the daughter of a carabinieri chief who looks like she's born for cuddles but not for Ruben, and Valeria, you-wash-the-dishes-I've-been-doing-it-two-thousand-years—and I get on the phone and convince my cousin Maurizio to come along, he's left school and works in a beer place and he's not quite with it, and when he gets there after an age of local trains & coaches he stands in the main room with its wide glass panes over the sea, struck dumb as he watches that transit of naked girls, and Sara Levi sticks her tits in his face and asks him is she sunburnt there in the middle, and he swallows and tries to be cool as his beers but he's horny as his customers and can't find his tongue in his mouth to say a thing.

Days and nights in order, like the squares on a chessboard, black-white, black-white in equal measures, the smell of the water and the noise of rubber shoes on the stone, soggy pastas with the same sauce every day, and down to the pier. And those who can kissing those who will, and some talking and some playing music and some thinking of who to kiss and some keeping their hand in the water to make small whirlpools among small fishes. So many guitars—and one day someone will explain to me why the girls all loved Lucio Battisti so much, all the more so when he killed them none too softly with his song about the blonde braided hair and the blue eyes, the red socks and what do you mean I am a woman now. You should see the dead-set faces on them as they sing it over and over again, looking over their shoulders and frowning like it's a war song. Ah, I get it—I know why they're always banging on with the ballad of the blonde braided hair. It's all about the refrain on that black and troubled black and troubled sea / you once were bright and shining clear like me: the brine-scented self-assessment of a tribe of fragile girls who have hardly learnt the old rule of the world and have to go out hard-faced to set the new rule—and they're scared that in the end no one will realize, no one will see they have an ancient heart.

And the girls have had another discussion between themselves, a negotiation—because holidays come but once a year
(we're like our folks, we use their same words when we fight),
only once for everyone, and everyone has the same rights, and I'm
a right: the right of those two bodies who feel the same hunger
as me, the same haste, the fear of running out of time before
being able to grab it all, the present sense of death all adolescents
share. And they've come to the conclusion that since we're on the
threshold of a new era we could do worse than sorting ourselves
out, that the stark force of things imposes a law, and they've laid
down the law—in the form of an alarm clock. A round, white
alarm clock with bells sticking out like jug ears, set to go off at
four o'clock every morning. No matter what time we went to bed,
no matter if I've made love or not, and to which one of the two,
when the alarm goes, I'm to jump from one bed into the other
and open my eyes next to whichever's down for the second shift—
romantic dawns on alternate days, black-white, black-white.

But I'm fine, I'm walking on sunshine and feeling pagan and
immortal. For a while. And then a languid evening comes, clouds
in the sky and our edges blurred by wine, an evening when anything seems possible, and Giuliana is still thinking of the curve of
my eyes, my long eyelashes—we're much closer now, the three of
us, a strange family held tight in that pact that is smudging like
make-up on a sweaty lady's face. And Giuliana is thinking of mascara, she wants to see my face made up like a woman's. Here I am
with summer's heat burning my skin, scarifying and sawing my
bones, with evening taking me in hand and undressing me—I
remember seeing a classmate dressing her boyfriend in her light
clothes during a school trip to Florence, and I was laughing and

looking on without judging, because we're shedding our skins and the New Man is not the male he has always been, he's learnt to cross over. It's hard work to be nothing but the line you're scared to cross—I dreamt of being male, and a warrior, but no hair would grow on my face and I had soft round curves which at times had landed me into trouble or made me so ashamed that I fled or burst into tears, no matter how I howled and growled afterwards. Like that time when an old guy on a moped sidled up and started rubbing my backside, calling me 'pretty little slut' and mumbling a toothless string of conditional tenses until I turned my full curly head around and said 'my cock's bigger'n your head' and he'd zipped off calling me a faggot. Or at the scouts shop, where I'd gone to buy a knife, and the lorry driver who was unloading had leant against the counter in a way that made the muscle bulge on his arm and whispered: 'What's the matter, miss—thinking of stabbing the boyfriend, are we?' Saved by the shop girl, who'd swallowed hard and said quickly: 'But he's a boy! You can see perfectly well he's a boy!' Or the worst of all, in Colleretto, walking home after stepping off the little Canavese train, and a pack of older kids had left the veranda of a beer counter on the square and started tailing me, whistling and catcalling to get me to turn around: I was terrified, ran up the road and straight into the blind alleyway by the church, and luckily they'd stayed lower, but one of them looked up at me and shouted: 'Come on, no need to be scared—we were just wondering if you're male or female,' and I'd yelled 'Male' and they'd laid off, somewhat let down. I'd felt totally rotten afterwards, bad enough I wanted to cry, but then not to cry because crying's for girls, and I was not yet male. Now I can hear the girls telling me I'm not scary: they're doing up my eyes, cuddling up to a hermaphrodite dream that's warm and reassuring enough for these raw women who are already hurting themselves plenty with their heads and trying at least not to hurt themselves too much with their bodies. Soon they'll grow and start taking their chances with the warriors, but for now they're hard put to manage the explosion, can't govern the body and its desires, and with the arrogance of children they are fashioning their own image from any substance soft enough to be moulded. Now I understand Marina's strange sadness as she applies to my eyelids the knowing movements by which she makes herself pretty, or Giuliana's as she dreams of the perfection my face could attain with a little help from her artistry. The sadness of growing up, the hazy awareness of those who are about to leave the happy kingdom of the indistinct, a pre-emptive nostalgia, a fear of what will come later, when man is man and woman woman and the days divided into workdays and holidays, when all of life is patterned on the chessboard, black-white, black-white.

That evening the early shift is Marina's, it's she who patiently does my eyes, then blushes powder onto my cheeks and more lightly on my forehead, pencils my lips in. I say, 'Wait,' and try to catch my breath, saved by the wine that's mounting from inside, filling my nose and blotting out its aversion to perfumes. Then she undresses me and I want her, I can feel her hands and want to grip them tight, I need to bite and grip, to get my own gestures back, but she smiles silently as I say 'Wait' and feel the fear mounting inside the wine, everyone is sleeping or making love in the oleanders and the other low, tough, fragrant plants, no one'll be looking but I can feel the eyes of the whole universe on me, I can feel something digging into my guts, and Marina gathers my hair in a ponytail clasped at the nape and looks at me with eyes wide open, taking good care to caress me, priming me, and I say 'Wait' and can feel something flowing away that I would want to hold back, feel myself falling and know I'll get hurt, I can feel something tearing and breaking, but she's looking at me with those eyes and constructing me, inhaling my fear, her gestures following their slow ritual, a sacrifice, since the night is rushing away and it won't be her who'll consume the body she's inventing, I'm breathless and she smiles, she breathes, 'You're shaking,' and I nod yes but say nothing lest I cry instead, she smiles and hugs me tight closing her eyes, I can feel her heartbeat, everything moving along as if fated, an act of courage with no reason to be. And onward, I'm shaking, she has me wear a long white tunic that she belts at the waist with a red scarf, she's stroking me, staying so close as to have me feel her breath on my skin, second by second. Now she smiles, 'Shall we go for a walk first? On the roadbed—no one will see us.' She smiles again, looks at me: 'You gorgeous boy,' and I'm grateful for that 'boy'. I walk along and keep quiet, listen to my own footsteps.

Giuliana: I don't give her any time to look or think, or any mouth to breathe, the alarm won't go off tonight, I grab her and swoop on her with all my strength, I force future and contradictory dreams onto her, spread her thighs with my hands and mount her and beat and beat against her crotch and won't stop even after I feel her orgasm and my sperm dripping between her legs, beating furiously from above, one hand on her chest to stop her getting any closer, staring in the brass headboard at my own eyes painted green. After hours of this I'm in the bathroom washing that night off me with water and with that chlorinated smell of taps at the seaside, then go back naked to a bed where I want to fall asleep and sleep for ever, or at least until sleep has stitched back together something that has broken inside me.

Instead, I hear their voices: Marina and Giuliana are whispering, but I can hear them, there's a curtain flapping and letting in slashes of sunlight that burn my eyes. 'I just meant for you to do him up—you've sent me a female.' Like a baseball bat swinging around my crystals cabinet. I decide there won't be another night. Gino Bonetti and Pasino have been on the beach for hours, the girls are somewhere flashing their tits around the cliffs. We're off tonight. Bonetti, Pasino and I are off to Rome for higher political reasons: Lotta Continua are sorting the five hundred thousand signatures gathered in favour of the eight referendums to hand them in tomorrow, they need extra hands and eyes, it will be a night spent drinking coffee and being of service, they need people in the sections if the signatures are going to get delivered in time— you expect us to stay here fucking around? No arguments against a militant choice: rucksacks packed, and off we go before dinner. Shouldn't we go earlier? Bonetti is easy: we're going to be up all night anyway, we'll get there in time.

DOM ARGENT (1975–1979)   Meanwhile the protagonist of this story is working away, well concealed from our uncertain gaze. There are people in town who will spare none but the protagonist. They live in great strongholds on the hill, or inside pedestrianized areas, and they split humanity into worthies and unworthies. They serve their servant, and the rest serve them. I need help if I'm to tell you about them: these are people who will tear the pillow from under the heads of still powerful men, people who count their blessings in this life and bear honorific titles, receive bows and applause from senators—they're clapped-out widows wedding anew, they've sores that a plague-house would turn away, but it's always springtime in their days. And they have a safe in the city.

As for us, we don't understand money: it flows far away along invisible channels, it clasps men's hands together and it rules. We can't intimidate it—but we can ignore it. The railwaymen's canteen, for instance: it shuts at eight, but you've got to be in by seven at the latest if you want to get a bite. In spring it's still light at that time—not very nice to sit at dinner in daylight, and then you've to queue up for the ticket that will afford you a slice of see-through mortadella or sallow cheese with holes, so thin the holes are real holes through which you can see the plate, one wide leaf of damp lettuce or one of those black slices of meat hardly touched by a curl of discoloured mash. The lights are neon tubes mounted on metal tracks and the windows are only to be found in the corridor, but they're black with the soot coming up from the tracks, no matter that coal is no longer used. The railwaymen's canteen is at the end of the flyover, at the bottom of Via Sacchi, past the headstop of the trolleybus to the factories. One wide room with plastic chairs where they sometimes do a cheap screening of some film. We go and get dinner there—not because it's much cheaper but because it's a secret and a smart thing to do: it shows we can use the city, that we have unsuspected resources. We assault all available space, go down into cellars and up old flights of stairs and conquer the city's third dimension, and not just that: in virtue of our young bodies, we are masters of time—hence we can ignore money.

But money won't give a fuck about that. Exactly halfway through 1977, as we're standing on the pier, it is celebrating spring-time and rebirth. In its sanctuaries politics steps back, bows and reverts to a handmaid's role. It had entered those sanctuaries one April morning, two years ago, when Avvocato Agnelli made his calm entrance into the boardroom where the shareholders were waiting for him to open the meeting. I can see him: elegant, with a folder full of papers he places on the table. I can imagine his voice (easily done—I'm from Turin). He speaks without prompts, with the sharp precision of a ledger book—but with grace. There's a grace about that fatal man. It is 29 April 1975, and he's come to announce a defeat. 'Gentlemen, for the first time our balance sheet is showing signs of an altered relationship with the banking system.' Time was when FIAT was so rich as to have no use for money: in fact it was lending to the banks, it had turned into a bank for banks, making profits on the interest. These days, 'an altered relationship with the banking system' means: we're in debt, it's time for us to ask the banks for money. None of the engineers ruling the great machine knows how that is done—none of them knows how to speak, whether as an equal or as a postulant, to the wizards of money. Avvocato Agnelli has already found the man he needs: a calm, inexorable tamer of the immaterial, mysterious flows of Mammon. And that man is already on the premises, destined for a fulgurating career. He is no engineer: his name is Cesare Romiti.

For years, figures have been juggled by sleight of hand: each year FIAT Plc sells off a piece and turns it into shares, in no time it will be a holding, it will no longer own a single shed or pay a single wage—just shares, flows, immaterial capital, speculum et aenigma. And as the FIAT group sloughs off its skin, stripping off sector after sector and shedding the physical bulk of the slow productive giant it was, the balance sheets are spread about. No longer one balance sheet for the entire group, but only partial ones, each to its own associate, and anything can be made to appear or disappear at will in that underwood, auditors like the paladins of France searching for Angelica amid the spells of sorcerers. A restrained silence descends on the subject of losses. Hundreds of billions, perhaps thousands: the company has been a sieve for years. Only now the three-cup game is over, the shareholders need to know. We're sinking fast, ever faster, it's time we asked. And not just for money either.

One tribe in particular cannot be kept in the dark about the disaster. These are the shareholders in the family holding, IFI, that holds the majority of FIAT stocks: the relatives, the Avvocato's solid constituency, those who passed on the sceptre to him when the company, faithful to its old chief Valletta, was rearing under his backside like a wild horse. That small forest of people called Nasi, Camerana, Elkann and Agnelli is the mantle of leadership. To them he has always granted support and wealth, even in the hardest times, when the workers were up in arms, when oil was disappearing, when politics swooped on industry to eat it alive. And even as FIAT was losing money, IFI was a happy parallel universe, the island of the rich, managing to pay a dividend to its shareholders every year: that was the pact between the captain and his people. Every year, Nasi and his satellites got their soldier's pay—at the cost of digging deep into the company's reserve capital, year after year, until it dried up. Nasi, as in noses—hard-nosed all right. In 1974, IFI's deficit is covered by nine billion taken from the last of FIAT's reserves, accumulated since Valletta's time and now shared out between the silent, hungry masters on the hill. But on that April morning in '75, as the Avvocato walks into the boardroom where the shareholders are waiting for him, every-thing's changed: not even IFI will be able to pay out any money—which means the crisis is also a crisis of leadership, of investiture. What's needed is a new agreement, renewed trust—even the hard noses will have to understand. This is the world turned upside down, FIAT no longer is what Avvocato Agnelli had inherited from Professor Valletta (titles are important, in Turin): no longer a meat-grinding military apparatus, the banner of the city and pride of its subjects, no longer the command centre of a huge ter-ritory between the four rivers that was formed and raped into its image. When it needed workforce, it took it, locking people by the hundreds of thousands in shacks and satellite towns without running water: through surveillance of the new ghettos, discipline bordering on violence, spies and filing systems, and above all through the proud conviction that all this was legitimate, the com-pany renewed the ancient military vocation of Turin. Images of garrisons, decimated divisions, soldiers tied to oak trees in the woods, parades along the great boulevards, braiding, white horses drenched in sweat and cast-iron cannons following. The Professor pushed the engines to the limit, worked the life force out of those who walk through the factory gates each day and walk home worn dry. He gave Turin its new face of throngs and violence, invented Rivalta, extended the field of Mirafiori beyond measure, stifled any voice rising against his model of a boomtown future, broke and cowed the unions, and forged with his own hands a leading class merciless as an army staff—a dark suit their uniform, a degree in engineering their coat of arms, and each of the city's command levers in their hands.

All of this, though, in the shadow of the prince, the ultimately noisome shadow of a young prince, the darling of gossip photographers and women on two or three continents: a forty-five-year-old boy who in 1966, the Professor having reached his age limit, came to claim his birthright. 'Will you tell Bono?' As legend has it, this is how Valletta responded to the prince directly telling him that he would be replaced. Bono Gaudenzio (surname first, like in the barracks) was the dauphin the Professor had chosen, the man who best represented the engineers' caste, and the caste had in fact already acknowledged and nominated him. The young man who has been a golden boy too long can sense the hostile breath of the great machine in those words. Those men in their dark suits of thick material, who have vanquished and tamed every foe, have no regard for the scion with French r's: they're lying in wait to catch him out, anticipating his first weakness, his first fall. Some are already dealing in private with the overlords of state holdings, rooting for a FIAT under the Christ-Dems' sway, a safe, Roman, papal concern. And he's given no time at all: petrol is disappearing like a card in a conjurer's hands and popping back up to set new rules written elsewhere. And in no time the awesome '69 explodes between his fingers: 'The Indochina War / has come to your shop floor'. One day in July, Corso Traiano goes up in flames: the imperial forum of FIAT Capitol, built to contain the new workforce and its awkward, messy, noisy relatives. And that autumn, Workshop 32 will down tools, remember they're alive and decide their own fate without asking permission. Sometimes you fall asleep in the afternoon and lose the sense of time, then you wake up all crumpled up with your window open facing the hill and the light is red and violet so you think you've been sleeping through the night and are watching the dawn, but then someone says it's about dinner time and it gets dark. The Avvocato speaks to the shareholders' nerves, says in his elegant language that this year, 1975, there won't even be any money to pay the 'thirteenth', the Christmas bonus that lights up shop windows in the town centre.

And so the time of politics has come. Avvocato Agnelli says he'll have to face colossal investments—so colossal that no company could carry them without huge, widespread consensus. He speaks of tax revenues, continental markets, planning, he speaks of the world that is and that will be no more—but several well-trained ears have heard that heavy word as it falls on the room and gauged its weight by the silence that surrounds it. Consensus.

What's needed is an agreement with the old foe: we need time, breathing space. Something is shaking houses to their roots, like those ultrasound calls inaudible to you that will have your dog prick up its ears and start running as if possessed, and the front-line city can feel in its belly the jolts of the world to come: once again, perhaps for the last time, it is a testing ground for what all the rest will be like in a while. The factory sheds its skin: under the new insignia of politics and finance, Cesare Romiti is going through it with a fine comb, spotting the leaks, the remedies, the potential profits. He's relentless, steaming ahead like Lenin's sealed truck. And the party of the communists does its job too, sends forth its economists, and in the drawing rooms some say, 'What nice people they are—who would have imagined it?' So competent, too. And the company has its falls and strokes of genius: one day, at the end of '76, a speechless audience is told about the arrival of a new partner who will bring 400 billion and acquire 13 per cent of the shares: Colonel Gaddafi—my father's bogeyman. Since that session on 29 April 1975, on the trails of consensus and power, FIAT has occupied society, and has done a lot of asking. It was only during one year, 1976, that the family kitty, IFI, defaulted on its duties towards the hard noses and the other relatives—but that same year, albeit by only a few million, the balance sheet was back in the black. The finance man is doing his job. And so are the politics men: Gianni Agnelli is president of Confindustria, and from that position he holds out a hand to the unions. And in that hand is a pen. There was this new smudge-free felt-tip just come available in stationers' shops, a welcome relief from the finger-staining fountain pens. The cartoon was in every paper: a caricature of Agnelli and Lama with the miraculous felt-tip, smiling as they sign away the contingency point. The much-maligned mechanism pegging salaries to living costs, the goal of the struggles of a workers' movement that had been gaining power, and ever since that signature, the main concern of great industry and of the great politics that has no say on money but handles inflation by devaluing the currency and producing new inflation. And 'inflation' makes its entrance in our lexicon of anxiogenic factors, in the murky menagerie of evil. No matter, we'll find a way to abolish the agreement—but the fact remains that it was signed, and any Italian can tell you about it.

And it's exactly halfway through 1977, as I'm fleeing from the Argentario and from my pact, that when the balance sheet of the holding companies is closed, money starts flowing again. Romiti sniffs the change in the air, the chance to win out. This year IFI will be able to hand out dividends again, Avvocato Agnelli is fast in the saddle, he can go back to handing wealth to the wealthy. So he has no more use for politics: the producers' pact, the war on parasite incomes, Confindustria, the ministry standing guarantor in case a government with the PCI should be needed—all that can wait. Time to go back to the shop floor, roll up our sleeves. Back to Mirafiori. There's something huge in the offing: cars, stuff that is produced in millions of pieces at a time. That's how we'll do politics now, we'll change everything, we'll face down the unions and the workers' rebellions. All we need is one person: someone who really knows how cars are made, an expert in works, sheds, assembly lines, people management. The turret of a huge tank turns unhurriedly and focuses on a new target.

DOGS ON A LEASH   Only one night in Rome—fever and dark thoughts each time I lower my eyelids, starting on the train that's now reaching the first suburbs, and here I am looking at myself reflected in the window, scared that a smudge, a dot of colour, a trace might still be showing. I've put a short-handled Hazet wrench in my rucksack, for a laugh, and Pasino is sleeping in his seat and Bonetti is watching the night that has almost grabbed the edge of the tracks. Termini station is an antechamber where voices ricochet, this is the city that shoots bullets, and the evening has a soft colour that takes the buildings from behind, there's people on the platform dressed like us—shirts, sandals, raggedy-assed jumpers. Bonetti is fibrillating, he hooks on to a guy: 'Hey, comrade!'

The guy looks at him neutrally. Bonetti hands him the can of beer he's been holding since Civitavecchia, the guy looks at him, drinks from it, says thanks.

'Are you here for the referendums?' 'What?' 'We're from Lotta Continua.' 'Yo, speak for yourself,' I say, and Bonetti snickers and carries on: 'This guy's a Stalinist, he's even got a 36-wrench in his rucksack.' 'Are you out of your wits, Bonetti?' 'Come on, you show him.' So the guy goes: 'Well guys, see you some time, eh? Thanks for the beer.' 'Are you going to Lotta Continua?' 'You must be joking—I've come for the Pope, there's an audience tomorrow.' And off he trots with his squeaky-clean pilgrim soul. We're looking at one another, Bonetti can't wriggle out of this one and gets the Dickhead Prize. Pasino reminds us that tomorrow there's also a rally with Almirante—look Bonetti, this is Rome, there's stuff going down every single day, and you go and tell the guy about the wrench? How big a fucking dickhead can you be? Bonetti is trying to glide over it, but if he was trying for leadership, he's blown it. We walk on into the night.

A fiasco from the start: at Lotta Continua they're working, there's a long corridor with yellow lighting, people rushed off their feet and doors slamming, it's tricky to even hook on to anyone and explain where we're at, they leave us there waiting for an hour or more by the side of the cyclostyle, then they say thanks and leave us to figure out that, well, we're kind of in the way. So off we go, back into the night, zero money—which means, starving. Well, OK, let's at least have a look around the great city, shall we. Random walking, nose in the air to try and see the end of those orange buildings stretching up into the sky, there's always a lit-up piazza where it's best to avoid the smell of fried stuff from the outside tables, we can probably manage arancini from one of the street-food vans along the Tiber, and then we're tired, flummoxed, and we stop someone (shtum about the wrench this time!) who tells us the youth hostel is in Piazza Maresciallo Giardino, so off we go to look for it, walking along wide boulevards full of headlights and whores, it's far, so far we get there too late, it's a concrete cuboid planted on a ring-road green, Brasília inside the Grande Raccordo, a gate of the folding sort normally used to lock up shop fronts, everything padlocked and as if decommissioned, like no one's been in there for centuries.

'Was this not also the city of the Coliseum?' 'Aw fuck off, Pas—I'm going to see if anyone's in here, OK?' And sure enough there was—all snoring. One beckons from behind the grid, says they open at six, we're welcome to wait on the green. We look at one another—not for us, thanks, best walk on, we'll think of something when the sun comes up.

'Happy now? You want us to go see the Coliseum?' I don't know how you get from Piazza Maresciallo Giardino to Via Veneto, but that's where we end up, innocent of La dolce vita: locked-up shops, waste paper blowing along the pavements. Pasino points to the nearby park, our eyes are flickering, we're staggering around more than walking, and aside from a few 'look at this' or 'look at that' for some balcony or doorway, we've stopped talking. So we take as our guides those huge exotic trees that grow bare and endless into the clouds and then open out a black balcony of pine needles: you can see those ones even against a dark sky, because before they put out so much as a tiny leaf they grow all the way up to a dot of light in the east—daybreak light. At one point we find ourselves in the middle of a track which

Bonetti says is for greyhound races, then we climb some sort of slope, get to some wayside shrubs that will keep us from the shameless eyes of passing policemen and finally keel over—but not for long, because barely above our heads the road is lit up by a sudden blast of burning rubber and sirens and we wake up with a mouthful of Chicago, like inside a TV car chase we have missed entirely except for the last bits of soundtrack that are now fading away. Never mind, that's enough to make us open our eyes that have grown accustomed to the place and discover that we've unrolled our sleeping bags and fallen asleep in one of the town dumps, deep in plastic bags oozing all sorts, a stench of carrion, the sense of something creeping about and grabbing what it can: a muffled curse from Pasino and up we get, queasy with broken sleep we blunder onward and crash out at last under a huge round tree in the middle of an endless green and I open my eyes again for one moment in the milk of the first light just to discover there's a job I didn't know about—we're surrounded by pedigree dogs led on leashes in twos, threes, sometimes fours by blurred shapes of subaltern humans, and it literally dawns on me that's what these people do for a living.

SUBJECT: COINCIDENCES   Listen to this: 'Boys! Don't miss this offer! All-expenses-paid space flight! Join now! For the fault of three exclamation marks I fell for it and found myself on Slabour, a mining asteroid, where the sky, an artificial atmosphere, was the colour of dry blood. As the contract said, the ticket for the flight was to be exchanged for six months' work under Boss Callow, but bed & board were not included. I made friends with Simon and Suki, a prostitute I loved from the start. Obsidian-black

hair, night-blue eyelids, a cheat at speckers: as soon as I turned my
head she rearranged the pieces, then pretended to be fixing her
hair. Only 281years' work, and I'd be able to leave Slabour and
marry her. But no one has ever survived more than six or seven
years in the Creelium mines, because of the red dust that will poison and kill you. I thought I'd pay my way out by stealing some
Creelium, the raw material for DHX-119-B, the synchronicity
drug, the one that can inspire a genius or stop a war. The problem
was how to get round the Impartial, the mechanism controlling
the exit from the galleries at the end of each shift. I had one of
the machines maim one of my hands and they fitted me with a
cheap bionic replacement (does everything your old one did
except feel) that would screen the Creelium from the Impartial's
eye. After this coup I drifted around on a life raft. I was picked up
by the luxury cruiser Maya. I told them I was a Junglabarian
hunter bound for Junglabesh. I had no trouble making up fibs, and
soon found myself the star of the tourist passengers, favoured by
the ladies and dining with the captain. By night, I would look for
information on Junglabarians, but no one seemed to know anything about them: Junglabesh was wrapped in a radioactive cloud
making radio transmission impossible, and those who had set foot
on it—well, they had not come back to tell the tale. Unfortunately,
some of the passengers were excited by my tall tales and
demanded we headed for Junglabesh: in exchange for a safari, they
would pay the (exorbitant) cost of my passage on the Maya. But
the environment scared off the cruise passengers, and they abandoned me on the unknown planet, at the edge of a clump of
fleeza, among horrid roots searching the ground: here I came
across a sort of pink melon laid on the ground, with a covering

of long dark hairs. Under the hairs I discovered a face: that was a human head. The roots came off the fleeza and hurled themselves at me. I fainted. When I woke up, I was numb and buried alive. One of the snakes I had mistaken for a root was speaking to me: 'We are the Urs.'

'What about the Junglabarians?'

'You humans—you are the Junglabarians.'

He spoke to me of the cult of freedom, sacred among his people.

'Actually,' I said, 'I don't feel that free right now. We outlawed slavery thousands of years ago.'

'You think so? We probe the minds of the humans who chased us off the planet: each and every one of them is in bondage to a corporation.'

The Urs had evolved spiritually because they had no hands: the source of their energy was a power stone that could project spirit to the far end of space. Then the humans came in their metal ships: they did not try to understand them but considered them monsters and hunted them for sport, burned the fleeza and dropped the power stone in a crater atop the highest peak on the planet. No one had ever been able to retrieve it: it lay submerged in the molten lava. It was the bionic hand that came to my aid again: I took the stone and became lord of the planet, I saw the universe with the eyes of my spirit, the truth as a web of brilliant connecting fibres. I had the other prisoners freed. The stone put me in touch with Slabour: I learnt that Simon had died because of talking back to Boss Callow and the Impartial malfunctioning, and that Suki had been taken away by the police. When I woke up, the fleeza had dried up and the Urs were dying. A silver pod descended on the planet, it was from TRANS-GALACTIC REALTY AND CONSTRUCTION. 'Sorry,' the men in overalls said. 'Weren't supposed to be any humans here. We got orders last week to fly up here and gas the place with Double M-437, then clean up and dig some foundations. We're building a nursery.' By threatening to report them for genocide to the United Board of Corporations we got them to transport us to New Panama. On the ship I made friends with Ben-Gotz. He was unbeatable at speckers and had a commanding attitude, and before ending up on Junglabesh had been chairman of Nova Spacecraft. 'My first act after the coronation,' he said, 'was to institute work-incentive bonuses. Urtz-Al, my rival on the Board of Directors, interpreted my plan as a form of profit sharing and therefore anti-capitalist— he denounced me at a board meeting. Then came the proclamation for the first quarter—production up by 8% . Profit omnia vincit—I was a hero, but Urtz began to scheme for revenge. During a trip on my private yacht he bribed the crew to slip some paralytic in my stimu-caff and dumped me on Junglabesh. He returned and told the Board he had found records showing I was an embezzler and that I had taken my own life.' Gotz asked me to help him retrieve the proof of his innocence: he'd had his yacht bugged, and the secret recording system had surely taped the scene of the betrayal. All I had to do was get the yacht: Gotz would wait for me in new Panama.

Thirty-four days later, I landed on Nova Center. As I went down into the Valley of the Workers looking for an inn, I heard a chant: 'I am worker born to suffer / Born to toil this sad life long / Someone has to weld the steel / To make the starships fly /

Soon I'll sleep in soft brown dirt / And let the worms do all the work / My soul will sit on the highest peak / of Management Hill, of Management Hill.' A throng of mindless people was singing inside a temple made from a disused Class C shuttle half sunken in the dirt: this was the Church of Bode-Satva, an ancient superstitious cult earlier than the Great Corporate Revolution of 2412. On each of the five walls there was a scene from the life of Bode-Satva, painted in a primitive style and showing phases of his life from childhood to martyrdom. One showed him as an adult on a ladder of golden ropes, a great jewel hanging in the sky above him: four hundred years earlier, Bode-Satva had recorded 168,896 tapes, one to be played each day beginning with the day after his death. The tape for the day, as the preacher Sava-Nanda explained, was No. 168,781, and carried the order to unbury Bode-Satva. I tried to tactfully explain that Bode-Satva had disappeared on an entirely different planet, but that didn't seem to impress them. In an inn I made friends with a cute chambermaid, Je-Nett, who kept me up most of the night demonstrating the screwing positions popular among locals ('Refuelling in Orbit'—the male ship extends his hose while the female rotates slowly, scratching his fuel tanks), and gave me the location of the junkyard where the yacht had been dumped.

I got the yacht. Doris, the ship computer, was happy to take care of someone after years of solitude, but had never heard of a secret recording system. During the journey I became ill, I searched the yacht's pharmacy and found a vial of DHX 119-B, the synchronicity drug. I stashed it away inside my bionic hand. As for Doris, I found out she had been a real, human woman. Her brain was surviving connected to a cybernetic system that made her immortal. 'I'm not supposed to talk about it,' she said, 'but since you're here and Benji trusts you . . . I am his wife.'

When I got back to New Panama, Ben Gotz confirmed there was no flight recorder. It was Doris he wanted: she was a far more reliable witness than any tape. He had married her because she was a fine speckers player, and the laws of UltraCapitalism say a woman's body is her husband's to do with as he pleases: only by marrying her could he turn her into a computer. Thanks to Doris and the tribunal, Ben Gotz took his place back at the head of the company. The shareholders had in fact been getting restless: Nova had failed to pay a dividend last quarter. Urtz was tortured to death. At the inn, one of the customers explained the reasons for the grim atmosphere: as soon as he was back on the throne, Ben Gotz had instated 'loafing deterrents'. Let's say you're late from lunch. Or you go to the toilet and the absence timer rings off the four minutes before you're back. Or you get so damn sick of soldering circuits that if you don't take a break you'll start howling and screaming and seeing little pink krombars everywhere. Well, in Gotz's cassette that's called loafing and it earns you a stick with a stinger. Gotz summoned me to inform me that Serendipity was a subsidiary of Nova: in his view, I was liable for conspiracy, theft, assault and contract violation. He granted my last request and told me the story: two centuries before the Great Corporate Revolution, curious 'crimps' in space were discovered—we call them warp-routes now—allowing mankind to populate the galaxy. There followed the greatest period of expansion in history, along with the most radical change in human consciousness since Descartes. We came face to face with alien life forms terrifyingly different from ourselves. The warp-routes themselves were disturbing, for they violated every known principle of physics. Men travelled them daily, but could not explain them. The human mind has a terrible need to explain. When it can neither explain nor ignore, it must change. And change it did, to a spiritual consciousness. For many this meant a return to superstition, to magic, but a select few, by studying the techniques of the ancients, learnt to train the spirit to travel between the stars on mysterious ladders of golden ropes. They were the Wanderers, the lost sect. The trouble began when the Wanderers discovered a stone similar to the power stone of the Urs, which could increase the psychic powers of all mankind if properly distributed. The stone was of gigantic proportions—an asteroid. It would allow every man freedom from his body and from the triviality of everyday life. All well and good, but it would also destroy the capitalist system which had been so carefully developed after thousands of years. Obviously the spacecraft industry would be the first to go, and electronics would follow shortly. There would also be a subtler effect: the entire economy of the empire depended on the purchasing of unnecessary items as an acting out of sexual, intellectual and social frustrations. With the stone, these drives would be fulfilled. A terrible war ensued. The UltraCap army won and exterminated the Wanderers guided by Bode-Satva. The few survivors were deported on Nova, and uses were found for the stone that would not destroy the economy of the galaxy: a minute dose did not sufficiently energize the psyche to allow astral travel—but it did create a harmony with the universe which manifested itself in the form of 'luck'. A sudden breakthrough, the solution of a problem, a coincidence, a rainstorm quenching the flames that threaten to destroy a building, that sort of stuff. So as to stop the Diggers sharing in that luck through contact with the stone, UltraCap scientists developed a red clay composed of certain rare minerals that neutralized the stone's energies, and coated the stone with it the way a live wire is insulated with plastic.

I got it: the stone was Slabour! I asked Gotz why it was so important to maintain UltraCapitalism. 'Because,' he said, 'that is what we believe in.'

I was taken to the gas chamber. At the first puff of poison I remembered the vial of Synch drug I had stolen in the spaceship, I took it and an earthquake plunged me to the entrails of the earth. I came out among the devotees of Sava-Nanda who mistook me for the reincarnation of Bode-Satva and offered me shelter in the spaceship-temple, which against all odds shuddered up from the mud and lifted off. Our programmed route was heading to Slabour. Brother Sava-Nanda was convinced that if rain fell on Slabour the clay would be washed away releasing the Stone's properties. Except no rain had ever fallen on Slabour. So he had the spaceship water tanks drained at twelve thousand feet.

Boss Callow was holding Suki prisoner and under torture. I surrendered, and he dug it in by stopping her Youthification: what he brought to me was a hobbled old woman with endless suffering in her eyes. They locked us up together. 'It's their wedding night,' Boss Callow said. I stroked Suki's high cheekbones, her wrinkled skin. She shivered at the touch, I said I didn't care, I raised her face to mine. 'Don't pretend,' she said. 'I'm not pretending.'

As I kissed her, I could hear a patter of rain pelting clay outside the cell.

That was the Secrets of Synchronicity by Jonathan Fast. But it's not the book I plagiarized.

SHORT FORWARD JUMP (1980)   No, he'll not come back into this story. After the fruit conveyor belt at Lagnasco, I saw him only one other time, but it was much later, everything had already come to an end. He died early, at twenty-five, on 18 April 1984. He slipped his head into a noose hung from a nail and let himself fall. He was the hundred and forty-ninth one. I heard about his death only a few years later: for a while I looked for a hint, an explanation, or at least an image of his last days. I'd found his name in a footnote to a page full of statistics. It was about psychic unease and suicide among workers on the lay-off schemes: I had sat there, glued to those figures, unable to think, waiting for those intimations of death that were sure to come—an emptiness, some sign of grief that was slow in coming. I thought about calling Saluzzo, maybe Mariano still lived there, or looking for his mother. Or I could hope it was a namesake, maybe it wasn't him, maybe I'd find the number and he'd pick up and start snickering at me and touching his balls like he did when we worked together in Signor Lovera's shed. But there was one memory which identified that hundred and forty-ninth laid-off worker almost certainly as my friend Mauro from Lagnasco.

It was precisely the memory of our last meeting, in October 1980, when the story I'm telling you had already come to an end. We'd met by chance, at night, in the heat of a drawn-out summer. He'd turned up on this noisy, raggedy-assed Ciao moped that must once have been some shade of orange, outside Gate 5 at Mirafiori, where I was heaping wood on a bonfire. He'd said hello to one of the old guys and started messing around as he was wont to do—a string of gags, winking, questions he'd reel off while swinging back and forth as he spoke. So I recognized him and walked up to him: he looked at me a moment, searching his mind, then leaped at me, hugging me while unloading a volley of punches onto my hips. 'Yo, worker boy,' he was shouting. 'So here you are, worker boy! Still touching yourself, are ya?' and as he shouted that he started making a show of rubbing his crotch. He wasn't on the pickets—just curious: he'd heard that the guys on his team were picketing the railway tunnel and had decided to go see them, and they told him that up here at Gate 5 was the old guy who'd been his teacher in his early days at FIAT, so he'd come by to say hello. Nothing to do in the evenings, he said, so he just rode around on his moped. Not that he was against the struggle, the blockades and so on, far from it—but he wasn't the sort to go on a picket line, and then at night his mum wanted to speak to him on the phone. 'You want to know something? I'm on the lists,' he said to me. 'And I don't mind a bit,' he added in a quiet voice so the others wouldn't get mad at him.

I was there by natural parasite instinct, with a few other students who had mobilized partly from solidarity and a lot from a need to stay outside in the depths of night—and also from nostalgia for the time of the war we had waged against the universe and that had slipped away from under our feet. This sort of appendix to our struggle had started with a leaflet ('Another September 11!') comparing FIAT's announcement of redundancy proceedings for 14,500 workers to the 1973 Chilean coup. Same date. A season of suffering and lay-offs was looming that autumn for the steelworkers of the FIAT group. There had been a general strike, the government had fallen, and Berlinguer, the secretary of the Communist Party, had gone to the factory gate to speak, explaining that the workers' hard struggle would find the PCI ready and participating (somewhat tentatively adding that well, yes, even if it came to occupying the factories, well yes, if it should really come to that, well, the party would not demur). So FIAT replaced the redundancy plan for the fourteen-odd-thousand with a full-time lay-off scheme for twenty-six thousand (and someone in the unions even cheered). The morning of 27 September, as the first shift was going in, workers in all departments of Mirafiori, Rivalta and Lingotto found the lists of names and surnames pinned to the walls.

'What happened to your leg?'

'Check this out,' he said as he started hobbling around the square. He was limping.

'Are you faking it?'

'No,' he replied, 'I've really gone and lamed myself.'

I asked him if it was a factory thing and he said no, he'd got smashed up while riding his bicycle. 'Under a van,' he added after a pause. His mother went through hell during the months when he was learning to walk again ('Hey, I'm back on the dance floor, even!'). Then, thanks to a carabiniere—an officer, actually—he got the right push to start at FIAT. That was spring '78: thousands joined FIAT every month, things were picking up, and people said the times were getting slacker—shift times, I mean. Mauro was proud as he said to me: 'Hardly two years in and I'm at Maintenance already,' and I thought, with that gammy leg he'll never make it to the lines.

So here he is, my friend Mauro, alive and limping, his destiny
finally played out: he's walked through that gate once and for all,
and he's got used to it. He hasn't changed, he talks of pussy, says
the factory's rammed to the rafters and then some. 'Hey, did you
know there's hookers inside as well?' Yeah, right. 'Cross my heart
and hope to die! There is! The year I got in was the year of all
sorts—you think it's just a load of tough old terroni workers,
right? Wrong. There's guys who turn up dressed in drag just to
get the foreman's goat, or just for a laugh.' Ah yes? And hookers,
too. 'That's right—they'll do you after the shift, get ahead on the
line and fit you in that way. There's guys fall in love with them as
well—like you would, surely.' Give over, Mauro. 'It's the Calabrese
bring them in, make up these little teams of hookers, they'll work
the bays for a while, then resign and new ones come in—keeps
the catalogue fresh. I told you, there's all sorts in there—doctors,
engineers, all workers now. The old guys can't believe their eyes—
never seen that sort of people in the sheds, sometimes they get
mad at the partying but they end up laughing, even the old guys.
Yo, nonno—fire a bit slack, innit? Shall I go and get you some
wood?' Here he is, our Mauro, hogging the limelight already. The
old guy he has just called Granddad, a piece of Quinta Lega history, looks at him like a bear would consider a flea and says there's
a lorry comes round for wood. The weather's warm: these are signal fires, there's a belt of fires all around the great sleeping devil,
pickets at every gate, people in no mood for sleep, words, and
above all the great stories, the myths, from Dien Bien Phu to
Stettin, Battipaglia to Corso Traiano. There was a guy from
Bologna, Serafini, a manager, I knew him from national student
assemblies—you could say he was my passport on the picket line,

sort of a guarantor for me: I get the feeling at times that the workers can't stand us really, and so does he, but he turns on the charm and knows how to get accepted. Serafini was the guy who could raise a laugh, on those nights around the fire he was the one who kept everyone awake telling jokes. Sometimes he'd turn to me out of the blue and go: 'Valle Giulia?' And I'd shoot back: 'We won.' 'Corso Traiano?' 'We won—fourteen hours' fighting, sir.' And everyone cracking up at our proletarian-marines skit. 'Tet Offensive?' 'We won, General Giap.' 'Very good, lad, very good. Piazza Statuto?' 'Er—I can't remember, sir.' 'Yes, well—go get some wood then.'

Behind Corso Traiano there's a building site where you go and nick a few pallets for the fires. Mauro comes along: 'I'll show you the love grove,' he says. I'd never noticed: just on the square of Corso Unione Sovietica, about halfway between the Quinta Lega and the admin building, there is in fact a little grove. Never seen it before—real trees, I swear, and little hearts, initials and love vows carved into the barks. 'Is this where the hookers come?' 'No, this is for the likes of you. Hey, you have a girlfriend?' Er—yes—no—bah, dunno. 'What are you doing these days—uni?' No, Liceo Classico—fact is, I got flunked a few years ago. The tarmac is shiny with the million feet that have trampled it since Corso Unione Sovietica exists, since earlier even. It reflects the big word spelled in four lit-up blue cubes on the roof of the admin building: F-I-A-T. Over on the left, screened off by a set of ten-storey council blocks typical of Seventies town planning, this side of where Corso Traiano arches over the tracks to land in front of the hill, there's a sort of muddy waste: it's full of discarded pallets, building-site traffic barriers, cracked planks—as if they're building something, or in fact as if they'd been building but paused a while and forgot all about it, and anyone with any wood to offload started dumping it there, without giving it much thought, perhaps just because the devil always shits on the biggest pile.

We needed a cart for this. 'You're the cart now,' Mauro says. 'Look at the shoulders on ya.' Well, I've been playing rugby. 'Good for you—now you're coming in handy for the wood. To think of the wanky little squirt you used to be, back at the fruit conveyor belts.' I bend forward and he loads a few planks onto my back. 'Don't worry, I'll get some too.' We walk back to the factory slowly, in my mind a question I can't ask: Is it really as I'd imagined back then, do you feel like your breath's knocked out of you as you walk through that gate? I've never been inside FIAT, I picture it as the devil asleep with a deep pain in his belly, kept at bay by the army of founders, welders, bodyworkers, painters, turners, I imagine it and stop on that borderline between factory and city that now, on those nights, is chock-a-block with frowny big marxs big gramscis big cheguevaras painted in red & black, and placards too, there's one at Gate 5 that says: 'The only noise a boss will hear is the silence of stopped machines.' And there's a weird myth too—a new one, I'd say, about those Lenin shipyards in Danzig where the workers rose up this summer, 1980, led by this guy with a big moustache called Lech Walesa who is as fashionable among Catholics as the new Pope to say the least. I think Walesa gets on my wick some, but over here many of the gates are hung with slogans such as 'Turin like Danzig', and Agnelli's got a bit more Europe on the shop floor: in '69 it was Indochina, now it's Poland—not bad as a forward leap. 'Hey, what happened to your Red Brigades, eh?' My Red Brigades? How are they mine? Anyways they've been keeping shtum all through this time of fires at the gates—they're not touching FIAT, and never will again.

My thoughts must have run away with me. In the next memory we're back at the fires, our hands stretched out to the flame, our faces orange, Serafini talking crap a few yards off and Mauro describing a factory that's nothing like I'd imagined it to be: 'It's a sort of buzz, like everyone talking under their breath—a hum—that's it, that's the music of Mirafiori these days.' The devil is no longer howling. 'It's fucking great—hey, what do you think the line is like these days? Like at the fruit conveyors, with you rushing around like a puppet to keep up, right? No waaaay. It's something else—you'd think you're in the middle of a film, there's trolleys moving by themselves, they know where to go, pick up the parts for assembly from the benches, look to see who's free and take the work over to you, and you're just waiting there, niiice and calm. The trolleys are robots, OK? Bzzzzzzz, here you are, sir—a couple of bolts here, a wee turn there, thank you very much and good-bye, sir, I'll send my robot colleague along next. All quiet—you wait for them and they come, when you're done you push the End button and send them off, and if you take your time with that you can even get a breather. Yeah, the old guys are still talking of how they used to work their asses off. If the next guy is still on something, the trolley will pick another bench and go there to get served: and there's no tracks on the floor, you know—they walk around right and proper, the robots do.' A web of magnetic tracks. 'The best is the digitron—fucking ace, the old guys used to do their backs in, eight hours on end with their arms up working on the overhead belt.' Conveyor, you mean. 'That's right, conveyor—on the overhead conveyor that moved the engines and body shells.

On the 131 line you can still see the pits—it's scary to watch the shells wobbling along, and you're standing in the pit, arms up to bolt the engine in. These days, it's a different kettle—no pits, just two of you handling the robot, and it's the robot does the bolting. Like, there used to be a hundred and twenty guys in the pits until two years ago, right? And at Rivalta they've got a robogate.' What's that? 'It's a tunnel full of robots with mechanical arms that build the whole shell from scratch—a tunnel of robots, can you figure? Bet you're feeling a right knob now, knowing you've been working on the fruit belts, ha? Much better here.' Mauro is full of pride. There's a few bottles going round, a guy brings some for us too, off to one side where we are.

Last spring all the leaders of the Communist Party came to Turin for the Organizational Conference. And the byword was: technology. See, they said, the bosses have failed to keep up with progress, the technology lag is penalizing FIAT, over the past few years they should have been quicker to start production renewal procedures. To hear them, you'd have thought the bosses had been standing in the factory turning crank handles and wielding whips. They were drunk on modernity: the workers' movement could teach the Agnellis modernity, recommissioning, new technologies. Maybe Mauro was dreaming when he spoke of his factory of robots. Either that, or these PCI guys have missed the whole robot thing, they can still hear the din of the lines and see sparks flying off the conveyors as the body shells wobble along overhead. 'We'll win,' Serafini is saying. 'The PCI has made a 180-degree turn, it's had to go along with the workers, the real workers this time—Berlinguer at the gates saying let's occupy! Look, this is the turning point—we'll win, my dear sirs.' Mauro is off, it's three or four o'clock in the morning and he says there's a woman waiting for him, she'll be getting mad—a whopper, clearly, but he just can't see himself without a woman or two, and off he goes on the yelping, farting moped.

Everyone knows what happened afterwards. One morning the radio speaks of the demo assembled at the Teatro Nuovo: sick of the picket lines, the bosses are marching to go back to work. The world upside down. The radio speaks of this silent march, ranked in concentric circles according to hierarchy: the manager surrounded by the deputy heads, surrounded by the mid-managers, surrounded by the line managers, surrounded by the familia. The police are saying there's fifteen thousand of them—which means seven-eight thousand, methinks. Then La Stampa writes there's thirty thousand, La Repubblica forty thousand. 'Yeah, right,' I say, 'make it half a million. And this is just a delegation, right?' Serafini shoots a black look at me, tells me to shut up.

On television: an afternoon programme, the image of a rainy day, the summer has waited until this morning before giving in and now we're full into the autumn, it's cold, heavy coats and fake-fur collars, a sea of open umbrellas in front of FIAT Meccaniche. 'Comrades, please—let's take our umbrellas down for the voting—only a few moments—umbrellas, please.' The voting is on the agreement signed by the unions that is sending everyone back home with no one allowed to even speak of defeat. The catch-phrase from Rome is: 'FIAT did not pass.' Umbrellas down: 'In favour?' A few hands go up at the back. Further back still a small crowd waiting patiently: white raincoats, the calm of winners—only a few more minutes. 'Against?' Hundreds of hands shoot up, most closed in a fist, words howled, one stands out: 'Abstained?' One hand, the camera zooming in on it. 'The agreement passed by a large majority.' It was 16 October 1980, and I thought of making a leaflet that said 'Another 16 October'—no, scrap that, that's student stuff.

And Mauro: a love story turned sour, doing a bit of cash-in-hand work to keep his lay-off scheme cheque, his mind still on the girl who'd sent him packing. People back home must have poked fun at him, maybe even the same women workers who'd look at us over the belts at the fruit shed. On TV they're asking a psychologist about all these suicides. He says the streets of Turin are straight, grey, all alike. That can cause anguish.

THE RAIN'S FALLING UP   Not just a communist, Dad—dressed in drag, as well. All I remember of that summer '77 are the rainstorms, as if the sun had burnt itself out over the stones of the Argentario. And certain restless dreams. I was having extra lessons with a young tutor who treated me as if she were rooting for me. She lived on Via delle Industrie, beyond the market on Corso Racconigi, a sort of snake made of stalls that splits the city from its outskirts on the side of the mountains. When I was a child, on Saturday mornings, my father would look at me with a sly look on his face and say 'We're going to spend, splash out and spree,' and then he'd walk me along that long double aisle of plenty, you'd get in on one side and think you'd never get out again, even when you got to the end, drunk with the colours of fruit and clothes, and you still had to go up the parallel aisle, stalls of spices and plastic knick-knacks. If you looked up, in between people's heads and awnings you could just see the tops of buildings. We'd buy a box of tangerines and I'd eat it all by the Sunday, ignoring anything else. My father would say that at least I'd never grow up to get cancer.

Now he's retreated to Colleretto to see the summer out with my mother, and I'm crossing the market on the short side without looking, walking despondently towards Via delle Industrie. Sometimes I catch the last evening coach and get to Colleretto at twenty past midnight—they're waiting for me I think, because they're always up when I get there. I like to get there by surprise and watch them as they try to hide how happy they are to see me. It's rare these days for me to want to spend time with them— mardy, stand-offish, all-knowing, little resident sacred monster that I am.

Yeah, all right, I did remember a few things. The deeds of Alcibiades, indirect intimation in Quintilian: I was studying, my tutor was happy, and then the sky lime-white, the air electric with rainstorms. The autumn will come in the end, it will bring revo- lution, taverns and unsuspected public breakthroughs. A figure at the window high up in the telecom building is also watching the world's end as it pours from the sky, the air is plague-black, rain- drops are being sucked upward. A blur of blue light at the win- dow—a woman? It's working hours, I put my hand out to see if my downturned palm will also get wet, I think she's looking my way: I'd risk nothing by raising my arm in greeting. She looks pretty from this distance, in her light-blue shirt. She turns this way again and makes a sign. She's far, far up. I don't respond. After a moment I turn and realize I can see her very well, reflected in the glass pane. I'm one up now: I can look at you, but you can't know. She turns and goes back into her office. I could have made a sign, called her, begun a splendid adventure. But in fact I've hardly even seen her go back, all I saw was a back-to-front reflection, all I have to do is stop looking at that window. Out I go. There must be someone left in town, tangled up in the tarmac. Barabba was shut down, our wee building with its porch on fat pillars now has barriers and padlocked chains on the gate. This is how things happen in summer: without anyone putting up a fight, by a sop and a promise. They say it'll be turned into a playschool, and we can't start fighting children, can we. They promise us a place on Via Garibaldi, a big house that had been empty for a while. Someone accepted: Who? Bah—I was at the Argentario, jumping on Giuliana in my nymphet get-up.

'If you want to come to the cinema, we've got a car.' Lucky she's around—Marcella, the thin girl with the long flower-print skirts, the girl of the long pendants of gold-plated wire, hair in a bun over her nape and a melancholy face, she'll not say much but she's thinking, you can tell by how she weighs her words, and maybe she already knows I've left the Argentario earlier than planned. 'Any news of Ciccio?' 'Nah.' Johnny—nah—Ninetto—nah—et cetera. But Albertino is around: good news. Albertino the reticent, the trickster, Albertino the card sharp. I'm saved. The film is gruesome: Sordi torturing his son's murderer for endless minutes. That's all right, it will remind me of the reasons why I started finding my own social class terrifying at some point. We're talking of September, the great gathering in Bologna, the French philosophers who've caught on to the army-tank atmosphere over here and have written a manifesto for Italy. September, everything will change: the movement is opening out to the world. Albertino is writing a song, a South American melody, F7aug: 'Piazza Maggiore, hippies hammering their strings and playing that old samba, mbambarambambà / a scream on the radio, Zàngheri the mayor speaking to the town-ah, mbambarambambà.' Albertino hitting the arpeggios, changing a chord or two, showing off his perfect pitch: 'In Rome the children of the economic boom / are taking lessons from Geronimo, ah-uhm / but in Bologna those who come will find / an island of serious minds.' If I was Marcella, I'd be his for the taking—but she's off to one side, cultivating some strange sadness of hers, smiling and thinking of someone else. At the old slaughterhouse there's a huge trunk lying on the ground, a plane tree with all its leaves still on—the rainstorm, I think. One night I get out of bed to write down a dream, because I know it'll be gone for ever if I don't. It's 3.57, the translations assigned by the tutor from Via delle Industrie are working on me in the dark: two Gaul chiefs are in love with the same woman, the dreamer seems to be her favourite, but enmity mounts and they start name-checking their respective alliances and lineages. Then the tribes are up in arms against each other, but Caesar's cavalry swoops on the field and brings the confrontation to a bloody close. The two youths, defeated twice, enter into a sorrowful friendship, all by night, in an endless city of stone and stairs, a small square hanging between slopes with a long balustrade overlooking the lower town—a sense of defeat grabbing everyone. At times I feel breathless, because as a child I suffered from allergic asthma.

Marcella is looking out for me. I walk her home sometimes, to a neighbourhood of low houses and narrow streets huddled together on a long road that joins the prison to the far outskirts. A working-class area, not many people around, a parked car and two old geezers talking, their backsides on the bonnet, the heat making clothes stick, a yard block in Turin. One of these wee houses is home to swivel-hip Billy, I'd shout him out of bed but I doubt he's around—smell of an all-night bakery, croissants and trays of cakes. Inside a smudge of light there's a girl reading a book, protected by the bars of a ground-floor window: sitting in profile on a wide stone ledge, legs together, hands like a book-rest in front of her chest, she is dark in the bright light. Nostalgia for the Argentario I rushed away from—or else for a life with no Argentario at all. Strange summer coiled in wait for the great September epiphany, rainy season, drizzling water and brown air. There are chords, harmonics, desires. On the coach to Colleretto I can see a barrier of light behind the Valle Orco, a dark wall of mountains closer than usual, it looks like a mountain face from the Levanne but it's a cloud front: the last rays of the sun are filtering from underneath and rising in a crown as if the light were coming from the ground. The coach driver is talking to the conductor and can't see any of that: maybe climbing this road every evening makes you used to miracles, or maybe his job is just too hard. I think of an atom bomb that's missed its target and is falling somewhere in the mountains, and me looking at the blast in the frozen moment when light precedes the sound.

Later, at night, air in a square tube—not square section I mean, but closed in on itself like a ring on a square plane. Hot air flowing heavily with exasperating slowness, exploding each time it reaches one of the four corners: a small hot burst crushing the lungs. I wake up breathless. Outside, more rain sheeting down, compact like a wall of frosted glass. One guy goes: 'It's not like you think, kid: you get used to it,' and he scratches his armpit, filthy as everything else with the black dirt that covers him. I don't know what to say, I want to puke, and he says what brings people here may be some big mistake like death or murder, but no one can imagine life out here from a distance. He's got used to the mud, the knives, the air-starved lungs, this sickly smell, the dim lights, and I want to sleep and the heat is flooding everything, splitting volumes, blurring colours, and then that heavy current resumes its crawling around the metal snake. I almost miss that dream, that elective inferno full of adventure: a penitentiary or a mine shaft, I don't know. One night I look to the side of my bed and can't see the window, there's a tangle of hungry plant life growing out of the floor. I wake up at home, crouched against the front door, badly bruised from bumping into walls and sharp edges as I ran away.

TINY MAGGOTS   Marcella says she dreams of the dead, sometimes she can see them standing at the foot of her bed and pointing their finger, trying to speak, and there she is, wide awake and petrified. The dreams vary, but it's almost always herself, alive in the presence of the dead. Once she is in a garden, and there's a sort of great conveyor belt with the dead in double file, silent and miserable as they take their place one by one into the niches along the side of the belt. She says she feels as if she's living on the far edge of things, in a parody of something important that has already happened. She's older than I am, she might be posing, but she's thin as an oracle. We're walking along the same walls as I would slip along when I used to exchange Zagor comics with Rinardi, the smallest boy in my class. A street door smooth as a coffin lid surmounted by the frame of a coat of arms that's no longer there, a stark windowless wall and the newspaper stand where I'd spent fortunes on football cards. The mould on walls, Albertino, Marcella's step a little further back, and she thinking of something elsewhere—some guy, probably, but still she stays here, calmly. An almost romantic evening, in the secret garden screened off by a gate in the second Via Roma, two wide greens separated by a hedged lane. From here you can see the great domes tracing a threshold of light in the black sky. Huge swarms of midges teeming against the air, falling towards the ground and losing their shape, swaying scattered for a while then taking off again in a flash, compact in one shape, an egg or a plume rising stiffly to add length to the treetops.

Dreading ridicule, I'm keeping my mind well fixed on the alcoholic prospect awaiting us in a few minutes, and my eyes pinned to the gleaming edge of small puddles. Nothing doing: I can feel Marcella's calm breath, high clouds, trees and swarms like pillars, and the park is a salon. Albertino is telling his story: it starts with a marble he swallowed, aged eight, to stop a bully stealing it from him.

He wasn't brought up by his nan—that's one of his lies: he grew up in an institution run by a mingey small-town hag who gets paid to drag up the children nobody claims. His mum a prostitute—his dad, who knows. Because of that marble he gets taken to hospital, on the plain of the Po: he's well behaved, he's their pet, he thinks he might even stay there and who knows, he might become a nurse in time—until the day when his heart seems to burst inside his chest: he gets scared, blood beating furiously against his ventricles, help. One of the medics decides that anxiety is a nasty illness, and he gets transferred to the neurological ward of a big hospital in the city—whacked out on medication, induced calm. On the ward they're all older than he is: they teach him to play cards and he learns to cheat, to adapt, to get people to like him and gracefully tell survival lies. But he's not ill, they can tell he's not like the others. If you're nobody's child, all it takes is a wisp of breeze to blow you off course with no return: a twist of chance, or the presumption of a medic in Vercelli, and your life is marked for ever. What do we do with a nobody's child in recovery, living inside a structure for mad people? Nowhere is home: no one asking after Albertino, no one paying for him. And so he ends up in hell: a place with the soothing name of Villa Azzurra, where a famous consultant will stick an electrode up your ass and wire another to your balls. That's his idea of order. Caught wanking? One electrode here, one there. He's invented a technique all his own, that he calls electromassage: not just one burst, like in all madhouses, but many low-voltage ones that will cut your breath, split your brain, have you accept anything. Singing in the yard? An electromassage, for the sake of quiet. Talking back to a nurse? Or not talking at all? Or aboulic, catatonic, indifferent? Electromassage. And then whole days, sometimes three or four on end, strapped to the couch, clamps at the wrists clamps at the ankles, a nurse who will sometimes leave a bit of slack and feed you with a spoon (now and again the kindest will free one of your hands and let you feed yourself). A brave journalist finds out about the goings-on at Villa Azzurra—or rather: everybody knows, it's just that he's got the guts to look into it and tell the story. And finally the consultant, the famous Dr Coda (Albertino says his name carefully, it's scary when he's like that), is caught, a judge starts investigating, the trial runs on for years. Someone, perhaps the journalist, notices Albertino: they put him in foster care with a rich, generous, unfathomable family, up on the hill of the houses with large glass panes. Albertino grows up among new brothers, sisters, mothers and fathers, they're elegant, present, he sometimes thinks they've got rich friends, houses full of wonders that someone could make off with and sell. He's saying all this because this August, just a few days ago, the almighty Dr Coda's brush with the law came to an end: he was sentenced, but then the case was statute-barred—and so the man who tortured Albertino returns to his place as one of the esteemed professionals of Turin.

The city is the dark interior of a palace, and next to me is the lady of the house, and she is saying 'You should cry a little now, Albertino, don't you think?' Instead he laughs and kisses her hand with a slightly off-key gesture, and then it's dark and we're sitting on a step watching the reflections on the edges of puddles and each is thinking alone—she'll be talking to death, he'll be composing songs in his head or planning a burglary, I'm trying to establish a sort of seance-style complicity through silence, trying to make it through the night. Marcella says: 'They're maggots.' She points downward and I discover that what we've been watching over are not the gleaming edges of some small water splashes, but the backs of tiny maggots teeming in the first pale light on the crumpled tarmac pavement. Albertino picks them up, I think he's about to eat some, but he turns towards Marcella and says: 'They're dew crystals.'

Then Marcella leaves, off on holiday somewhere, and I throw myself onto Via delle Industrie and the dry, impervious sentences in Tacitus. Summer is drained of all colour, and the day of my resit arrives. The bearded woman counters, discusses, harasses, but I parry her blow on blow, I feel strong, it's like a mental

homage to the honest woman of Via delle Industrie and her summertime work. And then I'm off, a couple of days in the mountains with Dino and Ruben who are back in town as the afternoons
begin to fill up with friends' phone calls, their suntans and their
'So, what have you been up to?' We climb to a mountain hut set
above Turin in a bare narrow valley with an artificial lake. We're
meant to make for the top in the morning, but shortly after midnight someone throws the bedroom door open and hurls something at my chest: a sturdy, slimy, clinging carnivore plant, three
tentacles hooked around my neck, gripping my shoulders. I start
struggling and fall off the top bunk, the monster's trying to
smother me, so I load all the strength of my arms into the punch
of a lifetime and aim it straight into the central sphincter of the
green beast. Dino is standing by the light switch and laughing,
Ruben is rubbing (ha!) his face and mumbling what a fucking dickhead I am, I have a dislocated elbow & knee—we head back down
at daybreak.

PALE, SO PALE   'So—you found the philosopher's stone?'

    'No, but I know how you do it—there's a book . . .'

    'Are you all right?'

    'Yes—you?'

    'Yeah, I'm fine.'

    'Where've you been hiding? We've not seen you in ages . . .'

    'Been busy.'

    'You're very pale.'

    'Give over, I've never had better colour.'

'Look, you're so pale it makes me sick to look at you—how did you find me?'

'You used to call me inspector, remember?'

'Yeh—that's right.'

'How's Marina?'

'Still thinking of her?'

'No, no, I have a partner these days . . .'

'. . . ?'

'Marcella.'

'Marcella? From Barabba?'

'Yep.'

'So.'

'So—Marina?'

'All good, all good.'

'Giuliana?'

'Yeah, good, she's always good, that one.'

'Hmmm.'

'Sticking around a bit?'

'Yes of course—where the fuck do you think I'm going.'

'That's right—Turin's not very big, is it.'

'That's right.'

SQUAD   A warm, dry September, clear sunlight and the exam results on the noticeboard. I walk over calmly, after a long sleep, and on the pavement I see the English teacher coming towards me—a guy who spoke to me of the Soledad Brothers and

Langston Hughes and John Giorno and Malcolm X. I'm with Swivel-hips Billy, and with Cocò, who puts a fright on you just walking by you in the street. The teacher is uneasy, he stops to look at the slightly intimidating trio in front of him, wipes sweat from his pate, says he's sorry, that they fought in the meeting, that he disagreed and so did the maths teacher. All right, I get it, walk up to the noticeboards—just a formality, as the fear of what might come later mounts inside me. Cocò is in no two minds: 'Fucksake, oh fuck—she's bound to have a car, this slut of a teacher, innit.'

Good job Igor's back—strange, cagey, looking askance and talking half as much as he used to and laughing almost never, sometimes just flashing the savvy smile that earned him his 'Inspector' nickname. These days he lives up to it by wearing a white raincoat. It looks to me like the new place on Via Garibaldi is not exactly for everyone: it's small, and we've lost that atmosphere of permanent assembly we used to have back in the spring. The toughs are around, and that's enough: each circle puts together a squad. Safe guys, no messing around: they're a defence for all the others, as Albertino explains to me. And are you in the squad. 'Nah,' he says, 'I don't like playing toy soldiers.' Johnny's the chief: 'At last he's got someone to boss around.' Albertino says that Johnny, if he could, would put together a supersquad with the most trustworthy from the squad and then a supersupersquad made of himself, and boss it over his own sweet self. Anyways, I wasn't told a thing. My age perhaps, I'm young—but then Billy's my age too. Fact: I've grown up sheltered, you can tell by the soft curves that my women like so much, I've not a whisker on my face—or on my balls, clearly.

Luckily this is a town where no one looks at you as you hasten towards such an ambitious and urgent task as the reforming of humanity, the beginning of a new love, the discovery of another sex. The avant-gardes have occupied the night, and you can be left outside, confined inside the afternoon, trying to see, trying to make out some shape as it moves through the dark, your eyes dazed by the wan light you live in. There's people change the subject when you get in, you who go back home to sleep at night and with each step you find yourself still in the skin you thought you'd left by the wayside, your ID card, the sequence of numbers you are: the afternoon is a place where you're seen without seeing. If you're a bourgeois you're a bourgeois—at a pinch you might come in handy some time.

Now and then Igor disappears, then reappears with a smile on his face. Something's brewing for 13 September, for Santana's concert. There are short, angry-faced women hanging on the warriors' arms, shared cigarettes and big eyebrows. Where was I while the human race was changing? It's not like Barabba has organized its own security crew: Barabba has become a security crew—or at least what's left alive of Barabba, what's still pumping energy and has some value. The rest is frills.

I come out of the hole on Via Garibaldi for a breather, the air is chilly already, it's like whitewash on the roofs, or instead of the roofs. This is how the summer ends. We'll go to Bologna to look for serious minds, as Albertino says, we'll take the city. Here I am outside, on the square, September air, lamppost. Over the bridge, the great, white, round church that watches over Turin: the Great Mother.

MINT SODA   Truth to tell, there was nothing to the night of the fires except running away. I've started awake and don't know what I was dreaming, but I'm awake now and I've a stone in my hand and playing in my ears is the staccato intro to Europa, Santana's guitar: ta ttara ttara tarattaaa. It's all very dark and the treetops are floodlit.

They've decided to broadcast the music outside via these huge speakers rigged up on the dome of the indoor stadium: that should keep us quiet—we've come for the music after all, haven't we? The air is murky, almost like trying to rain—aerosol rain. My problem is: there's a step, and I've to find a battle station. On the step or off? Off, and I risk stumbling when it comes to running away; on, and I get the feeling I'm out of the playing field. After all, I've been given an officer's role—or just about: the squad at the front, and me back here with the women, a stone in my hand, to cover the retreat. 'You watch over Marcella,' Igor said—which makes me an ensign at least, right? And there she is, God strike her down by lightning, stock-still and silent with her stone in her hand. Neither of my two has bothered to come—you don't just go out at night for the hell of it. Are those flames over there? No, no—Tatta-ra ttara tara taaa haha, the front rows look like those lines of paper soldiers you get when you cut a sheet after folding it and then open it in a child's face, and the murky air in front of the floodlights makes them look white. We'll hear the siren first, won't we? Taratattara taratàn, taitàn. It's cool to be here, back in school I can tell them I was leader of the stone-throwers—an ensign's role, that's what. Taratt . . . oh fuck, the paper soldiers have crumpled in the time it's taken me to blink my long eye-lashes: huge armoured vehicles are charging forward at top speed—blurred outlines, only darkness behind. And they attack right away, no one's thrown a single bottle, our guys too gobsmacked to fight back—now they're behind me while Ciccio is trying to reorder the ranks, this is the moment to throw the stones, they're closing in, you can throw your stone but it's more like getting rid of it than hoping to do any damage. Teargas going off much further away, much further behind us, because they're throwing in straight lines: if they just wanted to smoke us out they'd be lobbing them, but they're throwing to hit us. Then they stop two or three hundred yards beyond our ranks, we are vaporized in the aerosol drizzle, the bastards charged without any provocation—our rule book says police can never attack first.

One guy's saying these have come from Padua, they've brought them in by the vanload because Padua cops are the meanest and get even meaner after a stretch of motorway driving: I can see them, getting here with their stomachs turned from the journey and being ranked with nothing to eat, you can eat after you've made mincemeat of those kids, all right? Now they've stopped, in fact all I can see is vehicles, ambulance sirens are wailing, we've already heard that someone got hit in the chest with a gas can and is in a coma—who is it? Dunno, a guy from Grugliasco. Santana is making a racket, you can hear he's pumping it out like he knows, it's night again and we can see the wind in the treetops, birds flying across the shafts of white light. Now we can hear a few thuds—whup, whup, this time it's the bottles, our guys are attacking. Another charge: What the fuck are we doing here with no stones left? Now our squad guys are rushing back, faces covered, straight towards us and between us, someone stops for us: 'Go—it's getting ugly.'

We stop at the edge of the flyover that borders the park—a coach is ill fated enough to attempt a turn right before us, it slams down and stops. Albertino jumps in, two or three after him, then the others. Albertino gets the driver off: 'He's a comrade, he could have made it hard for us, but he's with us.' Might be—the driver walks off with his uniform hat on. I think, how can they drive all day with a tie on. At Albertino's request, the comrade driver has left the keys in. Santana has stopped playing, it's getting cold. Albertino is cursing and trying to get going, the coach shudders but won't budge, we look quickly back at the park, can't see anything in the pitch black: Are they coming, not coming? He's revving it up, fucksaking & chrissaking, the starter is howling and stalling, then the armoured vans come out of the black and Albertino twigs. 'Offuck-ing-ggod! The wheel lock!' Nice comrade driver indeed, the sonofabitch in his shit of a peaked uniform cap—too late now, they're swooping on us, those who can are jumping from the doors, someone gets stuck, never mind, we've to run as long as we've legs to, down along the three-lane boulevard. Over and above the floodlights, the Lancia skyscraper is lit up in the night.

They say a whole bunch got busted on the coach, nobody on the boulevard now, time to counterattack and I've lost Marcella—offuck, Marcella, I've a stone and hurl it away into the shrubs, offuck fuck fuck. And anyway we have to turn back, we're at the edge of the boulevard where the road meets the skyscraper—a huge tower, tight and upright, judging you: the street runs beneath it, into its belly, bows like the whole city does and then slopes gently down into Corso Racconigi, where the long market is. The Martians have stopped less than half a mile away, they're aiming floodlights from the roofs of their vehicles, lucky there's smoke between us and them and their steel shapes are only halfway out the clouds, they're looking at us but we see no humans, only spaceships. The guys from Autonomia are upending cars on Via Lancia, setting them sideways across the road: if we've to respond, best do it from here, on the boulevard we'd be slaughtered before we even begin to raise a barricade. Sirens wailing behind us as well. Off across the flowerbeds, running across the park in opposite directions, and here come their humans: dark, green and blue in the reflections from the flashlights, running like demons: these guys are tough, nothing like our Maresciallo Speranza, this is not the Digos, dear gentlemen, these are Triveneto thugs, they run as if possessed despite the plexiglass squashing their faces, and they hit hard. I don't know how but I manage to pass through the shrubs and cut across the police line and end up behind them, isolated from the fray. I can see the flames all right, now—they're burning some cars maybe, I don't know.

On the clearing now, only a circle of faint light in the shrubs, a small group of nervous people huddled around a bench. With them is Marcella. I want to fall on my knees and thank God. Also the Induno sisters, Chiara and Manuela—one solid, blonde, planted on the ground, and the other lank and dark, a long tall sally with an intellectual's slow, absent-minded eyes: they're the sisters of a well-known fascist bruiser—wonder what their family life must be like. So here we are, out of it all—what shall we do? There was a plan: if all hell breaks loose we'll regroup in Piazza Sabotino and sort ourselves out, see if to call an assembly or demo for tomorrow or lick our wounds and get a bit of breath and identity back, like that time at the market on Via Baltimora. Piazza Sabotino—easier said than done: the whole of Borgo San Paolo in the middle, and between us and Borgo San Paolo the three-lane boulevard, the skyscraper straddling a street, the bruisers.

Now I'm running through side streets, things popping out of the dark in silence, lit-up windows on the top floors, lower down people are locked in, you can feel their eyes peeking out at the street through closed shutters. We're running, there's not many of us left—or rather, it's not like we're running proper, but more like . . . you know when you're walking fast and both your feet are lifting off the ground together, but you're ashamed that you've taken two running steps so you put your heels down squarely and feel the pull in your calf muscle—well that's how we're stopping ourselves overtaking the faster ones, and I'm not one of them. At the bottom of a street on the right we can see a corner lit up through the glass front of a bar, Via Pollenzo. Outside the bar there's a crowd and they're looking at us: here even the ground floor windows are open, I say look, this is a working-class neighbourhood, let's turn that way, dive into the crowd and they'll cover us. They listen to me, and we rush straight into the arms of the people of Borgo San Paolo. Except the people are moving. They're making waves, swelling and catching us: 'So are you done burning our cars, you bastards?' You bastards. That's got to be a keyword, cause as soon as one says it all the others latch on and start rolling it around their mouths and you can hear they're loving it more the more they spit it out: 'You bastards!' And they're closing in—I hadn't noticed how brightly lit this Via Pollenzo is. Some are running already—time to leg it, and so much for finding a home in the working-class neighbourhood, those guys are yelling about what they're going to do to us, to the girls especially, and so having run off first and finding myself well ahead of the group I take heed and stop. Marcella rushes past me and almost all of them after her, where the hell are the Induno sisters? I'm standing in the middle of the road like an idiot with the posse of bloodthirsty good citizens charging towards me, I can see their veins bulging under the hair on their arms, I can see their arms bulging to burst in the rolled-up shirt sleeves, I can see a bruising in the offing and to hell with the Induno sisters, I turn round and take off like I've got wheels and pistons in my trousers but it's too late: Via Pollenzo is flying before me like a straight wide line lit up white by photocells, they'll get me for sure, it's full of doors and street doors opening and people hurtling out at the rhythm of 'You bastards', great big feet drumming away on the tarmac, I've had it, this time I've had it all right. I turn round to see the lynch mob and omiggod they've got their claws on my shoulders, tugging hard at my shirt, I've had it, I jerk my shoulder forward with all my strength, rrrrrrrrripppppp, there goes my sleeve, I've left it in the brute's hand, the shitface, thought you'd got me, you shitface, I'm running like I've no such things as lungs liver or spleen in me, an alley on my left, throw myself onto the bonnet of a parked car and roll off to the other side, off up the alleyway.

Clearly the Indunos are a more valuable prey: no one's followed me, the whole mass of bludgeons and clubs is off in a straight line along Via Pollenzo. No lights here, but I stop to check. Another straight road at a right angle, one of those where the tram line runs. No one there, it must be late. Now I can feel my spleen all right, I'm running on at random, turning every corner. Like playing street pinball aged twelve with my friend Mandrone, only this time it's at night and there's this new rule, you can find a policeman round the corner and then it's forfeits. More fun this way, no doubt about it—except I'd put on the mother of all shirts this evening, mandarin collar and all, and ripped up as it is by the Via Pollenzo vigilantes the mandarin shirt has gone up to twice, thrice its value, but you can only use it once: it's not like you can run around with a sleeve missing after the battle's done. So it's all the more urgent to find the women.

''xcuse me—for Piazza Sabotino?' The lady looks at me, she's at a loss but then explains, it's easy, just follow the tram tracks, except I was going the opposite way, more or less straight into the mouth of the big vans. Oops—about-turn and get walking, at the end of the street orange light spreading, the motorway floodlights again, very 'industrial-city', isn't it—the mayor must be crazy about them. Phew, here I am—Piazza Sabotino.

Empty. Not a soul. It's wide, with a cinema on the corner set inside one of those buildings with rounded-off edges that fascist architects used to love. Closed. There's a kiosk across the boulevard and someone's calling out to me, but these are not my comrades: it's a small group of kids in leather jackets, pointed boots, slicked hair. Great—all I needed this evening was a bunch of local yokels. The local yokels are an institution: they're the guys who rob you at the gate of your primary school, give you a shove and nick your snack or your Pelé footie card, then rob you again outside secondary school and nick something bigger, say a pen, your gold chain, the hat you really liked, and on a bad day you'll cop a kick in the balls for good measure. Once I ran into the worst two in the neighbourhood, Formaggino & Facciabruciata—as in Cheesy & Burnedyface, kicking down Via Montecuccoli behind the school in their bum-freezers, and they'd set eyes on us already, but I was with my mate Pino Folacchi, who'd spent his days as a small kid practising left-right kicks with a real leather football outside the church hall where I was going to scouts. We'd get there sporting our neckerchiefs and he'd start off with 'Oh fuck it's the boy scouts,' then carry on taking the piss, but in a smart way that made us laugh, sometimes we'd go at each other a bit, but mostly you'd just tell him to fuck off and walk on into the church hall. I don't know how we got to be friends later, but that day I was with him. So Facciabruciata says something to stop us in our tracks and Pino replies with some motormouth gobbledigook, 'Kalarmahulamakamuttefutte' or the like. And you can see Formaggino is thrown, but then he rallies and says, 'Anyway, Calabrians can all suck my dick,' lays a hand on Pino's shoulder and shoves him aside, doesn't even clock me, and goes 'Run along, matey, it's your lucky day,' but it's him who's running along, and me proud of my friend. Sorry, I digressed and got lost—but look, I'm finding myself right now: in Piazza Sabotino, with these guys who've jumped straight out of the night and are whistling and beckoning me to the kiosk and I'm thinking, all I need is the local yokels, and I'm also thinking: 'SOLFERINO! Offfuck-ing-god, SOLFERINO! How could I get that mixed up!' Here I am with the yokels of Piazza Sabotino staring at me, and I finally remember that our meet-up point was in Piazza Solferino. What can I do? I walk on, sad as I must be.

'You thrashed them?'

'Wha?'

'The cops, I mean—you thrashed them?'

'Nah. Bruised us, black & blue.'

'Your shirt?'

'Bah—dunno, it's not like I can remember . . .'

'Well done you. A beer?'

'What?'

'You want a beer?' I can't believe it. He's offering me a beer.

'I don't feel that good . . .'

'You've got to have something, you need it.'

'Oh all right—a mint soda, then.'

So he orders one from the kiosk guy, gestures that he's going to pay, and I think he's either about to skin me and wants to have a bit of a laugh first, or I can't make head or tail of a fucking thing. What's going on? The working-class guys want to hang me and the local yokels buy me drinks? I glug the mint soda in one go, I was right thirsty but too busy being scared to realize. He asks me do I want some more, another is saying I should put a tot of brandy in it, he's snickering and I'm thinking, here we go, but instead they want me to tell them all about it, they're listening, and I think it's cool to no longer understand a thing about the world, maybe things really are changing after all. That should be the last thought for the night: after that sort of thought you should just go to sleep.

FANTASTIC ZOOLOGY   But in the end it's the local yokels give me a lift to Piazza Solferino in one of their clapped-out cars. I get there in the dead of night, but there are still people by the fountain, I can see them from far off because the fountain is lit up at night—a huge ampoule with two fringed waterfalls on the sides and one central spurt shooting up high. As a child I was scared of that spurt, a blind force that can grab you and annihilate you. In winter, something strange happens on this square: when a veil of snow falls, you can see a geometric pattern forming on the ground, concentric rectangles with ornaments. There's an underground source of heat melting the snow, but I'm yet to find someone who can explain to me what it really is. Meanwhile the fountain is lit up, and in front I can see outlines of people catching their breath and the breath in small clouds—September does play this sort of trick sometimes. The snow will come, but for now the pattern of Piazza Solferino is resting quietly underground.

Get closer and you'll see them better: on the bench, sitting on the backrest with their feet on the seat, are Igor and Marcella. Igor and Marcella—we should get used to the sound of these two names falling together, because these two will be a lifelong couple. Igor smiles at me—in some way I've done my job. And right then I remember what I'd been dreaming earlier, when I woke up in battle stations outside the indoor stadium at the Parco Ruffini. It was something that had happened here, that afternoon, as we organized a meeting point for after the clash.

It was about Giuliana and Marina, and both of them had a strange light in their eyes, and they were smiling a little. Giuliana had only said that neither of them was going to come to the demo, nothing more. They wouldn't come because they could smell the stench of violence, and violence is a male thing. This was not an antifascist demo (crucial point), so if you're going out with clubs and bottles you're just playing at war, and it's time you grew up and changed inside. So they were not coming. And now Giuliana was quiet, but you could see she had something to say and was running the show. But Marina was jumping out of her skin: I'd got to know her by now, and I liked her excitement, the urge to enjoy the world that sometimes came over her, as happens with little kids when they're about to tell you a joke—it puffed up her cheeks. And now she's standing in the square, her boots right over the invisible tubes that draw frames on the ground in winter snow. In the autumn Marina wears boots with short openwork woolly socks, and for this alone I could marry her. And now she's even standing with her heels off the ground, rocking on the balls of her feet in those boots.

'So?'

'We've something to tell you.' Marina is the speaker, Giuliana the director. I'm expecting a 'Look, we've had a talk and—' but this time it's 'Look, we've made an experiment—' Marina is laughing with her eyes, making fun of me, making fun of herself, making fun of the whole world, thrilled to be in the world.

'What experiment?'

'Well—this is a weird situation, isn't it?'

'Which situation?'

'Ours, I mean—us three.'

'Oh.'

'And we've been thinking it's weird.'

'Ah.'

'It's even strange to say us three, don't you think?'

Hit below the belt: a reflection on language is not like Marina. What the hell's going on? But Marina is getting too playful, so Giuliana moves in on the scene.

'We have a relationship. Us two, I mean.'

'What?'

'Marina and I have a relationship.'

Do I need to explain to you what 'a relationship' means in the one-way youth language of my times? Hardly. So you can imagine my dumb-fish face as I look at them, waiting for them to say something, anything. I'm seething, but they say not a thing. Marina laughs and stamps a kiss on Giuliana's lips, right there, in the middle of the square, six o'clock on a summer evening. And Giuliana strokes her hair, then pulls her close, kisses her long, like a lover, and I can feel my belly plunge into my heels and my blood rise at top speed, I've always dreamt of that sort of thing, but it's not like you can say it, is it. Marina is greedy, she takes my arm and pulls me in, we are tangled up in a threesome, a strange beast, the sort of fantastic-zoo, trial-and-error creature that nature discards in the evolution of the species, but our bodies have shapes it's difficult enough to master in a twosome (which is why I've become a masturbation artist), so we end up as this sort of symbolic and probably silly thingummy where we have to stick our tongues out until our throats hurt to get the tips to touch, and there we are, licking away furiously without caring who might be there or passing by. Afterwards, Giuliana only says: 'At last.'

So that's how I got to be standing unawares in front of the police bruisers, and now it's night, who knows where Giuliana and Marina might be—laying out a dream palace for me, I think, so if the revolution backfires, there'll always be our dream palace.

It's nighttime and things are blurred by sleep, even the fountain. Marcella doesn't know where the Indunos might be, she says they got caught by the mob but she's not sure, she ran away without turning to look. Of course she couldn't have turned—that'd have been all we needed, what with me beating it up the alleyway. We wait, the Indunos know about the meeting point, we'll wait all night if necessary, under the lit-up fountain. I have a strange genetic gift: I can curl my tongue up in a clover shape. Once we used to run around and play circus, the four of us: I had my clover tongue, Ruben could shift his hair back and forth like a wig, Igor had six left toes and Gino Bonetti would finale with his special number—whenever he sings Lay Lady Lay, without fail, deterministically, he'll break down and cry. So now I'm listening to Marcella and trying to stay awake on the bench, curling my clover tongue— to myself, mind you. With my mouth closed.

I spend the night doing the clover, until in the morning the Indunos finally show up. They live two blocks away from the fountain, so they've come around to the square. Good that we waited. They tell us a strange story: they got dragged into a hallway behind a street door, and there people set up a sort of trial. It was turning ugly, someone even said 'Let's kill 'em'. Then a guy in the crowd, plain clothes, pulled out this badge and shouted everybody calm down. After a bit, a van arrived and they were loaded into it and taken to an office where a clerk took their ID cards, scribbled something on a sheet of paper and let them go with no further action. 'Saved by the police,' Igor tittles.

SAMBA OF ANSWERED PRAYERS   And the hippies are hammering on their strings and playing that old samba, no doubt about it. But there's not many of them, and they're huddled away in a corner, not quite digging the music. The evening news has split us into peaceful Injuns and violent autonomy fighters: two tribes I don't recognize. Here's a way to look at us without seeing us—we're used to that. Yet it's true that two worlds are coming apart: in assemblies we're at one another's throats, some are coming to blows, four-square militants miming a wrangling parliament, showdowns and blatant gestures lingering in the streets. So this is Bologna. The movement of dens, the great underground nation of equals without chiefs or hierarchies on one side, and on the other, reheated military idols, the summit, the base, the sweat and sacrifice—and the blood into the bargain. It ends with a demo narrated by the radios, walking and moving over a whole day, howling but not turning into battle, bang we're dead, all of us, like the people in Nagasaki drinking their coffee with the atom-bomb plane already overhead and their shadows on the walls more real than they are. We couldn't do it—the serious minds in Albertino's song did not come out.

Who knows how far we could have gone if we'd aimed for precision, rather than settling for our abstractions of desire. The agony of the dying world was so strong in our guts that if we'd armed ourselves with exactness, we might have been able to determine its destiny. But we settled for the warped, obscure language of our emotions. One of our newsletters now comes out with the heading: 'The revolution is over, we've won.' That's the most lucid thought in that whole season. Except it's biologically impossible to think of the end with lucidity: you can expound it, you can think you ought to be thinking it, you can approach it the way mathematicians do, in fact moving away from it into stellar distances, inserting endless, smaller and smaller thoughts between what was thought and what is unthinkable, and each of these thoughts says that to get there is impossible. We are faced with the end, the engine of every market, virtue of the banks, lacuna of utopias: money, through its immaterial channels, knows the twilight zones and can exploit their resources. We who are unsuited to the revolution because the place of revolution is infinity, the future, the dream of flower children in prosperous times, gone times, gone dream—we will pass from the endless power of our carnal adolescence to the endless frustration that pushes people to consume, whether it's merchandise they consume, or themselves. Or lives as merchandise. Lives of the dead, lost in tangles of rebellion, burglaries, hard drugs, guns, dejection or career. Some will end up deciding that survival means emerging, crushing, cutting and in the end devoting themselves to the rule of natural supremacy. Having started from far off, they will find moorings in the basic fascism of life lived as the rule of the best, the strongest man, the sexiest woman. Very soon now, many of us will be speaking like gangsters, proud to have made their entrance in the adult world: 'I fucked his woman'—'His mother's loaded, let's do his flat'—'Your barker oiled? Today we shoot'— 'He's a poof, no balls'—'He's got to die.'

It's full of people crying out for a forward leap. Clack! Nearly always the noise of a coffin lid. Albertino was singing about 'serious minds', but his are not the serious minds of firearms: he can see things that no one can, and later he'll not be aware of how clear-sighted he had been. He forgets himself, and will soon be lost, because he's seen a huge supermarket with lines of trolleys and square miles of parking spaces: if you've bought enough, you'll get free parking. He's seen the pension fund, the scrap heap, spring water, text messages, temp agencies and incentives to early retirement, DIY holidays, porn sites, amaretto seduction.

Work is extinct, we've won. Hence the most intelligent among us are extinct. The new world looks like us, we are the stuff of future leadership, those who will consume the most because they are most unhappy, those who will crush others' heads to survive. Ciccio, Albertino and the others are about to die, and they can see the survivors' future as a shattered mirror. They'll be spared the fork in the road that we'll have to face in a few weeks: either alone or enrolled. No wonder Albertino had a moment of melancholy before lunging ahead, no wonder that in his samba rain is falling. Bologna is burning, it's seething—with powerlessness.

GIAP. THE PHILOSOPHERS GO BACK TO FRANCE   There's three hundred people in jail for the clashes of last March, and there's a new law inventing maximum security prisons. Maybe Ciccio and Albertino are right, nothing left to do but die, maybe Giorgio is right, nothing left to do but run away, maybe Carletto and Zio Lupara are right, nothing left to do but shoot. I'll not find myself faced with that fork in the road. I've no hair on my face, I've a warm house in the town centre: so it's back to school, to my new class, I've spent the summer studying and I can read Greek and Latin better than my younger classmates. I've never dared ask about the tragelaph that joined its three heads only once, in Piazza Solferino: it died from functional inadequacy of its monstrous organism, like certain unfortunate creatures cross-bred in labs— too well or not well enough endowed to stay alive, to breathe and feed like less ambitious life forms do on a daily basis having been more effectively approximated over millennia of evolution. It looked like a deity, but clearly it had been born crippled, and so went off to die in some female den, in some broken-off discussions between Giuliana and Marina, in something unsaid I must have missed. So much for the eighteen thousand wanks I dedicated to the barely touched idea of making love as a threesome.

The squad mates are nowhere to be seen, but there's a free zone where the toughs won't come, because we all come from good families and we're all going to some sort of lyceum. Sure, there was social mobility at the time, high schools were not only for the children of professionals or shopkeepers rich enough to forget their shops, but also for the children of the FIAT village in Settimo and others like them. Steady on, though: no chance of people like Igor, Cocò, Billy or Johnny getting in, no matter that we lyceum kids were trying hard to look like delinquents. So we organize a nice assembly and decide that the times are tough and dangerous, that security at demos is far from guaranteed, that lyceum students must be represented, and what about self-deter-mination—in short, we're flexing our muscles under our fluffy jumpers. Which taken together and translated means we'll orga-nize our own security crew and get a few things out of our system. The lyceums: Galfer, Quinto and D'Azeglio out in phalanx (we Classics guys know what that means), showing their own military virtue on the street—in a minor key, of course. Bonetti appoints himself responsible (i.e. captain), and is immediately drowned in raspberries: no 'responsible' captains, this will be an autonomous, self-determined, collegial structure. But you can't expect Gino Bonetti to go home empty-handed, and so he proposes we use a password, a sort of street call. Giap. These days, that word has a broken, nightmarish ring as it flashes back through my mind: Giap! Giap! Giap! I can see Bonetti standing stock-still in the mid-dle of Corso Francia, holding up a heavy flagpole made from a pickaxe handle and yelling, 'Giap! Giap! Giap!' as teargas blossoms all around him. Until a guy running back in retreat slaps his shoulder and says, 'Hey, Jip Jop—time to run, not squeal.'

KAKI FRUIT   The news lands heavy into assemblies busy discussing the recent government bill for the opening of four nuclear plants. Nuclear plants—here's a whole new world. We had almost forgotten about the fascists for a while, and now here they are, bringing us back to something we had overlooked. For the past three days, in Rome, they've been setting off in squads from the Monteverde MSI section and shooting: on the first day, two kids sitting on a bench; on the second day, Elena Pacinelli, who had found herself in Piazza Igea having a chat with someone. Elena will not die instantly, she will take years, never recover—which is why everyone will forget her. And on the third day, Walter Rossi, aged twenty, who was handing out leaflets about Elena's shooting: he will die on 30 September. We're wanting a final showdown, some sort of revenge for the emptiness in Bologna. And here in Turin, we have the mythologized memory of that time early in the decade, when the MSI section in Corso Francia was attacked and closed down by the workers: we'll do it again, we'll do it this time. And the next morning the demo is huge, sullen and roiling as always happens when something's going down, there's workers, groups, students, the slogans are booming out among the houses of Turin, like in Rome last spring. It snakes slowly over to Corso Francia, that great diagonal blade of a boulevard that starts in the mountains, plunges into Turin's liver and comes up against the black angel commemorating the fallen of the Frejus. The police are a wall, attacking from far off, pre-emptively, a storm of teargas sucking the breath out of your lungs, we try to hold our ground, withstand the first charge, but it's clear from the start they're out in force and we'll not be able to get to the fascist section. Someone has already come up with another idea: we retreat, and Gino Bonetti, who has missed the import of the day, is left standing in a shower of teargas and shouting 'Giap, Giap' for as long as they let him. The demo has coiled over itself and is backing away towards Via Cernaia. The orange carabinieri barracks is on action stations, snipers at the windows, the bare kaki trees standing in the ditch: when I was small I'd go past it on the way back from school and always dreamt of the grand theft of those kaki fruits, a mighty deed that'd leave the carabinieri flabbergasted—I'd come down in a zeppelin, or up from the sewers in an antimatter motor, or parachute a three-hundred-strong professional orchestra into their yard to distract the guards, you name it. But for that day, the coup on the carabinieri's kaki trees is not on the cards—we'll go further. To the seat of Cisnal, the fascist trade union, where we've better luck: all we need to do is break in and smash the smashable. No one in there, of course. We carry on towards the town centre, slowly. Right into the town centre.

AN OLD WOMAN   One body advancing slowly along boulevards planned for celebrations the city has never seen, one huge body seething with one evil thought. Moving along the arcade, down the streets that plunge into the city, stopping now and then, perhaps in doubt, in front of the masked faces of a thousand policemen. The city is only a chessboard for those who don't know her: over here, everyone knows how many curves can be traced on the apparently symmetrical plane of straight streets, like in a

Chinese game of skill. Perhaps the demo is stopping to imagine those maps, perhaps some part of its shifting brain is tracing the design it will lay over the surface of Turin. One great animal, each cell sharing responsibility for the whole. And when, bloated with its prey, the animal gets nauseous and convulsed, its fugitive molecules, lying low in alleys, houses, taverns, under the beds, at school or at work, will all feel the same biting pain in their stomach: the smell of teargas marks the beginning of the day, the demo stops in Piazza Castello, silent as a snake. The Giap security crew has regrouped, we're linking arms, next to me is Marina (this is an antifascist demo), next to her a blonde girl by the name of Nadia, then the Rt Hon. Mr Bonetti, and others. After the retreat from Corso Francia we agreed to hold the cordons at all costs: we pull the grip of our elbows tight together with the stubbornness of children and slowly make our way to Via Po, stalls of books and beads under the long crumbling arcade, shutters down, soot at the end where the Church of the Grande Madre should be. Now we are standing halfway down the street, holding on tight together, looking ahead and seeing nothing beyond the wall of backs and shoulders. And then it's just one moment, the automatic blink of an eye: the whole demo ahead of us is dissolved into thin air.

Slow on the uptake, perhaps still burning with the shame of Corso Francia, we're standing stock-still facing the street as it's suddenly emptied, swept by the wind that blows free through the span of the arcade. A cold shiver, a thought and its opposite in the space of a quarter second: we're the front line, there'll be a charge and we'll get the police's fury right in our faces—we'll resist—let's run. We're the front line and the rear: just look back, no one left

behind us either. That whole mass of people has vanished in the
blink of an eye, now people are sheltering just inside street doors
or on the side streets, something should happen but nothing does
and that's exactly what fills us with fear, you can feel it, throat
hurting as you try to swallow, a taste like metal, the air buzzing
like when I was small just before Benedetta arrived, and then arms
unlinking, no need to look at one another even, our legs carrying
us elsewhere in a flash like we're faced with a river in spate. But
there's no explanation: from the side courtyards where we found
shelter, we can see the street, no one passing by, just scraps of
paper on the ground, dancing away.

Someone peeks out from the colonnade, we go back into the
street, reform the cordons. News travels with the authority of a
command among bewildered people: turn left towards Palazzo
Nuovo, assembly at the university, not one slogan in the air, the
background noise is a buzz, it's as if everyone's swallowing the
saliva congealed in their throats before the flight. As we double
back under the sooty arches of the church on Via Sant'Ottavio, I
look to my right towards Piazza Vittorio: a strange image prints
itself in my eyes. In the middle of the street, not far from where
it widens to find its estuary into the square, there's a bar chair. It's
standing outside the arcade, facing sideways, where cars usually
drive. And crouched on the chair is an old woman, a peasant
swathed in the sort of black shawl country women wear, a scarf
over her head. It's just a flash, because my legs are running with
the demo, and the image is left there, with its charge of absurdity,
a freeze frame without an explanation. A woman in black on a
chair, frightened people looking out from under the arcade, no

one daring to move close. We can hear sirens as we walk into the glass cuboid of Palazzo Nuovo.

FELT-TIPS   There are things not even I, not even in the climate of that time, not even with my amazing skill at eluding things and hiding, can begin to tolerate. One is the following: 'If the blue angel is you / I don't like this shade of blue / it was on a Saturday morning / that you burnt without a warning.' I feel queasy, even a quarter of a century later, just thinking of it—much as I know that revolting quatrain comes from unease, embarrassment, pity, teenage narcissism, female narcissism. I should feel tenderness, but it's shame I feel, even now, even as I tell you about it. That's precisely what was scrawled, in blue felt-tip, on an improvised banner in the foyer of Palazzo Nuovo, on Monday, 3 October, when we held the assembly that was aborted on the previous Saturday. That Saturday morning, we'd been trying to cover up the news, to read something into it—but apart from a few isolated idiots, no one had it in them to shout. We had killed a nineteen-year-old lad, a factory worker who did some cash-in-hand jobs to get by, a guy who might have been too naïve to dare set foot in the jungle of our circles, where you could end up skinned alive on a whim for want of star quality or native wit. The demo for the death of Walter Rossi was missing a strong, conclusive action: during a longer than usual stop along Via Po, a determined faction, one of the squads I mean, had broken off and rushed ahead under the arcade, zipping past the fat human snake bloated with its own size. There was a bar that had the whiff of heroin about it: no fascists, that was not the issue with the Angelo Azzurro. Back to the roots of our circles: war on pushers, a way to say we'll not be caught in the net that's snaring us, we won't walk down the path they've traced for us, or at least for those of us who cannot be kept safe by income and family.

Some of the Angelo Azzurro customers are pushers: that's a good place to hit, this too is antifascism, and may the god of partisans forgive us. The dynamics of the action is precise, correct: rush in through the door, announce what's going to happen and briefly explain the reasons. Then carefully get everyone out, the barman, the waiters, the customers, and when the place is empty, mark your passage by a couple of molotovs. There was no way of knowing what would happen, no way at all—yet strangely, after the 1st of October 1977, no one in Turin has been able to hide behind a sentence such as 'there was no way of knowing', no one can let themselves off or absolve themselves. Roberto Crescenzio was having breakfast, for sure he'd heard the noise outside, maybe he'd cracked a joke with the other customers, maybe he had plans for the afternoon, and when we stormed into the bar (I say 'we' because all ten thousand of us were present, even those who didn't know about it) he got frightened. Badly. And he thought things were turning ugly and reacted like a hunted animal: panic misled him into choosing the wrong direction and locking himself in the toilet.

He burned through endless minutes without a chance of breaking free, no one heard his cries because everyone had been evacuated, and when they pulled him out of the last room in his life he could hardly breathe, devoured in every part of his body, crinkled black like an old country woman, and no one knew what to do, no one knew how to touch him, they placed him on that chair out in the open, praying to some god for air to give him relief, and out there, slowly, weeping, he died.

No, we didn't have the words: we left in dribs and drabs and locked ourselves into our houses, thinking, thinking. And some of us don't know how to say that this is not going anywhere, no longer going anywhere, nothing doing, and so they look for words with the means of a twelve-year-old writing poems in her diary, finding resonance in a juke-box tune whose title recalls the name of the bar where we've killed a kid, and the name is Angelo Azzurro. Two girls with addled brains take a blue felt-tip, their intentions are good, they mean to call themselves out, to say the movement has taken them where they didn't want to go, they're acting as if there was any way back, as if we were able to say stop, that's it, no more. You want to free yourself from your pain? Free yourself from your destiny. Go back, change nature's course, grow young again, never get old. Thersites suggesting the impossible to the Achaean princes. Ulysses, the hero of a serious time, will expel him from the world of men, beating him with a stick and banishing him for doing something that after that morning in Turin would be spelled out as the rule of the new world: grow young again, never get old, never die, never become.

The girls with their felt-tip are not sly as Thersites: they're just bewildered, they don't know they've been handed over to life and to its double, from that moment onward and for ever, together with a whole mass of living bodies that are about to turn into ghosts. And perhaps those girls, on the edge of time, on the vacant day that separates two worlds, in the terrible, loud awkwardness of their gesture, for one moment, before they write, are still themselves, living in a more serious world than the one they're inaugurating. Marina and Nadia take a felt-tip and write their crass quatrain, and down to this day I cannot stand it.

RINGLETS   Bruno also died that October—Bruno, my child-hood friend. We were six years old together, then seven and eight and at least as old as thirteen, when I fell face first on the ground as I ran to the glory of a brawl between gangs of rival small towns on the Schools piazza. Colleretto, a scant mile of cart track running by the cemetery: flat country, a smudge of houses along a main street on the edge of the A road to Ivrea. A triumphal entrance with a red brick farmyard-castle in the shade of large dark horse chestnuts, a church and a square straight out of a crossword magazine. My mother's summers, a little girl in '39, wartime summers with the loft to hide what little meat they'd managed to scrape together on the black market and the basement with the trap door where Grandma once sheltered a partisan and then, like the pretty woman she was, had to make eyes at the German officer to keep him away from the cellar until in the end he wanted to take her back to Germany. So much for Granddad, a guy who would jump on his bike every morning and ride over fifteen miles to Turin to run a small asphalt plant and ride back every night, the fascist badge on his lapel until the day they ran to meet him at the Alice junction: 'Manlio, chuck the gobbet, we're free!' The gobbet being the badge. Then my father returning from Alessandria after the war, him and Mum setting eyes on each other and thinking of the city. And then our summers, a band of cousins of many ages in a creaking big house, the loft and basement full of ghosts and legends. And the lawn with the magnolia and the weeping willow and the dust road just so that when the ice-cream motor cart took the Turchia bend you could see it coming by the cloud it lifted and you had time to rush off to Auntie Carla for a few coins. A thirty-lira cone, chocolate: the wee ice-cream man was called Tredici owing to the thirteen children he'd fathered—though my maternal grandma, with her ten, hadn't exactly been messing about. At the edge of the road, instead of pavements, there had been sewer runnels—they were culverted now, but by long habit the thresholds of courtyards were still called 'bridges': Bruno's bridge, Federico's bridge, like that. Tredici would stop off at Milk-Federico's bridge, Bruno's bridge was where we'd be dibbing to see who'd be goalie, Nearby-Federico's bridge was where we exchanged comics—you know those summers, you too can recall them: lasting ages, humming with the buzz of insects, and you can spend a whole afternoon watching a bluebottle as it tries to burst out of the cold shade of the house into the full light of the meadow through a green mosquito mesh stretched across a window frame.

But this is a morning in October, and they're saying Bruno is dead. They'd bought him a moped: I know him, he's a yokel, he'll have gone off to do wheelies on the main road, the sort of guy who loved making noise, Bruno was—he had some ideas and strength in his legs to run, like when he got us to dress up as ghosts and ambush Nearby-Federico's brother on the building site. We had filled the hollow bricks with candles, then lit them and started singing a ditty that went 'Hocus Focus Tantus Pocus'. And the little squirt had jumped off the first-floor iron ladder so fast we thought he was going to be killed, except we'd be killed first, the way we were laughing. At night we'd go steal bottles of fizz from Berto's warehouse, that's the Emporio Gianolio, I think he left them out for us: there was always a couple of full bottles in a crate of empties, as if by chance or by mistake. I say he left them out for us, because by day Berto was no fool—and neither was his brother Renato, who looked like a singer and was surely the pride and joy of the housewives of Colleretto. We'd just go and say 'The usual', and Renato would scoop a ball of lemon ice-cream into a coke, then swizzle and serve—aficionado stuff. Oh fuck—Bruno. As wee kids we'd stay in, me and my cousin Maurizio, he'd catch flies and I'd eat them. But when we got older, we'd go off to the Grangia with Bruno. The Grangia of the Third Alpini, that is: a place that works like a restaurant, bar, lightweight gambling house. We'd go and play fifteen, which is a sort of kids' blackjack with folk card decks that Bruno had discovered, then we'd play footie with Giorgio, a peasant strong as a horse, and Adriano who worked at the Fina petrol station—our idol, but he hardly ever played with us, he had a motorbike already. Or we'd go and nick watermelons from the priest's field, I didn't like that cause I'm scared of plants and the watermelon plant crawls along the ground like a night snake, aghhh—or we'd go down into the valley, one dust road with two cart ruts and grass in the middle, plunging headlong, down behind the big farmyard with its small tower: we call it the Castle, not to be outdone. From there a whole world of adventure starts, dark shrubs and hilltop roads, the best thing about it is we're not meant to go there because of the fishing ponds where once a kid fell in and died.

Right, so now we've done our bit with summer memories, now the news is that Bruno is dead. He's not one to stand out, but he scored good goals because he was sharp and fast—not one of the leaders, but one who'd always be there. I've a stack of photos of me and Bruno, he's wearing those yellow or orange terrycloth T-shirts that were in fashion in the Sixties, I wore them too, and in one of the photos he's making horns behind my head and laughing. Now he got this new motor and shot out onto the straight cemetery road, except he didn't think of the set of lights at the crossing with the main road from Ivrea, and there a car ploughed into him at full speed, he had no time to realize, dead on the spot they said. Morning funeral, autumn sunshine, walking down the same road where the accident had happened, and for the occasion Don Rossano has set aside the lyrical flights of his sermons, quick mass and slow cortège, especially at the crossing with the main road, probably the better to savour the frisson: right there at the set of lights you can hear the whispers getting louder, pssssspssss over the idling engines, those waiting for the funeral to pass, the jokes at the cemetery gate like at all funerals, then I get back home as fast as I can with my aunt and uncle, and get car sick because I've an empty stomach. At school that afternoon there's a meeting and I go and everyone treats me like a workplace hero, present in the hour of need despite the grief and sorrow. Marina has been to a hairdresser and now she's in ringlets, 'I knew you'd come anyway,' she says, and kisses me, slides her ringlets across my face, smiles, it's Monday, and later we go to her house to make love. She is towering over me, laughing and saying 'You're thinking of death but my ringlets keep you holding onto life.'

And this is how we enter the age of Thersites—not because we're fucking, but because we're emphatically declaring our adherence to life as it is. Small and ghostly, we make our entrance into the empire of kitsch.

SUBJECT: CHEMICAL MARRIAGE   Alistair Crompton, chief tester at Psychosmell Inc., a leading company since the twenty-first century, when the evocative power of smells had been commercialized thanks to substances made available by space colonization. Thirty years old, meagre height, sharp nose, receding hairline. His Sundays are devoted to the study of Aristotles' Nichomachean Ethics, and once a month he slinks to a newsstand to purchase a magazine of salacious content. His personality is the result of a psychosurgery procedure called cleavage he was made to undergo at the age of twelve, when his violent schizophrenia went out of control. The two discarded personalities were given Durier-bodies (growth-androids with an estimated forty-five-year viability) and sent to foster parents on the planets of Aaia and Ygga so as to discourage reintegration at the legal age of thirty, which in Crompton's case would be rife with contraindications.

At the height of his career, Crompton robs the company and embarks on a search for his alter egos, chased by the curse laid on him by John Blount, chairman of Psychosmell Inc. During the journey he is contacted by the Aaian Secuille, who involves him in his Game: having reached Perfect Enlightenment, the Aaians, the oldest intelligent race in the galaxy, are bored—so they play the Game according to rules unfathomable to other species. Crompton will be a pawn in Secuille's game, and there's no way he can get out of this. The Aaian recommends a 'nu' attitude: so strange things happen—what else is new? One of the inhabitants of Aaia is Edgar Loomis, the fun-seeking, sensation-loving component of the scattered Crompton personality: he works daily at the Episodes Division of Pleasure Scenes Galaxy Spectaculars, specializing in the sexual preferences of humans, alinopods, gnoles, subquasfian tadies, barbizans, double-joined trelizonds, falsely smiling lunters and hyperproteic muns. After discovering the true identity of what they considered a complete albeit despicable man, Loomis' wife and daughter abandon him. Loomis takes the occasion to 'start getting around a little more' and refuses the reintegration proposed by Crompton. Not even the argument on the brief lifespan of Durier bodies moves him: 'I have always found that things have a miraculous way of working themselves out if you simply ignore them and go about your business.' So Crompton takes up residence on Aaia in the notorious Pigfat district, where he is mistaken for 'the Professor', one of the foremost con artists in the galaxy. Capitalizing on the prestige gained through this misconception, Crompton sets a young colossus named Billy Berserker, three-times-running Psychopatic Personality of the Year and striving to leave his profession as a bruiser to become a genius confidence man, on the track of Loomis. Billy, who has changed his name to Sammy Slick, sticks to Loomis like a leech, believing him to be a first-rate earthling confidence man on a visit to Aaia, and torments him until he accepts to run away with Crompton. Locked inside one body like two mutually antagonistic tenants in one rented room, the two set off for Ygga in search of Dan Stack, the sanguine component and third incarnation of the original Alistair.

On Ygga, an undeclared war smoulders between humans and the Yggans, a dying race ever since the Terrans sprayed their planet with Supercyclone B, a gas that induces sterility in reptiles and in certain rare types of moths. Stack, whose cruelty had him expelled even from the infamous elispice plantations where natives live as slaves, has robbed his foster parents of anything of value he could lay his hands on and set up with a jail-mate by the name of Barton Finch on Blood Delta, a wild region beyond the swamps. After a sequence of mutual attacks for control of the one body and adventures among gigantic carnivorous ferns, corrosive resins, great armoured creatures with crablike arms and hostile natives, Loomis and Crompton reach the Delta just in time to witness the hanging of Stack, accused of murdering his partner. In fact, Finch is not quite dead yet, but as the locals say, justice don't waste no time on Blood Delta, and Stack joins the other two personalities in a split second as his Durier body hangs from the noose. But Crompton discovers that Stack, who is also schizoid, had got another Durier body and fissioned: Barton Finch, the humour of phlegm, is the fourth and indispensable component for the real Alistair Crompton. With Loomis and Stack's help, Crompton manages to rescue Finch from the apathy he has fallen into after Stack's assault and to obtain fusion. But the overall personality remains split into several individualities vying for control of the body. At the end of a series of complicated adventures and sexual experiences the protagonists are not quite sure whether to technically define as 'orgies', Finch takes command and persuades a doctor to order a referral: Crompton is moved to Aion, the best-equipped therapeutic planet in the galaxy, a green and pleasant place landscaped to look like California. On Aion, the four witness the life of a community entirely governed by the laws, tics, paracultural attitudes and consensus rules of psychotherapy. They discover that even madness has its ranking order, and that a four-way split personality will guarantee a very respectable social position. One day, Crompton is summoned by Doctor Chares, who takes him through the necessary paperwork and informs him that the course of the therapy may result in death, dismemberment, irreversible insanity, imbecility or impotence. As he signs, Crompton finds himself imprisoned in his chair that begins to descend through a just-opened hole in the floor.

'Wait, doctor! I'm not ready yet!

'They never are.'

Loomis says: 'Let me tell you something Al, you're not smart, you're stupid.' The downward plunge stops at a surgical theatre, where personnel in white coats rush him towards a stretcher on which an anaesthetized body is lying: 'Do get on with the operating.' As Loomis gets busy chatting up a dissociated nurse, Stack emerges and the situation gets out of hand: Crompton suffers a momentary syncope and finds himself in a garden on a high cliff. At his feet a fissure opens in the ground, and in the depths he can see the sulphurous glow of hellfires. 'Daniel Stack!' a voice calls out. 'This is the hour of your reckoning!' Crompton hands control to Stack, who begins to haggle over a couple of murders contested to him that he won't acknowledge. His wheedling irritates the voice, who snaps: 'All right, black out the garden set. Christ, isn't anyone on the ball around here?' Crompton is now standing in a vast yellow room with a placard that reads Superior Court of Karmic Instrumentality, Section VIII, Justice O.T. Grudge Presiding. Stack is summoned, and Crompton appears for him, brilliantly defending him on the grounds of habeas corpus: there is no mind or body answerable for the alleged crimes. The judge appreciates the attempt but throws out the case, and Stack is forced to face the victims of his murders, whom he engages in a conversation not devoid of philosophical nuancing. In the end, he is sentenced to be hung upside down over a cauldron of boiling yak turds and forced to listen to Franck's Symphony in D minor played on a kazoo (a well-dosed mix of his most concealed phobias revealed to the court by his foster mother). Just then a procession of priests with shaven heads marches in and bows to Stack, hailing him by the title of Bode Satva. Stack buys time by mumbling 'Hunh' non-committally, but Crompton manages to take back control: the body they are venerating is his, not Stack's. The priests are not surprised: their Wise Ones, in their caves in Tibet and A-frames in California, have previewed the entire sequence. Crompton, Loomis and Stack are but developmental stages in the bringing forth of the Bode Satva-elect: Barton Finch.

'So that's why he was always so quiet,' Crompton thinks as the priests invite him to sink into nirvana to make way for the predestined one. Disconcerted by a direct question that is very unusual in their culture (and what is nirvana?) the priests become embroiled in a discussion interrupted only by the arrival of all the deities in the universe come to greet the Bode Satva: Thor, Odin, Loki and Frigg disguised as Swedish tourists; Orpheus in a chicano shirt playing a charango, Quetzalcoatl and Damballa. Thangranak, the envoy from the three moons of Kvuuth and from the Polka Dot Abomination, has come via contingencies too fleeting to be imagined to visit death on the Selected One and now demands blood.

At this point the priests, the judge and the deities disappear and for an instant all that can be seen are the glimmering gunmetal cubes that are the fundamental building blocks of reality. When the dust settles, in comes John Blount, chairman of Psychosmells Inc. His agents, disguised as grooks, pretty nurses, vigilante colonels and psychoanalysts, have kept an eye on

Crompton all along, preparing revenge. Blount has understood that overcoming Crompton is but a transient stage on the way to achieving a higher and more universal goal: to destroy the whole of mankind. The plan appeals to Stack, who takes control of the body and allies himself with Blount. As the forewarnings of the realityquake which alters everything, usually for the worse, begin to manifest, in comes the Aaian Secuille from the Committee for the Preservation of the Story Integrity, better known as Archetype Vigilantes. 'Blount, you really ought to be ashamed of yourself. This is Crompton's story, and you are only a bit player in it. The Vigilantes have decided to write you out of the story. How would you like to go—car accident? Massive coronary? Sleeping pills?' Blount repents, donates all his assets to the poor and retires to a cave in Bhutan. Secuille folds the Vigilantes into a brown manilla envelope and says good-bye. Crompton is plunged into a nothingness so empty that he cannot even understand himself. He grows frightened and decides to incarnate and get into duality. Everything feels more normal once he has a body, but that just isn't good enough, so he creates Earth as best he can and then takes a rest and surveys his handiwork. He sees he's made some gross mistakes and got the whole of North America wrong, so he decides to settle in Maplewood, New Jersey, in 1944 and await further developments. When he sees column after column of panzer tanks moving down the main road of his small town under the command of Field Marshal Rommel and Daniel Stack, he realizes he has been fooling around. He snatches the first images that come to him and throws together a defence made of Swiss guards, Viking berserkers and a detachment of Hungarian cavalry. While Stack's troops are stopped, Crompton flies south, with Stack in hot pursuit, in command of the Grande Armée reinforced by Gurkhas, Boers and Albanians. The battle is raging and reality starts shimmering as an unfounded illusion when in comes Loomis (who evidently was not quite the softie he seemed), in command of five thousand hashisheens armed with pikes and a contingent of Malaysians. Stack reacts by simulating the Golden Horde and Cromwell's Boneheads and spreading the plague, but Barton Finch descends on the battlefield with Emperor Ashok and assorted Arahantas and Pratyeka Buddhas. Stack tries to remedy the fall of Mindanao by simulating Dien Bien Phu (a bad mistake) and Madagascar (a very bad mistake).

Struggling, Stack is heard muttering: 'I'm a Freud that this day that began so Jung is getting Adler and Adler . . .' Now Crompton is alone, he is changed, he is gone. A new person opens his eyes, considers life and finds it good. At last, he can strive for love, sex, money, god and still have time for several hobbies. What should he strive for first? He thinks about it but finds no answer, sees that there are many things to do, many reasons for doing and not doing. He considers. A presentiment of disaster comes over him. He cries out: 'Hey, fellows, are you still there? I don't think this one is going to work either.'

That's the Alchemical Marriage of Alistair Crompton by Robert Sheckley.

4

The Straight Roads

(1965–1975)

FAMILY SNAPSHOT   'Dear Friend, my name is Amos
Spiazzi. It is not easy for me to write this letter, but I am certain
that those who are my Friends and know me will be able to understand.' This letter was not in my father's papers: it came addressed
to me after his death. I read it often, turn it this way and that in
my hands, try to mix it with certain memories that blur into the
acid polaroid colours of my childhood, orangey red, ochre, the
cyan too light, overexposed. 'Everything ended without any explanation for so much dogged enmity, without one word of apology!
I should like to spend a few years in relative serenity, without any
ambitions or any desire for revenge, devoting myself to my family
and my studies.' It's a strange letter, its tone now off-hand, now
proud verging on haughty. The signature includes an aristocratic
title (Spiazzi di Corte Regia), and at the bottom of the letter is a
postal order 'for any contributions'. It represents a state of despair
and a cry for help. 'I have lost my Mother and my Wife, and my
children's future prospects have been damaged . . . I make bold to
request of the Friends who will receive this letter an act of solidarity that would save me from ruin.' But then the sum that each
Friend shall have to contribute is precisely specified, and so are the
payment methods and the precautions the recipient shall be forced

to adopt should the necessary sum not be raised. Military method, in grief as otherwise. That figures: emotion with dignity, uprightness, pride in one's duty done. The letter ends on an affectionate, heartfelt note. We had met him in Verona, where my father was serving at the Special Weapons Bureau of the FTASE command. A season of raised glasses, blonde nannies, lovestruck orderlies, parties with American officers and back-combed ladies, a season of mini-golf courses, children's soirées at the officers' circle, the army twelfth-night gifts wrapped in glitzy colours (a machine to make rubber monsters, crown of all my yearnings, gifted by an English lieutenant, a gentle and very beautiful woman who with good reason I decided I would remember all my life). Special Weapons: Dad was working with laser cannons, X-ray pistols, paralysing fluid—he was building barriers for space interceptors. NBC defence, nuclear, germ, chemical warfare: once I'd been allowed to watch a video showing the atomic mushroom, the wind lifting waves of earth at 100 mph, gentlemen with thick glasses sitting in ranked rows on chairs bolted to the floor.

My father disliked weapons: he took time to explain to me that his work was about making sure they'd never be used again, he told me about Hiroshima and Nagasaki, the flash that kills, the agony of those who didn't die immediately, the cancers gnawing the skin away, then the guts, then whatever's in the guts while you're still alive and die in full awareness. One evening many years later, when we were close again, while he was busy dying of the same death he'd told me about when I was a child and saving my life with the patient, religious effort of a dying parent, he told me a few things about that time in Verona, and revealed a secret: our Sunday trips. Often we'd get in the car with a couple of friends and drive over to Austria for the weekend: they'd tell me stories about trench warfare as we drove across the mountains—and then, on the other side, those green meadows and towns neat as boxed chocolates, ancient and perfect musical-box towns with clockwork men striking bells on church towers and pastry shops of chocolate and orange. Sometimes it rained or snowed, but we'd be off anyway, staying overnight in warm, mysterious hotels, mulled wine for the grown-ups and hot chocolate for me, what's not to like. We'd be stopping everywhere and taking photos: my father would get us out of the car, often right on the edge of the road with the guardrail as a background, wherever he or his colleague fancied, and they ranged us in a nice row, the wives and me, and click away. It was the time of the Cold War (my father smiles as he says that, almost apologetic with the kind detachment of his last years): Cold War—those were different times, you know, and we had to change the minefield locations on the border of the Warsaw Pact on a regular basis. Our holiday mission was to photograph the zones to be cleared and those that would be mined.

I've only got one of those photos left, with Mum smiling behind femme-fatale oval shades, a light scarf around her neck and her hand on my shoulder. I look very smart in a Mickey Mouse Club jacket, crest on the chest pocket, shorts, white socks and blue lace-up ankle boots. You can see there's a light breeze stroking us.

NAMES   The name of Colonel Spiazzi (or Major Spiazzi to me, back then) now belongs to the litany of Dad's colleagues, a vague music accompanying the memories of ageing children: my names are Marchisio, Ferraro, Spiazzi, Monastra, Scarchilli, Muzzi,

Basso, Gallino, Russo—names that crop up at the dinner table. Gallino says we should meet up for dinner one of these nights, Basso's got tickets for the match, maybe I'll take Pietrino. Ah yes, Monastra's son—*he's* doing well at school, isn't he.

The everyday life of an officer in those years: the money tight, overtime, relocations with the family in tow, a mechanism that knew nothing of settled life. We'd sometimes have to set up house where we'd stay for six months or a year at most, then up sticks again, new friendships, new habits, new memories even: What do I remember of Ostia? Walks with my mother to the Capitolium of ancient Ostia, with her telling me stories of the Romans, the warrior geese, and me counting gobs of spit on the seaside road. My mother, turned acrobat like all army wives, capable of making any old hole into a home and then giving it up with the same light-heartedness with which she'd laid out the temporary furniture, Swedish stuff in wood and metal that'd be light to carry all over the peninsula. Of Cesano I can remember the blinding green, up and down sloping meadows and those hugely tall trees against the sky, impassable thickets, and my father always rushing around. I only saw him when he was on leave, he'd take me up to a hill that seemed lost in the countryside behind our house and lift me up on his shoulders, and behind the green, far off, past sheep spotting the grass, I could see the sea like a low dust cloud. The sea that I hadn't expected would be there. My father was like a steam engine, hurling himself into the future with the strength of a young lad, and I knew he was a chief, the guy who taught soldiers how to fight a war.

For a few months we even lived in Rome: my great aunt from Colleretto had married a carabinieri marshal and, I don't know how, they had this large place where they'd go and weather the cold months. We settled there one spring, in that house with huge curtains where I'd spend my afternoons with the orderly, a soldier taken off barracks duties to make me play and pass the hours until the evening. My father could easily hurt people's feelings: once he told the orderly off for buying me a toy. Not to speak of how stern he got at Christmas time: his soldiers' mothers would send him presents that he would invariably return with a note—or, if they'd been delivered in person, a sermon on an officer's duties. Which embarrassed the hell out of my mother, who'd pretend to scold him for being made to give up all that bounty: bottles, hampers of fruit, even valuable antiques sometimes. Only once, as I recall, was she genuinely relieved at my father's strictness: he had sent back a dead pheasant with all its feathers still on.

We never saw Major Spiazzi after Verona. He was a kind man, as some of my aunts remember him, a man privy to certain secret stories that were daily bread to many officers whose sense of duty towards the fatherland was also the means to provide for their families' future.

SANAGOLA   And when we finally settled down in Turin, the world began to fall to pieces. One of the pieces was Maurizio. We'd grown up together by dint of fillet steaks (my mother would call them Auntie Laura's Special so I'd eat them) and Carosello before bed (we'd have a competition, who'd guess what was being advertised before the spot ended?). But now my uncle was being transferred to Florence, at the head of the Lupi di Toscana, and by the end of the year my cousins would be gone too. Very soon I would discover Scandicci, the banks of the Greve, and also a chessboard with green onyx pieces they'd bought for the new living room overlooking the Tuscan hills—don't know why I've never forgotten that chessboard. As they made their preparations to leave, the house filled up with boxes, rooms with the furniture shifted away, walls bared of their pictures: at the end of primary, year five, they'd be gone, and I thought I'd be feeling really lonely. Over those first days of warm sunlight after the winter, Maurizio and I had occupied the balcony with our armies: its white ledge, streamlined curves painted ochre, the drainpipe hole to spy into the yard—we'd even miss the fat, overbearing caretaker guy. And as we waited for this impending quake, we'd lash out and do our best and worst, inventing dangerous games like climbing the outer metal fences of the Citadel bastion, slipping into unknown houses to see what the loft doors were like, bunking off the afternoon catechism (but in winter it's so dark that you feel high as you would at night) to go and hide under staircases eluding the care-taker—sharp filter-tipped Nazionali Esportazione, their taste like bitter wood sticking to your palate, like chewing on the coffee table, and no inclination to breathe the smoke in. Maurizio is going away, soon the neighbourhood will be dark and empty. What counts is the thrill at the cigarette counter. The thrill: that's how I was beginning to leave behind the self that had failed to understand how De Luca could nick a Pelé footie card.

The thrill: we'd felt it for the first time over the Christmas holidays, in Salice d'Ulzio, under the ridges of the Genevris and in front of the ramparts at the top of the Chaberton, a frozen stone fountain with huge icicles, narrow paved lanes with puffy snow on the banisters, the glorious smell of fuels in the great garage under the block of flats where the band of brothers- and sisters-in-law would rent a small flat every year. A horde of cousins splashing around in the snow below the bedroom balcony, playing Russian retreat, drinking hot chocolate and especially waiting for the night, because we'd be put to bed in a small room with two bunk beds on one side and three, no less, on the other, stacked in a haphazard way like the steps of a staircase. And then it was whole half hours spent jumping from one castle-bunk to the other, and the beds were enemy strongholds and vertical labyrinths for pillow-fight ambushes. And then sliding into sleep while listening to the parents' voices as they play at a green baize table, low lamplight and a deck of fabulous images for their card game: bottles, flask, volcano, herald, castle. When are we going to Salice? For Christmas. And Christmas, thankgod, lasts a lifetime when you're ten.

But that year it was not enough: the older cousins were off towards some adolescence and their talk was of girls, forget pillow fights—and even Maurizio and I were having more fun in town by now, dodging caretakers and smoking filter-tips. Our job was to push a little bit further into the city with every outing, elbow our way in like you would at break time on a school day. One after-noon we'd made carnival costumes with my mother's clothes and smudged her make-up on our faces, and I'd felt a strange thrill at that time too, as if it were possible to be a girl as well, but off we go, raiding the drinks cabinet—there is one in every proper home, and mine was superb—and making a lethal red swill that we'd called negroni because of that name we'd always hear around the living room: Negroni, Carlo?—could do with a negroni—hold out, it's nearly negroni time—and we'd slugged it down at the risk of dropping dead and paid for it by an afternoon of puking and headaches, and then strolling around under the arcade with the images of passers-by and shop windows blurring on the surface of my eyes and Maurizio a little way ahead singing as he swerves and staggers along. Still not enough. So during one of our stays in Salice, when we'd been sent out to the shops, we went to the baccy counter. Maurizio was meant to distract the guy by messing around asking for cigarettes for the uncles—and I, who had spent days planning the robbery, I was standing there, my tongue curling back into my throat, staring at the candy-box pillar. A stack of small, colourful cuboids in all sorts of flavours. We were aiming for the gummy squares in a silver-foil tube called Caramelle Don: in the half-time break at the parish cinema there was this advert with a landscape of caves, all encrusted with crystals and stalactites made of Don, and we were feasting our eyes on those King Solomon's mines. I hated to let my cousin down, but I was truly paralysed. He'd twigged and we'd left empty-handed, but I was ashamed, so I rushed back into the shop, asked for a box of matches, and as the old, grey, bespectacled guy turned around I took down three packets of Sanagola—the amazing throat-salve candy, soft but chewy, strong tastes: mint, lemon and my favourite, pine. Three packets, all ours, free of charge. I was feeling slightly queasy. We'd started stealing, so now we could almost jump on a coach without ticket, for instance. This queasiness, though—prob-ably because of the pine flavour, the same as my father would buy me on Sunday afternoons when he took me to the Cravesana cinema, second row behind the narrow wooden balustrade, to watch through the smoke and mayhem of the young thugs in the front row the fabulous westerns that we—me and him—thought were to die for.

DARING AND DUTY   I might have found the nerve to steal, but still don't dare ask my father what he's scared of. At some point something broke, and my father got frightened: he lived through years that must have been a nightmare, he saw something he disliked and placed himself between us and the world, accepting fatigue and loneliness, fighting for real, I think, and the stakes in play were—ourselves, our peace, my right to a future. Once for school I interviewed him, and I chose my favourite subject: his work. My last question, formally addressed as they do in TV interviews: 'Would you do it again?' He smiled: 'No, I don't think I would—even though my ideals remain the same as when I started.' Written out in fair copy on the A4 exercise book with the blue cover. 8/9 out of 10—not bad at all. His fear in those years when I was leaving the arches and corridors of my primary school to walk across the modern town centre, business, cars, skyscrapers and glass fronts, to arrive at my fantastic secondary, a concrete cube with a gym in the basement, no more Savoy discipline, grey tiles instead of stucco, no right-about-turn to go to the toilet, no Signor Maestro but a squad of teachers with different voices and tics and habits—his fear in those years must have been as strong as the frightening serenity of his last days.

I liked family stories, the ones about Granddad crawling under a barbed wire fence on a stealth strike and being wounded in action during his days with the Arditi of the special force. I knew he had also trained in the force: 'Dad, can I do special force training too when I grow up?' That time he got really upset, made me swear I'd never say a word about that again, either to him or anyone else, and where had I heard those words?

'What words?'

'Special force.'

'Oh—I don't know—from you, I think . . .'

'Impossible—not from me. So then?'

'From Mum.'

I immediately rued that confession: I could tell by his face that I'd just grassed on Mum, and now she was in trouble.

THRILLER   That time of the promise about the special force training must have been one of the last times I ever called him Dad: in secondary school I was getting more sensitive to people's opinions, feeling judged and inadequate, scared of girls, and suddenly here they were in my class, even sitting next to me, like this girl whose school bag had broken once and I'd fixed it for her and she'd said: 'Smashing' and I'd gone around all week repeating that word, 'Smashing', all the grown-ups cracking up and Uncle Beppe calling on the phone and asking 'How's Smashing?' He was my father's best friend, a guy who'd had no children but was perfectly happy with me, he'd teach me the secrets of football and laugh quietly at my stories about schoolmates. He was full of wrinkles but charming, a Fenoglio or a John Wayne, a country man landed in the city as the foreman of a maintenance unit at FIAT. He and my dad understood each other even over things my father would rather not say, either to himself or to Christian the hairdresser, or perhaps even to my mother. Now I think my father was relieved when my interest in all things military faded away: he loved me without words, got into my stories just when I began to realize it might no longer be a good idea to share them with him. I was conscious of the need to take on a tone of sorts, and decided it would be useful to have more spirited monikers for my parents. I couldn't find one for my mother, but I did for him: Guv'nor. From that day onward, I called him Guv'nor, and began to breathe a bit more freely.

That was a tricky year: end of primary school, Maurizio gone, my father sullen and withdrawn. Now and then he'd take me to his office, mostly leaving me in the care of a sedulous lance corporal who'd teach me to touch-type and initiate me to the mysteries of shorthand: but sometimes he'd take me on a tour of the auto-fleet park where he was king, or the workshops, though he never let me get into the high-speed 'gazelles'. I was cultivating evening reading and thoughts of girls, one was thin and dark and had played me something on her slot-in record player, ah yes, it was about kung fu and yes, my problem was to get permission to go out on a Saturday night and watch a kung fu movie. Still, at dinner, the evening news were punctuating our time like the beads of a rosary in an unchallenged ritual. My father was riveted to the news and Mum and I would make fun of him: as soon as Mario Pastore said 'Good evening' the house was expected to plunge into religious silence. But if I asked for any explanations, which happened more and more rarely, then my father would light up as if I'd given him the chance to recover the lost time he had not been able to spend with me. The evening news was our secret garden. He would explain the story of a judge they'd tried to murder. There had been a campaign in support of that epileptic dancer, remember? Of course I do—and of one of his friends who'd killed himself by jumping out of a window while being questioned at the police station in Milan. And this judge was in agreement with those who'd started the campaigns. You mean he thought the dancer was innocent? That's right. My mother had some strange ways, she had sorted herself out with one opinion and wasn't going to change it, so that kind of talk bothered her, sometimes she had even argued with Dad: she thought he was filling my head with quandary and that could frighten me, or worse. But a question from me would warm his heart, and I knew that. So, this judge—his name was Alessandrini, and he also thought the dancer might have had nothing to do with the bomb at the bank, and said that could have been the work of some secret service or other, forget dancers. So he got a bomb set outside his house, by the SAM. Squadre d'azione Mussolini. I'd heard of the Torino FC action squads, and as a Juventus supporter, I was ready to be against them. But the judge had survived the attack, and so they went and killed the chief of police, and now, as Dad explained, there was a search on for the killer, over in Switzerland.

This was cool—like a thriller: an innocent man under accusation, a hero investigating, a mysterious killer, a brave policeman who gets murdered. How will it all end?

'It will end with the judge being killed too.'

'That's enough now, Francesco!'

But that was our garden, and the story of the judge was a sort of secret pact between us. We'd watch the evening news with the faces of two kids telling each other a bedtime story.

FORTE FOIN   He had not foreseen he would be a widower, could not even have imagined it, what with his wife so much younger, so full of life. He was sure that at the right moment he'd be able to leave her all his instructions for later. But she was the one to go first, and in such a horrible way that he used up all his remaining time finding a way to disbelieve it and to imagine there would be another chance. It was surprise that did for him, even more than the grieving that would gnaw away his last years. And from that moment onward he stopped caring for anything, least of all living. That's why those documents I used to sneakily read as a child are still here, with me. I've never had the courage to throw them out. I'll read you some.

Commission C, Psychological Strategy Board, 1951: Covert Actions (Extracts). I wonder if my father ever thought this would end up in my hands. 'Progressive steps to remove communists from administrative positions in government ministries, in schools and in universities. Step up discrimination against firms employing communist manpower. Specific actions either administratively or through legislation to deprive the communist party of its material resources in Italy. This might include steps for the curtailment of assistance to communist-controlled co-operatives and export–import firms which contribute financially to the party. The US will work to discredit the communist party and prominent communist organizations and figures by undermining the party's respectability, compromising communists in public positions, discrediting communist efforts during the world war, inflating scandals involving PCI leaders.'

There's also the booklet by the American general, remember? Its title: Field Manual 30–31, Gen. Westmoreland, 18 March 1970. Listen to this: 'While counterinsurgence operations are usually and preferably conducted in the name of freedom, justice and democracy, the US government allows itself a wide range of flexibility in determining the nature of a regime deserving its full support. There may be times when host country governments show passivity or indecision in the face of communist subversion and react with inadequate vigor to intelligence estimates transmitted by US agents. Such situations are particularly likely to arise when the insurgency seeks to achieve tactical advantage by temporarily refraining from violence. US intelligence must have the means of launching actions which will convince HC governments and public opinion of the reality of the insurgent danger and of the necessity of counteraction. US Army services should seek to penetrate the insurgency by means of agents on special assignment with the task of forming special action groups among the more radical elements of the insurgency. These groups should be used to launch violent or non-violent actions according to the nature of the case. In cases where the infiltration of such agents into the insurgent leadership has not been effectively implemented, it may help towards the achievement of the above ends to utilize ultra-leftist organizations.'

And the Red Hands booklet. Author: Agency D, no name. A stapled, hand-written note: 'Return to Stef.' It would be interesting to return this now. Listen up: 'Any violation committed by the communists, for instance gaining entry into a "new government majority" or worse still penetrating, even if only with a communications undersecretary, into a ministerial cabinet, would constitute such a grave act of aggression as to warrant the deployment of a total defence plan. Which is to say, the direct, decisive and definitive intervention of the Armed Forces.'

Wait, one last one—the scariest. An army-style memo, no wasted words, no other title than precisely that: Memo. And underneath: 'Services Office, IV dept., V Comiliter, m. 8930/10200.

Subject: directives for delivery of materials and their return'. Another hand-written note: 'No trainer personnel'. Many acronyms: 'RM56, RVM, delivery no. 1 electrical generator, vehicle CL52, no. 8 pieces dept. RM radio equipment, no. 1 RVM piece, no. 1 comb. outfits. Aug 4–20, location Forte Foin. Order observation 1 off. & 2 non-coms. Depot Mar. Di. Chi., auth. inventory materials no later than August 22, 1970'. Handwritten on a separate note: 'ord. Francia Salvatore.'

Forte Foin. Aggressoria. This is my home.

SIEVE   My father's been dead for five years. I'm holding his papers in my hands, and as you can imagine I'm trying to decipher what I've left of him. Now I think that on those news-watching nights I might have asked him about the mystery of his fear. But I was already running off elsewhere. The fact is, my new school was fantastic—no, smashing: the concrete cube had been placed on the same square as a chubby-cheeked baroque church, with domes, rounded steps, a couple of those metal fences that'll keep you from ending up under a tram, and then the tram line, a double track running from the arcade to where a bunch of us would be sitting on the steps. It was near Porta Palazzo, a dangerous place where some of my new schoolmates came from. They were tough and full of sly charm, and after only a few weeks there was a group of three or four of us walking the walk together: a gang, the new crime kings—Roll over Al Capone, you're done.

But I still had a little time for him, in the evenings: a famous publisher was blown up under a high-tension pylon, another anarchist died in custody in Pisa, one evening they showed a banker who'd been named by the president 'the saviour of our lira' and described by the Pope as 'the man of divine providence'. That evening, my father had taken his head in his hands. And then the explosive Cinquecento that had killed three carabinieri. I thought, 'I got it—he's got good reason to be scared if they're killing carabinieri.' But he had other things on his mind. He'd been talking of a sieve—'Operation Sieve', I think. It sounded like a film title. His boss, Marchisio, had personally assessed the profiles of five hundred people and sent reports to the judges. Five hundred left-wing militants. He didn't like that, he was talking about it with Uncle Beppe: 'Look, we've got five hundred and ten National Front regulars armed to the teeth, five hundred and ten jail-birds in our pay ready to shoot anything that moves, and we're breathing down students' neck?'

'Well, but Macchiarini—'

'Get away! We've loads of men at SIT and FIAT, too. Audino has eight more to enrol, did you know?'

'Tough guy, Audino. Whereabouts?'

'In all departments. So these guys who've kidnapped Macchiarini—we can get them whenever we like.'

Engineer Macchiarini of SIT Siemens had been caught one day at 7 p.m.: they'd held him at gunpoint and photographed him with a sign hanging from his neck: 'Fascist—tried by the Red Brigades. The proletariat has taken up arms, this is the beginning of the bosses' end.' Uncle Beppe said he must have got frightened, but my father was pretty much laughing in his face: 'Look, you know he'd dropped his watch when they got him? They sent it back to his house. These are good guys—no match for our lot.'

He keeps hearing the drums, doing his duty with this city's working-class tenacity. And watching TV, and thinking of the Sieve that scares him. And trains start blowing up again, four bombs in Calabria that same autumn.

OBSIDIAN   Those bombs on the trains just wouldn't stop cropping up, we'd all pretty much got used to them, taking trains nonetheless. The judge my father liked had begun to prosecute officers and policemen. It was only a short time since the day when my mother had come to my school so we could see the results of my first year at secondary. I was strutting my pride down the street, I thought it was plain to see I was no longer at primary. We'd celebrated with ice-cream from Pepino on Piazza Carignano, because my new school was also near the part of town that had been planned around the castles, the black churches and the arcades near Piazza Carignano. Mum had just been to Mexico on a package tour organized by the company where one of my aunts worked. She had no money, so my aunt had offered to lend her some and have it back in instalments. Dad was against it but she was burning, feverish to go: she'd read up on everything before leaving and would tell me about the Precolombians (what a word, full of vertiginous downward slopes) and Olmec Toltec Zapotec Totonac, just like she'd done with the stories about Livy when we were in Ostia, with my father at the Cecchignola military school. For as long as she could, that strange woman built word bridges to reach out to me, even in my wildest years: precisely at the time of my most corrosive revolts, and in an almost casual manner, that ignorant woman would pass on books she'd held on to all her life: like the story of the sick boy who pleasured himself by pressing his thighs together while watching the images in a magic lantern. The ancient American people kept me going in every field: history, geography, Italian, arts & crafts, even—a fretwork Chichen Itza pyramid instead of a Far West fort. Back from her wondrous journey, she gave me some black obsidian heads that would turn green or yellow if I looked at them sideways. I placed them on my bedroom shelf.

Now there were girls in my class: not that I'd annexed them to my empire, but—well, I could see them all day every day, their legs under the desks, the way they dressed, the way they moved their feet. And the boys from Porta Palazzo or thereabouts: my favourite was Elio Mandrone. His father was a caretaker, a massive guy in charge of a block with gates and stairways and six court-yards, so big and labyrinthine that once in the eighteenth century they'd put all the town Jews in there, and they had lived there, holding markets and being born and dying behind those gates where now Mandrone Sr was locking up at night.

With these new friends I would conquer new streets: we'd go and see Sesca, the guy in the front desk, who lived in Syria or Turkey—you had to take the No. 50 bus to the end of the line, the city's edge, and across there's a square with a road in the mid-dle that's almost a motorway, and nothing beyond that but the horizon. That sort of place, you have to allow three quarters of an hour to get there, because the bus is slow and you always end up drenched in sweat, no matter that it's winter. And we'd spend our afternoons drawing cowboy comics or talking about football or Ferrari. Discovering earthly pleasures, the modern city, no longer lost in dreams of castles or endless pampas but taking things apart: all the fantastic constructs of childhood coming down one after the other—draw a cowboy and he'll lose his halo, Father Christmas is dead, the street can be dominated and it's even easy to get into the cinema on our own. With Sesca & Mandrone we'd go and see adult movies full of things collapsing and breaking apart and breaking open and bursting into flames, full of sinking ships and nosediving planes, and sometimes there were women in miniskirts lying on a male's bed. I remember L'Emmerdeur, The Pain in the Ass—yes of course we'd gone because of the title, and What's Up, Doc? on advice from my mother, though I'd never tell the gang that. After the obsidian trip, my mother had started this beauty parlour (but it called itself a salon) in a courtyard in the town centre, a modern and modernible place with little gardens planted inside cement beds under cement arches where you'd go up & down cement staircases. It was not far from my new school, near a skyscraper—well all right, it's fourteen floors, but that's a lot in our parts, and then it's got a gallery with windows full of those lava tubes with colourful bubbles going up & down and bunches of metal wires tipped with little lit-up spheres. Past the skyscraper there's a street heading straight into the hill, nondescript facades, you think, but look again and you risk getting swallowed up by a dark church, a level slab of funeral marble, lopsided statues, red tapers, shade, one of those monsters camouflaged in the symmetrical ranks of the facades of Turin—standing there on the pavement, looking innocent, and now and again gobbling up a passer-by. If you manage to get past it, you'll find my mother's futuristic oasis, next to a shop selling the cool furniture that's fashionable these days: it's like A for Andromeda, starships parked in the square of sky between buildings. The salon was called 'The Tube', and it lived up to its name:

the walls were dotted with round see-through holes of varying diameters in day-glo colours, ceilings hung with huge springs that uncoiled to the floor and you had to walk between them. There was a beautician, Monica, Christian the hairdresser who was a founding partner, and my mother who did massage, and I did my homework there with Monica's help and learnt the art of fixing backaches, but more importantly learnt my way around by walking.

And then, no more Signor Maestro but a teacher for each subject: the first year we only had this lady in a black pinny, she was big and tall but I don't remember much about her, one of these people trying to convince you that the only things that matter are found in the classroom. And then you look out of the window. Soon, I don't know how, everything changed: young new teachers, strange guys—the strangest of the lot does maths and science, says 'I couldn't care less' all the time, says he's a failed architect, smokes stinking stuff that clings to his moustache, but he's a street-cred devil. You know what, class? You won't get a mark in science this year unless you bring a proper project—serious stuff, OK? And you'll have to work on it by going out there (he points at the window, there where I'd be looking if I wasn't looking at the girls' ankles, just where the black-pinny lady never looked)— you mean with a film camera, sir? Can we do a film project? Good idea—what'll your film be about? Dunno—science, like. . . Look kids, science is in the street, in people's heads—that's right, go up to a few people with your camera and ask them what science is, and what science they might have in their heads and what they are experts in, and film their faces nicely, then go into the city and find out where experiments are made, film the landscapes, then you bring me the lot, and if I like the film, you'll get a pass. Fantastic. So we make this group—Mandrone, Prette, Vivalda, Sesca, Lucco & I, and off we go. Once we even get to the top floor of the skyscraper, on the roof terrace, with the caretaker's baffled face. 'It's for a school project—can you take us up?' And from up there Turin really does look like a film, and then we burrow into the basements of the chamber of commerce, in halls with microphone booths for simultaneous translation, and we scurry off among the legs of busy men and women. But then it was true that he couldn't care less, it was clear from the outset that he'd never watch the film—never mind, he'd given us an escape route. Ta muchly, sir. And yet another escape route came from the PE teacher, who'd realized volleyball was boring and so started teaching us other games—mostly handball. We had set up this team and went to train every afternoon at Sesca's or Vivalda's, on those outer limits where the city doubles over between houses that look all alike when you drive past them, where streets are named after musicians and green buses go by in a diagonal line. We'd stay there sweating it out at handball until the light turned violet and the tram headlights came on, we dreamt about winning a tournament, and the music was exploding. I never cared about it before, but now it was important to know a thing or two about the hit parade, Afric Simone or Carl Douglas, and sing a bar or two on the bus so if anyone hears they'll see you know your stuff. And the most dangerous of all was the Italian teacher, Signora Giannese. Because of her young-old face, because of her small, clear, piercing eyes and because she'd invite us to her house to discover the books on her shelves: all right, we had to read Fontamara, but after hearing her we read Bread and Wine and even Emergency Exit, and in one go, snatched from the home bookshelves and read belly down eating reinettes, because she was nudging us to dig and find out about things, she gave us confidence, made us feel grown up. She was mixing literature with the world, Manzoni with the evening news, and certain Black poets whose grandparents had been slaves, and into our heads went Governor Faubus and Mingus and translations of Bob Dylan's lyrics, North Country Blues, and Woody Guthrie, and so we were beginning to see beyond the film, America falling wide open and huge outside the screen. Signora Giannese would open her house to us in the afternoon and address us like grown-ups, and she too at last was handing us a key—or rather, a wrench: if all is well, you can use it to loosen nuts & bolts, and if not, bring it down edgeways, and get cracking.

TRACKS   Let me tell you how I was running in those days. I'd get up early, guzzle a load of black tea as breakfast, then rush out to school. Around that time someone had learnt the trick of phoning in with a bomb alert—not us, we weren't that smart yet. Anyways you'd have to wait a couple of hours or more on the pavement between the church, the tram and the stairway before they'd let you into the gym or send you back home. In which case Mandrone, Sesca, Lucco & I would work on expanding our bit of city, out towards San Secondo or Vanchiglia. I'd run to school every morning hoping for the bomb. Hardly ever: so up the regulation four floors, and sit down next to my mate Zaccaria. Signora Giannese would come in with a newspaper, and one morning a policeman had killed the student Franceschi—bullet after bullet, not just one, not by mistake. And one April morning in Milan, during a fascist demo, a policeman called Marino had been killed: the MSI secretary said this was the final clash with communism, the PCI secretary condemned the adventurist left-wing and the Christ-Dem secretary revealed there was an international right-wing plot to sink Italy. And hardly three days later, she called us after the break and she had the radio on: during the night they had gone and burnt down the house of a street cleaner called Mattei who was secretary of the MSI section called Giarabub ('Down on your knees, cameleer'). Two rooms plus kitchen in the Borgata Primavalle, petrol under the door, fire. Of Signor Mattei's six children, all had got out except the eldest and the youngest, a twenty-two-year-old lad and a child of eight. Stefano and Virgilio. They'd huddled close, giving each other courage until the end, Stefano hugging Virgilio's knees with a child's fear, Virgilio at the window—this can't be happening, no one doing anything—and then they'd died. I'd get back home, with Crovella & Lucco, stopping off for bread in Via San Francesco, nicking chocolate bars and biscuits, sometimes the baker lady would spot us and we'd have to run. Back home, the news was of a student stabbed to death or one dying from a teargas canister that had hit him in the forehead, and in May the anarchist Bertoli had thrown a bomb outside Milan central police station and killed four people, except then it looked like he was not an anarchist but maybe from the secret services—and my father sullen, silent—and a day labourer from Forlì beaten to death by a fascist bruiser, and a guy running off with a bomb in Reggio Calabria but falling and the bomb going off in his belly, and a charge laid on the tracks of the Milan–Ventimiglia line at Locate Triulzi, a derailment at 80 mph, the evening news speaking of a miracle. There was no time to stay home for long, PE twice a week at 2.30, so gobble something and off again—Did you hear? They've arrested Colonel Spiazzi—but he's a good man, they've got the wrong sort of guy! After PE there's a food riot in the Murate prison in Florence, police go in and start shooting, one dead, four wounded. All right, Mum, I'll go and buy you fags. A street seller killed in Varese by a bomb signed Ordine Nero, which will turn out later to be a state corps. Fags—yuk, I pick them up with my sweater sleeve pulled over my hand so I won't have to touch them (something wrong with that kid), ah, the good guys are out again, this time they got a judge in Genoa, after that it's children's TV but it gets interrupted by a special edition, a voice saying, 'Please stay away from the stage, please.' Brescia, a bomb during a union rally, eight dead, ninety-four wounded, a terrorist slaughter, they say—fascist slaughter, they say—state slaughter, they also say, I go to scouts club, yes by myself, the route is lined with all my childhood memories, I sniff around and look at shop windows, and at Pian di Rascino the carabinieri find a paramilitary camp and there's a shootout, one of the camp guys dies, by the time it gets dark two more fascists are killed in Padua in an MSI section, forget the good guys, this is the Red Brigades, this is blood, at dinner time a left-wing sympathizer is stabbed to death in Rome, in Enna a fascist stabbing kills Vittorio Ingria. First course, twelve dead, a hundred and four wounded—the Italicus, a train running along the Apennines, that was lucky. What do you mean lucky? Well it was meant to go off inside the tunnel and then there'd have been—how many dead? Pass the salt—Fabrizio Caruso, aged nineteen, a squatter in empty houses in Rome, killed like a dog, meanwhile in Lamezia Terme a fascist shoots at random and kills Adelchi Agrada, no time to count the wounded, it's the cheese board, there's a shootout with the Red Brigades and Marshal Felice Maritano is left dead, I'll skip the pudding, how can you eat pudding? There's a general on trial and Kissinger on a visit to Italy, rumour has it the heads of the PCI are not sleeping at home that night, you never know, but can I watch Carosello at least? Fanny Dallari, from Savona, aged eighty-two, killed by a bomb from Ordine Nero, beddie-byes now, school and swimming tomorrow, always in the pool, always that black strip underwater that takes me to one end and then somersaulting and away to the other end, in Savona a farmer is rushing straight at a train, waving frantically, screaming, weeping, and the engine driver gets it and pulls hard on the brakes, a lot of people injured but the Ordine Nero guys will be furious, because they'd set a bomb on the tracks and that farmer saw it and stopped the slaughter.

THE CHIEF　　But in the meantime my father was relaxed: he'd got a new commander, a smart guy, he was always talking about him. My father always swore as if in the barracks, and that's why we kids loved him, and he was back on form, in good cheer, an idol even to our great cousin Vittorio, who would put up little skits for him and allow Poldo the dog to bite his backside, but in a way as would make it clear he was running the show. About his chief, my father said he was a great big piece of shit—but he said that in a friendly way. His name was Carlo Alberto—he probably really thinks he's the king, runs the legion like clockwork, brings a breath of fresh air and squeezes the last drop out of everyone down to the flying squad drivers, he yells and sometimes humiliates people, but knows everyone by name and looks at them straight in the eye. And my father stops seeing strange things everywhere, he is reborn and works like a demon, gets back home very late in the evenings and says, 'He's a real officer.' He'd stopped taking me to the office: General Dalla Chiesa would not allow a kid to buzz around him, let alone around the workshops or car-fleet parks, and my father made it up to me by taking me to the Salone dell'Automobile in the spring or the Cravesana cinema on Sundays. To hear my father talk, the legion looked like a fort ready for war, and from his tone I could understand that this was the clean war he was ready to fight. Against the Black Prince? Run along, matey, what are you talking about? In the whisky & negroni living room the talk was of divorce and the Christ-Dems' troubles, and that divorce referendum really was changing Italy, and sometimes I'd stick around, not spying any more but busy being a grown-up, and they'd ask me about school and the swimming.

The man of divine providence, Filippo—water under the bridges by now. And one evening Mum had been invited to dinner by the general's wife—a ladies' evening for the girl she was, catapulted into life too soon as a wife and mother, as a Seventies woman, and then into a coffin at fifty, her face a grimace. Signora Dora Dalla Chiesa was hosting a reception—orchestra and cocktails—and Mum had accepted the invitation, taking a few days to steel herself before the impact with a world for which she was not ready. Signora Dora loved to show up differences, and had given a small present to each of the visiting wives, in descending order according to military or social rank. For my mother, a small box of painted cardboard—like a snuff box, but fake. Empty. In the hallway, the signora had noticed my mother's coat, the only woollen one. 'Not wearing your fur coat, signora?' And my mother had countered: 'Well, we have a saying in these parts— Keep furs and gloves tidied away / until the feast of All Saints' Day.' She was lying: the proverb says 'muffs and gloves', not 'furs and gloves'. But it was October anyway, and that time she'd been quick enough.

CAPRANICO   She was getting fed up by now with her beauty parlour, had been on another trip on my aunt's company scam: New York this time, Cary Grant crossing the road in front of a grand hotel, the top of the Empire State Building, a hippy T-shirt and bi-coloured flares for me, and a guy in Piazza San Carlo stopping me and begging me to tell him where I'd got them. She got an idea: Could she make her useless old diploma work? Yes she could: there might be a long application process but it would be possible for her to become an arts & crafts teacher. I had enjoyed my spring- and winter-time Sunday walks and was hoping they'd never come to an end; my father was at work: each to his or her own. Only once had I seen my father's face as dark as before. He'd just come back from a week's hard work in Alessandria: there had been a revolt in the prison, and the general had led the operation in person, with Dad in charge of the car fleet as usual—but he said the cars had come back with blood stains, that they'd slaughtered people in there, that because it all happened behind the prison walls no one would see it, no one would even think of calling it a slaughter. But I'd stopped talking to him or listening, I don't know why. It's not like I loved him any less, but a girl in school had told me I wouldn't be too bad if I'd been less of a babby, and especially in school everyone had started with that terrible game of slaps on your balls: they'd wait for you behind a door or the blackboard and whack, a hand landing hard on your crotch—horribly painful, and all you can do is react in the same way. There were ambushes, if you get caught by four or five of them they'll throw you down, one of them grabs your box and until you whistle the jingle from Carosello they'll not let go—you try getting through that jingle. Constantly on the alert, bruises on your balls—boys will be boys. My mother was annoyed because of a colleague in the new school at Mirafiori Sud, Strada delle Cacce, where she'd been dispatched (a rookie, and so straight to the worst place)—a guy called Capranico who'd make fun of her bourgeois qualms.

My father's mood was following sine waves. He still took a soldier's passionate interest in the news, but I kept to myself, mostly. Remember the judge, Alessandrini? He's just indicted a general, and now he's breathing on the bankers' neck. My father was watching the trials on TV and he recognized certain faces as they flashed on the screen: 'Look at that—the expert—remember him? Dantini! The Chinese-posters guy!' I'd say the news made him anxious. But then he'd really got into what was happening in America: there had been a scandal involving no less than President Nixon, the guy who'd played table tennis with Mao Zedong and sent the first men on the moon, a household name, as familiar as Mike Bongiorno. Well, he'd had some political adversaries spied on, bugging the rooms of a grand hotel. It was called Watergate, probably because (as you could see on TV) it was shaped like a broken circle, like the toilet seat in a water closet. I saw my father laugh at the news of the captains' revolution in Portugal: 'Let's see what Mario will do now,' he'd said. General Vito Miceli, head of secret services, under inquest for the coup, for the slaughter, for perverting the course of justice, serenely looks at Judge Alessandrini and says: 'Right-wing terrorism is finished. From now on you'll only ever hear about the Red Brigades.' My father roars: 'Yeah, right! When they're all in jail!'

Meanwhile, I was gearing up for the secondary school finals, then the Argentario holidays with Ruben and Dino, then high school. The city was mine by now, I knew the long roads that bisect it from north to south, knew my way around them. I knew the secrets of the ghettos: the Vallette, Via Artom, and the one hidden behind the railway tracks under the Mauriziano Bridge, Via Arquata—you can get in, but as for getting out, who knows. One of the first blocks has a message daubed on it: 'God created the world, but he forgot hell. So we have Via Arquata.' And then, the myth: Shanghai. The name is spoken in hushed tones, it's a well-kept secret, a corral of huge blocks on Via Bologna enclosed behind bars, with a few entryways guarded by dangerous gangs. You don't go into Shanghai, but you're someone just by knowing where it is: my mother says she's levelled a little local yokel in her class just by saying: 'My son hangs out in Shanghai.'

Straight roads, so long that you can see the horizon on bright days. They start from the town centre and reach as far as Nice, Milan and France, or Leningrad. They run parallel to the Mirafiori, Lingotto and Rivalta assembly lines, and parallel to them run the lives of Turin. Head north and you get to the Falchera, where the houses huddled together by the motorway have no water or electricity or even sewers, but the people who have squatted there don't seem to mind. The carabinieri are getting ready to attack the Falchera, but one evening it's a sworn security guard who sorts it out: he takes his pistol and shoots a squatter in the face, a

25-year-old called Tonino Micciché—a proper terrone name, right, Mum? We'd laughed at the terrone name, Micciché—and they say they're from Turin.

By the way, the Black Prince: he'd died—in Spain, I think, or Latin America. Killed by his friends with a poisoned coffee.

SUBJECT: NOW   The supercomputer is ready, it will serve all the galaxies with its superior intelligence. Billions of planets connected to witness the inauguration, and a scientist throws the lever that starts it. Then he jokes: 'Let's ask it the most difficult question—does God exist?' The supercomputer starts buzzing, the clouds burst open and a voice thunders: 'He does now.' The scientist understands and lunges towards the lever, but a bolt of lightning from the sky turns him to ash.

5

Zero Theorem

(1978)

ANTIMONY FUMES   Once I had this dream, in the hour of deepest sleep. First, Marina's face, with the expression it took on when she was relishing the peak of the union between two bodies, hers and mine. Her eyes feverish, greedy, her face distorted, elongated and slanted forward in a smile that opens her jaws, a sweaty grimace of complicit joy. And with that look I know well on her face, she's gazing at something she holds in her hands: something alive, wet from her body—and she's astonished, ravenous, fulfilled. Warm light and her laugh, the astonishment on her face as she looks at the newborn just come from inside her, stretching her arms out the better to see him. She is strong as she never was in life. And the newborn's hair is streaming out in all directions, bright and lively as a crown.

Five in the morning—nearly daybreak. I got there by crossing a gloomy night made of fitful sleep and grim, base-line dreams, then my belly kept me awake. In the milky blur of the kitchen, I meet Marina's ghost. I'm coming from a dust road among pine trees, howitzer fire, someone saying it's dangerous over there. It's raining and I'm heading into the line of fire: there is an arcade, and a coffin on trestles. Next to it, a plastic bag with the dead person's things, and the things speak clearly: in the coffin is my mother. 'Why did she come out?' 'They're taking her somewhere else.' Hell, this is my mother, I can't very well send her away like this, alone like a dog: I've to stay awake and follow her. And then my mother walks into the kitchen, she's turned grey and comes to quench her thirst, cancers inside her body that she's still unaware of. 'Not sleeping?' That's my fucking business, I think. For a while with Marina I'd been dreaming of a house, dreaming of us setting up home, we were dreaming of it even as we failed to invent the days that would fill it.

But now Marina is looking at me with rings around eyes that are open way too wide, and she says she also wants it. What do you mean, you also want it? I want what she has: I never had you in that way. What are you saying, what does 'I never had you' mean anyway, what the fuck are you talking like this for? I want you in the same was as she's had you, and she's kissing me and touching me and it's a while before I understand what she wants, though not why she wants it. She's turned greedy, her nose that I used to like because of its broken line is long now, her tired skin clinging to the septum bone, she's hungry and her eyes are feverish. She is demanding I prove something to her, my female side, she wants to keep me there, halfway, in her hands. Giuliana has had me as she had primed me in the house at the Argentario. I bristle at this orgy of the verb to have. She is seized by a need for possession, wants to live off me and continue to run, and has seen in the white tunic I wore that early summer the way to hold on to me. Her skin is cold, and when she's off guard this strange, half-grieved expression slips out and stretches her face like a bird's beak, it's the face of one who's on the run from a hunting party, who has not eaten and is scared of not getting to finish her meal.

This is how New Year's Day found us, the thousand friends from last spring gone, we are clinging on to a dream of normality and quasi-family set in Milan, the capital of myth, and plunged in a degraded carnal whirligig, she wants me to call her by Giuliana's pet names, paints my face, deforms my body to mirror herself in it, each of our encounters is catwalk and pantomime. Post-coital, our dreams of a quasi-bourgeois future spring up, we imagine Milan simply because Milan is not there, we eat to get our strength back, imagine our weekdays in our future Milan, she will do massage for accident victims, I who knows, but every night we'll make love until sleep comes. And then out in the street I'm ashamed, travel back home feeling empty and scared of myself on the No. 50 bus crossing the Dora downstream from the factories, where the mangey riverbank is the home patch of stubborn old sex workers tipping the scales at around two hundredweight. Grey heaps of snow along the road, watching the pavement draw lines as it files past.

Giuliana knows nothing of all this, she'll not ask, stay outside, determined to follow my every turn no matter how snaky, until habit will have grown bones for this skeleton, and then we'll look at each other and say 'So, how long have been together?' and she'll be able to say in a natural tone, 'For ever, haven't we?' with a smile that also means, 'forever more'. That's Giuliana's way: she just lets it happen. I'm thinking that this spring the movement will regain all its awesome strength and then we'll tear the world down, all we have to do is wait.

We celebrated the new year on the No. 50 bus, Marina and I—coming back from the cinema, she's talking of a pair of sandals she wants to buy, we say happy new year to the driver who replies wearily and can't wait to come off shift, and we're looking for a heavenly sign in the year that slips away on the bus.

Inside the city encased in her glass egg, some experiments were attempted: badly mixed organic and mineral masses are reacting together. During the patient work of transmutation, gases are released that no wisdom can harness—antimony fumes, arsenic traces. For the compound to be produced, the egg must needs be entered by death: this is the via regia along which some substances will remain inert for ever. But if, as may happen, death overcomes, then the work will be death work. The city is sombre in the wide-open autumn, the shadows of buildings weigh on the pavements, street doors are swallowing those who move without caution and sometimes not returning their prey. In the stone blocks, spaces and tunnels open for fugitives to find shelter, under-stairs in a luxury hallway, wells inside back yards, corridors between lofts, secret flowerbeds huddled against huge boundary walls, trackways gone to ground between forlorn ballast beds. The gas passes through these conduits, into the veins of small bodies that have lost their way and are doomed to fall into the holes and not get up again. Inside the mass of stone and flesh that simmers slowly, everything continues as before, solve et coagula: it's a slow process. But in the meantime, the substances from the death work are separated, and settle inert at the poles of the compound—lead and arsenic. Billy has disappeared, Igor is pale, Albertino is saying: 'Make history without me.'

FIAT has launched a New Machine, it's called robogate: a complete system for the automatic movement of parts. Automatic. It will pick up the metal sheets and place them along the line that will process them into cars. It seems capable of choice, incapable of error.

TINY MAGGOTS (2)   Can you hear the noise of a typewriter at night from the flat next door? Can you hear steps in the loft? Has anyone been coming to work with a strange expression on their face? There's a questionnaire being circulated in town, the brainchild of the district president, of the mayor, of Mr Ferrara: 'Do you wish to flag up any actual facts that would help magistrates and the forces of law and order to identify those who perpetrate terrorist attacks, crimes and aggressions?' As in, report your neighbour—distributed in twelve thousand copies. Thirty-five replies, twelve thousand beating about the bush, the city is squirming. One afternoon in December, four unmasked people break into the town centre surgery where the statute-barred consultant Giorgio Coda has resumed his private practice. A building with some figurative airs and graces streamlined by twentieth-century taste, marble hallway and globe lamps, double street door, glass door, buzzer. They get him down on his knees, lock his secretary and one client in the toilet, tie him spreadeagled to a radiator and shoot three 7.65 calibre bullets into him—right shoulder, left shoulder, left kneecap. On the way out they hang a sign from the consultant's neck: 'The proletariat will not forgive its torturers.' In medical terminology, a child who wets the bed is said to suffer from enuresis. Doctor Coda cures that with prolonged electric shocks to the genitals and the brain. He uses the same cure for alcoholism and catatonia. He also works in experimental research, electrifying corpses to see if they will bounce.

'It can't have been him.'

'No—but they did it for him.'

MALE FETISHISM   'Comrades, this is not about questioning one practice versus another: it's about a transformation of collective praxis, and it would be absurd to focus on any one circumstance. That would be a form of fetishism—in reverse perhaps, but still fetishism, even in exclusion.'

Run that by me again? As looks go, she's got the looks, no doubt about it—and you can tell she knows. She'll stare into the distance as she speaks. She'll listen to any objection: sooner or later, for instance, Johnny's bound to come out with a sarky jab that'll let you know he's got no time to waste with your la-di-da questions. She's gorgeous though—and she does listen.

'The use of force, even against an individual, is not a discriminative factor in revolutionary praxis: rather, if anything, it's the consequence of a contingent situation—'

'I'm sorry, but to me that sounds like more or less what the cops say when they cut a comrade down.' Albertino. But she's not thrown.

'I mean to say that questioning a single praxis, and a contingent one at that—since clearly no one enjoys killing a person, unless some of the men here do?—is a way to fetishize behaviours that are not defining of revolutionary action. In a phase of frontal, homicidal attack from the state, flexible behaviour is a condition for survival.'

Right.

She's bruised him black & blue, no doubt about that. Even Giuliana, who normally looks askance at her, gave a little jolt and a smile at the jab against the men. But 'fetishize', well. Does she get off on maiming words? Johnny gets off in a different way. But you can swear he'll waste no time when the next occasion to say 'fetishize' comes along. The civil war against the vocabulary has begun. In a few years, these comrades will invent 'desolidariza-tion'. They're off into a world of their own, and words like 'des-olidarization' form its landscape. 'Desolidarization' means killing a friend or grassing up on him. On 7 February 1980, at Porta Ticinese in Milan, William Waccher will be desolidarized, being in turn guilty of desolidarization. Ennio Di Rocco will be desoli-darized in the special prison at Trani on 27 July 1982. Arrested in January and tortured by police officers for nine days, he has resisted, following the code of South American guerrillas or the GAP: he holds out for seventy-two hours to give his comrades time to clear out of the bases he knows about. Then he breaks. But this is not the time of the GAP: this is the era of approxima-tion, and the bases were not cleared. Torture does its job, and some arrests are made. Ennio Di Rocco, battle name Riccardo, is sentenced to death by his own comrades and tried in absentia: the sentence is executed in the prison at Trani, during afternoon exercise. The murder of the tortured man is claimed by the 'Proletarian prisoners for the building of the mass organism in the Trani camp'. A debate will follow. On torture. On the 'increasing desolidarization'. But for now, we're still at 'fetishize': 'I mean to say that arms are not the armed struggle and that the armed strug-gle is not a cult of bearing arms. The proletariat has no need for warlords or killers.' Brava—gorgeous.

This is a meeting of the committee against repression taking place in a very exclusive location, an ancient building. In the city there are raids, arrests. One comrade had her house ransacked, they took all sorts, and then it was raids on the houses of all her acquaintances—all on account of a pair of gloves. Convent-school girl gloves, complete with student number, standard issue for the girls of the Sacred Heart College, up in the hills. Found at the Centro Studi Donati after a break-in claimed by Prima Linea: she says she lost them ages ago at the university. I'm getting sleepy, the gorgeous one is speaking of new social subjects and widespread organization. She's come from Milan, and next to her Johnny has got some of his old sparkle back. He's been passing a document around for a few days: 'Have a read, we might want to discuss this later.' Don't get a single fucking word of it: snake in the tunnel, multinationals—like it was written by a maths professor. I can never read that stuff, after twenty lines I have to stop. Johnny is looking straight through me. Ciccio, Albertino and even Giorgio are being pains in the ass, strutting and acting up, but the gorgeous one is never ruffled. Someone snaps: 'No need for killers, of course—if you don't have the balls!' Albertino jumps up, Ciccio stops him, they whisper to each other giggling like they're out of it. Albertino sits back down: 'The balls,' he says laughing.

Someone brings up Judge Alessandrini, who is now investigating Calvi and Sindona and is about to have a little meeting with my friend Johnny outside his house. The gorgeous one from Milan is explaining about the reform of the secret services, someone speaks of infiltrations: the Circolo Alice, for instance, is teeming with cops. Billy won't credit that: 'Sure—like the cops are scared of a bunch of scagheads.' My father says you don't infiltrate those you fear, but those you can use. Infiltrators: in the form of humans, like us, among us, callous and immoral. The very idea of their existence is an offence to the self-esteem of those who think themselves gorgeous. There can be no infiltrators in the ranks of the pure—as in ourselves, we who are only moved by our moral beauty and by the sharp, painful awareness of universal injustice tearing our flesh and conscience apart. An infiltrator's mindset is predicated on collaboration, conniving—or slack attention at the very least.

The gorgeous ones are building a world they will live in for ever, they're preparing the future, their future: the veteran's pride, the survivor's memories, the co-operative of exes, the memoirs of the gorgeous one. For a short, mind-blowing period, they'll have been an elite: that thought will obsess them, and they will always act along elite logics.

Billy is leaning against the wall and laughing, standing next to Johnny like an ensign. I'm pretty sure he doesn't get it, whether it's about the snake in the tunnel or the reform of the secret services—but there's no need for him to understand: Billy is cannon fodder. When the chips are down, his future will be pushing coke in the capital city. Cigarette smoke.

POTS AND PANS   Marina's face has changed, she's whingeing and snapping and bereft of her grace. Not so Giuliana: she has calmly built her network of relationships, she is sure of me, her younger fiancé. I'm thinking that we should take our teenage lives in our hands and break the legs of those who judge us from leaden newspaper columns, those self-proclaimed fathers who no longer see us. Journalist Carlo Casalegno is murdered outside his home on a November day—my wishes come alive and go walkabout through city streets, and they scare me, my dreams taste like puke. I'm holding in my hand a wodge on international finance and saying I don't understand as if there's something wrong with the document and not with me. I'm congenitally out of step with the front line.

Widespread illegality, that's what we'd called our way of standing on the threshold: a magic formula naming haphazard gestures, an open sea that gives a sense to lifting a football from a department store, ransacking a service station cafe, making a molotov cocktail, paying reduced proletarian prices, a brawl a couple of scams and a few lies to the girlfriend. It's the workshop for a new rule, the place where even our disembowelling of the male and the female or my waltzing around with my two fiancées acquire a sense. Mass illegality, collective violence I liked, because it was impossible: a dream of deferral, a model like the perfect sphere, a stratagem to put things off, a horizon of beauty and harmony that made us all artists and none of us murderers. The ambush, the gun, death by decree and appointment, a body suppressing another body, do not belong to that model. One year ago, a high-profile Red Brigades man escaped from prison in Treviso to continue the struggle. 'He has snapped his chains.' All right. He snapped them together with Vincenzo Andraous, a fascist from Catania who's a killer for the mafia. That's all right: nothing justifies a body imprisoned. I needed Johnny's voice, his calm: 'The state has begun its war, and it's a war of annihilation. Do you know what a maximum security prison is?' No, Johnny, I don't know. But the mafia fascist taking us by the hand—I can see that reality all too clearly.

Marina is missing our swimwear embraces on the mountain backbone of the Argentario, and one evening we decide to celebrate the memory in a paradise of rain and beer cans on the edge of a mangey green that in Milan gets to be called a park: a festival at the Parco Ravizza, a sad gathering reliving the rituals of a bygone spring. The fury of a rainstorm rescues us from debates and concerts, and we stay put, making love in the tent raised on the green with water seeping through, without hearing the words outside. Milan is tough: katanga, loden coats, cloth caps, iron bars stashed under the pullovers. They all move as one, you can see there's a centre to their gestures, some organization, geometry. They've taught discipline to wayward comrades—the likes of me—by hitting them on the head with pots & pans. Marina and I look at the panners of Parco Ravizza from the crack between tent flaps, the quaint lawns made for dog walking are filling up with garbage as she says 'Let's run away.' She's saying that and looking into my eyes with her special high-drama face. 'Let's run away to Milan.' We'll find a house and then there'll be a job, her dream is to be a physiotherapist, there's a school here she could go to after her finals or even now, and we could live together on the periphery of this centre of the world, it would be like a family, her family, and she says it's me she wants. She's saying this all in one go, all too much in one go, as if each word needed to grab on to the next to stop tumbling down and being forgotten. I should notice that, but here in our tent we've stopped the rush of time, in the dogs' flowerbed, while outside they're at one another's throats. We dreamed of a war in which no one died, and every clash would last for ever with no winners or losers, we thought of violence as an ideal landscape so as not to be forced to live inside it, and we keep using our star quality to live to hunt to own to overwhelm, to give shape to things and people, to gobble it all in one go. We are made to measure for the new world, a baby world mumbling pet names like some old people do when dementia makes them obscenely quaint.

We shall seduce, transgress, desire, all life long—babies in grotesque adult bodies.

ABOUT THE BODY   Oh that's right—I guess I should talk to you now about those bodies we come across now and again in passing, as we tell this story of bodies and fanciful desires. My father's, for instance—my father, constrained by a work ethics in whose face I loved to spit, symmetrical to mine or at least to the struggle I was part of, the attempt to formulate a future ethos that would only be tied to such duties as might be dictated by the fact of moving limbs.

My father, strangled, cultivating inside himself small monsters, crazy cells that take on fanciful names, I remember the doctors' euphemisms, remember polyps and diverticula, it's hard to fear something with such a name as diverticulum, no matter that it's there, lurking in the dark, growing, enveloping. My father and I had efficiently, punctiliously stopped speaking. And if I really couldn't avoid addressing him, I'd call him 'Dottó', because I knew that hurt him. 'Hey, Dottó.' We didn't speak, and there was only one exception to that—when Uncle Beppe died.

He was a silent man from the countryside around Asti, the very handsome man who had married my mother's eldest sister, who was the one with the degree in English. Beppe and my father had become friends quietly, without one wasted word, over a few glasses of wine on the Sundays I remember from the year Cagliari won the league, when Beppe would come to our house and I was allowed to stay up. And later they'd held each other up during the collapse of a family, my mother's, in which the men died one after the other and my grandfather's modest entrepreneurial dream faded away leaving behind a poisoned trail and the surprise of a newfangled poverty: and they had risen as one to guard my grand-mother's supreme dignity, that must be left intact.

Always with just a very few words—a bon mot here and there, a joke, a wrinkle on Beppe's forehead smoothed out by that laugh-ter in which you could hear all the peasant men he had been in a thousand previous lifetimes, and would be in the next thousand to come.

And then in spring '78 Beppe had died, and my father, out of the blue, had come to ask if I wanted to go to the funeral. I went with him, and even in the car we didn't speak, silence and the bell tolling once on a cold morning in the dead man's town on the plain, and then on the way back we were still silent, but a bit less hostile, and then a guy in a souped-up car comes screeching out a side street and almost drives us off the road, horns blaring and over-the-top exhaust, and the screechy guy starts winding up the old man at the wheel of the brown Alfasud, and gesturing, and flooring it then stopping dead as if to say 'come on, ram me', because he wants to show off his youth and the weight the souped-up engine puts between his legs. And then for five minutes, and never again or before in my entire life, I got a taste of how the old man could drive: five minutes the local yokel would remember for years, and then silence again, except for two words—'Fucking ace . . .'—that showed how impressed I was.

After those two words, more years of silence. Meanwhile he had already started growing those things, which will show up only many years later: the first one in his throat, around 1983, takes him into a hospital in Lione Bronne where his arteries are snipped and he comes out solid as before, holding strong, laughing and making us laugh just like back in the days of Gorilla Batungo versus Gorilla Baringo. The second one after only two years. Cancer—and no possible mistakes, in those years when it was still mentioned in public only as 'an incurable disease'. One of the doctors will have said neoplasia, tumour—sidling up to the unmistakable word. One consultant even says you can survive, it's something in your throat, and he says nothing. I remember my mother meeting the question in my eyes by simply nodding: 'It's that.' He books the operation, no wasted words, and goes off to Colleretto with a few friends—that army doctor who used to be the life & soul of the party sixteen years earlier, and the Sardinian major who's left the army to be a fisherman in South America but is there now, they're all there, as if by chance, even I am there almost by chance, and my father gets food going and we eat on the grass under a huge walnut tree that's no longer there these days, and he's counting the leaves.

I remember him at the hospital, getting the news that his mother had also died while he was in there, unable to give her a last greeting. They'd cut into his throat and taken everything out and now he was breathing through a hole under his chin: my father, a bare and partly shaven body, pale and worn, threadbare, hardly covered by the sheets, and he hadn't had any time to weep and still didn't, and even if he'd wanted to, he no longer had a larynx to sob with. They'd opened his neck at the front, a porthole rimmed by a metal ring that led straight into his windpipe. He breathed from there, blowing furiously, suffocating when catarrh formed, and then you had to grab hold of a device from his bed-side table, switch it on and stick a tube of hard plastic into the throat hole. I used to believe what doctors said back then, and did as they said, pushing the tube right in to where it met some resis-tance, and that resistance was his bronchia, and he was brave and let me get on with it, encouraged me to get the knack of it, but I was sticking that stuff into his bronchial walls and then turning a switch that hoovered air up with the catarrh and he felt the whole brunt of death by suffocation, no discounts except for the final one, and I remember his arms and legs flailing though he was spasmodically trying to hold them still, his willpower calming them for an instant and then the sense of dying pushing kicks out from his legs, and afterwards he'd say thank you.

He had a notebook by which he spoke in broken sentences, because as soon as we got what he had meant to write he'd stop, we'd answer and he'd start a new sentence, and so on: few words, no sermons, quotidian exchanges, hoping to be able to visit a farmer who'd been his roommate and had promised a salami, visits from a guy who'd been operated on before him and had learnt to speak in belches, comforting words for my mother, a strange sentence in which he tells her not to lose hope, that something always happens, look how we pulled through with Pietro, we didn't think we could, the way things were a while ago.

And most often, repeated every few pages, one sentence: 'You go home now.'

Almost ten years after the story of Marina and Giuliana and that losing ourselves into bodies without knowing about bodies, here it was, the old colonel's offended body.

He'd been well pleased when only a few weeks before the larynx operation they'd transferred him to civil defence: logistics officer, working in a consulting capacity with the prefect office for the pre-empting of natural calamities, and for a short while he'd been travelling around the countryside in the fresh air, making friends, pre-empting away. When he came out of hospital they told him it was over: retirement, rest. In two weeks he'd lost his voice, his mother, his job. When others spoke, all he had left was silence— what else could he do? Yes, he could make himself understood, ask for a drink of water or some bread to eat, but then? He'd been a happy man, a guy who laughs and sings and if he's got something to say says it outright, down to the last comma. So depression got him, the hideous role exchange, him silent and huffing away, the hole covered by a flap of surgical dressing, looking for a place to be in the house, the pantomime of a role, the torture of seeing him take my dish after dinner to go and wash it, the rage, paucity of the collapsing physical world, body imposing its commands and dictating emotions.

And the indignity, my mother drinking and when she drinks losing her mind, one evening I caught her beating him and he— I didn't see him, or perhaps I've forgotten: the mind is a good soldier. Screams and whole hours degenerating in that way, but by now the only voice shouting and cursing was my mother's, altered by smoke and alcohol, and I'd get my bike and go out to

275

the bridge where you can see the Dora and the Po joining and the waters mixing slowly, and I stood there looking, feeling calmness as it rose from the water and made some space back in my stomach.

Then the day comes—another two years have gone by—when it's my mother's turn: her bones are aching with rheumatism, he's still huffing around and taking antidepressants, I'm away working in Turkey, leaving the house behind. And the ache in her bones is a false trail: it's starting from the throat for her too, she's even worse off than him and he's alone, she says she'll never accept living through the nightmare that has hit him. So he pulls himself up by his vest straps, gets back into his ordnance clothes, quickly learns to speak by modulating with the mouth of his stomach, it's belching but approaches a voice, he even manages to give it some timbre, and meanwhile he takes up my mother's medical notes, looks after her, alters the reports, bravely gets her to carry on. She says, 'If I had to wake up with a hole in my throat I'd take a running jump out the nearest window,' and meanwhile the consultant has passed judgement: 'If she's to have a chance, we'll have to make a hole in her throat.' I recall a doctor who's a family friend coming out of her room and saying: 'What a nasty death she's in for.' And I'm away, Belgium or Turkey or the mountains, far away, and my father speaks to me on the phone with his erstwhile calm, in belches, he's negotiating with the doctor and she goes through the operation, they open her shoulder, paralyse one of her arms but get her to wake up with no hole in her throat, no respirator, no tube down her bronchia—and the two of them alone.

Here they begin a new life made of three-month periods, chemo, radio, and a slip of paper that says: All right, you can go, you're going to stay alive for at least three months, after which we'll see.

Two and a half years it lasts, and they might have been the best years in their life, because those two persons are hugging each other again, meeting each other in a newfound complicity made of holidays and travel, with each slip of paper they'd leave, France or Tuscany, following the car's headlights wherever it may lead, and somewhere along the road stopping at a restaurant or a hotel.

Until the day when the phone rings at my house, and my mother is speaking to me in broken, bamboozled sentences. From what she's saying I work out she thinks she's speaking to my uncle, so I figure she must have started drinking again. A wave of disgust washes over me, nothing but bother, and I go see them; but my mother surprises me, she looks at me all evening and smiles, and she's struggling to talk, spitting out the odd word now and again if she must, with the air of someone who's keeping a grip on herself.

That night I left their house with a claw twisting my guts upward into my solar plexus, and went out to see Dances With Wolves, a lousy film. Soon I would learn something about my mother that I had not known. She was being devoured by cancers unleashed everywhere, perhaps not even metastases from the first one, the one that had brought the gift of two and a half years of travel and joy in instalments: no, this was new stuff, coming from her colon and lodging in her bones and liver to throw a tentacle into her brain, a tentacle that kept her awake, stopped the morphine doing its work and prevented sleep.

It would last three more months, without the comfort of palliatives, and she kept on top of the pain as best she could as she

burnt inside: the night I'd gone to the cinema she'd been struggling to speak because she was holding it together by the skin of
her teeth, a patient stitching, just like that time—my father said—
when she'd nearly died giving birth to me at twenty-one but had
not said a word. There would have been other occasions for her
to scream, back then when the breath was starved out of her
thoughts and her dreams of a more complex life were smashed
against daily disaster; but as her body lay dying she pursed her lips
tight and attempted the ultimate adventure of control.

In the beginning, when she was still able to hold on to some
scrap of lucidity meshed in with relentless pain—in the beginning
she would worry about me: she sensed I was in danger, entrusted
me to someone, forgetting my thirty years and my arrogance. My
father spent his days, and whenever possible his nights, by her bedside, until an evil doctor sunk in his own role called me into his
surgery to tell me there was no hope, to explain to me about her
impending death made of stabbing pains and retching with no
outlet, to force silence on me by his perverted language, the but-
tery words that fill the mouths of consultants, words born of a
school in which the human person has no legal currency. He was
telling me I was 'the most grounded relative': I was floundering,
and had erased from my memory the time when I'd learnt to mis-
trust the maiming of words. With paunchy superciliousness the
consultant was explaining to me that I must not tell anyone, that
yes, I must lie, especially to my father, because he was too close
to her and would let the fatal word escape him and then she'd
understand and refuse treatment. We'll fit her with an artificial
anus, he was saying, and meanwhile just a few walls away her
brain was not responding to the morphine and she was going

THE RAIN'S FALLING UP

under the mace blows her intestine was dealing her, but of course we don't want her to refuse, if there is any hope at all we must act on it, mustn't we? Hypnotized, I was preparing to lie, to tell my father we'd get out of it and carry that tale around on my own as I looked at them from the corner of the ward—they'd put her on the ward—and they were holding hands and exchanging promises for later, and speaking of their next trip, drily.

In her last but one week she told me I should read Memoirs of Hadrian—I still haven't. Then she asked to go home for the weekend, I spoke to the doctor and got him to say yes, and I remember that last night: a Jerry Lewis film that she was watching with a little girl's stubbornness, determined to laugh, and then at 11 p.m. in the courtyard, halfway through the Domenica Sportiva, getting the car to take her back to the hospital, and my father grasping my shoulder and looking into my eyes: 'Tell me she's coming home,' and I promise, of course I promise, 'She is,' and know full well I'm lying and only want to get it over with.

And at the hospital she loses her mind, reverts to being a child, perhaps coming full circle on what had started with the Jerry Lewis film, she thinks she's three years old, looks at my bald pate and mistakes me for her father, climbs into my arms weeping and trying to turn her guts inside out, tries to stop herself screaming, to take courage, in my arms, weeping and trying to empty her intestine that is full of death. One week only and another doctor intervening, saying to me 'I will speak to your father' and telling me not to put her through the operation, not to draw out the agony, one week and she dies in my arms, saying 'Ciao' with one last smile and one tear from that bluest blue eye of hers, and not knowing what to do I eat that tear, the electrocardiograph beeping and they tell me to take her to the morgue and I follow the stretcher into the underground section of the Molinette, an endless subterranean corridor cluttered with air tubes and doors with emergency handles, dark, all the way in, so I can see them securing her jaw and tying a bow at the top of her head, like an Easter egg, and the last blasphemy of that sixteenth of May is a star big as a soup dish throwing a blaze of light into a turquoise sky, over the roofs just outside the hospital.

ABOUT WORK   This is precisely where the work begins. At a certain point in life, dying becomes a job, and that man strangled by his military work ethics understands it alone. And gets to work. In those days your father was going through his operation, in a different city—remember the downpour? My father tells me to go, and then does something that's not easy to do for a colonel: remember the moped I had tied to an apple tree at Signor Lovera's? Well, the same man who got me to go back all the way to fetch the dead moped now puts himself in the hands of a neurologist, tells him he needs to be on his own and come out of it, no drivel, tells him he's OK with taking pills if needed, pinpoints his limits and sticks to them with the lucidity of an honest craftsman who must deliver his piece of work.

And he tells me to go, that I must be with you, that he's fine with the neurologist and the pills, he knows if he goes under I'll go too, and then you'll be on your own. And so the work of years begins, made of equanimity and rabbit stewed in red wine that he cooks for the joy of seeing me. There'll be another tumour, the prostate this time, an operation and then the chemo, injections that I give him at his house in exchange for rabbit stew, good wine and sausage and the serenity he builds by fighting tooth and nail, speaking a language of belches and grimaces for my daughter's benefit, and there will be all the holidays he'll stay away from. He wanted to spend Christmas and New Year's on his own thinking of my mother, he was trying to get me used to the idea that he too would die. He had a plan, and was shaping his life by perfecting it. So he'd drop by on Christmas Eve or Boxing Day, quick, discrete visits designed to stop us feeling any guilt on his behalf as we went into the holiday or came out of it, he'd come on the pretext of a present for my little girl, he'd invite me to dinner for the next week or bring a fine bottle that he'd found at a good price in one of the supermarkets he knew. He'd lived through the full horror of my mother's hospital death and taken up the challenge: to prepare, to ease things, to prevent that horror happening at all costs. The horror for me, I mean: he was training his body to carry the full weight. It was a question of avoiding the repetition of that horror at any cost, a question of lightening my load.

Dying is a job and he's working, grinding away and working, chewing on it and grinding away. Until one day in Colleretto, I hear a noise in the basement and find him in the tub that had been dug into the floor, head turned onto his chest, no breath, his toes fanned out and yellow, and I smash into his ribs in an attempt at heart massage and give him artificial breathing through the hole in his throat, in short he makes it, the coronary unit gets in and he makes it, and with a good soldier's smile he says to me: 'You got me out and now I have to thank you—but I was dead and hadn't realized. When am I going to get that lucky again?' That's my old man. And then he's back to work: this is not work you can improvise, there are no shortcuts, it's method, effort, planning, leading to a summer day, not much later, when his breath cuts out and I can't convince him to go to hospital, he says stubbornly he'll have none of it, he knows his bronchitis, but then one of my aunts intervenes and forces him, and he goes in.

And then again, always, again, the euphemisms, then the sentence: mesothelioma, it will get his pleura, the other little monsters had spared him only to deliver him straight into the mouth of the worst one. He's working, grinding away, showing the joy each of my visits gives him, he says oxygen is important but seeing me is better than oxygen, walks his last steps to go and meet his granddaughter who's sneaked into a place where children aren't allowed: she's come to say hello, and he organizes these wordless little games in that exclusive language of theirs made of huffings and glances, and takes her the rounds to show her off a bit with the other inmates, he smiles and inexplicably stops eating and drinking. He's working. The doctor says he doesn't understand, there's no reason for giving up, he'll get debilitated. One day in August he gives in to thirst and asks me for some spring water, no a drink, and I bring him one of those with mineral salts, he takes one sip and regrets it, gets back to work: he'll not have another agony like my mother's land on my shoulders. Go back to work, he says to me, don't hang around here all the time, go back to your little girl—as if to say, let me be, can't you see I'm busy.

And he's thinking of the little girl too, of her mother, of the Bosnian lad who comes to visit him each day after his factory shift and has a new kindness every time: he figures an old guy who won't eat might like raspberries and brings him some—and he eats one, because work has its breaks, its finishing touches, and that sometimes calls for a counter-movement. Effort and commitment—the colonel puts his affairs in order. He asks me do I know when it will be, and I say it's not even certain it will be at all, that they'll drain his lungs and then an operation and then we'll know, and that time even I believe it, and he takes the space one morning for us to be able to say all the things we had meant to say, and he gives me space too: he'll not leave me with the regret of things unsaid, and we talk, clearly and affectionately, without reticence or falsity. And then he tells me I should go back to work, I was working in Milan, he's gone without food or drink for days, weeks, he sends me off and tries to die alone.

I get back there at breakneck speed, devouring miles on the motorway, and grab the last hours of his life by the hair: I find him unconscious already, hooked up to the cursed electrocardio-graph—yet each time I call him, that line the doctors would like to say is flat ('Strange,' they say, 'this is not normal,' each time they come to check and find him still alive)—each time I call him, that line leaps up, so I experiment, shift the bed, say something more, and the line won't do anything, but it jumps up if I call him.

And so he goes—calmly, greeting me, leaving me time to do everything, including seeing him into his last moment. He goes taking the whole weight of death on himself, and death means all the suffering in the world, he goes away working, finishing his work, loading his bag with as much as he can of my grief, my soli-tude. By dying, the colonel has won a hopeless battle. He has won, and I'm thinking of that phrase, 'by dying he defeated death', I think that phrase captures a vertigo, the point at which the expe-rience we have here on earth touches upon something else. The point at which our body itself indicates something else, as had happened in parody form back in our season of progressive wonders—except that this time everything's clear cut, there's no time left for attempts. Look, this story is frightfully embarrassing, and I don't know how to level with it: time to go back to the years of the aborted New Man.

NORMAN BETHUNE   For the rest, business as usual. Fascists blown up as they set off a blast, policemen, guards outside some factories, bursts of machine gun fire. And one of our guys is killed in the street, his name is Roberto Scialabba, and there's something strange here—one of those things that will have you say, OK, I'm dreaming, no doubt about it, I'm going to wake up any minute cause I'm asleep, either that or it's a trip pumped up with pills, because the murderer is Giusva. Giusva was the perfect kid in the TV series, remember? The guy your uncle would hold up as an example when you used to watch reruns in the after-noons after class at primary school. Giusva—what sort of a name is that, no wonder a kid like that gets on your wick, all blond and smooth and goody two shoes: we'd hated him from day one, like you hate Mickey Mouse because you love Donald Duck, or Tweety because you love Sylvester.

Igor won't come to the phone, his mother doesn't know where he is and he won't call back if I leave a message. And Ciccio is nowhere to be seen, ditto Cocò and the girls, the other girls I mean. Dino has some new friends, they speak in self-assured tones about Chinese economy: he introduces them, and I listen and now and again put a word in. And then they stop, calmly put down the pile of Fronte Popolare issues they're carrying for militant dissem-ination, and start laughing. Dino must be ashamed to be friends with me. Bah. It looks something like the snake in the tunnel: if I don't get it, it means there must be something big at stake. That's right—maybe the universe-to-be is made in China by hanging the Gang of Four, sweeping away a bit of sentimentality and deviant tendencies, giving up on holidays to bone up on Congress theses, learning to poke fun at those who don't know about the Great Leap Forward, in a loft at 20 Via Principe Amedeo, following the lectures given by a small moustached man in an army shirt who's been parachuted in from Milan (Milan!) to put us through cadre training (cadre training!) on the Hundred Flowers, on Hua Kuo Feng. And Giuliana follows me, comes to the lectures too, she's faster, leaps forward on me but then holds back and waits. There's even two real factory workers at our meetings, and one university student, all at catechism at the top of five flights of stairs with a wooden banister, serious and consequential male revolutionaries proud of having a girl in their midst—and a bright one at that. And Giuliana weighs her words and says her bit on Yunnan Province and on people's conferences and democratic Kampuchea even—with no mystery or exoticism, no Marco Polo or Genghis Khan. That's what I like, she's parachuting me in, I go in cautiously, Hua Kuo Feng is enough to satisfy my apocalyptic tension, five vertical flights of stairs, short of breath and light filtering through the roof tiles, issues of Xu He's political economy manual published by Mazzotta, read the chapter on Originary Accumulation for Monday.

Rinardi was the smallest of my primary-school mates, a wee thing who swam around in his uniform and you could see his gothic-arch knees pale above his socks. Hair always greasy, big nose, sad eyes, and perhaps he really was the worst off: he lived with his single mum in a garret under the arcade west of my magic square, and remedied life's dogged cruelty by a boundless knowledge of comics. He'd introduced me to Zagor and Tex. Later, the passing years had not spared Rinardi, and during my time at high school he'd often turned up shortly after lunch, punctual as a curse: he'd ring the bell and I could see him from above as he slowly walked across the gravelled yard, head hung low and the same greasy hair as ever. He'd come at that time and never leave, no matter that I had to do homework or see Marina. To put a stop to those gruelling visits I'd sometimes pretend I was going out: I'd see him to the door, but he'd follow me into the street, and then I had to find ever more complicated strategies, like disappear behind a street door and wait for him to go. My mother called him the Implacable: 'We haven't seen the Implacable for a while—is he all right, do you think?' And part of her was laughing, but on the other hand she was genuinely worried about him. He came for two reasons, and the first one was elementary: food. And wine, even if he was still a boy, because the misery and folly of his single mother leaning on him who was alone and unemployed meant he had not been spared alcoholism either. And then he wanted to still talk about comics—a wee bit more, just for today, come on—and then we'll see.

Rinardi had a natural talent: he was good at drawing, and in those afternoons at secondary school, when I was already hiding the wine bottle from him, we'd played with the idea of starting a magazine that we would fill with all the ghosts and ravished damsels we wanted—and also with our doubts about ever pulling through, later. Then I grew up nice & easy and he didn't—but he was still good at drawing, in fact even better, and so I asked him to do four portraits for me, stuff that I couldn't even find at the Marxist–Leninist bookshop on Via Sant'Anselmo.

He did them in sepia ink, on school drawing paper, and brought them over in silence, one day around 2 p.m.: Hua Kuo Feng, Deng Hsiao Ping, a young Stalin and Norman Bethune. Who's Norman Bethune? I'm the only one who knows: he's a Canadian doctor, a friend of Mao's—must have died in China. And meanwhile I'm getting used to people looking at you when you say you're a Marxist–Leninist and nodding gravely as if you'd said you've just lost a relative or that you got a degree in advanced engineering and then went to work for Alfa Romeo. A church like any other, ground under your feet, busy afternoons, and even the pleasure of being unable to go into the mountains when school's out because you've so much to do. No, it's not anything serious: it's a way like any other to sit it out during the movement's fitful sleep and powerful dreams. Andrea Pazienza draws a cartoon with a prophetic caption: 'There falls April seventy-eight / coppers' head will feel the weight.'

All we have to do is wait—and meanwhile my weekday afternoons with Marina are taken up with behaviours that my new Chinese fatherland would reward with lifelong imprisonment and hard labour. To dream of a perfect world on the other side of the world while risking nothing personal: well, that too is a way to exit history—and one of the least harmful.

SOFAS (2)   'You're sick again.'
  'I'm all right, stop worrying.'
  'I've been trying to call you.'

'Yeah, I know—my mother tells me every time.'

'Not that you'd get back to me.'

'Well—I do mean to—but there's always stuff.'

'Right.'

'The girls?'

'Giuliana—don't see much of her—she has her own life.'

'Right. Marina?'

'. . .'

'You're together, no?'

'Well—yeah—yeah. I'd say we're together.'

'And Giuliana's gone.'

'Right.'

'Right.'

Of course I'd tell him I'm not with Giuliana—well, practically I'm not with Giuliana—haven't touched each other in months—and so on, something like an old geezer's catalogue of miseries, you know the stuff: 'We're only staying together for the kids', 'I swear to you', and the like. It's a lie: we do touch each other every time we get together, and all told that's pretty often. It's just that I can't take her anywhere—at least outside Chinese circles, that is. A while ago everyone knew about the three-way pact: some envied me, all made a show of respect. And then silence descended—or rather, a low hiss that creeps around and stops as soon as you start listening, like when an adulteress steps into a small-town church. Ah well, that's what people are like, this is stuff coming back to the surface from where we'd sunk it when the annus mirabilis of our upended sky saw us announce the effrontery of our pact to the world—the small world of our friends. This year, the year of sudden backtracking, a three-way love is a fuckwit's trip.

And so, nothing for it but carry on in hiding. Though in fact I'm still a bit green: my weapons are not well honed, my age works against me and my lies come out awkward, shabby and loud. Sure enough, Igor puts up with them patiently. His face is pale, even paler than usual, and he nods like one who can't wait to wash his ears clean of the garbage I'm pouring into them, he's dying to turn around and go back to his suddenly inaccessible life. This was really too much, though: 'Haven't touched each other in months.' Like I can fuck around with Igor, expect him to sit through the sort of stale little yarn you'd crank out in a hurry for someone who's not worth you straining your invention any further. He deserves better—did we not use to be friends? He whips round, his eyes flashing like I've known them to: he's about to strike.

'So you've decided you're in love in the end—'

'What?'

'And does she love you?'

'Bah.'

'Does she love you or not?'

'Knock it off, Igor—we just like to be together.'

'She'd die for you, right?'

'Look, what are you trying to say?'

'Well—you know why Marcella dumped Billy—do you?'

THE SLUT   You want to know what I think? I can tell you now, twenty-five years' worth of detachment later. I think: 'The slut.' In fact I'm thinking up a whole generative algorithm of 'The slut', something like: 'The slut! The slut!! The slut the slut the slut!!!' On Ruben and Dino's sofa, in front of everyone—the slut! Imagine the simpering—he'll have felt like such a great macho, the little son of a slut with his swivel hips, and the slut sucking him up to a stiff peak. Oh but I'm going to cripple her soon as I lay hands on her—the slag. What's the matter with me? I've not felt like this in ages! I know you shouldn't say slut, you shouldn't even think it, it's not that—but I know what she'll say, and then where was I that Saturday (was it Saturday?), eh? Well—with Giuliana, clearly. But I hadn't told her, she couldn't have known, I'd probably told her I was playing football or spending time with my folks for a change. So she's the slut. Clearly.

Now, we have a problem here: how to give legitimacy to a thought embodied in an inappropriate word. My fake map of the universe is painted in gross colours: all Igor needed was to shoot one look at me—but then, Marina is gross too. So, let me try and reckon with this: Billy, of all people? Billy is not part of the pact—and besides, I'm faithful, aren't I. Meaning, she can't know I'm not, and so I'm entitled to expect her to behave accordingly. And even if she knew everything about Giuliana, would she be gracious enough to tell me when the pact expired? On what day? Have we ever sat around a table and said, look, it's not happening any more? Did you not also want to divvy up our times together into drug-store doses, with the little alarm clock at the Argentario? And could you not say something if you're not happy with it? As for me, I've never cheated on the pact—of course I don't like it, of course it's hard work, of course I've to put up (put up!) with a shitload of lies all the time, but I'm up for it, and I do my best, cause I do care. Do you think I've never felt like telling you both to fuck off, you and that other one who turn up at my place one day and announce you've decided that from now on I'm yours for the taking? You think I'm always happy with it all? What do you expect me to do, fuck the first woman I see in the street? No no nooooo, this won't do, you slut you slut you slut you slut, of course if she's got a slut head on her how do you expect her to go much further than that, she can't do much more than give it away, use it for what it is, which is: shit, garbage, slutface dog food. What the fuck's Billy got to do with anything? Igor, OK, I could understand, honest—but that turd! On Ruben's sofa, in front of everyone, in broad daylight. What the fuck's where I was got to do with anything? What matters is, I wasn't on that sofa, or even sitting around laughing with the others. At Ruben and Dino's house: might as well have been our bed (meaning, her parents', but for all intents and purposes it's our inviolable nuptial chamber). That little shit didn't even have to cross the road: the ice-cream parlour where he pulls his pudding into the vanilla is just there, forty yards along the arcade—take the lift up, walk up one floor to Dino's loft: his lovely little spurt saved up to shoot into my girlfriend, and a sigh of relief for the bourgeois who'll eat their croissants in peace today.

You slut, you slut, you slut—the algorithm by which I avoid saying what really is making my bad blood mount: she does me up as a girl, the slut does, all simperings and pretty words, makes all her pretty plans to set up the two lesbian housewives plus free-of-charge prick (mine), mewling about Milan and all, but meanwhile, just like that, just to remind herself what real cock is made of, she goes for the warrior stud—handsome Billy of the Swivel Hips. Fucking him with her eyes ever since that morning at the Tesoriera—fucking him right into his balaclava. And maybe the guy with the big gun was someone else entirely. But meanwhile he's cock of the walk and I'm pushed back into the coop, crestfallen with my painted-up feathers, and the others, the real guys, cracking up right left and centre. Mygggod, I feel like even the stones are laughing at me! I return Igor's look with an icy smile so he won't notice. Is he also laughing? Shit, does he know about the filthy stuff I get up to, got up to, used to get up to? Have I got a smudge of mascara left on me? And meanwhile I feel like a raging hurricane—so the male is back, and how: a male in a towering rage, ready to give the girl—the slut—a good once-over, she and her pact of the New Man.

ALL SORTS   He never apologizes. 'Come on, a sparkling white.'

Right. A sparkling white. Up your ass with the sparkling white—except I've not the nerve to say that to him, so we turn into the Quinto bar. It is the evening of the day, and the trees on Corso Palestro are shimmering.

'Where does he live?'

'Who?'

'Billy.' He laughs.

'You want to deck him?'

'Nah—just ask him a couple of things.'

'Good—or he'd have crippled you.'

'Fuck off, Igor.'

'That's my man.' He's changed tone, laughing as he used to.

'Knock it off—it's just that—'

'You'd not find him anyway.'

'. . . ?'

'He's legged it.'

'. . . !'

'That's right.'

He touches his finger to his nose to bid me keep quiet about it. I widen my hands and close my eyes as I turn my head to tell him that goes without saying.

'Johnny tells me you're in with the Chinese.'

'What the fuck does Johnny know.'

'Actually he does know a thing or two.'

'So—what's he saying?'

'He's saying that the next time they pan a comrade in Milan, you'll be found with your brain dripping on the pavement.'

'Yeah, right—and you tell him we'll—' He gestures to say, cut it out.

'Won't say a word to him—for your good. And anyway, I'm not on good terms with him any more.'

'. . . ?'

'That's right. '

'And . . . ?'

'I don't know.'

He's quiet for a while, downing his sparkling white. I call for another half, he's looking down and giggling, when he's struggling he giggles and looks around to stop people seeing he's struggling.

'They're a bunch of madmen, Pietro. Have you seen how they get off on it? They're getting whipped up, playing at it. It's a bunch of crap. They think they can change things with their magic guns. Motherfuckers—you've got to stay with things if you want to change them.'

'. . . ?'

'Remember the philosopher's stone?'

Why the fuck does he always have to treat me like a little squirt? The philosopher's stone, really! But he's away.

'Matter is transformed because the operator also is matter.'

'Right.' I keep a hard face, won't lower my tone.

'These guys, they dump everything and beat it. You want to change the factory, you've to stay in the factory, no? Want to change school—do you stay in it or not? What the fuck do you expect to understand about anything otherwise? Well—what they're doing is dumping everything and going off. It's an abstraction, a bunch of crap. Want to change things? Then stay with things.'

'. . .'

'Their whole clandestine trip—that's bullshit, matey.'

'Hm.' Matey. 'That why you're dumping them?'

'Dumping who?'

'Oh—sorry.'

Another half carafe. Another full one. He looks at me, straight into my eyes this time: 'My mother is ill. FIAT are hiring masses of people these days, it looks like things are picking up big time. They're hiring all sorts. Really, all sorts. And I need to work.'

VOLONTÉ   I'm walking faster, but I don't really want to get there. The same route as every day, late every day, along the plane tree boulevard. I hold the jump-into-your-clothes world record: wake-up call at five to eight, a slap of cold water in my face and I'm on my way, dodging the No. 5 tram. I'll cut diagonally across Corso Re Umberto and Corso Matteotti (must be something symbolic in this intersection, I'm beginning to think about it every morning, but then walk on), the regulation haversack covered in marker writing: in class by ten past eight at the latest, sleep in my eyes, the maths teacher pissed off because I've forgotten to bring my books again (honestly, how can you set maths as the first class in the day?) but anyhow I've made it. In class with a showdown scene running through my head, no, two, no fifty of them, all so violent and mashed together that I fear I might get badly mixed up: let that fatal s-word come out once and I'm fucked, I'm mulling it over and over, a thousand times in ten minutes, I've three or four different tones for my opening line but I'm losing them, losing it as I make the choice—in fact I've ten or twenty openings ready, each is as good as the other, the only certainty is the unutterable concept: you slut. Too mad to read science fiction under the desktop today, too far cuckolded, too ill at ease with my boyish side. If only I had one whisker of beard on my face—one! that I could cherish and grow and pull on to get it to grow. Nope— not one hair, lovely smooth chin and unblemished skin, never had a single spot even. So there's nothing for it but listen to the lesson, I'm putting my hand up like there's no tomorrow, asking questions, saying I'm not quite clear about this or that, just to be a pain in the ass. I'll get you in the break, girl, don't you worry.

Except there's no break, a guy's rushing around, quite out of breath, saying 'Extraordinary assembly called by the head, all gather in the main hall.' That's all I needed. And then, the head? Since when has the head been calling assemblies! What sort of shit has the world come to? He says that in Rome they've mowed down five policemen and driven off with Aldo Moro. Oh fuck. Very well, I'll get her at the assembly.

There's a film where Moro is played by Gian Maria Volonté, with a scarf and a slash of white in his hair, a film about the Christ-Dem underground: they don't say it's about Aldo Moro, it was Dino explained that to me, and so I laughed and pretended I knew (though the film is nothing to laugh about), and in later months, at meetings, I would do an impression of Volonté in the film and go: 'We-ell, mediation, mediation,' and people thought I was funny. This assembly—I sit through it without getting a single word. Never mind. No one will get anything about this question for years, I've just got a head start, that's all. They've upped the ante at last, I'm thinking. And the others? The guys who go on about armed utopia and the swivel-hipped violence of the body? They're keeping quiet. Best not to think about that, or I'll flash on Billy fucking Marina on Ruben's sofa. At assembly, she brushes past me. 'I want a word with you later,' I say, and she smiles, the assembly continues, my rage makes way for a sort of astonishment. I'm looking for some sign in people's faces, can't recognize any of the opinions voiced, no one's saying anything I might have expected, it sounds like everyone's gone and got wise on me. I need my Chinese paradise—but meanwhile, I've let Marina slip away.

CALL OUT   An afternoon hand in hand with Giuliana. Section update at the Marxist–Leninists'. No mention of China, this is an extraordinary call out—Moro again. From the central committee in Milan we get a new line: it's no longer true that 'there are no enemies in the left' as we'd learnt in cadre school, February meeting, a corollary to the Theses of the II National Congress (as a blatant paradox, Marina's presence and her embarrassing little notes during the secretary's exposé. Clear awareness that I'll never be a National Congress delegate: I'll spend a lifetime in the section—but with two women. Could do worse, China allowing. In any case, Marina will never show up at the Chinese section again: she'll put up with anything except boredom).

The new line leaves our two factory worker members somewhat cold—they say no one's exactly tearing their hair out over Moro: the unions called a strike at 11 a.m., but people on the assembly lines couldn't care less. The university student and the doctor guy are more boring: you can see they're bringing all their clever luggage into their frameworking, focusing & analysing. As usual, Dino is the most lucid: 'This is an action geared to attacking the movement. The Red Brigades have decided to burn the bridges with Seventy-seven and blow generically antagonistic subjects out of the game. Class is back at centre stage.' I can't understand if he's pleased with that or not. The working-class centre stage, the clash against the state. A good Chinese comrade should like that— and dislike movements full of druggies and pervs. Steady on,

Pietro—the hand you're holding here is Giuliana's, not Marina's, and there's no Carletto Ninetto Albertino here: no pet names in the section. So that means my thoughts are running off in the wrong direction—mostly in the direction of the great slut Marina. I know where to get her: it's five o'clock, all I have to do is make sure I leave here by six. Half five—I get my excuse ready. Quarter to six—nearly time to act. The secretary's turn to speak: he's refuting Dino, as far as I can understand, by saying he's a movementist. Six o'clock: I think I'd better go, my mother is—yeah, right—can't get a single word out: first of all, a Chinese comrade has no mothers, and secondly, you just don't leave in the middle of the secretary's piece. Quarter past six and he's still going on—Dino is unruffled. Twenty past and Dino is clarifying. Let's see—I'm afraid my mother is—no, not the right moment: it would be like saying I'm against Dino, and though he's not showing it he is a bit anxious—how can I take off while he's speaking? That'd be dirty. Half past six—perhaps if I run. The secretary is giving his riposte, two more people sign on to speak: the doctor and the steelworker—and oh shit, Giuliana. Can't budge until Giuliana is done, else I'm in for a home section meeting later—or a section whinge, more like. By this time the problem has shifted: dinner'll be ready at home—is this the time, you treat the house like a hotel, and on and on. All for a pain in the ass of a meeting on Moro! Honestly. Good job I'm still young enough, with muscle & nerve enough to sort out certain stinking questions on the phone.

LOVE   Cry. All she does is cry, just cry. Saying I can't understand, that I don't understand a thing. Crying, neither admitting nor denying, and I'm getting mad, screaming at her, don't give a fuck if my father can hear. I didn't say you're a whore, I said 'like' a whore: that's different. If someone tells me I did something stupid, it's not the same as saying that I'm—now she's slammed the phone down in my face. And I call back, again and again: cry, that's all she does. All right, look—tomorrow morning, before school.

'I'm not coming to school, I'm sick.'

'All right—after school, then. I'll come to yours.'

'Yes come, love.'

Love. Crying and calling me love. The slut. Back in the living room, on TV, they're covering the bodies of the five policemen with sheets. I have time to prepare my punishment with the proper care. Approaching her house now, the bridge on the Dora, here we go. Entry-phone, lift up. She's drop-dead gorgeous. What did I expect? Made up & dressed up like she's going out, and she's hugging me tight, pendants at her ears going bling-bling, she takes one of my hands and places it on her breast, 'Can you feel it beating?' I can feel all right, no question about that—except that over the heart there's one of those tits she's got on her, so I don't know what I can be feeling right now.

'Did you see that—about Moro, I mean?'

'I don't give a flying fuck about Moro, all right? We're hardly here to make conversation.'

She bites her lower lip—a tear down her cheek. She knows her stuff, and she's giving it her all. Says 'I love you', says it on my lips, says it to herself, in a low voice, you want to believe it. So I say 'I love you', especially towards the end, but only because that makes me harder. I'm looking at the window, its wooden frame over the roofs of the blocks of flats, not far from where I would play handball with Mandrone: not a bad idea to concentrate the mind on Mandrone. She's kissing me now, saying I've said terrible things to her. She kisses me, I kiss her. Shall we talk about Billy a bit? No, not now—there's time. We can do that on the phone, since we talk every night anyway.

LOW SUNDAY   In Milan, at the Casoretto, the mild breeze is keeping two kids outside, talking under a street lamp before going back home for supper. Their names are Fausto and Lorenzo—but everyone knows Lorenzo as Iaio. The police say it was en execution, but they'll never find the executors anyway. The section secretary says these are two of our dead, or rather, one of them was: he was in the organization. What I'm thinking: our dead was Roberto Crescenzio, the Blue Angel guy. Today the new special laws are being passed, the government is out in force, from the PCI to the fascists of Democrazia Nazionale. Marina is staying away from school, and it's better that way: what I need to tell her is best said on the phone.

'It's all off—no Colleretto this Easter.'

'Oh—but didn't you say we—'

'No can do, sorry—my cousin Maurizio's got the house.'

'Well, couldn't we—'

'No room.'

'Maurizio—you mean the guy who came with us to the Argentario?'

'Yes, that's right—why?'

DOM ARGENT (2)   Chorus: Aldo Moro is no longer himself, the PCI men depict him as a coward—discreetly in their press, overtly in the sections and on the street. And the great macho Party gathers all the female ones: there's no negotiating. They say he's begging, and they think real men won't beg. Marina is no longer herself either: crying, she's always been a crier, and greedy, yes, she's always been greedy—but these days she's clinging, demanding, wielding our shared dream of Milan as a bludgeon. And she's on target, because the dream of Milan is stronger than the dream of China. On Good Friday she took the coach and went to Colleretto, found my grandfather's old house, and who can picture the look on Maurizio's face when she turned up there—that was really our place, not at all her place. She got in, said she was hoping I'd be there, used tears the way she knows: they're tiny crystals, setting off her black eyes. I called Maurizio.

'Look, it's bullshit, she knew perfectly well I wasn't in Colleretto.'

'She told me terrible things about you—'

'. . .'

'But I won't believe her.'

'She's just a little shit.'

'She is.'

What does that mean? What has she been telling him about me? What is she after? And then, Maurizio doesn't know much either: his brother Vittorio was also in Colleretto over those days—the great Vittorio, idol to all the girls. And Marina sticking to him. Maurizio didn't see much of her in those days.

'What do you mean, didn't see much of her?'

'Well, she was always out—'

'What about you?'

'Well, you know—Vittorio gets around, doesn't he.'

Vittorio gets around. How fast does he get around? Faster or slower than Billy of the Swivel Hips? Right, so that's why she hasn't been showing up. Vittorio—no, please, not Vittorio.

'And then she wanted to come to Florence with us, but Vittorio wouldn't hear of it, I think they must have had a fight.' Maurizio's voice changes. 'And then she—'

'She what?'

'I don't know—she's strange—'

'What do you mean, strange?'

'She asked me for money. Vittorio said that too, that she was after money.'

CONTRACT KILLING   I think I must have wept. Why is she asking for money? She's fucked the great Vittorio, what more does she want? Why does she keep calling me and I can't say a word? It's an ordinary austerity afternoon, TV news and state firmness, Moro is slamming against the walls of his tiny cell, I'm walking again on the pavements of the great market at the city's edge, back to her place, so be it. She grabs me on the landing, smells nothing like her, stinks of fags that have been put out and saved for later, looks at me and smiles a spider's smile.

Afterwards I rush away in a rage, not caring for my trousers and the button that's still undone or for her unbearable lisp ringing out on the stairs, let her deal with her neighbours, and thtay, pleathe, love, don't go, pleathe darling, thtay with me. A shower and soap, loads of soap. She wanted to make my face up, I shook my head no, she was speaking to me like to a female, 'You're pretty—pretty girl, I want you,' I shook my head no, she opened me and took me, her eyes slitted, green lightning flashing through them. 'Pretty girl.' Stop it, I hate this, I hate your breath, and she's saying: 'There's this friend of mine, name's Carmelo, he wants to meet you.' A slap, that's what was needed—a slap and strong nerves, but all I can do to get out is ooze away like the mushy thing I have become. Out, I'm out, I'll never see you again, you can phone all you like and lay siege to my door and pester my mother and fuck my cousins and tell whoever you want whatever you want, you'll see how I'll lay the ground for you, let the phone ring and ring, OK? And good for you you're not coming to school, I'll set you up all right. 'Marina is pushing. Can't get off the shit and has no money, so she's pushing.' In my book, this is a death sentence. There was a law, wasn't there? A length of steel rebar through the skull for anyone caught pushing. Igor, Marina is pushing. Tell Johnny, tell everyone, I tell everyone, in assemblies, in the small groups standing around after school, outside the ice-cream parlour, I tell our old friends, the Chinese, those few left from Barabba we still see around the streets. Someone will see to killing her. Meanwhile there's a search for Aldo Moro in the alleyways of a small town called Gràdoli.

ONE　　My mother understands: she's seen and heard it all.

'What are you going to say about missing classes?'

'Can't you write me a note?'

'You need a medical if you're going to be away for more than—'

'Can't you ask someone?'

She nods and says no more, gives me some money, I can get to Florence that evening, Maurizio will find me a bed—though not at his house, I don't want to see the great Vittorio. And then I'll leave Florence, there's a comrade has this farmhouse in Pian di Sco, near Arezzo, and his granddad keeps pigs and has a special gift for curses in the vernacular, motherfucking sheep-butchering god, and I think they even saw a flying saucer landing in these parts some time. And then maybe Bologna, there's always someone at the university, after which we'll see. The search for Moro continues, they're looking for him in a frozen lake and the newspapers are not printing his letters.

So here I am, helping the granddad from Pian di Sco to push the pig out the pen, hanging around the university canteens and retraining my eye. And then it'll be all right, I've someone else on my mind already, one I've met in school, she's younger, looks at me through these big glasses and smiles a crooked smile, looking up at me, her jumper stretched over her breast. She comes to lower school collectives, the stage where I can play my part of older leader—because I got failed last year, if for no other reason. And she in her skirt & pullover, they've seen her hanging around with young Christ-Dems, normally I would avoid her. And at the end of one of those assemblies, as the younger kids were walking back to class, she asked me if she could hug me. Permission granted. But then she wanted to say something.

'What's the matter?'

'I saw the posters on Moro in the main office.'

'Which main office?'

'The Christ-Dems'.'

'Well, that's normal, isn't it?'

'No it's not—they're obituary posters.'

'. . .'

'Ready to roll out. They've buried him already.'

'Well—'

'They make me sick, Pietro—the guys on my side, I mean.'

Pietro. And I think she's about to start crying. For Aldo Moro?

ON TIME   The whole world is in the telephone. I'm talking to Igor, to Ruben. I'd like to talk to the Catholic girl—but no.

'That's right—no use whingeing.'

'Well—maybe it's some use to you—'

'What about you, eh?'

'Well, I'm all right—working.'

'Yes thank you, Igor.'

'What else would I say? It's not too bad—'

'OK—but where have they put you?'

'Rivalta. Paint shop.'

'Oh shite.'

'We-ell, it's always like that at the beginning. Then in a couple of months they might move me on to sticking the paper stripes under the shells.'

'That's easier, isn't it?'

'Yes it is—healthwise.' He laughs, and I don't understand.

'And otherwise?'

'Well, let's say the paint shop has more—more movement.'

'You mean comrades?'

'Hmmm. People with real balls. Counterpower is not just some bullshit chatter over here. So there's a sonofabitch of a shift boss who's laying it on and getting pushy? Well, the other day we made a banner for him. Give it 24 hours, and his car'll go up in flames.'

'Fucking hell. Is that not risky though?'

'Well—in the meantime he's changed his ways some. There's this comrade, Matteo, a tough guy—and he goes, "So what's all the friendliness about, boss—your new car arrived?" He didn't half get scared, I tell you.'

'. . .'

'Look, soon's any of them starts getting cocky there'll be an inside demo on the spot, people in balaclavas making blockades. When we stop, everything stops.'

'Cool.'

'Yes—you're inside things, over here.'

'Hmmm—'

'. . .'

'What about work rhythms?'

'Nothing like I was expecting—when I'm on the line I can get ahead and grab a coffee, more often than not.'

'I knew a different story.'

'Well, things do change. They say that back in the day the line was so fast that you'd risk shipping out—meaning, you couldn't keep up and missed the part. These days you can even pull up—

as in, walk up the line and go for the work, and you'll make a few minutes on every shell.'

'Cool shit.'

'Yes—everything's different. These days it's us control the timings—for instance, if we all go upstream on one line, we can even end production and the line will stop early. Even an hour early.'

'So you can go home?'

'Not so fast—there's the Impartial.'

'Who's that?'

'What, not who. When you get out you've got to press this button, there's a machine that says if you're going to get frisked by the guards or not.'

'Bet it's always getting the comrades.'

'No, it really is random, it's a mechanism—it can get anyone, even a boss, for instance. Hence, the Impartial. And anyway it sits right there where you clock in or out, so it's not like you can go anytime you like.'

'So are you all right or are you sick?'

'Better off—much better than I thought.'

'That's just what you say to sound tough, right?'

'No it's not.'

'So what is it you do when you've made some time on the line?'

'All sorts—even assemblies, for instance, but there's not that many of those these days, truth be told. We play cards—'

'Some counterpower! Two minutes ago I thought I was on the phone with Lenin himself, for fuck's sake.'

'See, I knew you wouldn't understand a fucking thing. That's praxis—it's nearly second nature by now, it's an immediate collective reaction to—I mean the unions, meetings, all that long stuff. All that is changing.'

'That's right. And so you play cards.'

'That too. So what? Look, spare time—we've talked about it some, haven't we?'

'All right, all right—only joking.'

'For instance, there's a guy buys all the papers and lays them out like a library. There's a drafts tournament, there's a market, you can buy all sorts with the stuff people take in—clothes, radios even.'

'Cool shit.'

'It's almost human these days. You can work at FIAT these days. The battle on time is fought in here too.'

'. . . I'm running out of change, Igor—I'll call you tomorrow or day after.'

'Do. And no shit-for-brains freaking out, OK? She's really not worth it.'

'I thought you were the one in love with her.'

'Pietro?'

'What.'

'Suck my dick.'

'All right—when it grows. Bye.'

'Bye. And no blubbing, all right?'

COCÒ   Except I could easily do some blubbing. Not for Igor, though he says he can even play cards. I'm back in Florence, since there's nothing I can say to anyone in the pig yard at Pian di Sco, or even in Bologna. If worse comes to worse, there's always Giuliana stuck to me like a limpet, with her bone—uh—China certainties and the whole world as nicely rounded and communist as her cheeks. On May Day I'm on Piazza della Signoria for the demo: people everywhere, in small groups more than cordons—a village Sunday. Under the arcade, suddenly, a familiar face, a friend—in fact, Cocò. There might be a few more of our guys too, I'm looking around but can't see anyone. 'Hey!' he turns around, shoots a nasty look at me. I move closer: 'Fucksake, Cocò!' He looks around, turns the other way to avoid looking at me. 'Cocò!' He turns around again, glares at me and hisses: 'Fuck off, you dick-head.' And then he turns and goes. Quickly. And I'm frozen to the spot. It's nothing really, a little shit like any other, a Carletto or Ninetto getting big-headed. But I want to cry. I go with the demo. At Orsanmichele, written on the wall: 'Free Curcio—or we'll free Moro at you.'

URANIA   And then I don't know what happened with Moro. Don't know if he's alive or dead, if he's got out and is speaking in the same tone as in the letters, if he's taken up a news night episode to explain about the real face of the world and start a new season for man, don't know if it's him at those funerals without the dead man. I don't know anything about that comrade either, the one the mafia has laid across the train tracks in Palermo strapped to a TNT charge, and L'Unità writing that he's a terrorist who's gone and killed himself. And the reason I don't know is, I've phoned home and my mother is crying and saying 'Come home on the first train.' Crying like a child, her vowels wailing open, not a pretty sound. And she's not saying what happened, but I'll waste no time asking questions—no use hanging around here anyway. A long wait at the station: the train leaves at five, I'll be home shortly after midnight changing at Pisa, and I have a Urania. I ought to be studying, I think it's back to school tomorrow, even, and I can't afford to lose another year. Fuck these polynomials—don't know how I'll ever get on with maths, can't understand the first thing about algebra. Polynomials in my brain, x over z times w open braces close parenthesis divide by alpha at the station of Santa Maria Novella. You need a form-equipped mindset—e.g., the zeros in a polynomial are the values which, when assigned to variables, bring the final expression to equal zero. They'll fill the hollows, even out the convex parts. This is it: I could do with a machine that dishes out my zeroes automatically—input me, output the zeroes. I have no such machine—I have a Urania.

Dead of night when I get home, and I can see something's wrong even as I walk into the yard: there's a glass pane replaced with some cardboard sheets stuck on with packing tape. I go up and open the door hoping to find my parents asleep. Light from the landing seeps in from the crack I've slipped through and shows up the blue cloud hanging one yard above the floor: they've been smoking as much as it's possible and impossible to smoke. Another thread of light, from under the kitchen door: my mother is sat at the table trying to write something—a letter. She jumps up to come and hug me, then backs away in restraint, or maybe it's me pushing her back with a gesture. She bursts out crying. 'Marianella—'

'Marianella what?'

'Go and see your Dad.' Just like when I was small and had done something wrong, and she'd send me off to beg for harmony and forgiveness. He's standing in the living room, leaning against the window. I have to wade through the smoke before I can see him. His right hand is bandaged: at least now I know what happened to the glass pane. He takes me by one shoulder and hugs me. I want to shrug him off, but let it go, wait it out: 'But what happened?'

'Did Mum not tell you?' Mum.

'No—what?'

'She's pas—she's dead.' His voice breaks. Not very military.

'What do you mean, dead?' He nods yes.

'Marianella is gone.' Images through my head, none of them about Marianella. 'You must be strong.'

Me? I have to be strong? Shows you're talking nonsense, Dad. I wish I could say something about anything—the broken window, maybe. And feel anything by way of a reaction—a tear would be enough. But no—nothing. Maybe it's just that I can't quite believe it. My mother has slipped into the room after me. She has not switched on the light. How many days have these two spent in the dark?

'She was shy—when she got on stage she couldn't—she needed it, you understand—to stay up and be able to sing.'

'No, look, I don't understand—please.' She's making an effort to wear a face suited to the occasion, looks for a teaching tone, she's going to act like Mum now.

'She used to take substances.'

'You mean she killed herself?'

'No—she made a mistake—she—' My father breaks in.

'Heroin, Pietro. Marianella was addicted.' So. A sentence like this spoken by him—I'd have expected it to come out in a contemptuous hiss. To come from as far away as a colonel is. But no. In a low, low voice, the colonel adds: 'It was her father.' My mother takes his hand as if to stop him. His eyes are swollen, he is huffing, and I think of Marina, of the spider's stare.

SMELL OF WATER (1970)   Box hedges, the usual cloying smell and white gravel as in any cemetery. And men in uniform pushing the coffin that won't go into the niche not meant for it. My father and Uncle Mario far off, and Aunt Rosalba whispering something as she strokes the stone.

'Hoooong Kooooong . . .' One of those voices struggling to get through the whorls of a stomach in the throes of heavy digestion, something midway between a belch and a lament. The same thick curtain of smoke, at navel height: my nine-year-old navel. Darkness. And loosened ties over bellies sprawled upward, low leather armchairs, spools whirring and two slim women rubbing against each other. One turns to face the audience and runs her tongue over her lips: she has slanted eyes. Someone notices I've crept into the room: the light projected from the crack as I opened the door showed me up, cutting across the room for an instant, falling on the base of the screen where the black & white home movie is rolling. 'Let the lad stay—he's a male: the earlier he understands the earlier he'll start getting busy.' But Uncle Mario is not listening, he walks over with his cigarette clenched between his teeth, tip pointing upward, shirtsleeves and braces: 'I'm sorry, young man—this is off limits for the troop.' He takes me by the arm and pushes me out, but he's not angry, he even gives me a friendly spank: 'Run along now.'

They're all night sequences—perhaps because that was the first time I'd been allowed to stay up late, apart from the moon landing. At the seaside you're allowed, at the seaside it's all right, and I loved to wait for sleep on the margins of their parties. All I remember of that Sicilian summer in 1970 is parties, and at night I was learning the smell of water and the call of cicadas that grated on my ears accustomed to the soft blowing of crickets in Colleretto. Marinalonga, villas embedded in plant life like hermit caves, a party behind every glass pane and streams of words at every party: 'This is the Athens of gossip,' Aunt Rosalba said to my mother, partly as a joke but partly to warn her. I stand watching the agaves, at night they're a bit scary, like great old animals made wise by age who might wake up again and resume the hunt. I steer clear of their toothed leaves fringing the braziers left smouldering until the morning for anyone who might fancy a bit of grilled meat, and stay on the shoreline where there are young girls running around who have large eyes and friendly ways. Empty white wine bottles, stained tablecloths, the long beach in Mondello, Aunt Rosalba steering my mother through the forest of people as if she were a child who must see the world. And the huts of Sferracavallo and Cinisi and Terrasini, and the great bonfires by the sea on the mid-August holiday. There was a gentleman who had become a great friend of my father's, an elegant man, very dark, with a broken nose. He made children laugh and stroked them, and he taught me all the secrets to pass the endless time you must spend at the table waiting for dessert: say a little star made of toothpicks that will open like a clam if you let a drop of water fall into its heart, or the toothpick jutting out from the corner of the table under the tablecloth to hold a bottle balanced over the void. Or the paper wrapper for oranges: roll it up in a cylinder, set it alight and it will take off one split second before the flame reaches the tablecloth. Or the dentures he would make for himself out of an orange peel to flash a sudden smile at me. A dinner-table airman, tamer of toothpicks, sit-down acrobat, vessel of wonders: I remember him because of this, but also because of the incident on the beach. One day we saw him with a bruised-up face, one eye stuck shut by a purple melon of flesh, his lips covered in scabs and his nose blackened and flattened out towards his cheeks, one arm in a splint, bandages across his chest under his shirt.

He says he was walking around the cliffs last night and slipped and fell, wears his usual face, but everyone's saying he got beaten up. He was in Terrasini last night. Was he perhaps meant to be meeting the comandante? The comandante is a ghost, a mythical character who is meant to come any evening but never does. 'I'll introduce you one of these nights, you'll see,' everyone used to say—that is, my father, Uncle Mario, the nice gentleman even, and they were telling me about the comandante's wartime adventures and how he did not betray the sworn allegiance to Italy. 'The women say we're jailbirds.' But if he ever did come, I was surely asleep.

The nice friend of my father's had named his daughter after the comandante: Signorina Junia. But Uncle Mario didn't get on too well with him: 'He's working for a communist newspaper these days,' he'd say. One evening a carabinieri colonel had come to supper at Uncle Mario's: a tall man with hair swept back from his forehead, and you could see he was an important guy, and I'd asked was he maybe. But no, not him—even though this was a strong, clever man who scared off all the bandits. Not a nice guy, though: I remember that he never spoke and left very early, and no sooner had he gone than the sluice gates of gossip flew open, the women especially were saying all sorts about Colonel Bogeyman.

The nice guy, the one who'd got bruised up, was not an officer: he was a journalist, and one night Aunt Rosalba had made him blush by telling everyone that he also had a future in the movies, there was an important director who had engaged him to shoot a film in the autumn. I told him I wanted to be a journalist too when I grew up, but that wasn't true: I wanted to be an officer. After the incident, his friendship with my father had become stronger, they were always together, even though Dad was younger. He was treating him like a sort of teacher, and they'd spend hours by themselves talking about anything, including their shared passion for Juve. And once—the mid-August holiday had been and gone and we were beginning to think of going back home—Dad had been away for two whole days and Mum and Auntie were talking thick and fast and you could see Mum was worried, but then she was always worried until she saw he was back home—her man. I was asking, and Mum was smiling wide, saying that she and I were on holiday, but Dad was here to work.

Mum was going out with Aunt Rosalba, as if hand in hand, and it seemed like she was always thinking up new ways to get in trouble. One evening at the restaurant in Sferracavallo there were three or four families of important people, they had arrived on two yachts big as clippers, and everyone was greeting them. They were deadly handsome, dressed in light colours, young, and you could see they were having a great time. If someone had told a good joke they would share it loudly around the other tables. On some evenings, Uncle Mario looked like the king of the world, and was holding my dad in the palm of his hand. 'My little bro,' he would say. But he was showing huge respect for those guys from the boat, kissing the women's hands and speaking to the men as if they were his elders. Well, that night at Sferracavallo, Mum put her foot in it for the fault of two men in white who had started trading words over a seating place: 'This was my lady's seat,' and you couldn't quite tell if they were horsing around or really fighting: they'd turn grim for a moment and then burst out laughing or wink at the audience that was gathering. 'Well, one ass is as good as another,' one of the duellists had said. 'But we're talking about my lady here,' and on like that for ever, firing their 'my lady' broadsides all around the veranda. Until one of the two contenders thought he'd get out of the hot spot by turning to Mum: 'Well, I don't know what we're going to look like with these ladies and gentlemen here, they come from Turin and are surely not accustomed to our wicked fights. Isn't that so, madam? What do you think of our argument?' My mother could lop heads off with a sudden icy glare, that was her main charm: 'What do I think? I think I've just witnessed a spat between two cretins.' Aunt Rosalba glided in on the double, parting the crowd with hurried steps, half like a mother and half like a raptor swooping on a sparrow, and she took Mum out on the balcony, and they'stopped to talk. Mum was laughing, Auntie not a bit.

That was the summer of Marianella dancing in the evening, the summer of her swimming costumes. And at night she'd go out late to meet her friends, because everything starts much later over there, and not much ends before daybreak. And before going out she'd stop with me and teach me about teenagers' things and tell me about boring friends and cool ones. I had one nasty secret I'd only shared with her: about the skipper who'd locked me into the changing room on the beach and pushed my head against his belly, then immediately opened the door and said 'Get,' and I'd run off to wash myself and didn't want to tell Mum or Dad. Marianella was like the fireworks on the mid-August holiday: if she got mad the whole world would know about it—and in fact she did get mad at her father nearly every night, and everyone stood to watch, she made such a show. But when I'd told her about the skipper her face had turned dark and she said she'd speak to my uncle and that the skipper would be sent away. 'At the very least,' she'd said. Then she'd asked me if Mum had never told me not to follow strangers—not scolding me, more with sadness. But I knew that skipper, he was the one who'd sailed us out to see the islands. 'That doesn't mean anything,' Marianella had said. 'You could have died. He could have done horrible things to you.'

SUBJECT: ORANGE   According to the teachings of Huang Po, Mind is the Buddha, while the cessation of conceptual thought is the Way. Hence, based on this premise, the rules of normalcy are temporarily suspended in favour of new rules of which no hints can be given. If, however, one wishes to establish a starting point, this would be best situated in the phase of crossing the Lesser Magellanic Cloud. Tom Mishkin's Intrepid III is tooling along the Cloud heading for the colony of Dora V with a load of frozen South African lobster tails. Then, the crash. Tom's pilot ear, always attuned for the Malfunction That Could Not Happen but always does, perks up. Malfunction in part L-1223: port side valve and retainer ring. Immediate automatic main drive shut-down. Up space creek without a paddle. Any attempt at restarting would result in the following consequences: (A) total main drive disablement; (B) implosion; (C) death; (D) permanent black mark on the service record of the pilot, who would also (E) be billed for a new spaceship. The only feasible option is to reach one of the caches of spare parts: the nearest is on Harmonia II, 68 hours' journey by secondary drive.

Use of 'multiple premises' termed confusing: Professor David Hume of Harvard declares that sequence does not imply causality. Professor Kant, in his Cal Tech study, looks badly shaken. 'This,' he says, 'has awakened me from my dogmatic slumber.' At a loss, Mishkin reaches for the Turn-off Bottle. It has a label that reads, 'If the trip goes bad, drink this', and another on the other side, 'If the trip goes bad, do not drink this'. He quickly drinks the contents of the Turn-off Bottle: it couldn't get much worse, he decides—which shows how much he knows. Then he issues his orders to the control board: 'We will proceed to act on the premise that we all are what we seem to be at this moment and that we will remain this way indefinitely.' This creates havoc. A voice from the control board intervenes: 'What would you say if I told you that I am a middle-aged psychiatrist from New York City and that your act of labelling me a control board shows where your head is at?' Anyhow Mishkin does land near the cache on Harmonia, where the control panel to the parts counter confesses to being in the middle of a trying time and informs him that the part he requires is about fifteen miles away: a decentralization dictated by security criteria, guarding against the chance of a disabled ship crashing on top of the cache. So human pilots in search of parts are forced to go out on the surface of Harmonia, an alien planet, which by definition is a Classified Dangerous Activity. For his safety and security, Mishkin is assigned a SPER (Special Purpose Environmental Response) robot specialized in responding to the environment. SPER is short and rectangular, has a most attractive scarlet case and walks on four spindly limbs. Mishkin figures that the robot knows what he's doing, but he's wrong: add SPER's ignorance to Mishkin's and you will get vertigo.

The first hallucination is a chef with a battered harmonica who is devoid of any criteria to tell the real from the unreal. Blasters in hand, the two find themselves fending off the mating dance of the proto-Brontostegosauruses: dangerous animals, since information relative to the intended subject of their passion takes a few minutes to get through to their brains, which entails the risk of being mistaken for the ideal mate. There follow cows disguised as tigers and other tricks. Mishkin and the robot cruise through the unknown, and following the potentially lethal consequences of a few mishaps, it becomes clear that SPER is programmed for Darbis IV and not for Harmonia. During the heated exchange that ensues, there appears a worm some twenty feet long, coloured orange, with black bands and five heads arranged in a cluster, each with a single multifaceted eye and a toothless, moist green mouth. The heads are called Vince, Eddie, Lucco, Joe & Chico Pagliotelli. Vince has become the head of the family after the death of Poppa Pagliotelli. They are fighting over whether or not they should eat Mishkin and the robot. Mishkin points out it is not good practice for intelligent creatures to eat one another. 'You trying to teach me manners?' Vince says. 'Me, intelligent? I never even finished high school! Ever since Poppa died I've had to work twelve hours a day in the sheet metal shop to keep the kids. But at least I'm smart enough to know that I ain't smart.' Vince confesses that what he really always wanted to do was study the violin, and advises the two to look out. 'What sort of things should we look out for, specifically?' Mishkin asks. 'Everything, specifically.'

Accidents. Fatalism. To measure up to the challenge, SPER takes on the appearance of a 1968 Rover TC2000. Labelled objects, labelled actions. Desert giving way to semi-desert. Many adventures, as karma catches up with us all. Enter Ronsard the Magnificent, the Great Thermos, the White Leather Man worshipped by robots of the Schenectady area. Grand space-opera scenes, voices from another level. The beast that kills by boredom is also found in these parts. His voice is firm and authoritative, his statements are unchallengeable, his appearance unimpeachable. He speaks to you in a reasonable manner until your impulse to wish him dead although he's done nothing wrong to you vanishes and you are snared in apathy and pushed to suicide. Just at this moment he is boring fish for his dinner by lecturing to them on their inalienable rights. Mishkin is spotted by a bill collector who knows every detail about his debts. No matter: the Life Systems

Support Mechanism tells him to stop taking dream medicine—a good idea, but contrasting with the intrinsic creatural (and therefore impermanent) nature of the Mechanism itself. Sub-assemblies spread and proliferate. Mishkin points out that his journey has a specific purpose and that too much is happening to him. Orchidius and SPER agree, and Orchidius explains that everybody is a bit player in the movie of Orchidius' life. Through a space-time continuum crossover we are now back on Earth. We see everything according to a different topology, so the reality apprehended by our senses is subtly altered. Ramsey Davis is impaled in the course of Premature Conclusions, the Mishkin Museum is a success, and old friends are writing to Tom. Repetition is inevitable, but it clearly has a decisive function in the structure of the narrative. However, distortions must be expected. Mishkin intercepts a recorded message to remind you not to forget. The plot thickens, loses any epic character but acquires some magic. The Man of a Thousand Disguises (MTD) sits in his temporary office and considers the problem of Mishkin and the engine part. Somehow the two will not come together: the MTD has been forced to invent himself as a deus ex machina and is now endeavouring to explain what is to himself still inexplicable. Having constructed himself, he is now stuck with himself. To simplify things, he quickly abolishes the necessity of explaining himself. He only has to explain about how Mishkin and the engine part will come together. He tries out a dozen alternative hypotheses, some deliciously improbable, including an attempt to revisit the reality principle. A few peregrinations and boating adventures later, Mr New Hero appears. Mishkin meets him but remains unimpressed. There's even a hint of Emilio Salgari. As for Proteus, he gets a chance, but it is clear from the outset that he is a cheap solution. The MTD writes Mishkin a dejected letter. This is followed by the Final Transformation.

'Tommy! Stop playing now!'

'I'm not playing, Mum. This is real.'

'I know. But you have to stop playing now and come home.'

'I can't get home, that's the problem. I need a part for my spaceship.'

'I told you to stop playing. Put down that broom and come into the house at once.'

'It's not a broom, it's a spaceship. Anyhow, my robot says . . .'

'And bring that old radio in with you. Hurry up, you have homework to do and the dinner's getting cold.'

'All right. But really, it is a spaceship, and it is broken.'

'All right, it's a broken spaceship. Are you coming in?'

'Yes, Mum, I'm coming in right now.'

It ends with a photograph of the 2nd battalion of the 32nd infantry, 7th division, 8th Army. The faces are all alike, but if you look carefully, Mishkin is in the fourth row from the bottom, third face from the left. He has a silly smirk on his face. He is in no way remarkable.

6

Options

(1958–1970)

OPTIONS BY ROBERT SHECKLEY   I started copying it
after Marianella's funeral, thinking it would make me look interesting to you: I wanted to win you, but was not able to rely on
myself. And I finish here: I've failed to think up anything decent
since beginning to write to you. I've no plan. I thought I'd propose
we should revive our old deal—I don't know how. I think it'd be
good to stick a bomb under the ass of the benevolent, paternal
boss who's sacked you—you know, just to follow the curve of
necessity, which is almost like leading it.

We are living in the age of Thersites, the world inaugurated
by Marina in ringlets and me as a fledgling standing at the grave
of my friend Bruno, who died a child. It is forbidden to grow old,
and today our world has its manifesto: a page in La Repubblica
where the children who have died under the rubble of a collapsed
school are called 'angels'—chronicles from the angels' funerals,
interviews, the thoughtful journalist at pains to show she actually
is on site describing the toys and little rucksacks left in the after-
math, the blood. There's even a column listing the misdeeds of
the administration: the skimping on building costs, the slow tim-
ing of intervention and aid—someone will be held to account for
this. And so they will—but within the limits of one and a half

sides, because the maximum visibility, horizontal lower half-page slot is taken up by a huge, pretty-young-lady stiletto: silent and incongruous, in pride of place, it is there by right, black on white, and no one's going to ask for its ID. No words, except for the brand: Prada.

By copying from the pages of a Urania I was able to level with myself a bit: I had discovered that my own good was outside myself, and I wasn't used to that. I stayed plunged in my own Urania, I think that all around a battle had been raging between the work principle and the body principle, and the body must have won. So I should have been happy, since that was the banner I'd been fighting under. But instead I had lost myself and would get further and further lost from then on, with no other guide than the black & white sequence of workday/holiday, workday/ holiday, workday/holiday. I didn't know how to approach you, and I went for a scam, a word-theft I thought would make me interesting. Another man's words: this was the first thing I ever did without my own self as a goal. To lie and be ashamed, to risk being found out, only to get close to you. And as you know, it worked. Of course I never told you, even in the years when we could have laughed about it, and I was hoping with every day that you would lose that very precious letter. We even made a lifelong pact.

Marina—I only saw her once again, having picked up the phone at the wrong moment, one afternoon a few months later. Her voice was dull, she was pleading, asking for five minutes' time, she wasn't even going to come to my house, just five minutes at the No. 69 bus headstop, Piazza Solferino. The sky was clear, she was already at the stop, looking tiny in that great big bus shelter in the middle of the square. She was wearing different clothes from the sort I knew—yellow toile trousers with a matching jacket, all too light for the season. Her face might have always looked sharp, but now it was a razor blade. And her clothes stank, like that last day at her house. I remember she ventured to say that she had not reached orgasm since . . . I told her to stop it, and after that I don't know what else either of us might have said. But I do know how it ended: with her crying and asking for money. 'Five thousand liras—and I swear you'll never see me again.' I made her repeat the oath and gave her the money.

With Giuliana it was easier. Shortly after Marianella's funeral, one evening my father told me they were screening Belle de jour at Cinema Alpi. He'd seen it when he was young, and had never made up his mind as to whether he liked it or not: against all that had been happening between us for years, he said he'd be interested in my take on it, and was wondering if I at least would understand what might be in the box that the Chinese guy shows Catherine Deneuve. We went the next night, driving in the Cinquecento. On Corso Siccardi, my father slowed down a touch and pointed his finger to the right: standing at the No. 72 bus stop were Dino and Giuliana, kissing with such passion it was clear this was happening at the same time every evening. I felt a surge of relief and went into the cinema. I couldn't tell my father what was buzzing inside the Chinese guy's box.

Johnny went up in the world, took power, killed Judge Alessandrini and some other people. He and his boys were overcome by the thrill of other people's deaths: they murdered a student (by mistake) as he was walking down the street, and a barman (by choice) because two of their guys had been killed in his venue. As for Cocò's strange behaviour in Florence, I would understand it a while later when I saw his photo in the paper: he had enrolled with Johnny and was scared he'd be recognized. And once, Johnny also damaged Igor: together with his mathematician friend from Milan, he wrote an extremely clever pamphlet on industrial policies in late Italian capitalism. Then, so as to give the pamphlet some audience, he killed a FIAT engineer. That was like a signal. The company stopped tolerating the ongoing warfare: sixteen woundings, and now the killing. The tank turned is turret once and for all and unleashed its fire power for all to see. On 9 September 1979, sixty-one redundancy notices were issued to union militants and political avant-gardes. The campaign was termed 'normalization of production'. Even the FIAT men were astounded at the weakness of the reaction: aside from a few bland words, the unions were accepting a fact that had been unprecedented at least since 1969, the year of the workers' resurrection. The sixty-one left, never to return to the factory. That was the dress rehearsal for what would happen exactly one year later, in the autumn of 1980. Even the conquest of time Igor had been speaking of that day on the phone had turned against him: those long pauses on the side of the assembly lines, those card games and all the rest were conclusive proof of an uneconomic use of machineries. It was irrefutable by now, and the humans had nothing to oppose but a few peevish moral arguments.

More answered prayers: the assembly lines outgrown, the end of Fordist alienation, the 'new way of making cars' (all the key words central to the workers' movement over the century that was going into receivership) had become realities, and realities to be reckoned with. Igor was one of the sixty-one expelled. I don't know if he'd already started flirting with heroin or if he began after that trauma, but those were terrible years, during which he and Marcella locked themselves in a garret and went through all the stations of that nightmare. They fought their way out of it, alone, with the strength of giants. Igor found a job with the council's funeral service.

So what about us? Let's look at the options: we can make ourselves at home in the ranks of consumers and fight for a place of power, or let ourselves be milked and then put out to pasture or thrown by the wayside without even a shred of liturgy—the watch given to the FIAT senior on retirement, say. Or maybe not. Maybe we've still got some time, maybe we've not yet understood which side we're on. After all, things only really make sense as a whole, and our lives will only be understood when they are over. For instance, you and I could have a child, since we can't afford to, and while the clock is still on our side. And pledge ourselves to that child for the rest of our days. Maybe that child will wake the army of the dead who have walked the pages of this story.

But there's yet a couple of things I have to tell you. Things that, in a sense, are on the verso of the sheet on which this story is written—in fact, they are this story itself, in the places where I cannot tell it.

ANTECHAMBER   As he sat waiting for his interview with Colonel Dalla Chiesa at the carabinieri legion in Palermo, Major Miasco was wondering whether he was gambling his career away or saving it. He had just gone through the hardest forty-eight hours in his entire life: hard as those he had spent by his father's deathbed, when he had caught himself praying for him to die.

Miasco Sr would have loved to see his less assertive son, the younger one who seemed to have no future, make headway in the armed forces with the same drive as his older brother—and Francesco had plunged into the military life partly to expiate his last, blasphemous, answered prayer. Now, as he sat in the small waiting room, he was thinking something different: perhaps his father would have liked to see him sacrifice his professional life in the name of the principles he had passed down. So many painstakingly upheld ideals had come to nothing but rubble, and a curtain of white poison stopped Major Miasco seeing himself. He was clinging to his sense of duty, but failing to find anything to give it solidity. He knew that to some, what he was about to do was 'treason'. The only thing that supported him was the idea, albeit abstract, of a duty superior to any personal considerations. His mind was made up. He was trying to keep his face inexpressive, reminded himself to stop biting his lower lip as he sat on a wooden chair, his back straight like when he was a schoolboy, his eyelids lowered but only slightly more than usual.

Gorilla Batungo and Gorilla Baringo.

Robert Kennedy's funeral: his son asking, how can that boy stand in the church so close to his daddy's coffin—is he not scared of ghosts?

The moon landing, Tito Stagno—we must wake Pietrino, he should see this, it's a historical moment.

The wind through the open windows of the Cinquecento, driving on the Gargano.

The cat following him like a dog, and two warrior geese guarding the house, and father not yet back, not back.

The wind, wind in his face, always the wind.

One night in June, his nose swollen from an allergy and Mariano outside the tent insisting they go out after women: 'Let me sleep or I'll shoot you.'

His father's death throes, Mario's absence, yes Mario's absence—Mario was at the Academy when father died.

Early morning, still dark, his cargo of pears for sale tied up in a tablecloth and slung over his back, those grown girls going down to the market and the shame of having to sell, the shame worst of all.

His uniforms—the first one, the last, the diagonal stripe for summer.

Poldo the dog going off to die in a sage patch.

That evening when Pietrino went out to get ice-cream and took for ever coming back.

'Ah, Miasco—good afternoon. Come into my office, I'm afraid this is going to take a while.'

'Sir—' Major Miasco had shot to his feet and was about to stand at attention. To his relief, Colonel Dalla Chiesa avoided formalities.

'Easy, easy, please. Would you like a coffee?'

'Yes please, sir.'

'Do come through.'

A CAREER   It had started with poverty, with his need for emulation, his urge to get out and away. His brother Mario had already been in Modena three years when Francesco Miasco finished the Liceo Classico. He was full of humanist fire and fanciful wishes that the military life stifled, year after year, denying him the company of any of those high-strung girls born for university and love stories. Mario was calling out to him.

Nothing to do with family tradition: old Miasco had been a sublieutenant in the WW1 and later a registered fascist in uniform—but his was a railwayman's uniform, and his ancestors had always been farmers, not so badly off either. But war, hunger, their father's purging had swept away any plans for further education the Miasco brothers might have had.

In Modena, the military academy is a guarantee of duty, prestige and a solid serviceman wage. Francesco joined in 1954 as a trainee officer in the eighth course. He showed all the determination of one who has to prove to his parents he's not the mistake of one night. It had worked for him: Francesco Miasco, a lover of cars and horses (two species unfamiliar to his previous life), came out top of his course, beautiful as a divine blessing, tall and strongly built, one of those excellent young officers who get noticed by their superiors.

Mario was always one step ahead of Francesco in the ranking hierarchy: he still called him 'little bro', but now the 'little bro' was good enough to show off as a trophy. Francesco was embarrassed by the pride Mario took in him, but respected his elder brother, a brilliant officer—decisive, selective: two much-prized virtues in their profession.

In 1958, Sublieutenant Miasco had a conversation with Captain Miasco which proved of much moment to his career. Mario was on assignment leading a company of alpini riders in the Alto Adige, and had asked his brother to take advantage of a brief leave permit he himself was going to provide and join him in the Val di Casies, where he and his division were quartered for a summer training camp. Francesco was on duty in Milan, and it was not without surprise that he found himself in possession of the permit his brother had mentioned. The meeting between the two happened one evening in June, after muster and the assigning of off-duty times and watch shifts. Mario and Francesco made their way to a tavern in San Martino in Casies.

They took their time, gave time to the clear Alto Adige wine and the meadow filling with fireflies. When the meaty soup in wooden bowls that gave the tavern its good name was served, Mario decided to get to the point. A hereditary restraint had kept them both away from childhood reminiscences, except for a few hints exchanged like they would do as children, in a sort of code known only to the two of them. Mario cracked a joke about the episode of the flight from Cuneo after the rout of the Decima MAS: it contained in unspoken form the whole of their father's destiny, the injustices suffered, the hardships the family was still having to face. Francesco got his brother's drift immediately. Mario saw his chance to change the subject: he started speaking of the communist offensive, said that the lesson of Hungary had gone unheeded. 'The military didn't just stand and watch, Francesco. From the outset a few thought about being prepared for a sudden communist attack. Did you know there are whole regions where a quarter of the population takes orders from the Slavs?'

Francesco nodded: these days, in '58, you couldn't even mention Tito's henchmen in public, for reasons to do with international political opportunity and routine Italian hypocrisy. Mario told the story of his direct superior, Colonel Olivieri, a former partisan in the Osoppo Brigade in Friuli. In '45, when the Osoppo had been disbanded, Olivieri and the other commanders had asked military authorities to re-arm their units so as to counter the beastly violence of Tito's men in border zones. Mario was telling the story of an organization called O, after Osoppo, that was still active under the command of Colonel Olivieri under the name of Stella Alpina: 5,050 men, 300 officers and nearly 500 NCOs. Francesco was fascinated by his brother's words, he liked to feel he was part of a state with steel nerves and keen teeth, he could feel the strength of the democracy to which he had devoted himself the day he had sworn allegiance to the republic.

'An elite unit.'

'More than that—Stella Alpina also works in peacetime, it has intelligence activities inside and outside the armed forces.'

'You mean you have some civilians?'

'That too. But we report to the V Comiliter.' Mario was laughing. 'And so do you, Francesco—except you don't know!' Politics is a swamp, the military is smothered in bureaucracy, if structures such as O were out in the open the public would stir up the usual hornet's nest, it would be no use. The wine was helping Mario and Francesco to bypass all the usual, slightly rhetorical comments that would have been necessary on other occasions, between different interlocutors. 'There are still some,' Mario continued, 'who trust the armed forces, the clean part of the country. Important people, Francesco—there's Costa with the Confindustria, Valletta, the Pirelli brothers, Mattei the engineer—'

Those names did not mean much to the sublieutenant eager for action: his new war ethics included a touch of generic contempt for civilians. His next comment was of a technical nature: he said this sounded like a tactical group, and well organized as it might be, it wouldn't amount to much in case of a civil war steered from abroad.

'There's not only Stella Alpina, but many units—Giglio, Fratelli d'Italia who liaise with the British, the Armata Italiana per la Libertà, Pace e Libertà. And then the structures for psychological defence of the ministry of the interior.'

'Paramilitaries, you mean.'

'No—the co-ordinating is ours. Let's say it's a military network making use of civilian personnel. Nothing odd about that— the mobilizing plans, division weaponry and materials are all in our and carabinieri barracks. Olivieri, for instance, reports directly to the Mantua division. Civilians are useful for private funding, but it's the central co-ordinating body that guarantees the dollars. Understand? It's us the Americans trust. They used to rely only on the navy, and in fact navy divisions have been covered since earlier times. It's all stuff written down in the Marshall Plan agreements . . .' Mario knew how to mesmerize his younger brother. There was a need for people like them, staunch anti-communists with proven military skill. 'It means working with the Defence College—a blazing career. And guess what, little bro: logistics officers are most highly in demand.'

Logistics officer Francesco Miasco had already decided to get on board, and Mario knew it: he had long cracked the code of the bony face across the table. After that, the evening grew awkward, as often happens between males raised with few words and unaccustomed by family tradition to the art of conversation.

FILIPPO (2)   Francesco returned to Milan the next morning. Mario had given him certain documents to read, pages and more pages in English and Italian. One read, 'SANDRO declares that the tasks of the organization are set out as follows: (A) in peacetime: control and neutralization of communist activities; (B) in case of a conflict threatening the border, or internal insurrection: anti-guerrilla, sabotage of communist fifth columns acting in support of the attacking military forces or insurgent forces; (C) in case of territorial invasion: partisan struggle, intelligence service.' The document was classified 'top secret'. Francesco was flattered that his brother would run such a risk to enrol him. Better a madman like Mario, he thought, than the mass of hapless civilians paralysing the forces of Italy's young democracy.

Francesco Miasco soon realized that something was changing in his career path. He was sent to the infantry school at Cesano Romano for special force training with General Aloja: something young officers mentioned often enough, but always in the hushed tones of people speaking of a legend. The training courses really did exist, they were as hard as Francesco could have imagined, and included every sort of update on techniques such as guerrilla, counter-guerrilla, psychological warfare, propaganda and counter-propaganda. After six months in Cesano, Francesco was promoted and transferred to Verona, at the disposal of Major Spiazzi. The network needed him, and he began to need the network: his job was to ensure that vehicles and materials were kept moving along the right corridors, at the disposal of the Stay Behind divisions. A secondary role, perhaps, but one on which his country's Atlantic fealty depended. He put all the enthusiasm and dedication he could muster into the task.

There were neofascist civilians. Francesco viewed them as little more than local colour: their ranks, all pennants and Nazi slogans, fed an easily influenced reserve list and an ideological network apt to involve certain professional technicians useful to the cause, and could also draw funding from a few rich and nostalgic industrialists—but all said and done, they were an awkward squad from the past, incompatible with the real finality of the operations.

In May 1965, Mario Miasco, a lieutenant colonel by now, took part in a conference on unorthodox warfare at the Hotel Parco dei Principi in Rome. There were civilian and military academics, both Italian and foreign: highly prestigious figures, as Mario would say later. The works had been promoted by a certain Istituto Pollio di Studi Strategici: a cover name for Defence General Staff. Francesco, the younger of the brothers, did not have access to that level, but on that occasion too his career was furthered by his brother's activities: Mario was at Parco dei Principi as a representative of the V Comiliter, and on that occasion he made some important contacts. One morning he was summoned by his commander about a confidential meeting to be held that evening in one of the hotel suites. Mario thought about it all day. As he listened to the presentations, he was scanning the room and the corridors opening onto the hall: they were teeming with that strange crowd in which combatants from the Repubblica Sociale Italiana that he had dreamt of joining as a lad were mixing with former partisans and career officers too young to have fought in the civil war. He would linger with his eyes on the small groups gathered at the edges of the meeting, and fantasize on the encounters those people might have had in the past, under totally different circumstances, perhaps with firearms in their hands. He knew that somewhere among them, not as one of the presenting speakers but as an honoured guest, was the supremo of the Decima MAS, the hero of his youth, Prince Junio Valerio Borghese.

That evening, in the hotel suite, he was introduced to the prince. He kept to a strict military code of conduct, refraining from any excess words, even though he would have wished to show the prince how much the meeting meant to him. But the comandante was not the main personage that evening: the meeting was overseen by a civilian, introduced by the name of Filippo: his remarks were brief and analytical, but sufficient to reveal a position in the hierarchy that was not subordinate even to the prince. Later, during the toast that closed the day's proceedings, Colonel Braschi, also an artilleryman, told Mario something about Filippo: he had been an eager young Salò hierarch, and distinguished himself in the repression of partisan organizations—after which (whether as an infiltrator or simply out of foresight, Braschi didn't know) he had managed to be credited as a Resistance fighter. He had worked successfully in the Oss, and although very young at the time, seemed to have had a hand in organizing the American landing in Sicily. In a way, he had been hand-picked by Jimmy Angleton as his successor. The fact was, Filippo was now the most important representative of the American secret services in Italy. Mario was wondering how much of what Braschi was saying while swirling Hennessy brandy around a crystal snifter might be true, and how much was legend. But he did understand why Filippo was treating the commander prince as an equal.

In 1966, on recommendation from his elder brother, Francesco Miasco was twice sent to the United States to attend further training in Washington and at the Fort Bragg Rangers base. By now he was a top specialist in the organization of parallel logistics. Mario was obviously pushing Francesco's career, but he liked to say that it was 'pleasant, albeit entirely unnecessary, to recommend a man whose skill and hard work are his best references.' Now a captain, Francesco Miasco was put in charge of most of the military supplies for civilian groups connected to the network, and tasked with accounting for such supplies: each single vehicle issued to the paramilitaries was to be meticulously registered in a ledger inaccessible to above-ground hierarchies but available at any given time to the occult logistic structure. Francesco's work was the pivot coordinating rapid-response units for the Stay Behind network: Stella Alpina, Stella Marina, Azalea, Ginestra and Rododendro. Each of these units was about 1,500 strong in peacetime, which could be doubled in an emergency. The 'soldiers' were not informed of the existence of any units other than their own, or the identity of most of their fellows. Francesco himself did not know any of the men or their trainers, but only the supply-chain personnel.

Francesco's skill and enthusiasm, and also his conviction that the worst deviousness of communism consists in the instrumental use of democratic legality, also brought him into contact with Prince Borghese. The prince was organizing his own political movement, the Fronte Nazionale, which he would formally constitute only in 1968 by a regular notary deed. It would present itself as a movement finalized to 'all activities useful to the defence and restoration of the greatest values of Italian and European civilization', but it would be organized in a two-tier structure: a visible level, and an occult one made up of armed groups. The prince did not make a good impression on Francesco, who disliked the violent fascists the old man liked to surround himself with and his dreams linked to the inhuman models of German national socialism, whose crimes, Francesco thought, were plain to see. He was not in the habit of discussing work with his wife, but could not help mentioning his meeting with the prince. When she asked him how it went, his only answer was: 'Hatred—that's what he lives by.'

But he was a soldier, and he had his orders: his superiors had put him in charge of 'taking care of Borghese and his structure' in terms of logistic support, control and 'intelligence exchange.' Francesco thought it would actually be no bad thing to keep an eye on those fanatics. Once again, he worked well: his Piedmontese origins, his knowledge of the terrain, the flexibility he had shown meant that before long he was in charge of a 510-strong Fronte Nazionale division stationed in Turin, which in turn meant, at the end of the Sixties, the transfer to the city he had wanted so much (for the family, for his wife, for little Pietro's future).

In Turin he was promoted to the rank of major, which involved consulting duties in the recruiting of civilians, a task he brilliantly fulfilled by overseeing the infiltration of a group of trusted individuals, hand-picked among former paratroopers and Decima MAS combatants, into the control structure at FIAT, with monitoring functions on subversive activities.

Some of the men chosen by Francesco worked efficiently within union ranks. He was at the top of his career. With Mario he was invited to a ceremony in a splendid palace in the vicinity of Arezzo as the guest of an elegant, authoritative man who was introduced to him, almost tongue-in-cheek, as 'colonel brother'. Mario told Francesco in confidence that he had met the man years earlier, under the cover name he used in the secret services: Filippo. His real name was Licio Gelli, and he had a prominent role in the freemasons too.

Francesco was not offered masonic affiliation: he would not have wanted it, though he could not help recalling that some officers of his rank had been initiated, probably on account of family connections. Yet Filippo did give him a few moments' attention that evening. They spoke vaguely of generic subjects. By a few brief hints, Filippo let Captain Miasco understand that he knew about several particular aspects of his work, asked him if he was available for a private interview, and made an appointment with him in Milan for the following week.

Miasco arrived in Milan escorted by his commander. The interview was also attended by two men in plain clothes, who did not introduce themselves or speak much. Filippo took his time sounding Francesco out on his opinions, repeatedly praised him and had his commander confirm his worth. Francesco was flattered, and understood he now found himself at another turning point. As they drove back to Turin, his commander told him that the 'colonel brother' was in charge of recruiting officers available for the instating of a 'colonels' government' along the Greek model. An effective government, free of any conditionings and corruption: 'A transitional government, don't get me wrong—for the purpose of reinstating democracy and cleaning things up a bit.' Francesco listened without interrupting. The commander told him that the Grand Master had initiated over the sword a few hundred high-ranking officers, generals and colonels prepared to take part in instating the new government. After that strange interview, and for the first time in many years, Captain Miasco felt he was no longer in control of the outcome of his actions. He felt at the mercy of events: he needed to speak to his brother again—and in deep detail.

TORA TORA   'You've seen Filippo again?' In the command office of the I ORE, Mario nearly let out a whistle. 'No stopping you, little bro.'

'Mario—what is Operation Tora Tora?'

'If you know the name, you know what we're talking about.'

'Yes—a coup.'

'If you want to call it that. But in actual fact, things are a little more complicated. A coup produces a dictatorship, but this is a different idea, don't you think?'

'Hmmm.'

Mario wanted no secrets between himself and his brother, and he could sense that Francesco's career had by now taken off independently of his own. He told him that the whole network was mobilized so as to contrast the ongoing destabilization, and that the times were ripe for a forward leap. Francesco was familiar with the theory of destabilization: he had worked with Spiazzi in NATO's Operation Chaos, which consisted of Europe-wide infiltration of far left-wing groups that were to be conditioned and pushed into actions geared to swaying the public towards support-ing the idea of an authoritarian turn. Once, Francesco had even had fun, when he and the officers in charge of that operation had decided to invent certain delirious Maoist posters that went to line the streets of Rome. Also, he was one of the professionals most competent in controlling right-wing extremists engaged in provo-cations. In Turin, 'his' Fronte Nazionale men were rearing to go, but Francesco was restraining them. Turin was a hotspot, the stu-dents were making mayhem, the university had been occupied: they were doing a great job by themselves, thanks very much—people were well fed up, and there was no need to unleash the Fronte Nazionale.

'There'll be many more things happening this year, you'll see,' Mario said. 'People are exasperated, all we need to do is lop off a few dry branches. This is hardly a South American golpe, with the caudillo taking power and getting rich. Think of a state of emer-gency enforced by some exasperated members of the military who say "stop" to this chaos. People ready to step aside as soon as necessary, asking institutions to make bold choices.'

'Actually, what I heard was about a government of colonels—'

'No, no—that's just a trick. A matter of a few days, then the carabinieri will step in and guarantee a return to democracy. There's an emergency plan in place already, all the corps com-mands have it—a copy in each of the barracks.'

'As in, Borghese does the dirty work and then the carabinieri step in and save the country?'

'Look matey, let's cut to the chase. Dirty work, right? In the end it's Borghese himself will call the carabinieri in, he'll play the part of the guy who heard the voice of the military when they were exasperated at the country's dissolution. It'll have been a show of force, but also a way to jolt democracy into doing its duty. The coup has a tactical value, the strategic objective is the change that's meant to follow. But meanwhile the military gets to a position of strength, it gets to a place where it can lay down conditions.'

'And you think the Fronte Nazionale will be able to hold all that stuff together?'

'Look, by the time Tora Tora is operational, the front's part will be minimal.'

Mario gave a rough explanation of the plan: a blitz on Rome by military and paramilitary divisions, simultaneous occupation of three key ministries (Interior, Foreign, Defence), control of the RAI and arrest of President Saragat (here, Francesco shuddered). The operational role of Avanguardia Nazionale, Ordine Nuovo, the Front and other organizations was still to be defined: perhaps they'd be part of at least one of the main operations, the taking of one of the ministries for instance. Their main task was to act in various areas of the country and around the capital, provoking disorders severe enough to call for the intervention of military divisions that would reinstate order, but later declaring loyalty to the provisional government. Rome would be covered by Major Capanna's Battalion of Public Security Guards, the Lancers of Montebello, the First Grenadiers Group of Sardinia, the First Regiment of Bersaglieri of Aurelia, a carabinieri division led by a lower-ranking officer so as to avoid compromising the top levels who would intervene at a later stage, and even the forest wardens. But that was not all: the whole country would see military manoeuvres, the whole nation-wide anti-communist apparatus would click into place at once. 'For instance, Spiazzi with his division will go and occupy Sesto San Giovanni, a hotspot, with the Lancers of Milan, while Verona will be covered by troops moved in from Friuli.' Stella Alpina, together with other outside divisions, was tasked with controlling the eastern border. All movements of troops from their habitual sites to the decentralized lines were responding to standard security procedures against enemy intelligence. Operational command would see Filippo in a strategic position, albeit behind the ranks: he, more than the prince, was the pivot of the operation. The provisional government would include numerous civilian personalities 'as a guarantee'.

'And you think the communists are just going to stand by and watch?'

'Well, the immediate operational phase includes enucleation—'

'Will you speak Italian, please.'

'All right. We have groups trained to arrest the greatest possible number of politicians and union leaders, not excluding certain intellectuals. There's a couple of ships ready to take them out to sea, and to camps set up in the Aeolian Islands or Ponza. We're going to blow them off the game before anyone can start any negotiations. And then, when everything's back to normal, there might have been a few accidents—by all means deplorable, but it will be in the past by then. You'll see—no one will be willing to block reconciliation. And we can name the odd square after them, or a school or something.' The filing of 'enucleation' candidates was already underway: 'Look, you've an example right under your nose: Turin is hard at work, the carabinieri legion has already laid hands on a few hundred names, addresses, timetables, routines.'

Once it was all done and dusted, things would be minimized. Mario knew he was breaching his brother's defences by assuring him that in the end the neofascists would end up getting what they deserved, looking like old mules that had bolted but would be brought back to the stables and then retired: 'We'll send them to the bully beef factory,' he had sniggered. This last operation, the dismissal of the fascists after use, would lessen any resistance from that part of the public who might share the purposes of the operation but would never condone its methods.

Francesco was not showing the same enthusiasm as he had during their previous talk, all those years earlier, in the tavern at San Martino. Mario felt it incumbent upon him to sound a warning: 'Look my lad, you've no time or space for doubts. You're in too deep, you're precious, you're one of the few who are able to see—almost in its entirety—a picture of which nearly all involved only see one or two details.'

Francesco thought that skewed expression, 'almost in its entirety', was concealing some essential bit of information.

FAKE BLASTS   Over the next few months, Francesco Miasco was listening hard—'to tell the real blasts from the fake ones', as he would say to himself. He was fully convinced that those he called 'real blasts' actually existed: communist-led subversive plans with unwitting executors such as the troublemaking students who went and occupied the schools. In the same way, he was convinced that the bourgeois most inclined to doze off in the face of clear and present danger could only be shaken by a few 'fake blasts'. The first blasts soon began to arrive, the following spring, and Francesco had no doubt: fake as fake can be. Yet they made him nervous. A few bombs had gone off in Milan, at the Fiera and at Central Station. Police were investigating the circles of a publisher famous for his extremist left-wings sympathies. Francesco Miasco was using all his knowledge of tactics and explosives to understand how those who set up the blasts could have been sure of not killing any innocent civilians.

The 'hot autumn' at FIAT took him by surprise. He kept silent, did not join his wife and her sisters' indignant comments. Deep in thought, and increasingly convinced of the necessity of Operation Tora Tora. The slaughter in Piazza Fontana cast him into despair, turned him suspicious, harsh, choleric. He told his wife he was suffering from 'nervous exhaustion', found himself weeping at night. He spent the next ten days in silence, watched in silence the huge unions' demo in Milan, the crowd in Piazza Duomo who knew what was happening, as he did. But the worst was still to come.

In June he was on a mission in the south, travelling through Calabria and parts of Sicily: hard at work, he was discovering a land of slow rhythms, its heat and intensity, and stubbornly seeking out its scents to contrast his dark forebodings as they took hold and grew, looming ever larger, haunting him. He disliked the people who worked alongside him organizing supplies—even the officers, his colleagues. He could sense a strange vein of sarcasm, of contemptuous detachment, of arrogance. They were menacing, even when smiling. Impenetrable. He watched on TV the revolt in Reggio Calabria—but more disquietingly, he realized he could not stop speaking, too much and with too many, about the train derailed at Gioia Tauro only a few days before those riots, about the six people killed that day. No one had heard the bomb go off.

No one, except four anarchists the secret services would soon find a way to disappear. More than five hundred miles away, Major Miasco was keeping a nerve-wracking tally of all the bombs—many—that cropped up on trains and tracks. He immediately realized the risk those mad people were running who had been summoned by the unions to travel the length of the peninsula by train and join the demo in Reggio Calabria. He learnt of the night in which trains had been inching forward at walking speed, union leaders standing along the track bed with lanterns to spot any explosive devices, and he heaved a sigh of relief when everything was over. He was feeling increasingly grim, often asking himself what more he needed to see before he finally walked away from that aberration. He tried to keep everything from his family, he was oppressed by a sense of doom, but he knew that one way or the other everything was nearly over. He had fought with Mario at least twice, but had accepted his invitation to spend the summer holidays together—a superior's order, more than an invitation. Mario had summoned him to the ORE in Milan and passed on his orders from the command: things were getting busy again down south. They'd spend the month of August and the last week of July in Palermo. Rosalba would look after the family, and they'd have time for fun too. Think about it—lovely for Pietrino to spend a good month at the seaside, no? And that's real sea, not the dishwater of Liguria. There'd be a lot to do, mind: Prince Borghese was going to spend nearly all of August in Palermo—there were many logistic details to define. Operation Tora Tora was set to kick off only a few months later: on the night of the Immaculate Conception, 7/8 December.

INTERVIEW (2)   'Colonel, sir—I've taken the liberty of making an official visit—'

'I understand, Miasco—you wanted to be safe. Let's say you have no trust in the corps—is it not so?'

'Not so, sir, not so. Yet—'

'Don't worry, I can understand you, in a way: you are young . . .'

'Thirty-nine, sir.'

Dalla Chiesa looked at him in silence. Now Francesco was embarrassed before that man whose charisma he could feel: he was even fleetingly tempted to justify the gap between his age and his rank (cover-up requirements connected to his work in the parallel network)—but no. Dalla Chiesa seemed to be reading his mind.

'Don't worry, De Mauro spoke to me about you.'

'He might not have told you everything, sir.'

'Then again he might.'

Miasco was trying hard to understand how far he could trust the man in front of him. Things had gone from bad to worse after Mauro De Mauro was assaulted on the cliffs at Terrasini: the journalist had opened up with Miasco, who had understood that the threshold had finally been crossed, that the time had come for him to quit. He had been talking to De Mauro, and the journalist had named that unusual officer to him. Miasco knew he was safe with De Mauro, and shared his doubts, connected to the central role of the carabinieri in the coup. De Mauro knew how to be persuasive: sometimes his looks (eternally relaxed even with his face covered in bruises) turned hard and his voice came out cold and sharp. 'It's different with Dalla Chiesa—and anyway, he's the only card we can bet on,' he had said.

'So you know about the landings, sir.'

'De Mauro is keeping me informed.'

'De Mauro is risking his life.'

'Every minute.'

Captain Miasco remained silent for a short while. Dalla Chiesa added, 'We're doing all we can to keep him safe. He's a wounded man—like you. He's seeing his erstwhile ideals placed in the service of something he finds repellent.'

Miasco swallowed hard. 'It's worse than that, sir—worse than that.' Dalla Chiesa changed the subject.

'Did you know he's about to start working in cinema?' At last the captain smiled.

'Yes, he told me—he seemed very excited. But that was earlier.'

'Well, at least that should keep him out of this whole business for a while.' It was Miasco who got back to the point.

'So, sir—you know about the matter, but you might not have all the necessary elements to frame it.'

'I imagine you're referring to this.' Colonel Dalla Chiesa spoke without emphasis as he passed an envelope across the desk. 'And I imagine you've no difficulties understanding English.'

'No.' Miasco was reading without moving a muscle. Dalla Chiesa decided to summarize.

'As you can see, this is a memo from the US Federal Bureau of Investigation. It lists names and surnames, and reading between the lines I think I can sense an ongoing polemic between different allied agencies.'

'Have you forwarded it to your superiors?'

'What kind of a question is that, Miasco—do you think I could hide this sort of material?'

'And how—how did you safeguard yourself?'

'How do I protect myself, you mean? I don't. I couldn't. And it would probably make things worse. Anyway, Procuratore Scaglione is aware—De Mauro trusts him. Have you seen the names?'

'Not yet—not all of them.' Miasco quickly leafed through the rest of the wodge.

'Let's get to the point, major.' For the first time the colonel had used the other man's rank as a vocative. 'The Americans are flagging up a heroin traffic—do you know what we're talking about? Heroin, I mean.'

Miasco nodded. The dust unloaded every evening at Terrasini made him shudder: he had read reports, knew about the chemical slavery. It terrified him, it was like dealing with the devil, an impalpable devil who gets you by taking your children. He compulsively searched for information on that devil, he thought of Pietrino, he searched for information even though he already knew what effect it would have on his stomach. That mysterious dust was haunting him like a nightmare, an agent of the end of the world: 'I always thought these were things that—the mafia, sir—' he could not continue. Dalla Chiesa did.

'Yes. You know that American saying? "Strange bedfellows". Now let's see: the US flag up a heroin traffic coming from the US themselves, under cover of some officers from the US Intelligence Agency, and entrusted, at least on our territory, to the mafia gangs of Palermo. A tricky situation, isn't it?'

'Even if it didn't go any further, it would be monstrous.'

'That's right. And we both know this is not just a criminal affair. But as you can see, not everyone agrees, as shown by the very fact that these papers are in our hands. I think I know what's on your mind—don't talk about it, Miasco. No one needs heroes. Here, read this.' The colonel had picked up the bundle again, leafed through it and passed it back to Miasco, open at the right page:

'Our American friends have not been sparing with their name-dropping. Look who they're saying is in charge of the whole operation.'

'Good God.' Miasco had turned pale, it looked as if he might be about to lose control.

'Michele Sindona. You know this name very well.'

'This means that the Rt Hon. Mr Andreotti—'

'Don't jump to conclusions. God's banker is more than enough by himself.'

'Of course you are aware of operation Tora Tora, sir.'

'I know what this traffic is meant to be financing, I know who the agents in play are, and you can rest assured we won't be standing idle.' Miasco understood the colonel meant to reassure him—but he didn't feel any less troubled. 'Anyway, major, you did the right thing by reporting, believe me.' Strictly speaking, this was an improper expression, since Miasco did not report to Dalla Chiesa, and since that interview, although obtained through official channels and with as much publicity as possible ('The more people know, the lower the risk,' De Mauro had said), could hardly be construed as 'reporting'.

'We're not the only ones keeping watch over this scenario, this is not solely an Italian question. And the state still has strong anti-bodies—you'll see.'

Late that afternoon, Miasco left the barracks. He felt at peace with himself and with his idea of a future for his wife and son. Less than two days later, with his family, he left Sicily.

7

Venus

ICE   From Turin you can see the glaciers of the Alps. From
the roads, and especially from the roofs. They are moving, but
look still from here. And on certain mornings in December, when
the sky is hard and clean as a crystal, the mountains are so close
you can see the shadow of the seracs. It is cold, but an efficient
ventilation system stops any condensation forming on the tinted
windows of the spaceship shaped like a squashed bubble and
poised on the roof of the old Lingotto factory, between the two
huge parabolic curves that for a century have been charged with
the dreams and desires of every adolescent male in Turin.
Avvocato Agnelli is alone, sheltered by the glass panes, immersed
in his colloquy with the glaciers.

A few minutes ago, the president of the republic, who had
wanted to meet him at all costs, left the spaceship. He would have
wanted to say something to the president, but realized his words
were getting caught in his teeth and just smiled the smile of kings
instead. The president understood, smiled back at him, and continued to smile even after leaving. He said to the journalists: 'He
is compos mentis.'

Avvocato Agnelli has remained in the presence of the mountains. He feels as if he can listen to their silence. At his feet, per-
pendicular to the tram tracks, the new world of flexible people is

teeming—it is built in the image of something he cannot think of right now. He knows he has done a good job, and the glaciers know—yet in his mind is an undefined woman's face, the outlines blurred no matter how he tries to focus on them; perhaps it's the face of many women locked inside a single image. He tries to concentrate, fails: he might have left something unfinished.

But then again, no—he knows he has done a good job. The glaciers know.

I leave you with a riddle. If you can't find the answer, I'll tell you tomorrow. Tell me: What is it that Adam brought with him from Paradise? What is it that children play with and then, as they grow up, throw away? What is the stone that's worth more than the cow it strikes? What is everywhere but none can ever see? What is the thing in which the poor are richer than the rich?

Notes to the English Edition

Albertino: Albertino Bonvicini, the author of the memoir *Fate la storia senza di me* (Turin: Add Editore, 2018).

The Alchemical Marriage of Alistair Crompton by Robert Sheckley was first published by Michael Joseph in 1978.

Aldo Moro: leader of the Christian Democrats and twice prime minister of Italy, kidnapped and killed by the Red Brigades in 1978.

Alessandrini: Emilio Alessandrini, a magistrate assassinated on 29 January 1979 by the armed struggle group Prima Linea.

Alice: 'Circolo Alice', a youth circle in Turin. Also 'Radio Alice', Bologna's independent radio station.

Almirante: Giorgio Almirante, founder and leader of the neo-fascist party Movimento Sociale Italiano (MSI).

Alpini: a mountain infantry corps in the Italian army. An 'alpino' is a member of the corps.

Amos Spiazzi: general in the Italian army. Tried and sentenced in connection with the coup attempted by Junio Valerio Borghese in 1970, he was later acquitted by the supreme court.

'anarchist died in custody' (p. 244): Franco Serantini, who died in prison in Pisa in May 1972. Having been tried and acquitted of any responsibility, the prison doctor in charge at the time of his death was shot in the legs by the anarchist group Azione Rivoluzionaria in 1977.

Anche gli angeli mangiano fagioli (Even Angels Eat Beans): a 1973 comedy film starring popular actors Bud Spencer and Giuliano Gemma.

Andrea Pazienza: the much-loved Italian graphic artist whose comix and paintings were part of the 1970s counterculture movement.

Andreotti: Giulio Andreotti, a Christian Democrat politician who dominated the Italian political scene for half a century and served three times as prime minister. Repeatedly prosecuted for collusion with the mafia, as well as the murder of a journalist, he was eventually acquitted and served as senator for life from 1991 to his death in 2013.

Angelo Azzurro (Blue Angel): the bar in which Roberto Crescenzio was killed shares its name with the title of a hit single released in 1977 by singer Umberto Balsamo. The banner made by Marina and her friend paraphrases the song lyrics (pp. 218–19).

Autonomia Operaia (Workers' Autonomy), also **Autonomia**: the far-left movement which played a central role in the social struggles of the late 1970s.

Avanguardia Nazionale (National Vanguard): a neo-fascist group which broke from the MSI and was linked to the Piazza Fontana bombing in 1969 and the Borghese coup in 1970.

Avanguardia Operaia (Workers' Vanguard): a far-left extra-parliamentary group active around 1968–78.

Avvocato Agnelli: 'The Lawyer', Gianni Agnelli, CEO of Fiat from 1966 to 1996. Also referred to as 'the young prince' owing to his mother's aristocratic title.

Avvocato Croce: Fulvio Croce, the lawyer who sat as court counsel to several Red Brigades militants tried in 1976, despite their having claimed the status of communist combatants and formally refused any defence. Croce was killed in late April 1977.

Barabba ('Barabbas', a word sometimes used to mean 'rascal' in northern dialects): Circolo Proletariato Giovanile Torino Centro, one of the many far-left youth circles active in the 1970s.

Barriera di Milano, also **Barriera**: a working-class neighbourhood sited in the area of a former customs checkpoint.

Battipaglia: the small town in the province of Salerno (Campania) where in April 1969 a strike was called to protest against the closure of two local factories. During the demonstration, a young worker and a schoolteacher who was watching from her window were shot dead by police, leading to widespread rioting. The two endangered factories were reopened shortly afterwards.

Beato Cottolengo: after Giuseppe Agostino Cottolengo (1786–1842), one of Turin's 'social saints' and the founder of a shelter for the poor and sick which exists to this day and has several sister houses worldwide.

Berlinguer: Enrico Berlinguer, leader of the Italian Communist Party (PCI) from 1972 until his death in 1984.

Bersaglieri: a unit of the infantry corps in the Italian army.

The Black Prince (also 'the comandante'): Junio Valerio Borghese, head of the Decima Mas corps during the war, hard-line supporter of fascism and organizer of an aborted coup in 1970.

'Boia chi molla' (literally, 'quitters are butchers'): originally a rallying cry variously used by Italian armed forces and later by fascist squads, this became the motto of a rebellion that took place in the southern town of Reggio Calabria from July 1970 to February 1971. Rooted in deep-seated discontent against long-standing divisive and exploitative national policies in the area, the revolt was finally ignited by polemics over which town would be designated as the administrative centre and seat of institutional offices for the region of Calabria. After an initial moment of unity, the communist and socialist parties withdrew their support to what they saw as a jingoistic struggle. While some left-wing and anarchist forces did take part in the revolt, local leaders and right-wing politicians took an increasingly prominent role, in an attempt to advance their own agenda. Systematically belittled by national media, the revolt raged for several months, with sustained road, railway, port and airport blockades, street riots and bomb attacks, leading to a large number of casualties including five deaths. Coinciding with its early stages, on 22 July 1970, was the derailment of a train travelling on a local line at Gioia Tauro, causing six deaths: while this was archived as an accident following early investigations, later witness statements and findings gave increasing credit to the thesis of a bomb on the track. A few months after the end of the revolt, on 22 October 1972, steel and construction workers' unions organized a huge demonstration in solidarity with the workers of the region, whose core demands they recognized as legitimate. In the night between 21 and 22 October, eight bombs exploded on trains heading to Reggio Calabria.

Bruno Pizzul: a popular sports commentator.

Calvi: Roberto Calvi, also known as 'God's Banker' because of his close connection with the Vatican. The chairman of Banco Ambrosiano, he was placed on criminal investigation in 1981 following a report on the bank's illegal activities. In 1982, his body was found hanging under Blackfriars' Bridge in London.

Carabinieri: Italy's national gendarmerie, one of its main domestic law-enforcement corps. Informally referred to as 'carambas'.

Carlo Alberto Dalla Chiesa: the army general killed in a mafia attack in 1982, shortly after being nominated prefect of Palermo. In the novel, Pietro's father's joke plays on the fact that the general shares his first and middle names with one of the Savoy monarchs.

Casalegno: Carlo Casalegno, a journalist killed by the Red Brigades in 1977, following a series of articles in which he voiced harsh criticism of their practices.

Carosello (Roundabout): the 'family-friendly' early evening programme comprising comedy sketches and adverts, broadcast on national TV in the years 1957–77.

Cesare Romiti: the economist and entrepreneur who served as CEO of Fiat, where he played a prominent role in breaking the 1980 strike set off by his decision to fire 14,000 workers.

Chinese-posters: a false-flag operation designed to weaken the PCI and involving the creation and diffusion of fake Maoist posters.

Cholera: an outbreak of the disease in late summer 1973 affected Naples and other Mediterranean cities.

Christ-Dems: members and voters of Democrazia Cristiana (Christian Democracy), the party that held power for over 50 years before splintering into several smaller parties in 1994 after a spate of corruption scandals.

Church of the Grande Madre, or the **Great Mother**: also known as Gran Madre di Dio in Turin, hosts the ossuary of nearly 4,000 soldiers fallen in the Second World War.

Cisnal (Confederazione Italiana Sindacati Nazionali dei Lavoratori): Italian Confederation of National Workers' Unions, right-wing trade union founded in 1950 and merged in 1996 into the General Union of Work (Unione Generale del Lavoro, or UGL).

Comiliter: Comando Militare Territoriale, or Territorial Military Command.

Comontists: a group whose stance might be defined as loosely inspired by Marx's notion of 'Gemeinwesen', council communism and situationism. Its stated aim was to move beyond a 'community of goods' towards a 'community of being' : hence the name, from 'community' / 'communism' + 'òntos'. It understood the critique of capital as a radical critique of both law and work, whence the slogan 'lotta criminale contro il capitale' (criminal struggle against capital).

Confindustria: General Confederation of Italian Industry, the employers' federation.

Corso Traiano: one of the thoroughfares of Turin, and the scene of violent clashes between police and workers assembled at the gates of Fiat Mirafiori on 3 July 1969.

Curcio: Renato Curcio, founding leader of the Red Brigades.

De Martino (Francesco), **De Marsanich** (Augusto): respectively the socialist and MSI candidates to the presidency in 1971.

De Mauro: the friendly journalist Pietro had met as a child in Sicily was Mauro De Mauro, an investigative journalist working with a Palermo-based newspaper *L'Ora*. The reference to his 'film career' alludes to the request he had received from director Francesco Rosi to do some research for *The Mattei Affair*, a 1972 film on the suspicious death in a plane crash of Enrico Mattei, the controversial chairman of Italian oil multinational ENI, who in the 1950s had negotiated a series of major deals set to break extant oligopolies. De Mauro disappeared shortly after beginning his research. His body was never found.

Decima MAS: commando unit of the Italian navy during the fascist regime, also active on land under the Republic of Salò in the repression of partisan forces.

Diciannovisti: from 'diciannovismo' (literally, 'nineteenism'). Coined by socialist party leader Pietro Nenni, the term refers to 1919 and describes the general climate of populist rhetoric, brash vitalism and widespread violence that led to the foundation of the Fascist Party that year. Thus, to label young people taking to the streets in 1977 as 'nineteenists' is to equate them to early fascist squads.

Digos (Divisione Investigazioni Generali e Operazioni Speciali): a special division of the Italian state police, tasked with investigating cases of terrorism, organized crime and kidnapping.

Dioxin: the chemical compound TCDD, that gained grim notoriety after the 'Seveso Disaster' of July 1976, when a highly toxic cloud escaped from a malfunctioning reactor sited in a factory owned by the Hoffmann-La Roche group in the Brianza region, north of Milan. While there were no reported human deaths, hundreds of people were evacuated and required treatment for poisoning and severe longer-term effects. It is estimated that 3,300 animals were immediately killed, while at least 75,000 were eliminated to prevent toxicity entering the food chain.

Domenica sportiva: a sports programme broadcast on Sunday evenings since 1953.

Don Bosco: Giovanni Bosco, a Catholic priest who worked to alleviate the hardships suffered by the underprivileged. Canonized in 1934, he was the founder of the Salesians, an order whose activities focus in particular on education.

Don Rodrigo and **Innominato**: the two overlords in Alessandro Manzoni's 1827 novel *The Betrothed*, the former brazen in his abuse of power, the latter converted to Christian gentleness—presumably representing respectively the greater and lesser evil on the Italian political scene, as seen through the eyes of orthodox communist youth circles.

Dorothees: a faction of the Christian Democracy party. Very much opposed to any agreement with the left, it took its name from a congress held in the Roman convent of St Dorothea.

Dottó: the truncated southern form of the word 'dottore' (doctor), often used for comic or satyrical effect.

'the Dutch guys' (p. 46): a reference to the countercultural Provo movement, whose ideas and practices had spread from Amsterdam to Italian cities, especially Milan and Turin.

Emilio Salgari (1862–1911): a writer of adventure novels who rose to huge posthumous popularity after a life of hardship that ended in suicide.

Epileptic dancer: Pietro Valpreda, falsely incriminated for the bombing at Piazza Fontana. The reference to 'one of his friends, who'd killed himself by jumping out of a window' (p. 240) is to Giuseppe Pinelli, a railway worker and member of an anarchist group in Milan.

Ermanno Lavorini: the 12-year-old boy whose kidnapping and murder in 1969 was sensationalized by local news channels. The crime was initially ascribed to a paedophile ring, but in 1977 the supreme court sentenced three right-wing extremists for organizing the kidnapping to raise funds for their group.

'explosive Cinquecento' (p. 245): a terror attack carried out in the northern town of Peteano (Friuli Venezia-Giulia) by neo-fascist group 'Ordine Nuovo', in which carabinieri were called out to inspect a Fiat 500 car that had been primed to explode on contact. Three carabinieri died and two were wounded.

'fallen of the Frejus' (p. 212): a monument celebrating the Fréjus tunnel that links Piedmont to France. Raised in 1879, it was (much later) dedicated to the workers who had died during construction of the tunnel.

'famous publisher was blown up' (p. 244): Giangiacomo Feltrinelli (1936–1972), the influential Italian publisher who was found dead at the foot of an electricity pylon at Segrate, near Milan.

Fanfani: Amintore Fanfani, a Christian Democrat politician who served as the prime minister for five separate terms.

Fantozzi: a hugely popular 1975 comedy film adapted from the 1971 book by Paolo Villaggio. Fantozzi is the name of the protagonist, a caricature of the average alienated office worker.

'fascist accountant' (p. 52): Mario Tuti, founder of the neo-fascist group Fronte Nazionale Rivoluzionario, who in January 1975 killed two policemen and was able to escape capture for a few months.

fiancé(e): in a language relying heavily on ironic appropriation, this old-fashioned term was more acceptable than the prevalent but slightly passé 'ragazzo/a' (boy/girlfriend).

Fontamara, Bread & Wine, Emergency Exit: *Fontamara* (1930), *Pane e Vino* (1936), *Uscita Di Sicurezza* (1965) are works by writer and politician Ignazio Silone.

'the French philosophers' (p. 184): In 1977 Jean-Paul Sartre, Michel Foucault, Félix Guattari, Gilles Deleuze, Roland Barthes and others were among the signatories of an appeal against repression of the Italian youth movement.

Fronte Nazionale (National Front): a neo-fascist organization founded by Junio Valerio Borghese in 1967.

FTASE (Forze Terrestri Alleate Sud Europa): Allied Land Forces Southern Europe, an Italian NATO command centre established in Verona (hence the reference to 'the years spent in Verona with the Americans' on p. 69).

Galfer, Quinto, D'Azeglio: the science and humanities schools in Turin, named after scientists Galileo Ferraris and Alessandro Volta, and statesman Massimo d'Azeglio.

GAP: Gruppi di Azione Patriottica, the action groups founded in 1943 as part of the antifascist resistance. Also 'Gruppi d'Azione Partigiana', a militant group formed by Giangiacomo Feltrinelli in 1970.

gazelle: a small or medium-sized carabinieri patrol car.

Giarabub: Jaghbub, Libya, the location of an Italian garrison since 1925, besieged and finally taken by Commonwealth forces during the Second World War. The fascist propaganda song 'La sagra di Giarabub' (The Saga of Giarabub) was released in 1941.

Giovanni Pesce: an antifascist partisan who fought in the Spanish Civil War and the Second World War.

Giulia Colbert (1786–1864): a French noblewoman and philanthropist who settled in Turin after marriage to Italian marquis Carlo Falletti di Barolo.

Giuliano Ferrara: an Italian journalist, TV presenter and politician who after early involvement with the PCI and socialist parties, joined Silvio Berlusconi's Forza Italia in 1994.

Giuseppe Arduino: one of the workers at Fiat Grandi Motori who lost their life in the occupation of the factories that sparked the insurrection leading to Turin's liberation (18–28 April 1945).

Giusva: Giuseppe Valerio Fioravanti, a popular child actor in the 1960s who later became a member of the fascist terrorist group Nuclei Armati Rivoluzionari.

Gràdoli: a town northwest of Rome which was indicated by Romano Prodi, at the time a member of the Christian Democrats, as the possible location of Aldo Moro after his kidnapping. Moro was in fact held in one of the Red Brigades bases in Rome, on a street named Via Gràdoli.

Grand Old Man: an image used in Italian political discourse to personify a system of occult powers manoeuvring events for gain or for the maintaining of the status quo.

Gronchi: Giovanni Gronchi, a Christian Democrat politician who served as the president of Italy from1955 to 1962.

I ORE: Officina Riparazioni dell'Esercito (Army Repairs Workshop).

Juve, Toro: colloquial terms for Juventus FC and Torino FC, professional football clubs based in Turin which compete in the Serie A, the top tier of the Italian football league system.

Katanga: the name of Congolese mercenary units, ironically adopted by the security crew of the students' movement in Milan.

L'Unità: during the timespan of this novel, it was the daily broadsheet of the PCI, founded by Antonio Gramsci in 1924.

Legge Reale: a law extending police powers, introduced in 1975 by the Minister of Justice Oronzo Reale.

Leone: Giovanni Leone, a Christian Democrat politician who won the 1971presidential election with the support of the MSI.

Liceo Classico: 'Classical Lyceum', a high-school course including humanities, Greek and Latin. Also known as 'Regio Liceo Classico' or 'Royal Classical Lyceum' at the time of its inception under the Italian monarchy

Lingotto: one of the most iconic Fiat factories located in Turin, now known as the Lingotto Building. Decommissioned in the 1980s, Lingotto was redeveloped over 20 years. The new building has retained the original rooftop test-track and added a small conference space known as the Bolla (bubble). Hence the reference to 'parabolic curves' and the 'spaceship shaped like a squashed bubble' in the closing scene of the novel.

'literature professor' (p 109): perhaps a reference to Alain Elkann.

NOTES

Lotta Continua: one of the major left-wing organizations in the 1970s.

Luciano Lama: general secretary of the CGIL (General Confederation of Italian Labour) from 1970 to 1986.

Lucio Battisti: the popular singer-songwriter whose 1971 hit 'La canzone del sole' (Song of the Sun) describes a young man's bewilderment and final acceptance at a girl's passage into womanhood.

Lupi di Toscana (Wolves of Tuscany): a division of an infantry corps in the Second World War.

Mani rosse sulle forze armate (Red Hands on the Armed Forces): a 1966 pamphlet written by neo-fascists Guido Giannettini and Pino Rauti—see also *Le mani rosse sulle forze armate* (Rome: Savelli, 1975).

Marelli: Magneti Marelli, a manufacturer of electrical components for the automotive industry founded in 1919.

Mario Pastore: a journalist and newscaster on national television.

Metropolitan Indians: one of the components of the youth movement emphasizing creativity and spontaneous action, named after their custom of wearing Native American–style face paint.

Mike Bongiorno: a popular quiz-show host.

Milena Sutter: 13-year-old daughter of a Swiss industrialist, who was kidnapped and murdered in her hometown of Genoa in May 1971.

Mirafiori: southern suburb of Turin which had been the seat of a royal residence and flower gardens (hence its original name, Miraflores or Millefleurs). Fiat opened a factory here in 1939.

Molinette: the main city hospital in Turin.

'Moroccan pusher' (p. 130): Abdellah Doumi, the 26-year-old Moroccan man who drowned after being thrown into the Po by a group of youths on the night of 18 July 1997. Armando Ceste documented this and other acts of violence against migrants in the film *Abdellah e i suoi fratelli* (2000).

Nero Wolfe: the protagonist of several detective novels by Rex Stout, played by actor Tino Buazzelli in the very popular Italian TV adaptation.

Nicodemite: from a 1977 interview in *L'Espresso* in which PCI leader Giorgio Amendola responded to criticism of the party's rigid stance towards the movement by labelling his critics with the epithet denoting the intellectuals who during the fascist regime had acted with outward compliance while hiding their true beliefs. Amendola's narrative thus conflates the angry demonstrations of 1977 with the actions of proto-fascist squads, and interlocutors such as Norberto Bobbio and Leonardo Sciascia with the figure of Nicodemus, depicted in the New Testament (John, 3:1–2) as a paragon of timidity.

Non è la gelosia (It's not jealousy): an ironic allusion to a 1928 hit song, 'Il tango della gelosia'.

Nuclei Armati Proletari (Proletarian Armed Cells): one of the far-left armed struggle groups active in Italy in the 1970s.

OAS (Organisation Armée Sécrète): a far-right French terrorist paramilitary corps formed in 1961 to counter Algerian independence; it engaged in a campaign of bombings and assassinations in both metropolitan France and Algeria.

Options by Robert Sheckley was published by Pyramid Books in 1975.

Ordine Nero (Black Order): a neo-fascist organization formed in 1974 after the dissolution of its predecessor, Ordine Nuovo (New Order).

OSS: Office of Strategic Services, a wartime US intelligence agency which was succeeded by the CIA.

panthers: the term associated with state police cars since 1952, originally referring to the fleet of Alfa Romeo 1900TIs.

Pdup (Partito di Unità Proletaria, or PdUP): founded in 1972 by independent socialists and communists. In 1974, it was joined by the *il manifesto* group led by Rossana Rossanda, Lucio Magri,

Luciana Castellina and Luigi Pintor, as well as by members of the student movement led by Mario Capanna.

'people's judges' (p. 126): lay magistrates in the Italian judiciary.

'per vedere di nascosto l'effetto che fa' (roughly, 'and secretly seeing what effect that will have'; p. 86): from the 1968 chart-topper 'Vengo anch'io. No tu no' (Coming With You—No You're Not) by singer-songwriter Enzo Jannacci that disrupted the stuffy world of Italian song contests despite partial censorship from national TV and radio channels.

Pertini: Sandro Pertini was a much respected socialist antifascist politician who eventually became president in 1978.

Petrovic, Vallanzasca, Turatello: leaders of rival criminal gangs operating in Milan since the 1970s.

Piazza Fontana: the square in Milan where 17 people were killed and 88 wounded in the bomb attack on the Banca Nazionale dell'Agricoltura on 12 December 1969.

Piazza Statuto: a city square in Turin which in 1962 was the site of violent clashes after a general strike following workers' refusal of the contractual terms negotiated by the unions.

Prima Linea (Front Line): one of the far-left armed struggle organizations active in 1970s, incorporating former militants of Potere Operaio and Lotta Continua.

Procuratore Scaglione: Pietro Scaglione was the chief prosecutor of Palermo; he was assassinated by the mafia in 1971.

'the producers' pact' (p. 162): Gianni Agnelli's words to define his proposal of a wide alliance between workers and factory owners that would 'modernize the country' and do away with 'parasite incomes'.

Quarta and **Quinta Ginnasio** (Gymnasium IV and V): respectively the first and second year in the 'Liceo Classico' high-school course.

Queen Elena: queen consort to King Vittorio Emanuele III (*r.* 1900–46).

Quinta Lega (Fifth League): a historical section of the steelworkers' union FIOM (Federazione Italiana Operai Metalmeccanici).

Quotidiano dei Lavoratori (Workers' Daily): broadsheet of the far-left group Avanguardia Operaia (later Democrazia Proletaria), first published in 1974.

Radio Città Futura (Future City Radio): one of the many independent stations that began broadcasting in the 1970s.

RAI: Radiotelevisione Italiana, the national broadcasting company.

Re Nudo ('Bare King', with a reference to the emperor's new clothes): one of the main countercultural publications, whose collective also organized gatherings and music festivals, including Festival del proletariato giovanile (Festival of Proletarian Youth) from 1971 to 1978.

Repubblica Sociale Italiana (Italian Social Republic): the short-lived fascist state whose duration coincided with the German occupation of Italy (September 1943–April 1945). Also known as Repubblica di Salò.

Rinascente: the oldest department store in Italy, with branches in several cities.

Rischiatutto (Gamble it all away): a popular quiz show in which contestants were required to stake their winnings.

Rivalta: a town located southwest of Turin where Fiat opened a manufacturing unit in 1967.

Salò: a town on Lake Garda that was the seat of the Repubblica Sociale Italiana.

Santa Marta: an eighteenth-century building in the centre of Milan that became a squatted social centre.

'the saviour of our lira' (p. 244): refers to banker Michele Sindona. Closely connected with Vatican and masonic circles, he was convicted of fraud and perjury in 1980, and died in prison in 1986.

Scuola di Guerra (War School): the Italian army officers' training academy.

'Se c'è una cosa . . .' (p. 105): Mandrone is attempting to undermine Pietro by levering on his own involvement with hard drugs. The lines are from 'Whisky Facile' (Whisky-happy), a 1957 song by popular Turinese singer Fred Buscaglione. Roughly translated: If there's a thing / that I find sickening / is water from a spring.

The Secrets of Synchronicity by Jonathan Fast was first published in 1977 by New American Library.

SHADO (Supreme Headquarter Alien Defence Organization): the hi-tech international military agency in the British sci-fi TV series *UFO* (1970–71).

'snake in the tunnel' (p. 267): a set of measures implemented by the EEC to counter currency instability.

Sordi: actor Alberto Sordi, who appeared in Mario Monicelli's 1977 film *Un borghese piccolo piccolo* (A Very Small Petit Bourgeois).

Stalingrado: an antifascist song released in 1975 by the Italian left-wing progressive rock band Stormy Six.

Standa, UPIM: department stores with branches in different cities.

Stettin: a reference to the riots of December 1970 in the cities of northern Poland.

'Sunday afternoons without cars' (p. 16): among the austerity measures implemented by the Italian government in the 1970s was a total ban on car circulation on Sundays, later mitigated by the introduction of an 'alternate number plates' system.

Terroni: from 'terra' (earth, soil, land)—a slur against southern Italians.

Tex: Tex Willer, the hero of a vintage comic strip created by writer Gian Luigi Bonelli and illustrator Aurelio 'Galep' Galleppini.

TG1: Telegiornale, the main news programme on RAI's first channel.

'thirty-two thousand ghouls' (p. 97): a reference to the anti-union march staged in October 1980 by Fiat managers and white-collar workers. Although the number of participants was a matter of contention, it became known as 'the march of the forty thousand' and 'made history' that broke a 35-day strike.

Tito Stagno: the newscaster who covered the 1969 moon landing for Italian TV.

TNT charge: a reference to Peppino Impastato, the left-wing militant and anti-mafia activist killed by an explosive charge after publicly denouncing the local bosses during the election campaign.

Triveneto: an old denomination of the north-eastern region of Italy, once also known as the 'Three Venices'.

Union valdôtaine (Valdostan Union): a centrist party in the small northern region of Valle d'Aosta.

Valle Giulia: a central area in Rome near the Faculty of Architecture, the seat of clashes ('The Battle of Valle Giulia') between left- and right-wing students and the police on 1 March 1968.

Valletta: Vittorio Valletta ('il Professore') joined Fiat in 1928, became CEO in 1939 and was president from 1946 to 1966.

Venus on the Half-Shell by Kilgore Trout (pseudonym of Philip José Farmer) was first published by Dell in 1975.

'War planes, some wee little payouts' (p. 115): a reference to the 'Lockheed scandal', involving huge sums of money paid by US aerospace company Lockheed to Italian politicians to ensure the purchase of their H-130 transport planes

Zio Lupara (Uncle Shotgun): 'lupara' is a sawn-off gun associated with mafia crimes, that takes its name from originally being used to kill wolves.